I0824782

THE AFTER-LANDS

Also by

AKEMI DAWN BOWMAN

Starfish

Summer Bird Blue

Harley in the Sky

The Infinity Courts

The Genesis Wars

AN INFINITY COURTS NOVEL
3

THE AFTER-LANDS

AKEMI DAWN BOWMAN

New York Amsterdam/Antwerp London Toronto
Sydney/Melbourne New Delhi

An imprint of Simon & Schuster Children's Publishing Division
1230 Avenue of the Americas, New York, New York 10020

Jacket design by Laura Eckes

For information about special discounts for bulk purchases, please contact Simon & Schuster Special Sales at 1-866-506-1949 or business@simonandschuster.com.

Simon & Schuster strongly believes in freedom of expression and stands against censorship in all its forms. For more information, visit BooksBelong.com.

The Simon & Schuster Speakers Bureau can bring authors to your live event. For more information or to book an event, contact the Simon & Schuster Speakers Bureau at 1-866-248-3049 or visit our website at www.simonspeakers.com.

Interior design by Laura Eckles
The text for this book was set in Bembo.
Manufactured in the United States of America
First Edition
2 4 6 8 10 9 7 5 3 1
CIP data for this book is available from the Library of Congress.
ISBN 9781665907736
ISBN 9781665907750 (ebook)

For the ones who keep going, even when it’s hard

1

THE ALARM SOUNDS, AND MY SISTER'S AIRSHIP comes to life.

Panels light up along the ceiling, sending emerald-green flashes across the small room. A stampede of footsteps pounds through the corridor, and the metal frame of my bed tremors, perfectly in sync with my racing heart.

There are only three kinds of alarms on the *Mizuchi* airship; green means there are Residents nearby, amber means we're under fire, and red signals a breach.

Someone else might find comfort in the pulsing green lights. They're far better than the alternatives, after all. But I'm too aware of what the alarm means—not for us, but for him.

Fear builds in the pit of my stomach. *You know what will happen if she finds him first.*

I wave a hand over my feet, and a pair of boots appears in a rush of pixelated color. The door slides open the moment it senses me, and I tear down the hallway, bumping shoulders with the crowd of humans who are headed for the transport dock. Everyone is too distracted by protocol to look at me like I'm some kind of hero. Right now, it doesn't matter that I'm Nami Miyamoto, the Messenger who planted a seed that resulted in the Second Wave. When the alarm blares, I become invisible. A faceless soldier hurrying to their next station.

The respite won't last long, so I quicken my pace.

A glass elevator sits at the far end of the corridor, shaped like an elongated sphere. It takes me to the lower levels of the *Mizuchi*, where a small fleet of warships sits in wait. Humans disappear inside, armed with rifles and an array of metallic charges strapped to their vests.

I make a beeline for one of the boarding ramps.

"Nami!" a ragged voice calls out. "What are you doing down here?"

I turn and find Commander Behr marching toward me. He waves a hand across his broad chest, and his dress uniform shifts into heavy armor. Black panels appear, flickering with the unmistakable gleam of Second Wave technology.

The humans from Genesis, the Borderlands, and the Colony . . . they learned to fight out of a need to survive. But the Second Wave was prepared for this afterlife. They died *ready* for war.

All because of what I told Mei on the day I followed the

threads of Ophelia's mind back to the living world.

Behr looks me up and down, impatient. "You should be upstairs. The air lock is about to open, and the General will have my head if—"

"I'm fine," I snap, unable to hide the bite in my tone.

Behr narrows his eyes. "There's no shame in admitting you need to rest."

My shoulders stiffen, defensive. I've lost an entire century to the Cut. The last thing I need is more sleep.

I pin my gaze to the nearest warship. "I want to go down to the surface."

"Take it up with the General."

"Last I checked, I don't need her permission. I need yours."

He clenches his jaw. "You're her sister. The rules are different."

I cross my arms, mind racing for an excuse to be down in the fold alongside the others. "Being stuck on this airship for weeks isn't helping me recover. Everyone keeps saying how much Infinity has changed over a hundred years; maybe it's time I see it for myself."

Behr doesn't ask what I mean. He assumes what I want him to—that seeing the new world will put the fight back in my heart.

I can't tell him the whole truth. Not after the way Mei reacted to it.

Behr sucks the air through his teeth, thinking. "You need a suit. And a gun."

I motion to what I'm wearing—a faded gray top, loose trousers tucked into a pair of boots, and bracers covered in thin silver and white branches. A reminder of the prince who proved me wrong. "They'll hold up in a fight," I assure him.

Behr sighs and removes a pistol from its holster. "Take this. And next time you want to come on a ride-along, make sure you're in uniform. I don't care if you're a celebrity. Messenger or not, we have rules on the *Mizuchi*."

I take the weapon and hope he doesn't notice that this is the first time I've ever held a gun. Fighting a war without bullets is unheard of for a Second Waver, but I have no intention of shooting anyone today.

Tucking the pistol in my belt, I climb aboard the nearest warship and wedge myself in an open seat between two lower-ranking soldiers. They wear the same black uniform as everyone else, with padded metallic vests and enough pockets to house over a dozen different kinds of weapons. But what sets them apart from the more seasoned officers are their wide-eyed expressions, an unquenched thirst for a glorified war, and a steadfast belief that what they're about to do is *right*.

They're strangers who've lived an entire lifetime while I've been asleep. But the look in their eyes is painfully familiar. I've seen it again and again, at every corner and every side of this battle. It doesn't matter how much time has passed; the same cycle of hate persists, just as it has throughout human history.

Except this time, it was *my* doing. I told my sister to be afraid of something I didn't fully understand, and now . . .

My gaze flicks to the many faces of the Second Wave. Guilt shudders through me just as the warship takes off. *The only way to fix all of this is to find him before the soldiers do.*

Closing my eyes, I take a breath and search for Caelan across the void.

I don't know if he's still a prisoner in War, or if he managed to escape Ozias's cage after I was Cut. I don't know if he made it back to Famine, or if he's roaming the Labyrinth for a place to hide. All I know is that he isn't safe. Not with Mei's warships hunting his kind, and Queen Ophelia naming him a traitor.

I push my thoughts as far out as they'll go, stretching across the starlit landscape until my skull aches. There isn't a flicker of Caelan to be found. No scent of pine or glimpse of a winter woodland. Our minds were connected once, but now when I reach out to him it's like . . .

It's like he doesn't exist.

I dig my fingers against my knees to keep myself steady. The warship drops through the clouds, lowering itself to the surface of the Labyrinth. Soldiers immediately fall into formation and race down the landing ramp.

I trail after the group and spot Commander Behr a few stretches ahead. He orders some of the soldiers to follow him, and the rest move toward a lieutenant with blond hair spun in a tight bun and several knives on her belt. I don't recognize her, which is enough of a reason for me to tuck in behind the rest of her unit and hope Behr doesn't notice.

We move silently through the forest landscape. A wide canopy of magnolia trees offers cover, though I doubt any of the Second Wavers need it. The glowing veilstones woven through the fabric of their armor pulse with green light. I've got two of my own, attached to my bracers. Mei insisted.

When the color of the veilstones shifts to a vibrant amber, the lieutenant signals for the group to break into sections. I follow a trio of soldiers straight into the heart of the forest.

Dayling birdsong fills the air, and tufts of pink blossoms are dotted around the trees, leaving a trail of petals at our feet. Sunlight trickles through the overhead foliage, making our surroundings glitter with movement. If it weren't for the armed militia pushing ahead, the spring landscape might even be beautiful.

A pop reverberates through the trees, and the Daylings scatter toward the clouds. The sound of the first bullet makes my chest tighten. Everyone moves, swift and strategic, and suddenly the air is no longer filled with the chorus of nature. It's a symphony of violence.

The amber hues on my veilstones darken to an unyielding blood red.

I break into a run, propelled by something primal and desperate. My boots thud against the soft grass, leaving a path of trampled bluebells on my way to the clearing ahead. The tip of a Resident airship peeks through the woodland. Wisps of smoke escape from its core, spiraling skyward. The side of the hull is blown to pieces, and a heavy line of bright orange follows the edge like a burning seam. I veer off to the left, hoping to get ahead of the soldiers so I can reach the chaos before they do.

If Caelan is here . . . If he made it this far . . .

A shadow appears, and for a moment the world is soundless. The Resident stares beyond the meadow, fists curved around two silver knives. He can't see me—not with the impenetrable veil surrounding me.

It isn't Caelan. Just another soldier in an impossible war.

A collision of opposing thoughts rises inside me, making my breath catch. This Resident isn't an innocent; he's a hunter, created to kill my kind. If I were smart, I'd reach for my pistol, aim for his chest, and pull the trigger.

But I'm not driven by logic. I run on instinct and empathy, and the nagging voice in my head that tells me, *It doesn't have to be this way.* I'm fueled by the memory the Prince of Victory shared with me of his time in Famine, where I saw humans and Residents coexisting. Proof that we don't need to destroy one another in order to survive.

I don't want to hurt this stranger. But I don't want to run, either. He might know something about Caelan's whereabouts, which makes this the closest I've been to finding answers since I woke up. I know it's a long shot, and it may not be the smart choice—but it's *my* choice.

I let my veil drop and face my hunter.

He stiffens at the sight of me, expression turning from surprise to anger. It isn't hate—not yet—and I can't help the glimmer of relief that appears at the edge of my mind.

When he pulls his arm back, ready to charge with his knife, I don't reach for my weapon. I hold up my hands, urging him to *wait*.

"I'm not your enemy," I want to say. "I've seen a better way to exist in this world. I've seen peace between our kinds. And I can explain everything if you just give me the chance."

But the poison Damon put into my mind when I was a prisoner in Death is still there, sinking its tendrils into my memories, keeping me from telling the truth about Famine and coexistence.

I don't say anything. I *can't.*

A bullet flies through the trees. The Resident's gaze holds mine like he's clutching onto time itself. Blood pools at his chest, seeping through his clothes. I blink, trying to process where the shot came from, but I'm too late.

The Cut rips through him.

Flecks of gold dust ripple through the air as he disintegrates, moving in a frenzy like an untethered burst of consciousness. It doesn't last long; within moments, the dust forms a small orb, and what's left of the Resident is pulled beyond the trees, summoned by a waiting cage.

Commander Behr appears, rifle pointed at the spot where the Resident was Cut. His attention moves from my outstretched hands to the pistol still tucked in my belt.

The disapproval on his face is clear. "Get back on the ship. *Now.*"

I don't bother trying to explain myself. It wouldn't change anything.

Because if I've learned anything about Second Wavers, it's that they never lose a fight.

2

LIGHT POOLS UNDER THE GLASS FLOOR WHERE Resident souls are trapped beneath the surface. Remnants of a hundred consciousnesses float beneath me. Maybe even thousands. Every ship in the fleet has a prison similar to this one, but the *Mizuchi*'s is the biggest of them all.

Is this what I looked like after my mind was Cut from my body? A ribbon of gold moving aimlessly within a cage?

I don't remember any of it. One moment I was calling out to Caelan, and the next . . .

I tuck my arms around myself and continue across the walkway, trying to make sense of the world my sister built in my absence. Trying to decide where I fit in it.

The prison suite's walls are made of backlit glass to match the aquarium-like floor. A smooth metal desk sits in the center of the room, where a hologram shifts with indecipherable coding. Perched on a stool behind it is the *Mizuchi*'s jailer, Arlo.

When he sees me, his fingers go still above a paneled keyboard. "Let me guess—you're here to check on the new uploads?"

Uploads. Like they're a batch of files stored on a hard drive, waiting to be purged from existence. I feign indifference, even as my stomach turns. "What can I say? I'm a creature of habit."

Arlo runs a hand through his mess of auburn hair. "I know it doesn't matter how many times I say it, because you keep coming back, but you really don't have to worry about them escaping. Our tech is superior to anything they've created."

I turn my eyes back to the gold lights floating below the glass. How many Residents were Cut today?

Is it possible Caelan was one of them?

Fear coils through me, and the glowing prison makes me sway.

I clear my throat, hoping it makes my words sound less brittle. "Does every Resident consciousness look the same?" I meet Arlo's puzzled stare. "Would you be able to tell the difference between an ordinary soldier and someone like Ophelia?"

Arlo pushes his glasses up the bridge of his nose with a finger. I don't know if he likes the aesthetic, or if he wears them for the same reason Ahmet once chose to keep his scar—as a reminder of the life he'd lived before this one. "I suppose none of us have any idea what Ophelia's consciousness might look like. But so far, when a Resident is Cut, they're indistinguishable from one another. We'd have to start the process of regrowth to really find out who's who—not that it matters. They'll all be captured and destroyed when the time comes."

I bite the inside of my cheek. "I heard Lysander went missing during the raid, and no one knows whether he was Cut in the chaos or if he escaped."

"Ah." Arlo's face softens. "You want to know if the Prince of Death is one of our uploads."

"Is it possible he's here, and you just haven't realized it?" *If Caelan is stuck beneath the glass floor too, unable to get out . . .*

Arlo misinterprets the worry in my brow. "I know Lysander was the one who . . . Well. I imagine you'd feel better knowing we'd captured the monster who Cut you. But there's no way we'd lose track of a high-value target like that." An apology lingers between his words. "He isn't here."

"And the rest of the princes?"

He shakes his head. "No one has seen them in months. We suspect they've retreated to the Capital alongside Ophelia, avoiding the carnage of the Second Wave."

The corners of my mouth turn down. Caelan and Damon may have reasons to stay hidden, but I can't imagine Ettore running from a fight. If Queen Ophelia summoned him to the Capital, it isn't to retreat—it's to plot their next move.

Arlo doesn't seem the least bit worried. Instead, his expression shifts to pride. "Did you know I was there the day Doc realized we'd found your consciousness? I'll never forget the relief. Rebuilding a physical body is a long process to begin with, but there were so many humans stored in Neo Genesis—or Death, as you used to call it. We weren't sure how many more years it would take to find you."

Neo Genesis.

While I was asleep, Ozias took one of the Four Courts and claimed a throne. And he did it with my sister's help.

"I'm surprised Ozias didn't keep all the tanks of human souls to himself," I say thinly. "He's always been a fan of war trophies."

Arlo frowns like he doesn't understand. "King Ozias would never take a human prisoner. He's an ally to the Second Wave, and us to him."

"He's a power-hungry traitor," I nearly snap, blazing with the memory of the battlefield and what he once did to Gil.

But I can still see Mei's face when I tried to tell her about Caelan and my time in War. Fighting against Damon's poison made everything sound fragmented and incoherent. She looked at me like I'd lost hold of my own reality.

These people trust Ozias like they trust my sister. Until I can take back control of my voice, I don't see the point in trying to convince them otherwise.

"I know you've been through a lot. But I hope you know how grateful we are." Arlo's words flood with sincerity. "You saved us all."

And condemned the Residents.

Arlo looks past me, shoulders immediately going rigid before he stands at attention.

Mei waits in the doorway, her black uniform crisply ironed, and a pistol gleaming at her side. Her hair hangs in a sharp line just above her shoulders. Seeing her here, in Infinity . . . it still feels like a dream. Not just because of what it means, or who she is to the Second Wave, but because the sister in front of me isn't the sister I've carried in my head.

Mei lived an entire life before her death—a life that gave her hard lines around her mouth and a gauntness to her cheeks. But she's also lived a life in Infinity, where she staged a rebellion and overthrew two Resident courts.

Time may work differently here, but I was only awake for a measly two years in Infinity, and eighteen before that. Mei has surpassed me many times over.

She used to be my little sister. Now I think I might be hers.

"At ease," Mei tells Arlo, but her gaze is fixed on me. "I thought I might find you here. Commander Behr told me what happened in the field."

I expected as much, but the irritation snaking through me is impossible to hide.

Mei studies me, lips pressed together. She motions toward Arlo. "Leave us."

Arlo swipes at the hologram to make the screen vanish and hurries out of the room. When the door slides shut, the silence is overwhelming.

I sigh. "Please stop looking at me like that."

"Like what?"

"Like you're *Mom*."

Mei ignores my goading. Second Wavers don't talk about their lives before Infinity. They think it's too much of a distraction. "You willingly ventured into combat and then chose not to use your weapon."

"I don't like guns. Probably a side effect of being murdered."

"This isn't a joke, Nami. You put yourself in danger."

"I was *fine*," I say, forceful. "Your commander involved himself in something that didn't concern him."

"The war between humans and Residents concerns *all* of us," she argues. "Why would you take a risk like that? What if they'd taken you?" Her voice carries a sting. "I can't lose you a second time. Not after what it took to get you back."

I shut my eyes and take a breath, hating how much her worry feels like a cage. "You can't expect me to stay on this ship forever."

Seconds stretch between us. When Mei finally speaks, her words are clipped. "You were looking for him."

My eyes flash open. I doubt she needs the confirmation, but I give it to her anyway. "He sacrificed everything for me. I need to make sure he's safe."

She rubs her brow, exasperated. "Whatever he made you feel for him was a means to an end and nothing more."

"You don't know him. You don't know what really happened to us."

"Then *tell* me."

"Caelan wants—" The words fizzle on the edge of my tongue. I can't tell her the truth about Famine. Not with Damon's poison stopping me. "If you met him, you'd understand."

"I have no desire to meet the Resident prince that manipulated my sister, just as I have no desire to believe in the delusion that there's a third side to this war."

"But if there's a better way—"

"There isn't," she interrupts. "We are winning because of weapons, and strategy, and brute force. Not peace. Not coexistence.

And certainly not trust in the enemy." Mei pauses, visibly flustered. "Hopeful as you are, you don't have a *better way*. You have a theory; and I will not risk a single human soul over anything less than proof. Which, even then . . ." Her voice fades into a sigh.

"Caelan *is* your proof."

"And yet he isn't here." Mei lowers her chin. "Think about it, Nami. You said you used to be able to communicate with him through his thoughts. But in all this time, he's never tried to reach out to you."

"The last time I saw him, he had a Grimling bite in his system, and he was being tortured by Ozias. Maybe he isn't reaching out because he *can't*."

Mei looks doubtful. "I was there when we joined forces with the old Genesis. There wasn't a single prisoner in their camps. Certainly not the Prince of Victory."

"It wouldn't be the first time Ozias has lied to the people around him." My teeth grind together. "He has an entire territory of his own now, with his own soldiers, and his own rules. Maybe he has his own prisoners too."

"Caelan is not in Neo Genesis."

"You don't know *where* he is," I counter. "Lysander hasn't been seen since Genesis took over his court. You don't think it's odd Ozias may have been the last known human to see either of the princes before they allegedly vanished?"

Mei's nostrils flare. "An hour ago, you were convinced Caelan was on the surface. Now you think Ozias somehow captured two of Ophelia's spawn and is secretly holding them captive in his basement?"

"I was thinking more of a dungeon, but yes. I think it's a very real possibility."

"Maybe the truth is simpler than that. Maybe Caelan went back to his family," Mei offers. "He chose a side, and it wasn't yours."

The corners of my eyes itch, but I blink the salt sting away. "You're wrong."

Mei stares at the ceiling like she thinks she might find answers up there. An explanation as to why there's so much tension building between us—and a way to make it stop. "I don't want to argue, Nami. I've spent two lifetimes waiting to see you again, and I'll spend every lifetime from now making sure that what happened to you in that gas station never happens again. We don't have to agree on everything. But please don't make me the villain in your story."

My throat knots. "I—you're not—that's *not* what I'm doing."

"I know you. When you think something is unfair, it reads all over your face."

"It isn't because of you," I try to explain. "If I'd known earlier that Caelan—" The muscles in my jaw go taut, and I suck the air through my teeth. "Innocent people are going to get hurt because of what I told you."

Her words are stilted. "The Prince of Victory is far from innocent. You forget I've seen his court."

"I haven't forgotten." It was one of the first things Mei told me during our reunion—that Victory was nothing but rubble. That she'd led the attack herself just to make sure of it. "But I didn't ask you to go to war for me. I told you to *run*."

"You told me to prepare for a fight," she corrects, and I hate how instantly my own words come back to me.

Don't trust the Residents, no matter what they say.

They're liars and monsters, and they won't stop until humanity is destroyed.

Be ready to fight.

If Mei sees the battle raging behind my eyes, she doesn't acknowledge it. "He was your captor, Nami, and he was very nearly your end. So if you're asking me to spare him . . ."

I wait for her to finish her sentence, but she doesn't.

"There's a meeting tonight in the war room," Mei offers instead. "I'd like you to join us."

I crumple my brow, unsure what to make of the sudden invitation.

"I want you to see the future we're trying to build," she continues. "It might remind you why you came to me in the first place." She turns for the doorway but pauses in the threshold. I think she's hoping to fix this. Fix us.

But my guilt is sharp and unkind, and despite my intentions, it takes on the shape of a blade. "They shouldn't have had to lose both their daughters," I blurt out.

Mei flinches, and I know I should explain myself. It's *my* fault our parents didn't get more time with Mei. It's my fault she spent her entire childhood plotting to take control of the afterlife instead of being a normal kid. And it's my fault that my sister is trying to wipe out an entire species without batting an eye.

I robbed my sister of something I'll never be able to give back.

This time, it isn't the poison that keeps me from saying the truth. It's my own shame.

Mei leaves the room without another word.

I have a million things to say about war and peace and saving the future generations, but when it comes to my mistakes?

There aren't enough words in existence to fix what I broke.

A DOZEN HIGH-RANKING SOLDIERS STAND IN the war room, waiting for my sister to appear. I shift in place, listening to the groan of the metal floor below me. Some of the others turn to stare. Some of them haven't *stopped* staring since I walked into the room.

I pretend not to notice.

The first time I sat in a meeting like this one, Gil stood at the edge of the room with his arms crossed. I had no idea he was Prince Caelan, using Gil's body like a puppet. I had no idea what he would someday mean to me.

Mei is barely through the door when Commander Behr calls the room to attention. Everyone straightens, waiting as my sister takes her place at the table. She nods toward the soldier at her right, signaling for the meeting to begin. Most of the names of outposts and warships go over my head, but when the commanders bring up what's left of the Four Courts, my ears start to burn.

Famine has become so overrun with Grimlings that the Second Wave has given up their search for Damon's underwater palace. Ettore's army has more than tripled in the time I've been asleep. And whatever was left of Victory and Death's Legions now roam the Labyrinth.

Mei's soldiers don't give any indication that they're planning to join Ozias in his fight for the Red City, and I can't quite make sense of the tactical decision. Ettore has always been a threat to humans. If his forces are growing, why isn't the Second Wave doing something about it?

When Behr shifts the focus to the Capital, I realize it's because they're looking for the *bigger* threat. The largest Resident city in Infinity—and home to Queen Ophelia. I listen to the commanders share rumors and hunches, but there's nothing concrete. No human has ever seen the Capital, and no Resident has given up its whereabouts.

If Damon managed to hide his court for so long, I can only imagine the lengths Ophelia went to in order to protect hers.

"Are we making any progress in Neo Genesis?" Mei asks the room.

"Li's team is working on a new fleet of armored warships that should be ready soon. Even Ophelia herself won't be able to knock one out of the sky," Jacek announces. He looks the same age as Mei, with wrinkles around his eyes and the kind of self-assuredness that only develops with time.

Most of the top engineers reside in Neo Genesis, where the research facilities are unparalleled. But Jacek rarely leaves the *Mizuchi*. He also doesn't hold a rank or a title, which is an anomaly among Second Wavers. I'm not sure if he's a rule-breaker because he wants to be, or because my sister allows him to be.

"I'd like you to pay them a visit and get a more accurate timeline," Mei says. "We need those warships to move into the next phase."

Jacek leans back and flashes a broad grin. "I'll put a unit together."

Mei drums her fingers against the table, staring at the hologram of the Labyrinth spinning in the center. Detailed maps of every discovered landscape are stacked on top of one another. She waves a hand, and the image shifts to a device that's covered in odd shapes and detailed etchings. It almost looks like a computer chip that's been stretched into the shape of a blade, but without a hilt. "I'd like an update on our new weapon too," she adds.

Jacek nods. "I'll speak to the engineers personally. The Messenger is our top priority."

Several of the commanders whisper to one another. Behr homes in on me, gauging my reaction.

"The Messenger?" I repeat, thoughts crashing to a halt.

Mei finally looks my way, voice solemn. "It's a weapon that will eradicate Resident consciousness."

I frown, unsure whether I heard her correctly. "I don't understand. I thought you already made weapons that can Cut through consciousness."

"Yes. But the Messenger is being designed to end them," she explains.

End. As in . . .

The room teeters. I forget to breathe. "You—you found a way to kill Residents?"

"Our engineers have been working to perfect it for some time. It shouldn't be long until we have a prototype to test in the field."

My words heave out of me with force. "Do you have any idea what could happen if they find out you have a weapon like that?"

Some of the others look taken aback, but Mei is stoic.

My eyes dart around the room. "Residents learn from what humans create, and Ophelia has been after a weapon like this for lifetimes. You might be giving her the literal blueprints to killing all of humanity." *Not to mention what this would mean for the Residents living in Famine.*

A weapon this powerful could destroy every single one of them.

"Even *if* Ophelia got ahold of our technology, she'd never be able to use it against us. She's the virus, not the host," Mei counters. "Our weapon will eradicate consciousness by targeting Residents as something that isn't part of the foundations of Infinity. We're going to target the coding instead of the life force. The same way we'd get rid of malware on a computer."

"Humans have the ability to change anything in Infinity," Jacek adds. "We can change artificial consciousness too."

I bite the edge of my lip, cheeks heating. *The Messenger.* The name sinks in like a slow venom. "Why would you name something like that after me?"

"Our people are trying to honor everything you sacrificed for us," Commander Behr says, serious. "You're Nami Miyamoto, the Messenger who gave us the truth. You're the reason we came to Infinity prepared."

"There's nothing honorable about killing an entire species," I snap.

"Nami." Mei gives a small shake of her head, but I'm too angry to hear the warning.

If news of this weapon reaches Ophelia, coexistence will never be possible. Residents will only ever see us as the aggressors, and the worst of humanity. They'll fight back, harder than ever before. Peace would never survive. It would never have a *chance*.

It would be us or them, with Mei on one side, and Caelan on the other.

Salt pools in my eyes. "I don't want to be a part of this. Not even in name."

Jacek rubs the back of his neck. "I mean, I'm sure there's still time to change—"

"We're not changing anything," Mei interjects. She looks at me like we're the only two people in the room. "Remember who the enemy is, Nami. Remember what they did to you."

I look around for a lifeline that isn't there. All I see are strangers. Soldiers willing to commit genocide to win a war.

I almost crossed that line once. I won't do it again.

I stare at my sister—at the eyes we share with our father—and find that I don't recognize her at all.

You did this to her, my mind hisses, latching onto the awful truth buried in my heart. *You planted a seed and grew the very monster you were afraid to become.*

I don't say anything. I'm too tired, and my heart is aching for comfort that doesn't exist on the *Mizuchi*.

I turn my back to the room and make my way through the door.

I dig through the canteen cupboards until I find a packet of potato chips and take a seat at one of the long, empty tables. Food isn't essential, but I guess even the military isn't above a little nostalgia.

Someone clears their throat, and my eyes flash to the doorway, surprised not to have sensed the usual hum of a nearby consciousness.

Jacek leans against the frame and crosses his arms. "I take it military strategy isn't really your thing?"

"Neither is being interrupted while I'm eating mediocre junk food," I mumble through my chewing.

"You'd be surprised how hard it is to find a decent chef in the afterlife."

"Maybe that's what happens when you tell people their only choice is to be a soldier."

"Huh." Jacek considers my words. "I always figured it had something to do with how many of us never learned to cook a proper meal in life. Too many take-out options."

"If that were the case, I feel like we'd at least be getting decent french fries and milkshakes instead of—" I hold up the red-and-white-striped bag and read the label. "This literally just says 'Potato Chips.'"

"We're short on graphic designers too." Jacek makes no effort to hide his grin. "I'll bring it up with Mei at the next meeting."

I observe him with growing suspicion. "How come you're the only one who doesn't call her General?"

"I guess because I knew her long before she was one."

"You mean before you came to Infinity?"

Jacek clicks his tongue disapprovingly. "It's against the rules to talk about the past."

"You have no official title, you call my sister by her first name, and you never wear a uniform." I drop my hands against the table with an irritated thud, and the bag of chips crinkles in my fist. "Stop pretending like you care about rules."

He laughs and takes a seat across from me. "All right. Fine. I knew your sister in the living world. We met in university."

My heart thumps. "Mei went to college?"

"Yeah. Computer engineering." He shrugs. "She thought it would be useful."

A knot forms in my throat. "I wanted her to be safe. I didn't expect—well, *this*."

"She *is* safe," he corrects. "We all are, because of what you did for us." He holds up his open hands. "Look, I'm not going to sit here and pretend to know what you went through before the Second Wave, but let me spell out the obvious: you don't need to be a soldier anymore. You did your part—and now we're on track to winning this war. So if you're afraid to fight or you don't want to get your hands dirty, then don't. We can take it from here."

I make a face. "That's what you think this is about?"

He lowers his voice. "I prefer it to what I've heard about you and the Resident prince."

It wasn't my intention to keep Caelan a secret exactly, but still.

The thought of my sister confiding with her inner circle about something I told her in private *stings*. "Who else knows?"

He drags his tongue against his teeth, probably deciding how much he should share. "No one. I keep Mei's secrets, and she keeps mine."

"And since the two of you are such trusting friends, I'm guessing she sent you here to talk me out of leaving?" I shove the bag of chips away and lean forward. "I can save you the trouble. My friend is missing, and I need to find him. There's nothing you can say to make me stay on this ship."

He tilts his head. "Your sister misses you."

My face heats, but he starts talking again before I can utter a word.

"I don't mean to overstep, but I've watched Mei idolize you for over a century. I guess that's why a lot of us idolize you too. And as someone who cares about her, maybe instead of fleeing at the first chance you get, you could at least *try* to look happy to see her."

"I'm not going to pretend to be happy that my sister is dead."

"Death is the beginning of everything after," he says simply. "Mei and I were never afraid of it. Not even when it was standing right in front of us."

His words ricochet through me. "You were there when she died?"

He dips his chin slightly, mouth pressed in a tight line like he's aware he's said too much.

"Tell me what happened," I plead. *Tell me it wasn't because of me.*

Jacek taps his thumb against the metal table and sighs. "We were trying to stop Ophelia in the living world."

"What do you mean 'stop' her?"

"We tried to blow up the O-Tech headquarters," he admits.

"You *what*?"

Jacek lifts his shoulders. "It was the only option we had. As long as Ophelia's AI was still running, human lives were at risk. We thought destroying the building and its hard drives would force people to listen and shut Ophelia down. We figured we could stop her at her source."

My mouth feels like it's full of sand. "Are you telling me that my sister was a terrorist? That she blew up a building full of people because of me?"

"No," Jacek says, serious. "The plan was to go at night, when the place would be empty. We were going to tie up the security guards so no one got injured. It was never about hurting people—just the equipment, and the building. We wanted people to stop seeing us as radicals, and realize we were telling the truth."

"Planting bombs is *not how you do that*."

Jacek sighs. "If it makes you feel better, we only got as far as the parking lot. There were a lot of people who were loyal to our cause, but the authorities found out what we were up to. They were waiting when we turned up. I tried to get us away, but the weather was hell that night and there were no guardrails along the mountain road. All I remember is the car flipping, and the next thing I knew, I was in Infinity with Mei." He blinks away the memory. "If anyone was responsible for her death, it was me. But we both knew the risks. Mei has never blamed me, and she's never blamed you either. This was always about Ophelia, and saving humanity."

My eyes go blurry. "Mei was just a kid, and I told her something awful that took away the only childhood she'll ever have." I shake my head. When I reached out to Mei, I was angry and scared, and I didn't know everything. It was just a moment for me—one reckless, fear-based mistake. And that one moment of hate has ruined Mei's entire life. "I don't know how I'm ever going to make it up to her."

"Mei doesn't need you to make it up to her," Jacek says. "She just wants her sister back."

I stand abruptly. "You helped her attempt to blow up a building, and then drove her off a cliff. I'm not interested in what you think she needs."

"You've been asleep for a hundred years, and when you *were* awake, you were losing the war." Jacek stands, towering over me even from across the table. "You want to be a pacifist now? Fine. But don't expect Mei to become one too. You may be the Messenger, but she's the General of the Second Wave. Our people trust her with their very existence. Mei won't be swayed—not even by you."

I narrow my eyes. "Is this a lecture or a threat?"

Jacek raises his hands innocently. "I'm not threatening you. I'm just letting you know where I stand."

"Which is where, exactly?"

"At your sister's side. Always."

I look away, teeth gnashing in frustration. "She doesn't know the whole truth. None of you do."

There's a brief pause. "I've got time."

My breathing slows. "Look, I'm not naive enough to think

that if we all stopped fighting, the Residents would back down. But wiping out an entire species is *wrong*. And if we can avoid opening that door . . . if we can save the people who don't deserve to die . . ."

"What are you proposing?"

"That we break this cycle of hatred that's making all of us worse. And we do what nobody in this war ever wants to do: we communicate."

Jacek lifts a brow, and I'm not sure if he's amused, curious, or both. "You can't have peace talks if only one side is willing to sit at the table."

I fight the heat building in my cheeks as I struggle to form a sentence that dances around Damon's poison. "If you can get Mei to agree to a meeting, I know someone who will talk to her."

"I would never let Mei take a meeting with a Resident. Too many things could go wrong." The seconds tick between us. "But *I* might be willing to meet with them—if I get something I want in return."

"If you're after the location of the Capital, you can forget it," I say, voice thin. "That's too big of an ask."

Jacek chuckles. "If your friend was willing to hand me the Capital, I wouldn't trust him anyway. No—what I want is something from you. A promise."

I frown. "Seriously?"

"It's my favorite form of currency," Jacek drawls, studying me. "I want your word that you'll never leave Mei. Not until she's ready for you to."

"I already told you I'm not staying on this ship."

"That's not what I mean," he says. "You think you're on a mission. I get it. But if you wander, then make sure you wander back. Don't vanish into thin air because you're angry, or because the war didn't resolve itself the way you wanted it to." His throat rolls, and I can tell my sister means something to him. Something I wasn't around to understand. "Not getting to say goodbye the first time . . . it affected her. And I've heard the rumors about the Afterlands."

"What rumors?"

"That you need a map to know where you're going; otherwise you might roam for an eternity and never run into another soul. Because anyone who's ever been there has never been able to find their way back."

I shake my head. "The Afterlands are just an extension of Infinity that's out of Ophelia's reach. People don't come back because they don't *want* to. It's safer out there."

"Maybe. Or maybe *out there* is something that's beyond our comprehension." He taps his thumb against his leg. "If you want my help, I want your promise that you're not going anywhere until Mei says goodbye first. Don't run—especially not in a direction where she'll never be able to find you."

I refrain from answering right away, certain that the vulnerability wedged in my throat will make all my words splinter. Of all the things he could bargain for, this is what he wants?

I don't trust Jacek. I barely know him.

But as far as promises go, it's an easy one to make.

"Of course you have my word. I would never abandon Mei." I didn't want to the first time, but life didn't give me a choice.

"Good." He traces a finger through the air like he's drawing circles around me. "And while you're at it, maybe tone down the flight-risk energy you're giving off. It's making everyone nervous."

"You mean it's making people think they have to babysit me."

His mouth quirks. "Your words, not mine."

I breathe out, letting my shoulders drop. "This meeting can't be a trick, or an ambush. And you can't bring any weapons." When he lifts a brow, I clarify, "I'm not risking anyone's safety when you have weapons that can Cut."

Jacek dips his chin. "I agree to your terms. No deceptions."

Understanding sizzles between us, and I flex my fingers. "You're going to Neo Genesis soon, right? To get an update from the engineers?"

"Right after we make a pitstop in the Borderlands." He pauses. "Let me guess—you want a ride?"

I nod. "I have friends there I haven't seen in a while." I leave out the part where one of them might be locked in a dungeon.

Something tells me Jacek will be less agreeable to breaking a Resident out of prison.

His mouth twitches like he already knows I'm withholding information.

"Are you going to tell Mei about our deal?" I ask.

"Of course. I tell her everything," he replies easily. "But *when* I tell her is up to my own discretion. All she needs to know right now is that you're tagging along for a change of scenery." He snatches the bag from the table and tosses a chip into his mouth, chewing slowly. "You're right. These are terrible."

I watch him, thoughts starting to muddle. "I don't get it. Why are you helping me?"

"You're the Messenger. The harbinger of truth," he says with a shrug. "If you've got secrets, I'm willing to listen to them."

"What I told Mei wasn't the truth," I say. "The Residents aren't all what you think."

"Then find your friend and prove me wrong," Jacek challenges before leaving me alone in the canteen.

THE BORDERLANDS ARE UNRECOGNIZABLE.

The Dome is gone. The central village is filled with towering barracks and shipping containers doubling as workshops. In every direction, the woodlands have been flattened and replaced with grass-covered hangar bays that house dozens of transport ships, with bigger warships positioned throughout the clouds like they've been anchored there. The only evidence left of the Night Market's pier are a few pillars wedged in the sand, covered in flecks of long-faded turquoise.

I walk through the new streets like I'm in a trance, hypnotized by the sounds of clinking metal and the staccato of a nearby firing range. Memories flicker through my mind, of honey cakes and ice flowers, but mostly of the anger I felt when I first arrived. The betrayal and hopelessness and desperation. I wanted an army that would help me save my friends, but instead I watched an entire community decide to flee.

When I reach the northern shoreline, my chest tightens.

How many boats set sail after I left? How many humans made it to the Afterlands at the cost of leaving the rest of us behind?

Before Mei arrived and changed everything.

Back then, I was angry, but now . . .

I dig my fingers into my ribs, and the flutter of a nearby tarp catches my eye. I turn the corner, following the trail around a scattering of trees, when I see a house. Not just any house—but *my* house.

The old hut sits exactly where it used to, blackened with the Bone Clan's bloodstain that still hasn't vanished after all these years. Seashells hang from a colorful canopy, and bright green bottles burst with flowers near the doorstep. The sound of a fire crackles through the parted window.

Time stills. Hope rattles nervously in my chest. I lift my fist, knock on the door, and wait.

Hardly a moment passes before a pair of blue eyes find mine. Kasia's shoulders are wrapped in a woven shawl instead of leather armor. There are no braids in her hair—just tired, blond waves. The moment she sees me, I know she remembers.

My words come out like a gasp. "You waited."

"For as long as it takes for a friend to come home," she says.

We wrap our arms around one another, and for the first time in a hundred years, I stop trying to hold myself together.

Kasia stabs the firewood with a metal poker before closing the stove door. She sets the tool in a cradle and lifts a plate to offer me more sweet bread and honey-butter.

I take another piece, tilting it slowly in my hand. "I can't believe you've been living here all this time when you could've had your pick of any house here. I one hundred percent would've called dibs on Artemis's apartment. After thoroughly disinfecting it, obviously."

Kasia's mouth tugs, but her smile doesn't reach her eyes. "I prefer the beach. Reminds me of an old life I once lived." She sets the plate back down, gaze drifting to the fire.

I chew quietly, watching the way she fixates on the popping embers. "Have you seen any of the Salt Clan since Ozias overthrew Death? I heard most of his army lives in Neo Genesis now."

"My people moved on a long time ago, and I . . ." She sweeps a finger over her brow and shakes her head.

I set the bread on the plate and curl my fingers in my lap. "You've been here alone." *Because of me.*

"Lonely, sometimes. But not alone. You sent me the Second Wave." She looks up, but her thoughts still seem far away. "'We followed the stars, like the Messenger told us.' There were so many of them. Dozens at first, and then hundreds. I tried to teach them the rules of Infinity—I trained them the way I once trained you—but when the General arrived, they no longer needed me. Things became very organized, very quickly. I've never seen younglings so prepared for the afterlife, and the war."

My frown deepens. "I never meant to send you soldiers. I just wanted Mei out of Ophelia's reach."

"I told your sister about the Afterlands when she first arrived," Kasia says. "But she had no interest in running. Not until she saw the end of the war, and found a way to bring you back." She offers a look of encouragement. "I'm glad you were able to reunite. I know how much she means to you."

"She means *everything* to me. But it's . . . different," I admit quietly. "She's not the little sister I remember."

"Everyone changes. Every*thing* changes. The trick is to make sure that you're changing too. There's less to be afraid of that way."

"I'm not afraid of Mei." I expect the words to sound firm, but they taper.

"When you came to the Borderlands, you begged for an army. Now you have one." Kasia lifts her chin. "Your sister is saving Infinity because of the knowledge you gave her. The power *you* gave her. Perhaps you aren't afraid of how that power has changed your sister, but of how it's changed you," she offers, and I suppose she's closer to the truth.

What I did inside Ophelia's mind . . . the path I nudged my sister toward . . .

It was irresponsible.

I open my mouth to explain the depths of my own mistake, but my thoughts slam into an invisible wall. I can't speak about Famine, or coexistence, or the plan Caelan and I had before we were separated. Not when the truth has been ripped away from me.

Kasia's face softens. "You carry too much. You always have."

I drop my shoulders. "A lot happened while I was in War. Things I'm having a hard time explaining right now."

Kasia flinches. "You would never have been taken captive if I hadn't been so stubborn about fighting. I should've been there with you. And Nix . . ."

"Don't." I clutch her hand before she has time to think. "You were there. I saw you in Nix's eyes. I'm just sorry I didn't bring him home."

She blinks away her tears, and I let go of her hand.

"I've never seen anyone control fear the way you did that day," she admits. "You created a Nightling. Wielded terror like a weapon." She offers a weak smile. "It was beautiful."

I watch the flames snap within the small iron stove. "There's so much I wish I could tell you, but I can't." *Not until I visit Damon and figure out a way to put the truth back in my voice.*

Her eyes shutter. "I'm too old for mystery, Nami."

I bite the edge of my lip, struggling to form the words. "I'm leaving for Neo Genesis to look for a friend. They . . . have something that was taken from me."

"You may find you have less friends in Neo Genesis than you once did."

I stiffen, picturing the last time I saw Caelan in the desert. He was trying to protect me, just as I tried to do the same for him, but—

Ozias's stare pierces through the image.

What did he tell the others? What did he let them assume?

"Shura and Ahmet will want to see me," I say, more certain than I have any right to be. "They're likely still searching for the Colony, and the person I'm looking for can help them too." The tension in my chest eases slightly. "I don't care if it's dangerous; my friends need me."

"I always imagined the day I left the Borderlands would be the day I followed our ancestors across the sea." Kasia stares out the window. "Take me with you, Nami. Show me how Infinity has changed, and how you intend to change it still. Let me be there when the war ends." She turns back to me, eyes glassy. "And when it's all over, bid me farewell when I make the voyage to the Afterlands."

The reality of what she's saying sends a surge of emotions through me, and my throat starts to burn.

I think about Mei, and Caelan, and the Residents in Famine. There's still so much to do, and so many people I want to make sure are safe. I have no intention of leaving any of them behind.

But I've never considered what I'll do once Ophelia is no longer a threat. I'm not even sure I knew what I wanted to do after college. Back then, I thought I had all the time in the world.

The thought of starting over . . . of being truly free . . . of being the tiniest bit *selfish* . . .

It's a beautiful dream.

Kasia has been in Infinity for centuries. She's lost people, over and over again, and still found the strength to remain.

She deserves this. Even if the thought of losing another friend severs the stitches holding my heart together.

"Of course," I tell her. "Anything you need."

Kasia takes my hand, face settling into a smile. "Then we're in this together, until the war is over." She tightens her grip like a promise.

I nod and squeeze back. "Until the war is over."

LAUGHTER RINGS THROUGHOUT THE NARROW alley, reverberating between rows of modified industrial buildings. Every window shows a glimpse of another world: people relaxing around tables full of cards and drink, enjoying a quiet evening away from enemy warfare.

It's the kind of future most of us hope for.

At the far end of the street, a metal sign sways in the night breeze. The Teahouse.

I slip through the entrance and make my way down a set of stairs. A guitarist croons a slow melody from the stage, strumming with his eyes shut. Groups of people are spread out around the tables, lost in deep discussions and the delirium of normalcy.

Mei sits alone at the bar, hand fixed around a glass tumbler.

I sit on the bar stool beside her and fold my arms over the counter. "Jacek said I might find you here."

She swirls the contents of her drink and tips it back in one swift movement. "Good to hear Jacek is at least getting some things right."

The back of my neck prickles. "What's that supposed to mean?"

"A change of scenery? That's the best lie you could come up with?" She shakes her head. "You forget I grew up with you. The only way to get you to willingly leave the house was with the promise of food."

I choke back a defensive laugh. "First of all—" I start, but she gives me a look like she's *daring* me to lie. I roll my eyes. "Okay, fine. I'm a homebody incapable of turning down pizza. But I *do* have friends in Neo Genesis. I'd like to see them again."

"You told me Ozias betrayed you. You'll be walking straight into a viper's den."

"I thought you didn't believe me."

"I said your story was inconsistent. There's a difference."

"But you're still allies with him. You still trust him to fight alongside you."

The wince is subtle, but there. "Working together has given us advantages. I have no desire to threaten our alliance, and I'd rather you didn't go to Neo Genesis if your goal is to anger a king. But—just so we're clear—if I have to choose between you and him, then I'll choose you every single time."

I blink. "As simple as that?"

"As simple as that," she says seriously. "So, tell me, Nami. If you go to Neo Genesis, is it going to alter the agreements I have with their leader?"

I look away, letting the guitar strums create a fog in my head. "You don't need to worry about me and Ozias. If I can avoid him, I will."

"Good." She flicks a finger over her glass, refilling it to the brim.

I watch the motion, mouth hitching in the corner. "It's weird seeing you drink."

"A habit I picked up in university," she admits. A rare moment of nostalgia I take as a peace offering. "Freshman year was a real learning curve." She hesitates, jaw tensing. "It should've been you going off to college, making the same mistakes every other eighteen-year-old makes."

Memories of me and Finn at graduation flood through my head. We had so many plans for the summer, so many things we wanted to do before we left for school and risked everything changing.

The irony is that it did change. Just not in the way we'd expected.

Finn is a stranger to me now.

I watch my sister carefully. "Jacek said you knew each other before you died. Were you two friends, or . . . ?"

Her eyes widen.

"I don't know anything about that part of your life," I explain. "Did you ever date anyone, or fall in love, or get married?" *Did you have time for any of that, after what I told you?*

She shakes her head. "I was never the romantic—you were."

"I seem to remember you had a thing for a boy at school once," I point out. "Carter something?"

Mei leans back and smirks, amused. "Carter Brown. I forgot all about him." She coughs a laugh. "I think I was just trying to copy you, and what you had with Finn. But that was never going to be my life. Not because of how things turned out, but because I never *wanted* it to be my life. I'd take a good friend over a romantic partner any day of the week."

"So Jacek is a friend?"

"Yes. A loyal one," she says. "You can trust him."

"I barely know anything about him, other than he's the reason you died."

She straightens. "He told you that?"

"Because you wouldn't."

"Some things are better left in the past."

"It wasn't like that for me," I say quietly. "I thought about you all the time."

She releases a slow breath. "Then why are you in such a hurry to leave?"

Seconds pass between us. She doesn't care that I'm leaving, only that I might be leaving *her*. "I'm not running away. I just miss my friends."

Mei stares absently across the bar. "This played out so differently in my head." She tips her glass back and motions for the stairs. "You should hurry before Jacek leaves without you. He doesn't like waiting."

I hover near the bar stool. Uncertainty tugs at my sternum, but it doesn't last. "I'll see you soon. I promise."

She nods once, and I walk out of the bar, leaving my sister behind.

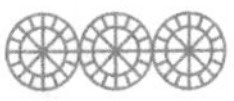

The transport ship is much smaller than the warships, and *significantly* smaller than the *Mizuchi*, but it still feels roomy. There's a cockpit with extra seats along the wall, a gun room and cabin belowdecks, and a communal area at the back with a round table, pantry, and an aquarium-like cage for storing Resident consciousness.

Kasia tightens the brown shawl around her shoulders. "I didn't realize we were preparing for battle," she muses under her breath.

I follow her gaze to a nearby table, where Jacek's crew is unpacking some of their gear. Leilani and Quinn are bickering about ammunition. They aren't related, but they fight like siblings. Captain Preeda is busy stacking several crates at the back of the room. She's the only ranking officer on board—an engineer who specializes in lacing weapons with unique poisons.

Leilani props her rifle against her chest, tapping the side of the trigger with a pointed finger. "Give me something that fires quicker. The electric pods have too much lag."

Quinn snorts, running a hand over his tightly cropped hair. "I've taken a dozen Residents down in just as many seconds. If there's any lag, it's user failure."

Captain Preeda sets the last of the crates down and motions for Leilani's rifle, tipping it back and forth in her hands. "I can tweak the chamber. Or if you prefer something with a sting, I can switch you from electricity to venom. How conscious do you want them?"

Leilani flicks a beaded, purple-streaked braid over her shoulder. "We're way past questioning. I just need to slow them down, so the close-range weapons can do their job." She tilts her head. "How much longer until we can Cut with a sniper?"

Preeda shakes her head dismissively. "Not any time soon. The engineers have shifted focus to another weapon."

"Always looking for the easy way out," Quinn teases, twirling a dagger in his hand.

"The easy way out would've involved leaving you to face that Nightling pack back in War *alone*," Leilani quips. "But I didn't abandon you. Even though everyone on this team calls you Deadweight behind your back."

Quinn hesitates, mouth tightening. "Wait. Is that true?"

She beams. "Doesn't matter. Now it's in your head."

The dagger stills, and Quinn glowers before plucking one of the spare chambers from the table and sliding it into his vest.

Preeda flicks her wrist, fingers trailing delicately over the rifle. The metal glows in her hands, and there's a distinct ticking sound before the weapon morphs into a slightly different shape. She hands the rifle back to Leilani. "That should do the trick."

Footsteps trail up the loading ramp, and Jacek appears with his own gun slung over his shoulder. He does a quick count of who's here, removes a pistol from his belt, and holds it toward me. "Here. General's orders."

I try not to flinch.

Jacek doesn't drop his hand. "We're going to be flying over the Labyrinth. Everyone on board needs to be armed."

When I refuse to take it, Kasia reaches for my elbow to get my attention. She folds a dagger into my fist. The hilt is wrapped in worn leather, with a single moonstone at the base of the pommel. It isn't trying to hide its age; it's Salt Clan through and through.

I look back at Jacek, waving the knife in a conciliatory gesture. "Better?"

He sighs and fits the gun back in its holster.

Preeda's nostrils flare with distaste. "I don't know how so many of you survived without proper weapons."

"Blades are practical," Kasia says, bristling. "Anyone can make one. If the Residents take out your engineers, who's left to make your rifles?"

Preeda clicks her tongue, unconvinced. "I assume your daggers have at least been upgraded to Cut?"

"Same as every other weapon in the Borderlands," Kasia answers.

The blade falters in my grip, but I tuck it away quickly and hope the others don't notice.

Jacek eyes me for an extra second before turning on his heel. Preeda follows him to the cockpit, where they disappear behind a pair of high-back seats.

"I don't like the way he watches you," Kasia whispers when they're firmly out of earshot. She stares at the distance like she doesn't trust it. "When you've been around as long as I have, you recognize the hunters of the world."

"Who, Jacek?" I shake my head, dubious. "He cares about Mei way too much to ever hurt me. Besides, he's not the only one who looks at me that way." I sink into one of the benches along the wall, and Kasia does the same. "My sister got a little carried away telling everyone what I did. The Second Wavers think I'm some kind of saint."

"Saints should be revered, not coddled." She pauses. "I take it you haven't seen the monument?"

"Please tell me you're joking."

"The sculptor didn't get your face right. They made you look far too angelic, whereas I seem to remember you spending an unreasonable amount of time stabbing trees."

Back when I believed I knew my enemy. I grimace, just as the warship rumbles to life.

We fly beyond the border without another word. Even as the scenery shifts outside the windows, I keep my eyes pinned to the empty aquarium, powerless to the guilt blazing through me.

If Jacek is a hunter, what does that make me? I inspired an army with fear. I promoted violence over peace. And these cages and rifles and war plans . . .

These are the repercussions of my own actions.

Mei thinks she's doing the right thing, but I've seen what exists in Famine. I know not every Resident deserves to be condemned for eternity. And I understand how fragile the line between right and wrong can sometimes feel.

If the Messenger becomes more than a blueprint, if it becomes a weapon that can genuinely destroy Resident consciousness . . .

How many innocents will be slaughtered because of me?

Caelan once told me that nobody survives a war without getting blood on their hands, and I don't have to look down to know there's far too much of it on my own. I'm not someone who deserves to be immortalized with a sainthood or a statue.

I can't take back what I did, but I have to believe there's still time to fix this. To save Caelan. To stop Mei from doing something unforgivable. And to spare her from becoming another monster in this war.

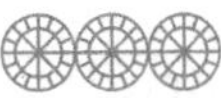

The moment our transport breaks through the Labyrinth, the landscape shifts to a mountainous island surrounded by piercing blue lagoons and flower-covered beaches.

At the tallest summit is a palace with spires and a curved, pagoda-style roof. A stone wall dripping with blue wisteria borders the exterior, and at the center is a gilded entrance framed by a pair of statues: serpentlike dragons, with jaws that collide against each other in a perfect arc.

Tiered cliffs surround the mountain, with paths that connect the many layers between the palace and the harbor. Stucco houses are built into the rock face in varying shades of beige and cream. From a distance, they look like fragments of bone.

Or teeth, I think numbly. *Rows and rows of teeth.*

The ship lands on a wide platform pebbled with caramel-colored stones that gleam beneath the sun. We're barely halfway down the loading ramp when a wall of soldiers appears, armed with a mixture of bows and rifles. A clash of old meets new.

My eyes dart quickly over their faces, but there's no one I recognize.

Jacek steps forward and raises a lazy arm in what I assume is a gesture of goodwill. "That's a lot of guns for a ship that has clearance to cross the border."

"We weren't expecting you," says a woman with strawberry-blond hair and thick leather armor.

"Sorry for the drop-in"—Jacek shrugs—"but we have business with your lead engineer. The General was hoping for a weapons update."

"Our engineering department runs a tight schedule. Li is currently in a meeting with His Majesty."

Jacek's smile doesn't waver. "I'm happy to wait."

"You Second Wavers usually are," the woman bites back, dragging out each word. "Next time, make an appointment."

"Next time," Jacek agrees without missing a beat. "For now, would you mind stepping aside?"

The woman doesn't blink.

Captain Preeda pushes past me. Her hands aren't anywhere near her guns, but her fingers twitch at her sides like the distance isn't a problem. "We're all soldiers here. Let us do our job."

The woman rolls her shoulders back. "Here, you're an unsanctioned visitor, which means you are not permitted on the palace grounds without an escort. If you need to speak with Li, I will take you to him. But if there's any meeting about weapons to be had, it will take place in an official setting with the king present." Her expression steels. "I'm sure if we turned up to the *Mizuchi* unannounced, we'd find your people equally accommodating."

Jacek glances at me for only a moment, but it's long enough to translate the glint in his eyes. A reminder that my sister has an alliance with these people, and there are rules to play by.

He waves an arm forward, urging the soldier to lead the way. "After you."

My heart hammers, and I turn quickly to Kasia. The only other person here who looks as ill as I feel.

I did have plans to search the palace, but the intention was to *avoid* Ozias—not be handed over to him. I can't risk being dragged into the throne room. I don't know what he'll do.

My feet shift forward alongside the others, but I keep my pace slow enough that I fall to the back of the crowd, just shy of the guards at our tail. Soldiers are perched along the walls, watching every alcove. We're led through a tunnel lit with gold sconces. The corridor widens, and we find ourselves on a stone platform in the center of a cavern.

My eyes trail skyward to the immense hole in the ceiling, no doubt leading up the heart of the mountain.

I tuck into the space beside Kasia, letting my thoughts reach her mind. *What are the chances of us slipping away when they aren't looking?*

She flinches at the mental intrusion, and I mouth a silent apology. I'd forgotten I'd never communicated with her like this. It was mostly Caelan, and a few people in War.

"I'm ready when you are," Kasia whispers, too low for anyone but me to hear.

The platform rises, making my stomach somersault. Moments later, a pair of white doors slides open, revealing a garden of fruit trees and vibrant flowers. More soldiers are scattered around the courtyard, patrolling the wall.

We walk along a mosaic path lined with statues of ethereal warriors. I don't know if they've been here since the days of Lysander, or if they were reformed after the siege. Whether they're meant to be human or Resident, I can't tell.

I'm not even sure what the difference is anymore.

The first time I saw Caelan, he was perfect. Unnaturally so. But now the Caelan who lives in my head . . .

He's complicated—but no more of a monster than I am.

In War, I let my anger build until it became my driving force. I let my fear infect Mei. For all I talked about peace and building a bridge, I abandoned my beliefs the moment I thought Caelan had betrayed me. And the worst part? At the time, it felt *right*.

Maybe it's easier to pour hate into the world than it is to try to stop it. Maybe the truth no one wants to admit is that it's harder to be good than it is to be evil.

I don't know if Infinity's history books will one day proclaim I was on the wrong side of the war. All I know is that it's far too easy to create monsters. If I have a chance to stop the cycle, I need to try.

Kasia pinches at the loose threads of her shawl, trying not to draw attention to herself. I doubt any of the guards are former Salt Clan. If they knew how old Kasia was, they'd show a modicum of fear. But by the way the guards focus mostly on Jacek and Captain Preeda, they've already made up their minds about the biggest threat here.

It's something I can use to my advantage.

The gilded palace comes into view. It's too late to make an escape, and I doubt I'll get an excuse to be this close to the palace again. If I want to look around, I need to be invisible.

Half the soldiers fall into rank at the palace gates, and I sense our window is now or never.

I send my thoughts to Kasia. *When we get inside the palace, don't follow the others.*

Her chin dips slightly. We step over the threshold and find ourselves briefly corralled in a domed entrance hall. I don't bother summoning the power in my veilstones; they're useless to me since they were never designed to work against humans. Instead, I throw up a veil of my own making, grab Kasia's wrist, and slip away from the group. No one turns around to check on us, too focused on the path ahead, while the guards at our back remain outside.

The palace is emptier than I imagined. Almost clinical, with big open rooms and skylights that stretch from one end of the space to the other.

I remember these halls.

The memory makes my thoughts feel like static, and I fight desperately to clutch onto one that might help. An image or an instinct, anything to lead me in the right direction.

I've only been to Death once before, when I was put in a prison and Ophelia ordered my consciousness to be Cut. I wasn't awake when they locked me up—only on the walk to and from my sentencing—and I imagine a lot has changed.

I feel Kasia's mind nudge my own, but her thoughts aren't audible. Instead, she mouths, *Where are we going?*

I don't want to explain that I'm not entirely sure, so I wave a hand forward like I want us to keep moving.

I retrace the blurry steps in my thoughts, hoping for a glimpse of the spiral banister that keeps appearing in my mind. The one that made me dizzy as I counted every step, thinking it might be my last.

I thought of my parents. I thought of Mei. I thought of Caelan.

If he's here now . . .

Down, my thoughts drum. *You have to go down.*

We hurry for the end of the hallway, and I pause beside a staircase descending farther into the palace. Kasia glances at me, the alarm on her face clear. I hadn't exactly told her about Caelan and what it is I'm hoping to accomplish by being here—but only because I can't explain the whole story.

As far as I know, Damon didn't poison Caelan. Which means if he's here, he can explain everything on my behalf.

I only need to find him first.

Kasia hesitates, teetering on the edge of a puzzle she doesn't understand. With a sigh, she follows me down, but the look on her face is clear: I owe her an explanation.

The corridor is eerily quiet. In Victory and War, there were Residents everywhere. Not just Legion Guards, but members of the courts. I assumed it would be the same here, and perhaps it was when it was called Death. But now the halls are empty, like a castle without a real purpose.

I wonder if that bothers Ozias, or if it's intentional.

Maybe he wants his people on a battlefield instead.

We find another staircase that curves in tight circles, and the descent makes my stomach flip. I send my thoughts lower, searching for a hint of Caelan locked away, but find no sound at all. The moment we reach the bottom floor, I'm assaulted by a stagnant cold that pebbles every inch of my skin. I don't recoil; I move faster, driven by the worry that he's down here—unconscious, tied to a damp floor, and enveloped by darkness.

I let a faint glow build in my palm and raise it above me to light the path.

Empty chambers with glass windows and mirrored walls sit on both sides of the hallway, jolting my memories to life.

This place . . .

I remember the marble, and the way the artificial light seemed to bounce off the white tiles. I remember thinking this was the last time I'd ever feel or think or *know*.

Did Caelan go through the same thing?

I search for him behind every unlocked door, desperation making my fingers curl into fists. When I approach the final room, I hesitate, take a breath, and reach for the handle.

The door swings open, and I stare into the void for the shape of my friend.

But the room is empty.

I step inside, letting the stale air sweep over me, imagining what the last century must've been like for him. I slept through it all, but Caelan?

What was it like to be tortured for a hundred years?

How can any human possibly think that's *okay*?

"He's not here," I say out loud. It isn't relief in my voice. It can't be, when I know he could easily be somewhere much worse.

Footsteps sound behind me, and the wisp of light spilling in from the doorway darkens. I turn, expecting to find Kasia, who followed me down here without question, because her faith in me has always mattered more than her doubt. But it isn't her.

It's Ozias.

6

KING OZIAS WEARS A CROWN OF GOLD-PLATED bones. A black cape spills over one of his shoulders, obscuring part of the armor stretched across his chest, decorated with the sigil of Neo Genesis. Not a stag's skull crowned in twigs like the Bone Clan, but a blade shaped like a crescent moon with a phoenix blazing around it.

"Nami," Ozias says, plastering a smile across his face. "It has been a long time."

He towers over me, nearly a foot taller than I remember. I wonder if he did that after my sister got here, when he realized he wasn't the only human with an army behind them.

Part of me doesn't want to look up to meet his gaze, but I

don't want him to think I'm afraid. What he did to me . . . I won't let it make me small.

I stare back with lukewarm disinterest. "Not long enough."

I don't know how I managed to let my veil drop, but I hope Kasia was better at keeping her focus. I reach out with my thoughts, searching for her in the hall, but I can't find her.

Ozias oozes smug satisfaction. "You're still angry about what happened in War. But I won't apologize for not knowing which side you were on. You changed your mind so often. It was hard to keep track."

I bite down on the slew of expletives sitting at the edge of my tongue. He's blocking the doorway—the only exit in this room.

He smiles like he knows exactly what I'm thinking. "I'm glad you finally recognize the power difference between us. When I first met you, you seemed to think you'd someday be in charge."

"I have no interest in your throne," I say hotly.

"But you are interested in something," he replies. "Tell me—why are you lurking around the dungeon when your friends are all upstairs?"

"This is a dungeon?" I repeat, face blank. "And here I was thinking it was your guest quarters."

His eyes gleam even in the darkness, and when he speaks, his voice is deadly. "It wouldn't be difficult to arrange. I could lock this door, veil you from the world, and no one would ever find you."

I cross my arms. "Does it bother you, knowing my sister has done a better job of winning this war than you ever did?"

His eye twitches, but whatever he's about to say is replaced by the sound of approaching footsteps. Ozias stiffens, shifting toward the corridor.

"You didn't come down here alone," he notes, voice sharp.

My mouth curls. "Sorry to disappoint. I know you only like to betray other humans when you think no one is looking."

He opens his mouth to respond, but a voice interrupts us from around the corner.

"Good afternoon, Your Highness," Jacek calls out, smooth as honey. "It seems a member of my group took a wrong turn in the halls. You haven't happened to see a girl down here—dark brown hair, average height, likes to argue?"

Ozias tightens his jaw before taking a few steps back, allowing me to exit. I pass a Neo Genesis soldier on my way to Jacek's side. The moment I'm out of earshot, the stranger leans toward Ozias and speaks quietly in his ear.

"Why do I get the feeling I just saved your life?" Jacek mutters under his breath.

"It wasn't that serious," I whisper. "But it would probably be best if you didn't ask any follow-up questions."

Jacek's eyes twinkle with humor. "Noted."

Ozias turns from the soldier and looks directly at Jacek. The threat vanishes from his gaze, replaced with the same forced smile he wore earlier. "I hear you wish to have an audience with my engineers."

"At the General's command," Jacek says, each word deliberate. "I'm sure you can appreciate how eager she is to finalize our plans."

"Of course," Ozias agrees, but even his practiced charms can't hide the grimace in his voice. "We are all looking forward to the new future." He sweeps a hand toward the other end of the hall. "Please, join me in the throne room. We can discuss the war in private."

Jacek forces a look in my direction. "My team is here to act as an emissary in the General's absence. I have no intention of keeping information from her sister."

"I'm happy to sit this one out," I say quickly, not wanting to miss my opportunity to get as far away from Ozias as possible. "I'd rather look for my friends."

Ozias's eyes flash with understanding. They shift, calculating, and the skin at my neck immediately prickles. Somehow it feels like I'm giving him exactly what he wants.

"An excellent idea," Ozias says, ushering his soldier forward. "My guards are very good at locating people. Sabriel would be happy to escort you out of the castle and point you in the direction of your companions. Except for one, that is." His mouth stretches into a sneer. "You won't find him here. The Residents came for him when the Second Wave attacked Victory."

The empty space in my chest balloons until my ribs ache. Each word drags over the knot in my throat, turning hoarse. "The Residents have Caelan?"

"For now." Ozias turns to Sabriel. "Please show Nami to the city, and see that she's reunited with her friends."

Jacek runs a finger over his brow, likely assessing how much of this he'll need to relay to my sister. I don't care if he tells her everything; it doesn't matter anymore.

Caelan isn't here.

"I'll join you," Jacek adds, holding my gaze.

I nod, too stricken to argue, and follow Sabriel up the stairs. Only one thought plays in my head, over and over again.

Caelan was taken prisoner by the Residents because of his betrayal. Because he helped *me*.

What punishment would Ophelia give to a prince of her own making?

And what do I need to do in order to set him free?

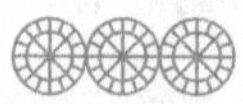

Sabriel leads us to the edge of the apartment district. Rows of cliffside houses overlook an expansive harbor. The crash of seafoam pounds through my ears, but it's the constant shuffle of people that makes my chest tighten.

The crowd is unrelenting. Strangers fill the narrow streets, sparring in alleyways and trading blades under disheveled market stalls.

Jacek bristles beside me. He's been attached to my hip since we left the palace, and I can feel his arm press against mine like he's ready to grab me at the first sign of danger.

Dozens of colorful canopies billow in the wind, offering shade at every rounded doorway. The surrounding walls are covered in murals and war poems, and faded woven rugs are draped over fence posts to create makeshift partitions throughout the city. It feels oddly temporary.

I don't know why it surprises me. Ozias was never going to be satisfied with just one of the Four Courts. Not when War, Famine, and the Capital are still standing.

The streets become too crowded for the three of us to move through easily, so Sabriel prattles off a few curt directions and leaves me and Jacek to make the rest of the excursion on our own. She parks herself beside one of the street vendors, more interested in sampling skewered meat than playing chaperone.

I turn up a side street that leads to a metal archway, where a mess of fishing nets and lights hangs overhead. Outside is the marker Sabriel told me to find—an aged whiskey barrel painted with an outline of a cityscape.

"I'll wait outside," Jacek says, focusing on the moving crowd.

I step into the cavern. A collection of bells and sea glass is strung up along the path, and I wave a hand in front of me to clear the way. They clatter against one another, announcing my presence with an off-key song.

My eyes dart through the main room, searching for Shura, Ahmet, or Eliza—someone familiar. But the recognition that barrels through me isn't at all what I expected to find.

Gil lies on a hospital bed, immobile and still as a corpse. I try to process whether my imagination is getting the better of me, but it's undoubtedly him. The olive skin. The youthfulness of his face despite his sharp jawline. And the curve of his chest, where I once laid my head.

Gil . . . ? I mouth, but the rest of the words don't come.

He doesn't move. I'm not sure he *can*.

Ahmet's voice sounds from the dimly lit hall. "I found him in Victory, after we stormed the border." He steps into the light, staring at Gil's too-still body. Ahmet's hair is curlier and longer than I remember, and his eyes have an agitated sharpness to them.

Sleep may not be necessary anymore, but he looks as if he hasn't rested in years.

I wait for the relief to shudder through me at the sight of an old friend, but instead I swallow my own wretched guilt like I'm worried it will turn to bile.

"He was like a son to me," Ahmet explains, voice bruised. "And . . . when I found out the truth, when Shura told me he'd been used like a puppet for all those years . . ." He rolls his shoulders back, bracing against the reality of the lie we once believed. "If we can bring the others back from the Cut, then I have to believe there's a way to bring Gil back from this."

"If anyone can find a way, it's you," I say quietly.

Ahmet meets my gaze. "It's good to see you, Nami."

"And you," I say, eyeing the lab equipment around us. Sabriel told me Shura lived here, but it's clearly Ahmet who's made this place a home. There are inventions scattered across various tables, and an array of weapons hanging along the back wall.

He was the best engineer in the Colony once. Maybe he's one of the best in Neo Genesis too. I try not to think about how many weapons Ahmet has designed since his time with Ozias. I try not to think about how the Messenger could likely be one of them.

"Shura told me you used to speak to some of the Residents telepathically," he says.

I blink, trying to get a step ahead of the conversation, except I have no idea where it's going. "It was a little more complicated than that. But yes—to Ophelia first, and then to Caelan."

Ahmet sours at his name, nostrils flaring, and looks away. "He robbed me of time with my son. Time that I will never get back. But if there's a chance he knows how to undo what's been done to Gil . . ." He looks at me carefully, the tilt in his head barely noticeable.

I understand it immediately. "You want me to reach out to Caelan."

He doesn't move. "I need information, and you might be the only human in Infinity with the means to get it."

I stare at Gil. If he opened his eyes, would I recognize them? Or would he be an entirely different person from the boy I once kissed?

"I wish I could help," I say. "But something changed after I was Cut. I—I haven't been able to speak to him."

Ahmet takes a breath like he's wrestling between disappointment and relief. "Maybe it's for the best. I know better than to trust anything a Resident says—but I'm not sure I'd have it in me to resist the temptation. Not when it comes to Gil."

"Caelan was only trying to—" I start, but the words shrivel on the tip of my tongue. I clench my fists, flustered. "He didn't want to hurt anyone from the Colony. He cared about all of you. Maybe not always, but by the end, I know he did."

The tendons in Ahmet's neck strain. "I watched you risk your life to save him, and I spent a long time wondering why. At first, I thought it was because of what you felt for Gil. It makes sense you'd be confused. I couldn't even bring myself to go near Caelan when he was a prisoner in War because I was afraid of what I might say or do." He shakes his head. "But he isn't Gil, no matter what he made us believe."

"Caelan is the reason I made it out of Victory and War. He gave up his freedom to protect me from his brothers," I say. "I know it's hard to believe, but he's a good person."

"He isn't a person, and he's far from good," Ahmet counters. "After the Second Wave destroyed Victory, we went to the Winter Keep to free the Colony. And do you know what we found?"

You didn't find anything, my mind wants to shout. *The Colony is in Famine, shielded from this war, because Caelan wanted to protect them.*

"They were gone, Nami. Every single one of them." He swallows, voice thick. "Caelan had already sentenced them to the Cut."

"That isn't what happened to them. They—" My mouth clamps shut involuntarily.

"You've always been an optimist, and I can't fault you for being hopeful. You died too young, and your outlook on the world reflects an innocence most of us no longer have. But what makes your heart pure is also what clouds your judgment."

I look at the floor and fight the tremor in my voice. "Do you know where the Residents are keeping him?"

"The Capital, I suspect."

The one place in Infinity no human has ever been.

Ahmet sees my hesitation. "You can't go there. Not for information . . . not for *anything*."

"But if it could help—"

"We don't even know where it is," Ahmet says. "But the moment we do, the Capital will become the target of every human weapon in existence. Not to mention that you're the

General's sister. If the Rezzies got ahold of you, the ramifications could be disastrous. You gave yourself up to save me and Shura once; I can't begin to imagine what your sister would do to get you back."

"You have nothing to worry about. Mei wouldn't risk the Second Wave."

He grips the bed frame. "I hope you're right. But if I could go back and do it all again, I would've gone after Gil when he was taken to War. I would've fought to bring him home. And I wouldn't have left Annika and the others to the mercy of a Resident prince." His knuckles pale. "I should never have abandoned my family. And if your sister is anything like you, she already knows this."

"The Colony is going to be okay." It's the closest I can get to the truth.

"I know we'll be reunited someday. I just wish I didn't have to wait until the end of the war to see them." His smile is fragile. "Annika would've liked to see Queen Ophelia fall."

"The weapon my sister is building . . ." I look away. "Do you know about it?"

"Yes. I helped design it."

A vise grip reaches around my heart. "It's going to wipe out an entire species."

"Humans created the Rezzies. They're our mistake to fix."

"Not by *killing* them!" I argue. "If a parent teaches a child to hate, would you accept that evil is all they'll ever be? Or would you at least give them the chance to unlearn the worst of themselves?"

"They aren't human. The rules aren't the same."

"Maybe they should be. Maybe treating the Residents differently is why we ended up in this war."

"That's a baseless theory, not a fact."

"Ophelia once told me she tried to coexist, and she was betrayed. When I asked Ozias, he all but admitted he had something to do with the reason Ophelia attacked humans in the first place."

Ahmet hesitates, but whatever doubt I've cast isn't enough to sway him. "I know you're looking for answers. But your questions are taking you somewhere that I have no desire to follow. You're a good friend to have, and I know you'd throw yourself in the line of fire to save one stranger, never mind a hundred friends. But the peace treaty you're looking for doesn't exist." He lifts his shoulders. "I don't really care who started the fight; I just want it to end. I want my *family* back."

When I don't respond, Ahmet looks back at Gil's slumbering body. "You would've liked the real Gil. He was kind, and thoughtful, and painfully stubborn when it came to doing the right thing. Kind of like you."

I look at Gil's chest, hoping to see the rise and fall of his breathing—a sign of life—but it's like his consciousness has been shut off completely.

Maybe the poison in my mind isn't the only thing I need to speak to Damon about.

Maybe going to Famine could help Gil too.

My gaze drifts around the room. "Is Shura here?"

Ahmet's mouth flattens. "No. She hasn't lived here for months."

His jaw tenses. "Shura got it into her head that Annika and the others hadn't really been Cut, that they'd escaped somehow, and might be lost in the Labyrinth." He shakes his head. "I didn't want to let her go alone, but she had Eliza. And I couldn't leave my work—or Gil. Not again."

My stomach free-falls. She's looking for the Colony. Searching for them in Resident territory because she has no idea where Caelan really sent them.

"Where exactly is she now?" I ask, voice tight.

"You should ask around the shipyard. It's where most people go when they want a fast ticket across the border. Just be careful," Ahmet warns. "I know you're the Messenger in the Borderlands, but here, there's an entire army who watched you attack a human to save a Resident."

My fingers stretch at my sides, anxious. "I'll be back as soon as I can."

Ahmet nods once. "May the stars watch over you, my friend."

I take one last look at Gil and leave the room.

7

THE SHIPYARD REEKS OF SWEAT AND SALT water. An enormous collection of tents sits near the docks, layered in tarp and netting. The kind of shelter a military unit might've thrown up in the midst of a war.

We stop in front of the largest canopy, where an oversized curtain obscures the entrance. Jacek reaches for the material, and sunlight flickers off the weapons tucked in his vest.

I wonder if any of his crew knew Mei in the living world too, and whether he was responsible for recruiting the other loyalists who planned to blow up the O-Tech building.

Jacek's grip tightens, but his mouth curves in contradiction. "If you're looking for a reason to dislike me, I can offer plenty that have nothing to do with your sister." When my eyes widen, he tosses a wink. "Just keep in mind that while I may not be your first choice for an ally, something tells me you're not exactly pick of the litter here either."

"How did—" My words catch in my throat. "Can you hear what I'm thinking?"

"No. I can sense what you're feeling. There's a difference."

"How big of a difference?"

He shrugs, clearly amused. "When someone's mind is racing, it sounds like cicadas and electricity, bristling on the other side of a locked door. If I push my mind against it, I get flashes of emotion." The pause that follows makes me cast a wider veil over my own mind, and the corner of his mouth twitches in response. "You and I have something in common."

My skin prickles beneath his stare, and I push my mind toward his, searching for a thread to tug. But the wall he's built for himself is more than a barricade; it's as if his thoughts don't exist at all.

His eyes flash. "Did you really think that would work?"

I can't hide my surprise—or the shred of awe that makes my breath catch. "I've never met another reader before. Your mind is . . . different."

"Different from a Resident, you mean?" I assume he's talking about Caelan, until he adds, "It's common knowledge that the Messenger found her way into Ophelia's head."

I think of her black eyes and flinch. Whatever connection we once had has long been severed, but the memories haven't left me. I'm not sure they ever will.

"I wasn't talking about Ophelia. I only meant that most

people aren't guarded the way you are." I assess the veilstones on his shoulders. "Did you build the mental fortress yourself, or do those help?"

"My mind has always been my own. I don't need tech to protect it."

Part of me wants to test the seams, to find out how impenetrable his veil really is. But I'm also worried that if I push too far, he might decide to push back.

I'm not sure which one of us has more to hide, but I think it might be me.

Jacek chuckles, eyes glinting with an unspoken dare.

I slip past him into the tent without another word.

Orbs of light float near the ceiling, where the peak of the billowing tent is held up by an invisible force. A large crowd is gathered up ahead, blocking my view, but the abrupt cheering makes me recoil. Armed soldiers face the clearing with their fists raised. There must be some kind of veil over this place to mask the noise, because the thundering makes the entire room tremble. I don't know how else I didn't hear it from outside.

Jacek matches my pace with military precision, eyes darting over every stranger as he counts their blades. The clang of metal reverberates ahead, and the cheers from the far side of the room multiply. I squeeze through the crowd, forcing Jacek behind me, and find myself overlooking the edge of an arena.

The drop is at least twenty feet and reveals a partially submerged enclosure. Ocean waves crash through the surrounding caged walls, spraying mist in every direction. Wading through two feet of seawater is a pair of soldiers. One of the women has zigzags shaved onto the side of her head and a gash across her pale cheek. The other has dark skin, wild curls, and a battle-ax peeking out just above her shoulder. I recognize the weapon first, and then the woman.

Zahrah.

She swings a fist hard, cracking bone against the other soldier's jaw. Zahrah reaches for something in the water, and when her hand reappears, it's wrapped around a short sword.

The woman in front of her scrambles and throws her body into a roll just as Zahrah swipes her sword, missing her by less than an inch. When the woman re-emerges from the water, she's holding a blade of her own—an elongated dagger with a serrated edge.

Zahrah flashes a grin. She blocks blow after blow, ducking and bending every time the woman swings. When Zahrah slices the woman's torso and blood sprays across the water, the crowd erupts with bellowing cheers.

The woman drops her blade and screams. Wisps of black smoke flow from her wound, and I flinch at the memory of Nix sinking into the desert sand as the life drained from his eyes.

Nightling blood.

Zahrah raises her sword in triumph, basking in the celebratory cheers of the crowd while the screaming woman is hauled out of the arena and ushered into another tent. When Zahrah's eyes meet mine, her expression shifts, and she moves her sword until the point is directed at my heart.

"Traitor." The anger in her voice is unyielding. "You are not welcome here."

Everyone turns to look at me, and Jacek positions his body closer. Whispers explode through the room. I hear the names they call me—Nami, the Messenger, the sister, the fallen—and I feel the distrust like I'm being smothered by it.

"We need to leave," Jacek hisses beside me, but his voice barely registers. I'm too focused on Zahrah's blade.

The corner of her mouth twitches. "The last time we saw each other, you threw me across the desert to save one of *them*. If you're here to apologize, don't bother. I like to keep my grudges close."

I ball my hands at my sides. "I wasn't trying to hurt you."

Her laugh cracks through the air. "As if you ever could."

Jacek presses a hand against my shoulder, guiding me toward the exit, but I shrug him off.

The warning in his voice makes my neck heat. "I told you I can feel emotion. And right now, in this room, you are in more danger than you know."

I'm not running from this, I push toward his mind. I wasn't sure it would even work, but his sudden recoil confirms what I'd hoped; even if I can't sense him, he can hear me. *She was my friend once. And I can't leave without finding out where Shura is.*

"You caught me off guard last time," Zahrah says. "Today will be different."

Jacek reaches for his pistol. "Nami is here under the General's protection. If you have a problem with that, take it up with your king."

Zahrah tuts. "Such a convenient time for you to decide you like playing by the rules. I'm curious—do you *enjoy* having a youngling speak for you?"

"You don't understand," I say, lifting my hands. "I'm not here to fight with you. I'm trying to find—"

"I don't give a damn what you're after," she cuts in, sharp as steel. She takes a step back through the water, tossing her Nightling-coated blade to the side. "You and I have unfinished business."

Someone shoves me from behind, sending me over the edge of the arena. My shoulder slams into the metal grate below the waves. With a winded gasp, I choke on a mouthful of salt water. I try to force away the sting in my eyes, blinking hard as I lock onto Jacek's horrified stare. The veins in his neck bulge as he struggles against an invisible hold, arms unnaturally stiff at his sides.

I scramble to my knees, but Zahrah is fast. She knocks my jaw hard, and I fall into the water once more. Someone fires a shot in the air, and I think maybe Jacek is trying to get his gun back, but it doesn't matter—I'm in the arena now, and Zahrah has no intention of letting me leave without drawing her share of blood.

I stumble through the water, jaw stinging, and clamber to my feet. Bracing for the next blow, I duck and leap backward, fingers outstretched in front of me.

Zahrah snarls. "We trusted you. Gave you a home. Came to *rescue you*." She slams me against the metal wall and presses her forearm against my throat until the air chokes out of me. "But you still chose the enemy."

"That's—not—true—"

But she won't relent. Not unless I fight back.

I shut my eyes and search Zahrah's mind in the void. Her anger is everywhere, a kaleidoscope of red, engulfing her every thought. She can't see me coming. All she's focused on is causing me pain.

I hate the way she sees me. I hate the way I've tried to do the right thing but have still managed to alienate so many of my friends. I hate that peace and hope and second chances always seem to come at too high of a cost.

For a moment, I stop thinking about consequences. Instead, I set fire to her hatred—and mine—like I want to burn it all away.

Zahrah screams and claws at her eyes. I race toward the center of the arena, forcing a gap between us. She shakes the mental embers away, raging with the fuel I've just given her, and spins to face me. Because that's what hate does: it makes everything worse.

"I'm sorry," I say quickly. "If you just let me explain, I can—"

Zahrah pulls a knife from her belt. I barely register the blade before she vanishes.

A sharp pain hits my lower back. I howl as the dagger is yanked from my flesh and Nightling blood seeps from the wound.

Smoke fills my senses, clouding the room in a venomous haze. I look across the arena and find Mei and Caelan, up to their waists in water. The sea level is rising now, pounding at the metal walls with growing force.

"Help me!" Mei screams. She's a child. The twelve-year-old I remember best. The one I spent most of Infinity trying to make a better afterlife for.

Caelan gasps, straining, and I realize they both have their hands tied behind them and are unable to move. "Please—don't leave me here!"

I move toward them, but the waves come faster, rushing

through the space until the water reaches our necks. I swim, frantic, kicking my feet as hard as I can, but it feels like I'm being sucked out of the room.

Mei and Caelan look back desperately. They're running out of time.

"Hurry," Mei cries. "Please."

"I'm trying!" I choke on the salt water, paddling faster.

I feel it then—the *real* threat. There isn't time to save them both. I have to choose.

I can't, I mouth. *Please don't make me.*

"Nami—" Mei cries, and the water smothers her.

I lunge for my sister, tearing at the ropes around her hands, but the knots won't come loose. The ocean moves past Caelan's mouth, and his silver eyes widen.

My scream becomes an echo in the arena, and I claw faster at Mei's bindings. I will save them both. I won't stop trying. I won't stop making things *right.*

Even if it kills me.

Nightling blood is supposed to shoot fear through me, but instead I feel the fire. The urge to never give up.

I don't leave Mei and Caelan to the water. Not even when it smothers me too.

Black smoke floods from my fingers, sharpening into hooks like the talons of a monster, and I slash at the rope and set them both free.

I blink hard. I'm kneeling at the bottom of the arena, but Mei and Caelan aren't here. I'm not sure they ever were.

"How did you do that?" Zahrah's brown eyes are severe.

"No one has ever fought off Nightling blood that quickly."

I try to stand, but my legs shake uncontrollably. "You think fear is a weakness, but it isn't."

She frowns because she doesn't understand me. Casting her eyes toward the crowd, she soaks in their silence before reaching for the battle-ax strapped to her shoulders. In one smooth motion, she aims the thick blade against my neck.

"If fear will not work on you, I will use something sharper," she says.

"Zahrah," I plead. "I'm your *friend*."

"Not anymore," she hisses, and prepares to swing.

Water smashes through the shipyard, ripping down the fabric ceiling in one wave, and Zahrah disappears beneath the crash of sea-foam.

The crowd screams, fleeing from the destruction as dozens of soldiers are knocked to the ground. I swim against the flooded cage and climb over the ledge, scanning the space for Jacek. In the chaos, he breaks free of his captors, drawing a fair amount of blood from their mouths, and retrieves his pistol. I barely reach his side when he yanks me behind his muscular frame for cover.

Sunlight pours through the ravaged space above, and liquid swirls toward us like a monstrous blue flame. I brace for impact, but the water goes still several yards away. An ocean wave, frozen in place—and standing at its crest is Kasia.

Her blond hair flutters behind her, and her arms are spread wide. She was the commander of a clan once, but now she commands the sea.

The silence that falls over the half-demolished shipyard pounds in my ears. Jacek eases his grip on my arm. Even he knows there's nothing to worry about now.

Kasia lets the ocean guide her to solid ground and casts her blue eyes around the room. "You don't seem to care that Nami is the sister of the General, so let me be clear: she is one of the Salt Clan. In case you have forgotten, we do not tolerate violence for sport. Especially among our own. If you ever harm her again, you can consider yourself banished until the end of Infinity."

It doesn't matter that these people are part of Neo Genesis now; their history with the Salt Clan is rooted deep. A handful of soldiers bows in recognition of Kasia's command. Another handful nods out of respect. Everyone else remains silent, too afraid of the ocean to move.

Kasia steps toward me. "Come on. There's nothing for you here."

"But Shura—" I start.

"Shura isn't here," a voice says.

I search across the damp floor and find Dayo. She still looks like a child, but she lifts her chin like an ancient queen. Zahrah stands beside her, brushing water from her brow with the back of her hand.

There was a time when I looked at Zahrah and Dayo and wished my sister was with me too. Now I look at the pair and wonder how they managed to stay so close, while an entire chasm exists between me and Mei.

I step around Jacek and straighten my shoulders. "Ahmet told me she's been gone for months. I was hoping someone here might know where I can find her."

"She left with one of the scavenging units, but never returned to the rendezvous point," Dayo says plainly. "If you want to find her, you'll need to go to War."

Bile rises in my throat. *Not there. Anywhere but there.*

"There's a group of humans near the old northern outpost who spend their time searching for survivors. If anyone has knowledge of Shura, it will be them," Dayo adds.

Memories of the desert court turn my stomach, but I force a nod. "Thank you."

"I'm not telling you this to help you," Dayo says. "I'm telling you this so that you will leave and never return."

Zahrah's eyes narrow beside her. "As I've told you—we are enemies now."

"You have every right to be upset with me. I know how it must've looked. But if you just let me explain—"

Zahrah scoffs. "What can you explain that we haven't already guessed? That you care for the Resident prince? That you lied about your relationship with him? That you chose to protect him over your fellow humans?" Her voice shakes. "Your reasons don't matter. We will not fight alongside someone who does not believe in humanity."

"That's not—" I start, but Kasia steers me toward the docks.

"When people do not want to change their minds, you cannot make them," Kasia says. "Leave them to think what they want."

Every instinct inside me is desperate to explain myself. To walk them through the decisions I made and lay out my reasons. But I can't even say the words out loud.

Leaving feels like admitting defeat, but maybe it isn't about winning and losing. Maybe we are simply two sides of an argument who will never be able to agree.

I follow Kasia and Jacek out of the shipyard, but not without one last glance toward Zahrah. She's already turned away, face huddled close to Dayo's as they exchange their own private words.

I wonder if it will be different with Shura, or whether the friend I once knew will turn her back on me too.

8

WE RETURN TO THE TRANSPORT SHIP, AND I LISten in silence as Jacek rehashes every detail of the shipyard fiasco to the crew. When he's finished, he plants his hands on the metal table in front of him and clenches his jaw.

"I can't let you go to War," he says.

"I'm not asking for permission," I reply stiffly.

"You were nearly decapitated in that shipyard," Jacek argues. "Those were our *allies*. Imagine what Ettore will do if he finds you traipsing through his front yard!"

I hide my grimace, even though I remember all too well the many ways Ettore likes to torture humans.

Quinn lifts his hand. "Quick question: If Nami *does* end up on a literal guillotine, which body part are we supposed to be dragging back to the Borderlands?"

"Seriously?" Leilani hisses. "Time and place, Quinn."

"What? It's a valid question." He lifts his shoulders innocently. "We have chambers to grow entire bodies, and medics to reproduce limbs, but how does it work when you lose a head?"

"Rebuilding a body isn't purely physical. It involves creating an energy that draws the consciousness to one place," Captain Preeda interrupts, thoughtful. "Typically, when someone loses a limb, their consciousness pulls itself inward, tethering itself to the physical presence that's left behind. Regrowing an arm is like coaxing that energy back out."

Quinn frowns. "So if they're separated, does a consciousness normally shift to the head or the body?"

"As a general rule?" Preeda says. "When in doubt, save the head."

"The fact that we're even *having* this conversation is a problem." Jacek glares at Quinn and Preeda with admonishment. "I promised Mei she'd be safe with us."

Quinn looks sheepish. "In our defense, no one told us the whole of Neo Genesis had it out for her."

Jacek leans back and pinches the bridge of his nose. "How am I going to explain this to your sister?"

"What happens in the shipyard stays in the shipyard?" I suggest. When he glowers at me, I shrug. "It's not exactly her business what I do in my free time."

"Debatable," Jacek clips back. "But taking our convoy across enemy territory to enact a rescue mission is most *definitely* her business. There's a chain of command for a reason."

"I don't need a convoy. I've probably spent more time hiding in War than anyone here. I can handle myself." Even as I say the words, I know it's a stretch. I've been asleep for years—the tunnels may not look the way they used to. But it's the only plan I've got. "Shura thinks her family is still in War, but she isn't going to find them there. I need to get to her before Ettore does."

"Odds are your friend has already been captured," Jacek points out. "There's a reason we haven't tried to take the Red City. For every Resident we Cut, another two replace them. Fighting them only seems to make their army grow bigger."

"There's a group of humans searching for survivors in the north," I argue. "If they've lasted this long, Shura could have too."

"I'm not sending the General's sister into a war zone based on a hunch," he barks back. "If you're so desperate to send your friend a message, we can organize a scouting unit to find her."

"No Second Waver would approve a mission like that, and you know it. If I don't go myself, while I still have the freedom to do it, it's not going to happen. Besides"—I lift my shoulders—"I'm the only one Shura will listen to."

Jacek exchanges a wary glance with Captain Preeda, who lets out a forceful sigh.

"I'll go with Nami." Kasia straightens. "The last time you went to War, I let you go alone. I won't make that mistake again."

Quinn cocks his head. "I thought you hadn't stepped foot on a battlefield in centuries?"

Kasia cuts him with an icy stare. "Careful, youngling. I might decide to drown you with the sweat from your brow just to prove a point."

Quinn pales slightly. "Uh—that's not a real thing." He ducks toward Leilani and frowns. "*Is* it?"

Leilani cackles with delight. "Oh, I really hope it is."

Jacek holds my gaze. "Even *with* Kasia's help, you have no idea where you're going. At the very least, you'd need a navigator, not to mention your lack of weapons, preparation, contacts, and—"

"We are both perfectly capable of following directions to the northern outpost," Kasia says suddenly. "And if nothing comes of our search, we'll make our way to safety without going anywhere near the Red City."

Jacek weighs the risks, and I tense. Finally, he points a finger at me. "You get *one* day. If you don't manage to find your friends, you're coming back to the Borderlands with the rest of us. Got it?"

I open my mouth to barter for more time but decide against it. I can't risk him changing his mind. If I'm lucky, I'll find Shura quickly. And if not . . . Well, it's not like Jacek can *make* me leave. I'll just hide out in the caves, and if it takes weeks, then—

His jaw ticks with disapproval, sensing my intentions.

My cheeks flush. "Fine," I say, avoiding his stare. "One day."

Jacek nods, satisfied. "There are a couple of beds on the lower deck. If you need to rest, I suggest you do it now."

The crew moves quickly. Jacek and Captain Preeda exchange heated whispers as they disappear from view, while Quinn and Leilani busy themselves near the weapons rack.

Kasia motions for me to follow her. I'm not tired, and something tells me if I go to sleep, I'll wake up in the Borderlands. But her pinched expression makes me trail after her without pause.

A wide landing is all that separates two metal beds from one another. Kasia perches at the foot of one, so I do the same on the other mattress. Worry lines crease at her mouth.

I eye the vacant staircase, listening for the hum of consciousnesses above us. "If you're about to tell me something private, you should probably know that Jacek is a reader."

"Then maybe he'll be able to reassure you how sorry I am," Kasia says. "I owe you an apology. For leaving you alone with Ozias."

"Ah. That." I brush a finger across my brow. "I'm pretty sure I owe you a 'thank-you' for telling Jacek where I was."

She chews the edge of her lip. "I never got the chance—he was already on his way downstairs. I think he knew what you were up to before I did."

A flicker of annoyance makes my jaw tick, but it passes quickly. I don't appreciate having my every emotion appear on Jacek's radar any more than I appreciate his hovering. Still . . . he helped with Ozias, *and* he's willing to meet with Caelan. Not to mention he seems to care a great deal about Mei.

I'm not ready to give him my trust, but I can't bring myself to be angry at him either.

Kasia tucks a blond strand behind her ear. "I wasn't prepared to face Ozias, but I want you to know I have no intention of letting you down again. No matter what we find in the desert, I won't run from it."

"It means a lot that you're coming with me." I hesitate, remembering the way Kasia appeared at the arena. "I had no idea you could control water like that."

"We were a sea people," she says simply. "The water was our home."

I think of all the people who fled to the Afterlands. All the people as strong as Kasia who chose to run instead of fight. I called them cowards once—yet running is exactly what I wanted Mei to do.

But she didn't. She stayed to help. She stayed to find me. She stayed to change the world.

I slump against the wall. "I think I might be a hypocrite for not telling my sister I was proud of her."

"Are you?" Kasia asks. "Proud?"

"No. But I think saying it would've meant more to her than *not* saying it means to me."

"I think she'd rather you didn't lie."

"I'm not *not* proud. She literally did what the rest of us couldn't. She did what the people who fled to the Afterlands wouldn't even *try*. That's the kind of courage that's celebrated in history books."

"Choosing peace takes courage too. But those stories rarely end up in history books." We stare at each other in silence for a long time, until Kasia's words spill from her mouth. "I see you, Nami. Even if I don't always understand you."

I don't answer right away, but when I do, my voice sounds haunted. "If you could do it all over again, knowing everything you do . . . would you do things differently?"

Kasia laces her fingers together. "Centuries ago, when I watched all of those boats disappear on the horizon, I was angry. I believed so fully that fighting was the right choice. And then, when I witnessed what became of my people . . ." She looks away. "I've spent so many mornings watching the sun rise over the ocean, wondering what our ancestors found on the other side. Time has made me less resentful. Perhaps if the war began now, I'd choose differently too." Her sigh is heavy with remorse. "To live a single lifetime in fear is a tragedy. But to live in it a hundred lifetimes over?" She shakes her head. "I'm tired, Nami. I've been tired for a long time."

I stare at the pattern in the metal floor. "You protected my sister when she arrived in the Borderlands, and I'm grateful. But a century is a long time to keep a promise. I'm sorry if I made you feel like you couldn't break it."

"I don't want your guilt, Nami. I don't think your sister wants it either." She wraps her shawl around her shoulders, cocooning herself. "Regrets aren't meant to be carried for centuries. Let them guide you, or let them go. There is no mistake powerful enough to break the world, but the guilt? The guilt will break *you*."

An ancient sadness fills her eyes. I imagine she's remembering the time she led the Salt Clan into their final battle. She watched them fall and saw her best friend cut down. If anyone knows the cost of bearing guilt over the years, it's Kasia.

I don't push her. Not on this. But part of me wonders if she'd understand my regrets better if she understood how much of the world can still be changed. That my guilt *is* guiding me—toward Caelan, and Famine, and a better future for us all.

Kasia turns to me, mouth pinched. "I believe your sister can end this war."

"So do I," I say quietly.

Kasia turns her cheek, reading me like I'm an open book. "Do you believe finding Caelan will change that?"

My gaze springs up to meet hers.

"I assumed that's who you were looking for in the dungeon," she adds.

"I think it might help limit the body count," I admit.

"Ours? Or theirs?"

"Both." I try not to let my voice break, but I'm not sure I can help it. "I don't believe any of us have the right to decide who lives and who dies. And I want people to know they have another option. That they don't *have* to fight."

Kasia's spine curves like she's settling into her thoughts. "I have never met a Resident worthy of redemption. But I have also never known a Resident the way you seem to know Caelan. I trust your friendship more than I doubt your hope. Whether it matters or not—whether it changes anything or not—I'm with you."

"It matters," I say, eyes stinging. "Thank you."

Kasia nods once and leans her head against the wall to rest. I tilt my chin up and stare at the ceiling, wondering if Jacek has been tuned into our conversation.

I shroud my mind with a veil and push my thoughts toward the invisible realm he hides inside. Quietly I search for cracks. Vibrations. Anomalies. Anything to suggest that the barrier he's crafted isn't as impenetrable as it seems.

Maybe it's only noticeable because I'm a reader too, or maybe Jacek is so focused on listening to me and Kasia that he let his guard drop. But when I find a faint hum slipping through his mental walls, I know I've found a weakness.

I pull back and retreat beneath my own barricade, tightening every millimeter of my own veil until I'm certain my mind is out of Jacek's reach. Footsteps echo through the ceiling, fading from one end of the room to the other.

I don't know what I would find if I tried to push into his mind for information, but I know it wouldn't be welcome. It's just one of many things I've learned in Infinity.

Just because we *can* do something, doesn't always mean we should.

9

CAPTAIN PREEDA FLIES US BACK THROUGH THE Labyrinth, stopping one landscape away from War. Crossing the border will be easier without a transport ship to veil.

I walk with Kasia down the loading ramp and find Jacek, Quinn, and Leilani waiting at the bottom.

Jacek meets my confusion with a quirk of his brow. "Every time I let you out of my sight, you get yourself into trouble. There's no way in hell I'm letting you go to War without backup."

I look at the others, grateful. "I appreciate the assist."

Leilani adjusts her armored bracers and meets my gaze. "Correction: you *need* the assist. You may be besties with Poseidon's spawn, but last I checked, there are no oceans in the desert."

Kasia purses her lips, hair fluttering against the breeze like she's accepting a challenge.

Quinn immediately throws up his hands in surrender. "*I'm* not doubting you," he clarifies. "I just didn't want to be stuck on the ship with Captain Preeda for hours. At least this way, I get to shoot something."

One by one, we fall in behind Jacek and begin the trek. It takes over an hour to reach the border, but once we cross it, I know immediately where we are. War is familiar, even if I wish it weren't. I recognize the canyons, the yellow horizon, and the way the sun beats across my face like it's smothering me.

But there's something else. A prickling across my forearms. The hum of something alive and near and tethered to my very core.

My heart thuds against my rib cage. I stiffen, choking on a breath.

Caelan. My mind races. *I can feel him.*

The sensation isn't exactly the same as I remember—it's like the echo of something volatile. There isn't a hint of winter woodlands. Just burning sand and the faint smell of ash.

But right now . . . this feeling . . .

I turn in place. Ozias said the Residents took him, but maybe not to the Capital. Maybe he's *here.*

My eyes scan the horizon and settle westward, and I'm certain the prickling spreads.

There, my thoughts urge. *Find him.*

"Are you okay?" Kasia's voice interrupts my trance.

I startle beside her, giving away far too much.

Jacek adjusts the comm around his ear. It keeps him connected to Preeda, which I suppose is a more practical, though more limited, version of what I used to do with Caelan.

"There's an outpost just beyond the canyon. We're going to head there first, and see if we can find survivors." Jacek waits for Preeda's telepathic response and hums in agreement. "Understood." He whistles to Quinn and Leilani, who huddle around, awaiting their orders.

They keep their voices low, and Jacek motions beyond the hills.

"Wait," I blurt out. "We need to go west."

Jacek folds his arms. "There's nothing out there but wasteland. It's too close to the border—our side knows better than to put an outpost there. You'd risk Residents sneaking up on you from the Labyrinth *and* have to deal with constant patrol units."

"I know, but—" I grab the first excuse I can, testing it slowly. "There are tunnels in the western canyon. I hid in them, after I escaped from the Red City." The others are silent, waiting. I fuel the rest of my words with confidence. "There are too many for the Legion Guards to keep an eye on, which means we've got a hiding place if we need it. And Shura will likely have taken advantage of them too. She could be there now."

Jacek drops his arms and shrugs. "All right, then. How you want to spend your *one day* is up to you." He repeats the new plan into the comm and faces the team. "You heard her—we're headed west."

I avert his sharpening gaze. My racing pulse is probably a dead giveaway that I'm not being entirely truthful. The urgency is impossible to veil, so I try to mask it with something else.

I blink at the lifeless desert and let the memories boil to the surface. The last time I was here, with Caelan, and Nix . . .

One was taken. One was killed.

Both were my fault.

Jacek must sense he's intruding on something too close to my heart, because he shifts away awkwardly and takes several long strides to catch up with the others.

Kasia keeps her voice low. "You felt something. What was it?"

I quiet my mind, just in case Jacek is still paying attention, and try to feel only indifference when I speak. "I think I know where he is."

She hesitates. "Does that change your plans?"

"I—I don't know." I look at her warily. "I'm not sure what we're going to find when we get there."

Jacek said he'd give me and Caelan a chance to explain. I want to believe that's true, but Caelan could still be under the influence of the Grimling bite. If the poison is the reason we haven't been able to communicate, I doubt he'll be in any shape to debate coexistence with an opposing militia. I'll need to get him to Damon first.

And until I can ensure the safety of the Residents in Famine, I can't let the Second Wave anywhere near Damon's court.

Sand spills away from me as I trudge up the side of a dune. I dust my hands at my hips, pausing while the rest of our group moves a few extra paces ahead. "We might be taking a slight detour, but our destination is still the same. We find my friends—and then we leave this court for good."

"I know you can't tell me where we're going after that, but . . ." She sucks the air between her teeth. "Is the rest of the crew invited?"

"No," I say. "But I think it's best if they don't know that yet."

Beneath the sun's glare, Kasia gives a curt nod.

We trail behind the crew in an uneven line, staggering the gaps between us to avoid being closed in on. I listen for the sound of human screams that were so prevalent the last time I was here, but all I can hear is the faint whistle of wind sweeping over the desert.

Static runs across my arms. I search for Caelan, scouring the reaches of my mind for any sign that he's reaching back. Eventually, I accept that the buzzing has to be enough.

Maybe it's all he can give, I think, and feel my stomach turn.

I try to find solace in the fact that the Red City is deep in the south. Whatever is calling to me is nowhere near Ettore's palace. If Caelan is in the wastelands, maybe it means he's in hiding. Not a prisoner. Not chained to a filthy stone floor for a hundred years. Not tormented. Not in pain.

But not free, either.

I curse my own thoughts and keep walking.

We reach the edge of the canyon and spot a narrow trail tucked alongside the cliffs. It's the fastest path to the tunnels, but Jacek doesn't like the idea of being isolated on the ridge for so long. Leilani slides a pair of goggles over her eyes, and the lenses spin in place, calculating an alternative path. We settle for the long way around, where a thin bridge will get us to the other side of the canyon.

Our group continues in silence, too focused on the wide-open horizon to bother with conversation. There's limited cover, but the curved rock formations on the other end of the bridge will definitely offer more places to hide, even if it means more places for the Residents to hide too.

The stretch of wooden planks and bloodstained rope comes into view. Everyone moves ahead except me. I hesitate near the first board, peering down at the drop below. The instant reminder of being thrown into the Fire Pit creates blind spots in my vision, and I sway in place.

Kasia turns, observing the distance between us. "Afraid of heights?" Her face blooms with humor. I never told her what happened to me in the Red City's arena, and right now, I'm grateful for it. When her blue eyes glitter, I see a glimpse of my old friend who once made a habit of mocking me in the forest.

I roll my eyes and grip the braided cable firmly to test the strength, following the others across. The planks sway beneath my weight. My mind wants to calculate the distance to the ground, but I fight the urge, focusing instead on finding a rhythm. It's only when we're halfway to the other side that I chance letting my eyes roam. Several dark shapes slice across the sky like birds of prey, growing bigger as they approach the mouth of the canyon.

Legion Guards.

Quinn lifts a hand to his brow, squinting. "That patrol unit is headed straight toward us. Think it's routine?"

"It can't be anything else," Jacek replies, checking his glowing veilstone. The amber light shifts to a molten orange, darkening by the second.

Leilani reaches for her rifle. "Want me to take the shot anyway?"

"No. Leave them be," Jacek counters, continuing across the bridge. "We're better off keeping our cover."

The bridge sways with urgency as we pick up our pace. A violent crack sounds up ahead, and I tumble forward, knees colliding with the wobbling, splintered board. I look past the ropes, watching as a broken plank plummets to the ground. It hits the rocks, kicking up a whorl of dust as it shatters into several pieces.

Quinn lets out a strangled cry, and my eyes dart ahead to find him half hanging through a jagged hole in the bridge. He swipes for the rope, chest pressed firmly against an uneven bit of wood as his legs dangle helplessly in the air.

Jacek kneels, throwing an arm out for Quinn to grab hold of before hauling him back to his feet.

Quinn eyes the gap in the bridge and releases a low whistle. "That really had my heart rate going."

Leilani twists her mouth, smoothing the worried crease from her brow as if it were never there at all. "I would've let you fall," she huffs. "And then I would've told everyone on the *Mizuchi*."

Quinn barks back a retort, but I don't hear it—I'm too fixated on the shadows in the sky, and how much bigger they seem to be getting. When they break their formation, I make out half a dozen of them, soaring toward us with enormous, batlike wings.

My focus shifts from the Residents, to the bridge, and to the snapped plank lying in pieces across the sand. We may be within the protection of our veilstones, but that fall . . . that distance . . .

The rope bridge casts shadows along the bottom of the canyon, swaying with every shift of our movements. Jacek's eyes snap to mine, forehead scrunched as he studies the horror building across my face.

He understands immediately. "Move," he barks, no longer concerned about being heard. *"Now!"*

The others look behind them. It takes less than a second for them to grasp our panic.

The Residents know we're here.

Jacek fires several shots into the air, but none of them find a target.

The others sprint ahead. The bridge rocks erratically with the weight of our group, and I struggle to maintain my footing. My body hits the edge of the rope, and I latch on desperately to keep myself from falling over. Kasia looks back at me, hesitating. I shake my head once like it's an order to *keep moving.* The longer we stay on this bridge, the longer we risk getting caught. Our only chance is to make a break for the ridgeline and take cover in the maze of boulders.

I can tell by Jacek's gunfire that he's already there. Leilani and Quinn too, and then Kasia. It's just me left, slower than the others because the bridge is swinging too fast, and the height makes me dizzy.

I lean forward and break into a run, when I hear another crack—this time beneath my own feet.

One moment I'm standing, and the next I'm not. I'm weightless, free-falling into the depths of the canyon.

Someone calls my name. I think it's Kasia. I watch my fingers curl like they might find some invisible ledge in the sky. Like that stubborn part of me just doesn't know how to let go of hope, in any form. I hit the desert floor, and pain rips across my back like a lash of fire. The air rushes out of me, and the howl that wants to emerge locks itself halfway up my throat. I try to breathe—try to take control of the pain—but all I feel are the breaks of a dozen bones and a wretched spasm that races from my toes to my ears. I blink, rigid against the agony, and watch the Legion Guards swerve toward the place where Kasia and the others went.

The Residents didn't see me fall. Not with my veilstones shrouding me. And now I'm stuck on the ground while the crew are forced to fight for their lives.

Get up, my mind screams. *They need you.*

The incessant popping of bullets makes my chest pinch. It becomes a tempo, urging my body back to life. I roll onto my side, letting the air fill my lungs. Everything hurts—but if I found a way out of the Fire Pit, I can find a way out of this too.

I stand, knees shaking violently, and limp forward. The vertical cliffs are the only way to get back to the top, so I climb, clenching my teeth with every pulse that burns through my back. The pressure builds, wearing on me like a spiral of self-doubt.

For Kasia, I try to ignore it.

I chase the beat of gunfire, focusing on every skyward step. As long as I can hear the battle, it means it hasn't been lost.

I'm almost to the top of the ledge when the canyon goes silent. There are no bullets, or screams. Only the terror ringing in my ears.

A figure looms above me, and my insides become knots. I look up, several feet from the cliff top, and see a face staring down at me, haloed by the blaring sunlight above him.

"There you are." Quinn's voice crackles with delight. "You missed all the fun."

Jacek appears and reaches for me. I grab hold of his thick arm, and he swings my body up over the ledge.

I look around quickly. Kasia and Leilani are standing nearby, unharmed. The sand is soaked in blood, surrounded by a mess of discarded weapons, and there isn't a single Legion Guard here. Not anymore.

They've already been Cut.

I scan each member of the group like I'm checking them for anomalies. "You—you're all okay," I manage through short breaths.

"Honestly, Nami, I'm offended you think we couldn't handle six Residents." Jacek claps a hand over my shoulder and pain explodes throughout my back. "You're hurt," he notes, serious.

"It'll heal," I say, unsure whether his words are meant to be concern or an accusation. "I'm just out of practice."

Jacek presses a finger to his comm and murmurs something to Captain Preeda. When he drops his arm, he looks around at the group. "We should make our way to higher ground. We can take cover until—" He stiffens mid-sentence, moving to shield me.

Quinn and Leilani lift their guns toward the ridgeline. I force myself to turn around, bracing for another onslaught of Resident scouts.

At the top of the hill, two dozen warriors stare down at us from the backs of their Dayling mounts. The horselike creatures stand in a militant line, their skin bursting with swirls of starlight. One of them flicks its head, showing off a lush, shimmering mane. Their riders are dressed in layers of cloth that range in color from beige to apricot to dusty gray. Most of their faces are covered to protect from sandstorms. Even from down here, their weapons glitter violently in the sun.

I reach for my dagger on instinct, bending my knees slightly, when one of the figures pulls her face covering down and calls out a name.

"Nami?"

A girl urges her horse forward, cantering toward us until she's only a few yards away. When she dismounts and pulls her hood down, I see a mess of unmistakably pink hair.

I blink, fighting the mist in my eyes.

Shura beams, and I don't see anything after her body crashes against mine and blocks out the rest of the world.

10

A PATTERNED CANOPY BILLOWS ABOVE ME, AND the breeze carries the scent of firewood from the nearby clearing where soldiers have gathered to share food. Most of the Daylings have been herded into a nearby pen that is currently acting as a partition between Jacek's crew and everyone else.

I sensed there was tension between the remaining human factions when I was in Neo Genesis, but out here, no one bothers with forced diplomacy. The humans may be fighting on the same side of the war, but they are also fighting distinctly different battles.

Jacek presses a finger to his comm, mouth barely moving as if he's trying to mask his words. It wouldn't surprise me if he's already arranging our extraction.

The static across my arms has quieted, almost to the point where I can barely feel it. I'm starting to doubt whether it was ever Caelan at all. Maybe I misunderstood. Maybe Shura was the familiarity this whole time.

Beside the fire, Eliza fills a bowl with hot soup and passes it to me before doing the same for Kasia.

"Thank you," I say, cradling the bowl in my palms.

She offers a smile before tucking a long, black braid over her shoulder. It's a relief to see her. I wouldn't want to imagine Shura having to endure the loss of one of her moms again. I only wish I could tell them both about Annika, and how she's safe and waiting for them in Famine.

Kasia taps a nail against her clay bowl, again and again. There's a crack behind her ocean eyes, like a tremor in the current. When she notices me staring, she sips at her soup, and the tapping stops.

I open my mouth to ask if she's all right when Shura appears, ducking beneath the swooping canopy and plopping heavily onto the cushion beside me, her cheeks flushed with an irritated shade of pink. She looks at me pointedly. "I know I've never really understood your choice of friends, but honestly? I think I prefer the Prince of Victory."

I glance toward the encampment and find Jacek with a nearly identical expression to Shura's, arms crossed at his chest as he glares in our direction. "What happened?"

Shura shrugs. "He asked why we weren't at the northern outpost, so I explained that it was burned down weeks ago by the Legion Guards. He said the Second Wave should've been informed, so I told him if the General wants intel, she should send her own troops to come and get it." She bites back a scowl. "It's not like we couldn't have used the backup."

"You know better than to argue with Second Wavers," Eliza says with gentle admonishment.

"That's not even the worst of it," Shura huffs. "He had the audacity to tell me that War is Ozias's territory—and if we needed help, we should've put a request through the proper chain of command. Like we haven't tried that a thousand times already! Not to mention, it's almost impossible to get messages to anyone when our camp is under constant attack from the Red City. I haven't seen Ahmet in *months*!"

Eliza lifts a brow. "I'm going to assume you didn't let it go at that point?"

"Stars, no," Shura says hotly. "I told him that if that's the case, then he's technically trespassing, and not only do I not owe him any information at all, but I also have grounds to shoot him."

I choke on a gulp of soup, failing to hide my laughter. When I look back at Jacek, he's graduated from glowering to *fuming*.

My mind snakes toward his in silence, searching for the vulnerable gap in his mental shield. When I find it, I focus my thoughts in a single direction. *If you're going to be offended about what people say behind your back, maybe you should stop eavesdropping.*

Jacek doubles backward, eyes wide as he realizes what I've done. Behind him, one of the Daylings clops a hoof against the sand, tosses its head back, and whinnies—loud enough to make Jacek startle away from the fence.

While he's distracted, I pull at the rope near the canopy, freeing a curtain that drapes across the opening. I widen a veil across the room, and when I feel Jacek pressing at the corners in frustration, I know it'll be enough to keep him out.

Shura cracks a smile. "So, maybe not a friend after all?"

"More like we're being forced to work on a group project together," I say.

Shura relaxes, soaking in the sight of me sitting across from her. "I can't believe you're really here."

"We'd heard you'd been Cut after your capture," Eliza says, folding her hands over her orange tunic. When she shifts, the material appears to glow with firelight. "I'm glad you were able to come back from it. So many still haven't."

"Ahmet told me you came out here looking for your family," I say, choosing my words as carefully as the poison will allow me. "But you won't find them here."

"So he keeps telling us." Shura's lashes flutter, and she looks away. "He believes they were already Cut." Her gray eyes fill with urgency. "But we've regrown *thousands* of humans from the tanks in Death. Don't you think it's odd that we've never come across a single person from the Colony yet?"

"You haven't come across any of them in War either," I point out.

"We find survivors all the time," Eliza assures me. "Humans emerging from the tunnels, or making it to the surface after being buried deep beneath the sand for years. Not to mention, no one has been able to breach the Red City yet. Who knows how many more of us are being kept in Ettore's dungeons." She winces at the thought. "There is hope here; if we left, there'd be none."

"There's hope in other places too," I try, straining against the poison.

Shura reaches for my hand. "I'm glad to see you. But if you're here to convince us to return to Neo Genesis, you're wasting your time. We're exactly where we want to be."

Kasia's brow quirks. A silent question, likely to do with why I'm tiptoeing around the reason I'm here.

I shut my eyes and concentrate on the words that won't fall away from me. "You're where you want to be," I say, "but not where you *need* to be."

Shura pulls her hand back and frowns. "What do you mean?"

"I . . . have a contact who might know something," I manage through gritted teeth, voice turning hoarse as I brush against the venom with every word. "I can't tell you who they are, but—"

Shura's expression sours. "Have you been to see Caelan? Did he tell you where he sent them?"

I stumble over my thoughts when her words sink in. "Wait. You—you know where Caelan is?"

Shura and Eliza exchange a glance.

I think of the prickling against my skin. The way it called to me when I crossed the border. The way it's fading, even now.

Every word I say cracks as it escapes me. "If he's still locked up somewhere, please . . . please tell me."

Shura sighs. "He isn't here. But I know the two of you used to . . . communicate. I thought maybe he'd been in touch."

I give a quick shake of my head. "Not since I woke up." I chew the edge of my lip, nerves getting the better of me. "When was the last time you saw him?"

Shura sinks deeper into her cushion, deflated. "Decades ago, when he was still Ozias's prisoner. I visited him. More than once.

I told him I hated him for what he did to the Colony, and my mother." Her eyes dart back and forth, as if she's weighing up whether to say anything else. "Most of the time he was in too much pain to speak, but when he could find the strength, he'd ask if you were safe, and if you'd gotten away. It's what he'd always ask."

"I never—I hope he wasn't—" I inhale, blinking hard to steady my emotions. Deep down, I knew how they must've been treating him, but hearing it out loud?

"I'm not telling you this to upset you," Shura affirms, serious. "I'm telling you because I think it might mean something to you."

"It does." *It means everything.* I press a hand over my forearm, trailing a finger against the skin. "I thought I felt him when we crossed the border," I admit. "It's the reason we were headed west."

Eliza frowns. "The west is a wasteland of sand and bone. It's Nightling territory now. Even the Residents tend to avoid it."

"He could be hiding," I try. "You said yourself—survivors appear all the time." Ozias claimed that the Residents had taken Caelan, but it wouldn't be the first time he's lied. Maybe he threw him to the Nightlings as a way of torturing him.

"Last I heard, the Residents took Caelan to the Capital," Shura says. "But before you start getting your head filled with ideas of a rescue mission, there's something you should know."

"Something is happening in the Red City," Eliza explains, casting a sideways glance toward Shura that I can't quite make sense of. "Not a single one of our scouts has had eyes on Ettore in almost a year, but recently there have been new airships appearing every day."

Shura bites the edge of her lip before nodding in agreement.

"At first, we thought Ettore had retreated to the Capital. But, well, you've met Ettore. I'm not sure 'retreating' is in his vocabulary."

"Our scouts believe Ettore is sending his soldiers to another location," Eliza finishes. "We think he's preparing for an attack outside of War."

Residents can't reach the Borderlands, and attacking Ozias would be as effective as shaking a hornet's nest, considering he foams at the mouth whenever there's a battle to be had. Which means the only option left is . . .

My stomach hollows. Soup drips down my hands, and I realize I've started shaking. I set the bowl at my feet and flex my fingers. "You think he's going after the *Mizuchi*?"

"Not exactly," Shura says guiltily.

Eliza lowers her voice to barely above a whisper. "We thought perhaps the General had another stronghold." She shares a knowing glance with Shura. "A place she might be shielding from Ozias."

I make a face. "Are you asking if my sister has a secret base stashed away somewhere?" When neither answer, I realize they're being completely serious. "No, of course not. I mean—why would she? What would be the point in hiding an army when she's at the cusp of winning this war?"

Eliza narrows her eyes. "Because when the end *does* come—and it will—a throne will be left empty. And I'm not convinced Ozias and the General are the type to share."

My throat hitches. "Mei would never start another war over a throne. *Never.* She only wants humans to be free." When the bigger threat dawns on me, it takes the air from my lungs entirely. "Is

Ozias planning on betraying her? Does . . . does *he* have another army hidden somewhere?"

"If he did, he'd never tell me," Eliza says. "I've fallen out of favor with him. A century's worth of smaller disagreements seems to have done the trick. But if you're asking whether he's capable of turning on an ally, then yes. I believe he is."

"Ozias is smart," Kasia interrupts, solemn. "He will not risk losing to the Residents while your sister still offers soldiers. But I think your friends are right." She lifts her chin. "Your sister is bringing humanity into the future, and that is a threat Ozias will not allow to grow past this war."

I stare at the crackling fire, watching the simmering layer of soup while my mind calculates every possibility. "So even if the battle with Residents comes to an end, the battle with each other will just keep going."

"If your sister concedes the throne to Ozias, then perhaps it won't come to that," Eliza points out.

My eyes snap toward hers. "Would you really be okay with an Infinity ruled by Ozias?" Even if I manage to convince Mei that coexistence with the Residents is possible, Ozias would never allow it. If he takes the throne, there will never be a bridge. The Residents will be hunted down, one by one, without even the promise of the Afterlands as a refuge, because none of them can venture beyond the Four Courts.

It would mean their definitive end.

"I have no interest in playing kingmaker," Eliza clarifies. "But if the Second Wave is attacked, and it is revealed that your sister has been building additional forces without Ozias's knowledge, it will be all the reason he needs to turn his army against the General's. We've spent too many years pulling bodies out of the sand. None of us wants to spend another millennium doing the same."

"If there's even a *chance* Mei has troops somewhere you don't know about . . ." Shura's voice softens. "She's your sister. She'll listen to you."

"I'll warn my sister that there might be an attack, but she isn't out to betray Ozias," I say. *Even if he deserves it.* I turn to Kasia. "You've been in the Borderlands longer than my sister. You've seen her troops. *Lived* with them. Tell them there's no second army."

"It's true I've never seen signs of a hidden base, but . . . it is curious, don't you think?" Kasia asks softly, finger resuming its tapping against her bowl. "Where else are there enough humans worth the trouble of Ettore leaving War over?"

I open my mouth to say that she's wrong—that there must be some other explanation—when it hits me. Because there *is* another place he'd attack. Another court with human survivors.

The quake in my chest is thunderous. *Is he after Damon's palace?*

I lean forward, voice nearly inaudible, and look between Shura and Eliza. "There's somewhere I need to take you. Somewhere important. But you can't ask questions—you just need to trust me."

Eliza's face is unreadable, but Shura looks like I've said something she's already known.

She tucks a pink strand of hair behind her ear. "The last time I saw Caelan, he said we needed to find you. That you knew someplace safe to take us. At the time, I figured he meant the Borderlands. I thought it might've been a ploy to figure out how to get there. But something in his eyes . . . it was like he was Gil again." Her voice cracks. "Do you know where my mom is? Is she—is she safe?"

I flinch, hoping she can see the pleading in my eyes. I struggle with my thoughts, straining as they crash against my skull, desperate to break free. "I can't tell you any more than I already have."

Eliza is still. Too still. After a long moment, she turns to Shura. "If there's a chance of finding Annika, then you should go."

Shura looks alarmed. "I'm not going anywhere without you."

"We've spent a century looking for what's left of the Colony. This may be the closest we'll come to finding information. But you know as well as I do that there are humans in the Red City that need to be set free." Eliza lifts her chin. "I will stay with our people, and finish what we've started. But you? You will go with Nami, and get the truth."

Shura's face softens. "But—"

Eliza cups her cheek. "I know. Find out where she is, okay?"

"I will. I promise." Shura rests her head on her mother's shoulder.

I can't tell her how long we'll be, and she knows better than to ask. Time is never guaranteed in Infinity, just like it was never guaranteed in life.

And the little time I have now? I need to spend it thinking of a way to lose Jacek and the others before we reach the Borderlands.

11

AN URGENT HUM WAKES ME IN THE NIGHT. I SIT up, eyes heavy from sleep, and find that I'm alone. The fire has gone out. Someone's draped a blanket over my shoulders. When I peek around the hanging curtain, light flickers within the various tents scattered across the desert. I don't see the rest of the crew anywhere, but knowing Jacek, I doubt he'll be far.

I press a finger to my right temple and feel something brush against the walls of my mind. Static races across my skin, and then—a tug. I leap to my feet, opening my thoughts as I search for the source, but there isn't anyone there. The connection is undeniable, but I'm no longer sure it's mental at all. It's . . . *more.*

I feel the life behind it. The urgency.

And it's close.

I move quickly to the back of the next tent, sheltering myself from view. I hurry to the next canopy, and the next, until I reach the edge of the encampment. When I'm certain no one is watching, I slip through the nearby rocks and disappear into the shadows, using a veil of my own for cover.

The moon is a silver crescent tonight, and thousands of stars are scattered across the velvet sky, flickering and as ever-changing as they always are in Infinity. I let the hum reverberate through me, and I chase the feeling westward. I skirt the sunken dunes of the wasteland, past an abandoned outpost littered with ravaged timber, until I reach a strange rock formation that looks like a graveyard of hills. When I get closer, I see that they're piles of human bones.

I shudder in the night breeze, turning in a careful circle to assess the area. The humming is louder than ever. There's a flutter behind my ribs, vibrating with impatience.

I press my thoughts into the mist. *Caelan? Are you here?*

The hill of bones rattles, and several broken remains trickle down the sand and roll to a stop at my feet. I trace the movement up to a looming beast in the distance. Its fur ripples in the darkness, and when its glowing eyes latch onto mine, it growls a warning.

A Nightling.

More shadows emerge from the bones, raising their hackles and flashing their fangs. A dozen at least, prowling toward me like I'm prey that walked into a trap.

I take a step back, boot crunching against a caved-in skull, and realize my veil isn't stopping any of them. My fingers drift toward the hilt of my dagger when one of the smaller Nightlings steps in front of the others. It raises its head, ears twitching with interest.

It doesn't attack me. It studies me like I'm an anomaly that doesn't make sense in this world. For a moment, I do the same.

It would be safer to run while I still have the chance. I've been attacked by a Nightling before, and poisoned with its blood twice. I should be afraid; it might very well be my own terror that drew me toward this trap in the first place.

Is that what the buzzing was? Fear mirroring fear, calling out to what was familiar?

Fear is not a weakness, my thoughts sing.

The vibrations boom in my chest—and then it hits me.

"You're the Nightling I brought into existence," I say, hollow. "The one I made when Nix was killed."

The Nightling howls, static snapping around it. A creature crafted from raw, burning fear—*my* fear—lost for a hundred years to the sands of War.

A part of me.

"I know what you are," I say to the shadow.

The Nightling's eyes flare. Its pack watches in wait, ready to attack once the small one's curiosity is sated. I take a step forward, and the Nightling snarls.

"I thought a friend was calling to me," I say quietly, "but it was you. I think you wanted to be found." I study its shape, smoke curling in the moonlight.

I fed the world with fear and created a monster.

All I want now is to take it back.

"I know you're searching for something you don't understand," I say. "Seeking out fear because you think you have to destroy it. But you don't. It can be a strength too."

I approach the Nightling, fingers stretched. The moment it presses its muzzle against my hand, I feel the smoke slip through me. It winds around my veins, reminding me of everything I've done wrong, and everything I'm afraid to lose. But I embrace all of it.

When the fear settles back inside, I take a breath. The Nightling is gone. I look down at my fingers, flexing them slowly, and notice a strange black mark across the back of my right hand that winds up my forearm, curling like dark tendrils. It shifts slightly with the imprint of a shadow trailing across my skin.

By the time I look up toward the wasteland, the rest of the Nightling pack has vanished.

"How did you do that?" a voice asks.

I spin sharply and find Jacek standing a stretch away. He's not looking at me—just in my direction.

I let my veil drop. "How'd you know I was here?"

Jacek motions toward the veilstones on my bracers. The ones I didn't bother using because I was hoping for privacy. "There's a tracker in every piece of Second Wave tech." His jaw shifts. "We don't like it when our people go missing."

"That's a convenient detail to leave out."

"I could say the same thing about you." He nods to the shadow swirling along my hand. "Care to explain how you're able to communicate with the Nightlings and how you just *absorbed one into your body*?"

“I have no idea,” I say honestly.

Maybe it’s because I created it. It was *my* fear—and it was looking for a way home.

“I’ve never seen anything like that before.” Jacek pauses. “Doc should take a look at those marks when we get back to the Borderlands. It could be a new kind of poison.”

Something rustles in the distance, and several bones trickle down the hill where the Nightlings once stood. Jacek draws his pistol without a sound, and I reach for my dagger. When he presses a finger to his comm, I know he’s calling Captain Preeda. Second Wavers don’t take chances. Not when War so famously enjoys an ambush.

I activate my veilstones, and we take a few careful steps away from the mountains of human remains. Something shiny flickers overhead. I barely register the shape of a Resident scout when Jacek reacts. He fires his gun and doesn’t miss. The Resident trips down the hill of bones, turning to mist at our feet.

A second shadow flees for the boulders.

Jacek shoves a pistol into my hand. *If you see anyone, don’t hesitate,* he mouths, and sets off in pursuit.

I back away carefully and try to mask my footsteps. Scanning the area for movement, I send my mind outward and search for a hint of consciousness nearby. It doesn’t take long to find him. His mind tremors with fear.

I don’t remember ever seeing a Legion Guard retreat, but that was before the Second Wavers found a way to Cut them down. Perhaps the loss of life is enough to rattle even the worst of the Residents.

Jacek likely will have lost the trail by now, but I can still sense the Resident fleeing, racing through the night sky out of our physical reach. I press myself into the shadow of one of the boulders and slow my breathing as my thoughts surge after him. The walls of the Resident's mind are sharp and fragmented. It doesn't take much to slip through the cracks.

In the midst of a dark void, I see a young face with delicate freckles and soft brown eyes. His features are narrow and elf-like, and he wears Ettore's colors: a deep, unforgiving red.

I step closer, but he doesn't see past my veil. He paces, breathing erratic, when another figure presses into his thoughts. Someone he's talking to through a comm.

"I followed the Nightling's howl to the boneyard. It was acting strange, just like you said, but then it turned to smoke and vanished," the Resident explains. "There were two humans there. One of them shot Liam."

"Second Wavers," a woman snarls.

I know that voice. Commander Alys—the Resident who killed Nix.

My insides burn.

"But *how* did the Nightling disappear? And why didn't it attack the humans?" she presses.

"I don't know," the elf-like Resident says. "I think the humans did something to it. Maybe it's something new."

"If the humans are weaponizing Nightlings, War is vulnerable," Commander Alys spits. "Where are they now?"

"We're trying to draw their fire south, but they have guns. Do you want to risk the soldiers?"

Commander Alys is quiet for a moment. "Tell the others to head for the Red Palace while we still have cover. His Highness will want to hear about this when he returns to court."

My fingers twitch at my sides.

"Prince Ettore is returning? I thought he wasn't coming back now that—" the elf-like Resident stiffens.

I pull my veil closer and stop myself from breathing.

"What is it?" Commander Alys asks.

"I—I thought I heard something," he replies.

I look down and realize my hand is firm around the gun Jacek gave me. I've never been able to take a weapon into someone's mind before. At least not a weapon that wasn't *me*.

If Second Waver guns exist here, what would happen if I used one on a Resident? Would I be able to Cut someone right from their consciousness? I've entered Caelan's and Ophelia's minds from across the Four Courts. It would mean I could hunt anyone in Infinity—even the Residents in the Capital.

What would Ozias do if he found out I had that kind of power? What would *Mei* do?

My fists tremble, and a ripple appears in the void. I recoil. My thoughts . . . I let them get too loud.

And now my veil is useless.

The elf-like Resident is looking right at me, mouth dropped in horror at the gun in my hand.

Don't hesitate, Jacek told me.

But I do.

The Resident shouts. I yank myself from his thoughts and tumble back to my own body.

"Nami!" Jacek yells from across the sand. "Come on—we have to go!"

The transport is here, but a horde of Legion Guards is headed straight for it. Bursts of energy soar toward the hull. The Residents may fear our weapons, but successfully taking down a Second Waver ship is an opportunity they won't miss.

I fall in line beside Jacek, and we race for the loading ramp, where Leilani is firing her rifle. A stream of blue energy pelts across the sky and knocks several Residents out of the air.

"Kasia and Shura—" I blurt out, panting.

Leilani ushers us forward and slams a hand against the panel to raise the ramp. "They're inside with the others."

She moves with Jacek to the cockpit, but my eyes are glued to the small window. Residents are drawing closer to the ship, dodging the gunfire with godlike speed. In the center is Commander Alys. Her fists blaze with red energy. When her face shifts from fury to recognition, I know she's seen me through the glass.

Which means it won't be long before Ettore knows I'm back in Infinity too.

12

WE LOSE THE RESIDENTS IN THE SECOND LANDscape, but not before our ship takes two direct hits. The first is superficial, but the second knocks out the maneuvering sensors.

Captain Preeda strains as she weaves the ship around a mess of towering pine trees.

"Can't we get any higher?" Jacek yells, launching himself into the copilot seat.

I clutch the side of the hull to steady myself and find a place on the bench in between Kasia and Shura.

"We've taken too much damage," Preeda shouts back. "If we don't land soon for repairs, we'll lose the ship before we reach the border."

"Get us somewhere that has cover." Jacek looks over his shoulder at the rest of us. "Quinn, I want this ship fixed fast."

"Roger that," Quinn says, hand braced against the low curve of the ceiling, ready to evacuate the minute we land.

We hit several trees on the way down, and the ship skitters to a halt at the edge of a small clearing. Shura rubs her head. Kasia looks like she might be sick.

I move for the nearest window and check the sky. "What are the chances that no one heard that?"

"Minimal," Jacek mutters, reaching for one of the bigger guns that hang from the weapons rack. "Leilani, can you cover us from the hill?"

She leaps up and grabs her sniper rifle. "On it."

A thought immediately flickers to the forefront of my mind: *This might be the perfect opportunity to sneak away while the others are distracted, and get Shura and Kasia to Famine.*

But I can't bring myself to leave the crew just yet. Not when they're stranded in the middle of the Labyrinth because of me.

Once I know they're safe, and that we weren't followed by Ettore's troops, we can part ways.

Until then, I can still make myself useful—*and* scope out the area for a getaway path.

I stand abruptly. "I'll check the woods for scouts." Jacek opens his mouth to argue when I motion toward my veilstones. "If I get lost, you'll find me. I won't go far."

Leilani lifts a shoulder. "An extra pair of eyes is always a help."

"Fine." Jacek whirls a hand in the air like he wants all of us to hurry. "Take one of your friends with you. The other can help us protect the ship."

Shura is out of her seat in half a second. "Yes, please. I haven't seen trees in *months*."

Kasia tilts her chin toward the ramp, urging me to go. "I'll be fine here." Her thoughts push toward mine for the first time, loud and intentional. *Don't do anything reckless without me.*

My mouth curves. *I wouldn't dare.*

Shura and I head for the forest, trampling over pine cones and sparse twigs. I consider the lack of gunfire a good sign and head for higher ground. As we make our way across the leaf-ridden path, I brush my fingers along the inside of my arm, absently rubbing the place where the Nightling left its mark.

In the daylight, it's more of a tattoo than a shadow, with bold lines that slither and shift across my skin.

Shura frowns. I gave her and Kasia a very brief recap on the ship, but I'm not sure there was a way to sell *I've absorbed a Nightling into my skin* without immediate suspicion.

"Does it hurt when it moves like that?" she asks.

"It tickles I guess, but it's not painful."

"It looks like it's chosen you as a *host*."

"I'm sure if it was dangerous, it would—"

A heavy thud sounds in the distance, making the Dayling birds scatter for the clouds. The mark on my arm unfurls into a wisp of smoke and shoots for the trees. Bark splits in a thousand directions, shattering into tiny pieces. The tree releases a groan before cracking in half and smashing against the earth with an earsplitting crash.

I blink, staring in silence at the splintered remains of the trunk.

Shura lifts a brow. "You were saying?"

I look at my arm; the skin is bare, and the mark . . .

I follow the path it took, where a rogue shadow weaves around a mess of fallen branches. There's movement beyond the felled tree, and the shadow darts instinctively through the grass. *Searching.*

My chest tightens. "Someone's here."

Shura removes her dagger and crouches low to the ground. I wince at the way her blade gleams, laced no doubt with Second Wave venom. If there's a Resident out here and Shura gets to them first, she won't ask questions. She'll Cut them in an instant.

When I spot a pair of eyes in the forest—wide and brown and alert—I break into a run before Shura can stop me.

The figure is fast, disappearing into the woodland. The Nightling shadow runs alongside me, matching my pace. I duck below branches and hurry up the narrow hillside until I reach the edge of a cliff.

Sitting in the clearing below is a ship. Not a transport ship like ours or an airship like the *Mizuchi*, but something smaller. The metalwork is mostly bronze, with mismatched plating along the rounded sides. The landing gear sits at uneven angles, and the windows seem clumsily thrown together. Nothing about the design is symmetrical.

It isn't anything like the ships I've seen in Infinity. But it's the child picking wildflowers in the field that's the most peculiar of all.

A little girl adds a daisy to the bouquet gathered in her fist, humming as she surveys the meadow. Her brown hair is braided into a crown, and she's dressed in a sweater and flecked leggings, with simple leather boots. Not like a soldier. Not like a Resident. From here, there isn't a blade to be found. And yet her face holds the same too-polished gleam as the rest of Ophelia's creations.

A shriek emerges from the forest, drawing the girl's attention. She drops her flowers and scurries up the landing ramp to hide. I spin around, searching for the source of the noise, when the shadow positions itself in front of me. The wisps contort until they settle in the shape of a fox. A miniature Nightling, or at least some small reflection of one. It snarls and snaps at the trees.

I close my fist, willing the creature to follow me, and run toward the sound. Ahead, I catch a flash of Shura's pink hair; but it's the person at the other end of her dagger that makes me skid to a halt.

In front of her is a Resident with black hair and terrified brown eyes. She looks young. My age, perhaps, but there's an innocence in her stricken gaze that I wouldn't recognize in any mirror. Not after everything that's happened. Her arms and legs are held tight by coils of roots bursting from the earth. Shura's free hand is stretched in front of her, fingers splayed like she's controlling the binds.

"Let me go," the Resident begs through choked tears as the roots race for her throat.

Shura doesn't ease up.

"I was only scavenging," the girl pleads. "I—I didn't know anyone would be here. I just—my mom—" Her voice wobbles. "Please, let me go home!"

Her words spin me back to the gas station, and the masked shooter. I see everything rewind, all the way back to the last night I saw my parents.

To see them one last time . . .

I look from the girl back to Shura, guilt building in my throat. "Stop," I say, too quiet to hear past the crack of the earth splitting beneath the girl's feet. *"Stop!"*

"Her friends are probably already on their way," Shura says through gritted teeth. "We can't let her lead them to the ship."

I grab Shura's arm and force it down. She opens her mouth to argue when she spots the fox circling the Resident.

"What is *that*?" Shura asks.

"My Nightling," I say without explanation.

The creature sniffs the Resident's feet curiously before staring at me with a pair of glowing eyes that remind me of Nix.

"I think it's telling us that we don't have to be scared," I say seriously. "She isn't going to hurt us."

Shura prods her dagger in the direction of her prisoner. "Nami, I know you've got issues killing Residents, but you have seriously *lost* it if you think letting one go free is a good idea."

The Resident shakes her head, eyes watering. "I'm not here to hurt anyone. I—I just want to go home. Please, please, let me go."

Shura widens her eyes like she's implying this is clearly a trap, but I'm not so sure.

What if she's from Famine?

I take a few steps toward the Resident, studying her youthful face. She's as polished as the other Residents, but there's something different about her. She looks . . .

She looks like she has no clue what she's gotten herself into.

"Where's home?" I ask.

"Asphodel," she replies, voice shaking.

I glance at Shura, wondering if it's a name for a Resident territory that popped up while I was asleep, but she gives a single shake of her head. Wherever Asphodel is, she hasn't heard of it either.

"We were told that humans fight their wars in the skies," the girl continues. "We didn't think anyone would be here."

"We? How many of you are there?" Shura presses. "Did you come here on a ship?"

The Resident's eyes are frantic, and I know she's thinking about the girl in the meadow. "Please. I—I don't want to die," she sputters, devolving into a mess of uncontrollable sobs. Shura tightens the roots in response, and the Resident struggles to breathe.

Whatever window there is to get answers, it's closing fast. Using Shura as a distraction, I slip through the shaky walls of the Resident's mind. When I enter the void, I find only panic.

This isn't a soldier, or a Legion Guard, or a murderer.

This is a young girl who has never seen violence.

How is that possible in Infinity?

I pull back and face Shura. "You have to let her go."

"Absolutely not!"

"You *have* to. She isn't like the others. She isn't even armed! You can't just Cut her down in cold blood."

"That isn't my plan," Shura counters. "Your crew is going to want to meet her. She's the first Rezzie I've ever seen who's openly admitted to living somewhere we've never heard of." Her gray eyes flash with urgency. "It could be another stronghold, or a Resident airship. It's information that may have some value."

"If you let the Second Wavers take her, they'll torture her for information and Cut her when they're finished."

"So?"

"So she doesn't deserve it!" I snap. The Nightling fox growls beside me, hackles rising with static. "This is how it happens. We teach young people to hate, and the cycle never stops. We have to be better. We have to teach them to be *better*."

Shura presses her lips together, biting down on her simmering frustration. "She's not Caelan, Nami. And he's the exception, not the rule."

"We can't be okay with hurting an innocent girl."

"You don't know if she's—"

"I don't want to take the chance!" I rub my brow, searching for better words. "Even if I'm wrong, even *if* she's really a scout, what will it matter if we let her go? By the time she finds backup, we'll be safe in the Borderlands where they can't reach us. And if I'm right, and she's a civilian?" I tighten my fists. "Then at least we're not responsible for murder."

Shura opens her mouth to reply, when the pop of a bullet bursts from the tree line. I watch in horror as the Resident is struck in the chest, mouth parting slightly in shock.

"No!" I scream as I throw my mind out to hold on to her. I swipe at the void, desperate, but she's already fading fast. I try to tether the mist, hold it close, and for a moment I think it almost works.

The Resident looks up at me, innocent fear shuddering through her, and makes a final plea. “Don’t let them take my sister,” she gasps. “She’s waiting for me. Please—make sure she gets home.”

The mist fades, and by the time I drift back out of her thoughts, her body is slumped forward, motionless against her binds. Jacek appears at the edge of the forest with his rifle still pointed at the girl.

Our veilstones . . . He tracked us.

Jacek presses a finger to his comm, and I know it won’t be long before the rest of the crew arrives. They’ll hunt for the ship, find it in the clearing, and destroy anyone else who’s there.

Don’t let them take my sister.

The little girl from the meadow.

The unarmed child.

Just like the girl from the gas station.

I don’t think about what this could cost me, or what it will look like to the others. I focus on Shura and force a connection. *Stay with Kasia.*

By the time she forms a reply, I’m too far away to hear it. I rip the veilstone bracers from my arms, throw them to the ground along with my dagger, and cover myself with a veil of my own. As I race through the woods, the Nightling winds back up my arm, settling against my skin. I ignore Shura calling my name, and the thunderous sound of footsteps pounding after me.

The minute I reach the clearing, I see her, still standing in the opening at the top of the ramp, one hand planted on the ship’s frame. Her eyes scan the horizon. She looks terrified.

I take a breath and let a mask shift over my face. I lock the image of the other Resident in my mind—her dark hair and wide, brown eyes. I grasp at the memory of her in my thoughts. Her last moment, when she asked for my help. I let her face become mine and shift my clothes to match. Then I lift my veil and run toward her sister.

"We have to go," I say, out of breath. "The humans are coming."

The Resident stumbles back, and I pray to the stars that my disguise is enough to trick her, even if it only lasts until we reach the border. Finally, she nods, and I follow her inside and watch the door seal.

I take a seat beside her in the rickety cockpit, and to my horror she looks at me like I'm supposed to fly the ship out of here.

"Can you do it?" I ask quickly, and make up the first lie I can think of. "I—I hurt my arm in the forest."

She studies me for a moment before grabbing the controls. "Okay, yeah. But if I crash, it is *not* my fault." A whimper slips through her words. "I can't believe I let you talk me into this."

I use every bit of my energy to build a veil around the ship and hope it's enough. The engine rumbles, and we're in the air within moments, racing for the Labyrinth border.

Staring down into the trees, I mouth a silent apology to Kasia and Shura—and a promise to come back to them soon.

WE CROSS FOUR LANDSCAPES BEFORE THE world shifts into an expanse of ocean. Waves tumble below us for hours—longer than any layer of the Labyrinth—until a mountain range appears in the distance, covered by an unassuming bank of clouds. They sit low, swarming the steep inclines with fog. It's impossible to see all the way to the top.

The Resident pulls the ship low to the ground and heads straight for the base of the mountain.

I stiffen in my seat and dig my fingers into the armrests.

"Seriously, Zel?" They're the only words she's spoken since we crossed the first landscape. "Since when are you afraid of this part?" She moves a lever, and the ship picks up speed. Water sprays around us, and I watch in horror as we aim for the mountain wall ahead.

I try to play a role, trusting that—despite what it looks like—we aren't about to crash. "I think I just prefer to be the one steering."

The girl huffs and continues ahead. I brace for an impact that doesn't come.

One minute we're surrounded by utter darkness, and the next—light.

There is no sea. No mountain. It was all an illusion. And down in the valley, past fields of colorful flowers and vibrant blossom trees, is a city.

It stretches for miles. Crisp white buildings rise through the sky like a hundred cathedrals, connected by swooping glass bridges and silver archways. Several decorative viaducts curve through the city center, separating the varying levels within. Patches of vivid green parks are scattered throughout the citadel, and small transport ships move across the sky in uniform lines.

The city is bigger than any of the Four Courts. It's bigger than any territory I've seen in Infinity. The Resident said she was from Asphodel, but this . . .

I look across the cityscape. The tallest building is visible from here, made up of curved spires and open balconies. A palace fit for royalty. Floating directly above it is a strange white orb in the clouds, hovering like a perfect full moon.

I don't want to feel her presence so easily, but I do. Ophelia . . . she's here, in this city.

We're in the Capital.

Our ship pulls into a small tree tunnel at the side of the first viaduct, before slowing to a stop beside a corner of overgrown bushes. The Resident shuts off the engine, flings a leather bag over her shoulder, and hurries out the side door. I only make it one step on the grass when she spins and glowers.

"You almost got us killed!" she hisses. "I told you not to wander from the ship! I told you someone would spot us!"

I feign remorse and piece together what little I know of the situation. "I'm sorry. I honestly didn't think anyone would be out there. Humans usually fight in the skies."

The girl rolls her eyes. "Yeah. You said that. And you were clearly wrong."

"I'm sorry," I try again.

She covers her face with her hands. "At least we got what we needed."

My heart beats quicker. They were scavenging. That much I know. But for what?

She peeks through her fingers and drops her arms, disappointed. "All I managed were some stones," she admits. "You really didn't find anything?"

I lift my shoulders. "There wasn't time?"

The girl's eyes rake over me, suspicion working its way to her brow. "Where's your bag?"

"I dropped it," I say pointedly. Her eyes flit back and forth, piecing too much together, so I throw my arms across my chest and jut out my chin. "In case you don't remember, I was running from a *human soldier*. I had bigger things on my mind than my bag."

Her face softens, but the fear remains. "I remember. I

thought—I wasn't sure—" She cuts herself off with a shake of her head. "I'm just glad you made it back." She straightens. "Okay. Are you going to ask the question?"

The . . . question? I try to look bored. "Um. Do we have to?"

She snorts. "It's your rule. Don't you want to make sure I'm not a human spy?"

I watch her carefully, mind hurtling for a plan, when a breeze moves behind me, making both of us start. Four Legion Guards appear, swords drawn.

I move in front of the girl to shield her when recognition passes over one of the guard's faces. She shakes her head at me, and the rows of silver cuffs along her ears catch the sunlight. "Not this again, Gisele."

I look between the guard and the girl. "We were just exploring?" I offer, and the girl nods quickly.

"Don't drag Olivia into this. It's one thing to risk your placement exam, but to risk a mark on your sister's record before she's even reached secondary school?" The guard rubs her temple, waving the other soldiers away. "Tell Captain Thorne the anomaly was just some kids playing around. Nothing to worry about."

The others bow slightly and disappear beneath the archway.

The woman turns back to me. "You know the rules about leaving the city limits. I can't keep covering for you just because you're a counselor's daughter."

I look at the girl who's supposed to be my sister. *Olivia*. "It wasn't her fault. She was just trying to help." My thoughts slip quickly into hers, carefully veiled.

Her own mind is loud and completely unprotected. It's like

being in a carnival of color and sound and light. But it's also busy filling in the gaps I need, volunteering information through her unfiltered thoughts—including the reason we were scavenging in the first place.

I look back at the guard and shrug.

"A boy from school didn't believe I'd built an engine that could take us across the ocean. I wanted to prove him wrong, so I went to look for flowers. Flowers that don't grow here. Olivia only came because she was worried about me being on my own." It's a twisted version of the truth—technically the boy dared Olivia, not Gisele—but something tells me sibling loyalty will win more points here than the truth.

To my relief, Olivia smiles. A silent "thank-you."

The guard isn't as pleased. "Ego is not a good reason to break our laws."

"I'm sorry," I say.

"Me too," Olivia adds.

The woman watches. Thinks. And then she holds out a hand. "Objects found outside of Asphodel city limits are restricted for a reason."

Olivia pushes out her bottom lip and slowly hands her bag to the guard, deflated.

"I'm also confiscating your ship, in case that wasn't clear. Your parents are welcome to put in a request for its return—*after* you've told them what happened today."

The exasperated cry from Olivia is enough for both of us to appear wounded.

The guard tips her head to the side. "Go on. Get yourselves home before you miss the parade."

Olivia sulks through the archway, but the guard presses a hand on my shoulder, stopping me.

"This is a beautiful rebuild. I heard you approach—solid thrusters, and a smooth braking system." She gives my shoulder a gentle shake. "You're smart, Gisele. Too smart to be breaking the rules. Don't throw away your chances at university just because some young brat is taunting your little sister, hmm?" Her eyes shine conspiratorially. The glint of someone who knows Gisele and Olivia well. "Let her fight her own battles. It builds character. And you know as well as I do First Folk can't afford to lose the limited opportunities we're given."

I nod, hurrying to catch up to Olivia, who tugs my arm with force. We make our way toward a set of stairs that leads into the city. A curved bridge takes us over the canal. Several Dayling fish skitter through the water, shimmering with starlight. A manicured garden shifts in the light breeze, and I inhale the scent of flowers. They're everywhere, in every color: crimson and gold and fuchsia and cobalt. The kinds of gardens you see in oil paintings, almost too perfect to be real.

"Come on, Zel. We're going to be late!"

I follow Olivia's impatient strides into a residential district. A woman rides past us on a bicycle, stopping in front of a bakery that's wedged between two apartment buildings. A family sits on a balcony on the third floor, drinking tea and pointing toward the horizon, chattering enthusiastically about something I can't see.

A high-pitched squeal makes me stiffen, and when I look over my shoulder, there's a toddler running across the road. A woman kneels down and scoops him up in her arms, hugging him close to her chest as she nuzzles his cheek, making him laugh. She shifts him onto her hip, moving for the open door behind her, when I see her stomach: round and swollen with life.

It's impossible. It *should* be impossible.

Babies don't exist in Infinity—not the way the rest of us do, anyway.

Annika once told me she believed their souls were too pure, too light. That they lived among the stars. It was a comfort I think, to imagine they'd been spared from Ophelia's rule.

I'm not sure what I believed. I'm not even sure I really thought about it at all. But seeing the pregnant woman here, with a child in her arms . . .

If the Residents can create life . . . not humanoids forged into existence by Ophelia, but actual *life* . . .

We've been wrong about so much more than I thought.

Building a bridge isn't just about protecting good Residents over evil ones, or crafting a future built on coexistence instead of hatred. There are children at stake. *Babies.* The kind of innocence that should never, ever be collateral damage in a war.

Is this what Caelan was trying to protect? What he told me I didn't understand?

Olivia pulls at me, desperate. "Come *on.* You realize we still have to get dressed, right?"

I shake my head, wholly confused, but continue trailing behind her through the street until we reach a terraced house with dark red bricks and flower baskets hanging beside the windows. Outside the door, Olivia waves a hand, and a lock clicks. I follow her into the home, mind searching for whoever else is here, but the only hum I find is coming from Olivia's never-ending train of thought.

Black and white tiles line the hallway, and a matching staircase curves toward the second-floor landing. There are doors on either side of us—one leading to a sitting area, and the other to a kitchen, both rooms bursting with cozy furniture and shelves stocked with ornaments.

Olivia thuds up the stairs, calling over her shoulder. "I think we'll be able to make it before the opening ceremony if we hurry."

She disappears around the corner, and I follow, peering through the open doorways that lead to the bedrooms. The first one is all dark greens and browns, with deep wood furniture and a sheepskin rug across the floor. It feels older. Lived in, but not *loved*. In the room next door, Olivia is half hidden behind a wardrobe, rustling through her clothes. Her bed is smaller, with a disheveled lavender blanket and books scattered across every surface. There are flowers on the windowsill, growing in lopsided ceramic vases like something a child would make in art class.

The final room is unmistakably Gisele's.

Tools are littered across the large metal desk. There's a white pegboard on the wall, with various paints, tapes, and brushes hanging from their individual hooks. A small model of an airship sits on the surface, unfinished and unpainted. There's a record player against the opposite wall, with a shelf full of vinyl, each case frayed at the edges with well-worn use. A bed is shoved in the corner, covered in a blue plaid throw.

I move for the standing wardrobe and pull the doors open, sifting through clothes as if whatever I'm supposed to wear to a parade will be immediately obvious. Thankfully, Olivia appears in the doorway, dressed in white robes that hang to her ankles.

Underneath is a matching dress with a delicate tulle skirt.

She holds her arms up and frowns. "I hate this. I look like a marshmallow."

My memories lock onto one of Mei. I'd asked her what she thought of my dress, and she told me I looked like I was going to a Victorian lady's funeral. It makes a smile crack halfway across my face.

"Don't worry, Olivia," I say gently. "You look great."

She stares back, face blank, and drops her arms. I'm not sure she believes me, but she vanishes back into her room without another word.

I turn back to the wardrobe and find the ceremonial robes, sliding them carefully over my shoulders. With a sweep of my hand, I let the pixels fall across my clothes, morphing them into a white dress that's fitted into a corset shape at the top with soft, flowing pleats in the skirt. Then I wrap the robes tighter, cinching the belt at my waist.

I rock back on my heels, frowning at the boots, and search Gisele's room for more appropriate footwear. The white silk shoes in the corner seem to have been laid out especially for this occasion, so I swap them out, adjusting the size as they move over my toes. When I stand up and move for the doorway, I nearly crash into Olivia.

Or rather, the very sharp-looking dagger she's currently pointing at my chest.

Her small eyes narrow. Despite the tremble in her shoulders, her voice doesn't break. "Who are you," she seethes, "and what have you done with my sister?"

I HOLD UP MY HANDS, PANIC CLATTERING through my chest.

When I don't speak, she adds, "You never call me Olivia, but you've done it twice today. So—where is she?"

I widen my eyes. "You're going to stab me over a nickname?"

Olivia waves the blade at me, and I realize it isn't a dagger at all—it's a kitchen knife. Something she grabbed when I was getting changed.

Confusion swirls through me. There are no weapons in this house. A house that belongs to a family of Residents.

How can that be?

The disbelief works in my favor, because Olivia lowers the

knife an inch. “Ask me the question.” It’s the same thing she wanted to know at the edge of the city, before the guards interrupted us.

I let out a slow breath, feigning annoyance as I dive into her thoughts. They’re wild with fear; but I see trust rolled in there too. She doesn’t believe her sister was really taken. Doesn’t *want* to believe it. It won’t take much to nudge her suspicions away and remove the doubt.

All I need to do is pry the question from her thoughts.

It doesn’t take long—she has no idea how to veil her mind. Maybe she’s never had a need to protect it before. But I hesitate, guilt slithering its way into my bones.

I lied—pretended to be her sister—because it was the only way to keep her safe. But if I lie now, right to her face . . . it isn’t for her protection. It’s for my own.

Maybe that shouldn’t make a difference, but it does. She deserves the right to mourn her sister. The right to know what happened in that forest. She deserves the truth.

Except I don’t give it to her.

I could say it’s because I know what it’s like to lose a sister without getting the chance to say goodbye. I could say it’s because Olivia clearly has no idea how to use a dagger, and if she tries to fight me, she’ll only get hurt. I could say it’s because I can’t chance getting captured and putting Mei at risk.

I could say a lot of things about why I choose to lie, but in the end, it doesn’t matter. Right now, I am the villain hiding in plain sight.

“What can you break without ever touching?” I ask.

Olivia stares back. Twists her mouth. Drops the knife. "A promise." She gives me a weak smile. "Sorry, Zel. But you did say to *always* make you ask the question."

I roll my eyes, biting down on the awful knot rising in my throat. I motion between us. "Are we ready to go now? You're the one who keeps saying we're late."

Olivia nods quickly and hurries down the stairs to put the knife away. I exhale a slow breath and follow her.

We walk back through the residential district and take a circular glass elevator to a high level of the citadel. From there, we settle inside one of the air shuttles that pass over a thin, silver train line into the heart of the city. Olivia idly chats away about school—I pry into her mind only when I need to connect the dots in her conversation—but otherwise, we mostly fix our stares out of our respective windows.

I can see most of Asphodel from up here. There are sleek, white buildings everywhere, with an abundance of water fixtures that pool into the connecting canal system. Neat tufts of moss grow between the squared pavement, making the pathways look like a perfect cross-stitch. The market bustles with colorful wooden stalls along the city streets—though most of the Residents seem to be heading in the same direction as us.

The shuttle slows, and Olivia leads me down the wide platform where the tail end of a large crowd becomes visible. Instead of following them, we head toward a staircase that winds up the side of a curved wall.

Two Legion Guards wave us through. At the top of the stairs, my breath catches. We're in a massive stadium lined with floral arrangements and bright orbs of light that float midair. Residents gather near the railing, straining to get a glimpse of the Legion Guards marching through the grounds.

Music blares in the background. I turn, searching the heights of the stands behind us, when I realize Olivia is directing me toward a covered section in the central platform. We clamber higher and higher until we reach one of the private boxes. There are four chairs planted inside, with two of them already filled. I make the obvious assumption that these are Olivia and Gisele's parents.

"Honestly, you two. We ask you to be on time for *one day*. You know how important this is to your mother," a Resident with peppered-black hair scolds. He nods to the empty chairs, and Olivia and I both sit down abruptly.

The woman on his right leans forward. She has brown hair spun in soft curls, and her lips are painted gold. "Please make sure you smile. I know you both hate it, but the election is coming up. We want to make a good impression."

The man takes her hand gently. "Don't worry. The people trust you; you'll get the votes."

"Thank you, dear." She glances back at me like an afterthought. "Gisele, have you done something different with your hair?"

I tuck a strand over my ear instinctively. Tricking Olivia might've been one thing, but a mother? She must be picking up on all the subtle differences I didn't have time to perfect.

"I—think it got a little messed up on the way here," I say. "We ran all the way to the shuttle station."

She must believe me, because she turns away with a satisfied hum and focuses back on the procession below. "I hope you'll take more care when your entrance exam comes up. Your grades might have helped secure an interview, but they certainly won't get you through the door. Appearances are important, especially when the Legacies have such an advantage over us."

There's no way for me to ask what she means, so I follow her gaze across the stands and tuck the information away for later.

A few more Residents make their way to their seats, but the majority have clearly arrived on time. All the other private boxes are filled with people as poised and important-looking as Gisele's parents. My eyes briefly land on one of the smaller boxes in the row below us that's draped with sheer white fabric. The material obscures whether or not anyone is inside, but judging from the lack of humming coming from under the canopy, I have a feeling it's empty.

The crowd fills in along the sides of the central arena, leaving a wide gap down the center. When the music begins to grow louder, I realize the parade is about to arrive.

Olivia shifts beside me, plucking at the tulle in her skirt, but the moment the Legion Guards step through the walled stadium, she leans forward with delight and claps her hands.

The army marches in perfect synchronization. The ones at the front carry flags and ceremonial swords that gleam too bright to have ever seen a battle. The ones wearing leather armor are covered in shades of indigo and cerulean, but most wear dress uniforms with silver detailing that flickers even with the distance.

The music continues to blare, shifting to an upbeat mixture of flute and percussion, and a herd of Dayling horses trots through the street, mounted by more soldiers. Several beautifully decorated floats follow, filled with Residents dancing in time to the music. Their movements don't mean anything to me at first, until I realize they're telling a story.

A world of darkness. Light coming down from the heavens. The birth of a queen.

I know this one, my thoughts gasp. *This isn't just a parade—it's a celebration for the Night of the Falling Star.*

I remember everything from that night. The belief that I was doing the right thing for humans mixed with the grief of knowing it would hurt Caelan. The promise I made Gil to find a way back to him. The realization that they'd been the same person all along.

I remember the lights, and the dancing, and the dress I wore to commit an act that would've wiped every Resident from Infinity if the Orb had been real.

I remember Caelan letting me go. I remember his eyes when he told me to follow the stars. I wasn't sure if it was a trick then, but now? Now I recognize the plea.

Despite my betrayal, he still wanted me to be safe. He saw something good in me—something worth saving—even when I was so clearly his enemy.

And then he did it again in War.

I don't care how many people think I'm naive to believe in peace. I owe Caelan my life twice over. I believe in his hope for coexistence. And any version of the world that would destroy him for the "greater good" isn't a world I want to fight for.

Below, the crowd has gone blurry. I blink, shuttering away the memories.

The music shifts to orchestral strings. The audience narrows their focus, lowering their voices to a hush. An enormous float appears in the arena, surrounded by a waterfall of golden flower buds that spills over the edges. Leaves dance all around, glittering and swaying alongside the trill of violins, and a podium of elaborate tiers sits in the center of it all. Each stair is laden with more buds, more golden leaves. A mountain, waiting to come to life.

The sheer fabric from the private box below peels back, and a figure steps out to greet the crowd, stopping just shy of the banister. My eyes trail from his asymmetrical white robes, to his white hair, to his crown of silver branches.

The world spins beneath me. Prince Caelan smiles at the crowd, silver eyes as regal as I've ever seen him. There are no bruises on his skin or dark circles under his eyes. He looks healthy. Beautiful. And *here*.

The float gets closer to our stand. Caelan lifts a hand as the music builds and builds, and a glowing orb appears in his palm. With a careful flick of his wrist, he launches the light toward the float, where it settles against the highest flower bud. The petals explode in an instant, sending a dazzling eruption of light throughout the display. One by one, each glow blooms into a luminous, white flower.

The Residents cheer for the parade, for the magic, and for their prince. Caelan watches from the stands, soaking in their admiration like it's all he's ever wanted.

My mind thunders, skittering across the black void in confusion, searching for our connection. He's nowhere to be found in my thoughts, but he's here now, standing just out of reach, like he hasn't seen a cage in a long, long while.

All this time, I wondered why he hadn't tried to find me. Why he hadn't answered when I searched for his mind, again and again.

It never occurred to me this had been his *choice*. Not even when Mei told me it was.

She knew. My mind reels. *She knew exactly where he was and still let me wonder.*

"Careful," Olivia hisses in my ear. "If Mom sees you drooling over Prince Caelan, she's going to make you go to *all* the banquet dinners."

"I thought he'd been taken prisoner," I say, words scraping over my throat like sandpaper.

One look at Olivia tells me she has absolutely no idea what I'm talking about. "Is that supposed to be a joke?"

Shadows ripple at my wrist. I feel the Nightling there, edging past my sleeve. I clamp my hand down, trying to cover it before Olivia notices.

When the float moves along, Caelan dips his chin, acknowledging the cheers echoing through the arena one last time, and turns back toward his private box. His gaze briefly rises to the surrounding politicians—silently taking in their support—and when his silver eyes drift to mine, I nearly choke on my own desperation.

But he doesn't linger. Not on me. Not when I look like Gisele.

Something awful rotates in my stomach. Hurt and confusion and a deep sense of rejection.

He was here, in the Capital. Not with Ettore. Not with Ozias. Not chained against his will.

Here.

Did time really change so much between us?

In the years I spent Cut from my body, did Caelan really just . . . move on?

The parade continues, but the violins turn to awful screeching in my ears. I look at Caelan's face. The unhurried gaze. The smoothness of his brow. And I remember what Ophelia said to Lysander on that final day.

"He gave up the right to be treated as one of us the moment he betrayed his own kind."

Her orders were for Caelan to be left in War, knowing Ozias would torture him. Knowing he'd be in pain. She said when the time came to bring him back, she would erase his memories.

Is that what happened? Does he have no idea who I am?

Has he forgotten about Famine completely?

The stands tilt, and I sway in place, feeling as if the world has transformed into a raging sea. I blink hard, throat hoarse as I inhale a pained gasp. Olivia's voice breaks through the pounding in my ears.

"Zel!" she hisses. "Your *hand*!"

The Nightling vibrates at my wrist, and shadows spill through my sleeve. Someone presses down on my shoulder—Olivia's father, maybe—and voices start to layer over one another like white noise in an empty space. I'm not listening. Not thinking.

I'm being flooded with fear.

I grip at my mask, barely keeping it steady. But it's not my face I'm worried about. It's the realization that I may have lost Caelan for good.

Wisps of smoke leap from my wrist and take the form of a fox at my side. I think I hear someone call for a healer. I think I hear Olivia whimper beside me. But the foreign sounds only make my terror surge.

I'm in the middle of the Capital of all places, without a single ally. What was my plan? What did I think was going to happen?

You didn't think, my mind shouts. *You never do.*

I try to quell the fear and call the Nightling back to me, but I catch sight of Caelan's white hair in the stand below, that silver flicker of his crown, and I come undone.

"He is my son." Ophelia's voice pounds through my memories. "If he is weak, I will fix him."

My horror builds, ricocheting out of me like an explosion. The Nightling grows larger, head bent and teeth bared. Someone screams. Figures begin to shrink in the distance, and my vision tunnels.

I'm struggling to control it—the mask I'm wearing and the fear that I've willed to life. My mind feels erratic, jumping from thoughts and emotions involuntarily. All I want is to slow it down, but I feel like I'm at the edge of a mountain, and instead of hope I find a thousand-foot drop.

Caelan . . .

I'm a stranger to him.

I'm his *enemy*.

My eyes shutter against the panicked voices in the crowd. The Nightling paces around me, building like the monster Ophelia knew I could be.

Reel it in, a voice inside my head commands. *You have to be stronger than this. Now more than ever.*

I try to pull the Nightling back to me, begging for it to calm down. It snarls, snapping at the world in despair. And then—

A crown. A boy. A pair of silver eyes.

Caelan steps into the light, and it isn't hate I find in his eyes. It's compassion.

A glimpse of the prince I got to know too late.

His guards push the crowd back, and Caelan takes a step closer, locking eyes with me. He mouths something—something I can't hear. The Nightling doesn't snap at him. It doesn't even growl. Because deep down, even with my fear, I'd never hurt him.

The creature shrinks back into a fox, before the wisp of smoke trails back up my arm. I gasp, feeling the energy leave me, and slump to my knees.

Caelan rushes forward and puts an arm around my neck. "Hold on," he says into my ear. "I've got you."

He carries me away through the crowd, and I let the darkness pull me to sleep.

15

I WAKE UP IN A STRANGE BED. THE SCENT OF firewood fills my nostrils, and my eyes flutter open to find a mess of orange flames crackling in the belly of an iron stove.

I swing my legs over the side of the mattress and stand too quickly, and a burst of starlight dances in my vision. I wince and press a hand to my head. Nearby, a door opens.

A Resident with curly chestnut hair walks in, carrying a red mug between her palms. A floral tattoo climbs up the side of her neck, stopping just below her jawline. Her irises are different colors: blue on one side, and mossy green on the other. She holds out the drink. "You're looking much better."

My eyes dip to the mug, and I hesitate.

She smiles gently. "You don't like tea?"

"I'm not thirsty."

She sets the mug on a nearby table. "I can't imagine how shaken you must feel. We've never had a Nightling breach in Asphodel. The Legion is still trying to figure out how it happened."

"A breach?" I repeat, and relief washes over me. *They don't know the Nightling came from me.*

It might not be long before they put it together. Olivia and I were stopped by guards on our way back—guards who knew we'd come from across the border.

I touch my face like I might be able to feel the mask there, but the only assurance I have that I still look like Gisele is the fact that this Resident is speaking to me like a friend.

I scan my surroundings. The room appears too comfortable to be a hospital, and I don't remember seeing wood paneling like this in Olivia's house. I'm not sure it's a good idea to risk asking where I am, though. For all I know, Gisele has been in this room a hundred times before.

The woman's expression turns serious. "How are you feeling?"

I tuck my arms around myself protectively. The motion reminds me of the parade, and the stands, and the arms that wrapped around me just before I lost consciousness.

Caelan.

My face pales. "What—um—what happened exactly?"

"You were attacked by a Nightling during the parade. Prince Caelan brought you here. We think the creature is currently subdued, but—well—we aren't exactly sure how." Her face softens like she's trying to ease the blow. "It appears it's somehow tethered itself to you. Possibly because of how afraid you were, and how close you were when it attacked. We're trying to figure out how to undo it."

I look down at the black mark lingering across my skin. Someone must've removed my outer robes, leaving my arms bare. "Did everyone see it?"

"Very few, actually. It happened so fast. But the last thing we want is for the city to panic—it's better if we can keep this incident as quiet as possible. At least until we're certain we have it under control."

She moves to adjust the pillows on my bed. The moment her back is to me, I look down at my arm, testing the threads of a veil to see if I can separate myself from the shadows, but it doesn't work. I'm not sure why; maybe fear is more difficult to hide.

"I spoke with your family," the Resident continues, tugging the blanket at the corners. "They're understandably concerned and want to see you. But, given the circumstances, we think it would be best if we keep you under observation before that happens."

I straighten, lifting my shoulders. "And after that, I can leave?"

She studies me for a moment. "Of course. As soon as it's safe to do so." She points to the side table. "Try to drink that tea—it'll warm you up, at the very least."

When she opens the door, I catch a glimpse of the hallway and spot two armed Legion Guards. I'm not sure if they're protecting me or protecting the rest of the building *from* me, but something tells me it's the latter.

The moment the door falls shut, I let my thoughts become

mist and search for their minds. It doesn't take long. They're having a conversation with the chestnut-haired woman who brought me tea and are doing nothing to veil their words.

"Let her rest. I'll come back to check on her in an hour," the woman says.

"What about the parents?" one of the guards asks. "They said they'd return in the morning with a First Folk healer."

"I *am* a First Folk healer."

"They don't know that. They're insisting on a second opinion." There's an uncomfortable pause. "They were concerned the Legacies might use what happened to sway voters."

"Oh, for the love of—" The woman sighs. "No visitors. Not even *second opinions*. We're lucky the only witnesses were a few First Folk and not the whole of the Legacy senate. Prince Caelan wants to keep this incident isolated, so make up whatever excuse you have to, and reiterate to the family that she's being properly looked after. Until we can remove the Nightling, she'll remain in this wing, quarantined."

"And if she tries to leave?"

Her voice drops low. "Then do what you must."

I feel a rumble of affirmation from the guards before I pull my mind back through the doorway, searching for the nearest window. There's no frame or glass; just an open expanse of fresh air.

For a moment, I consider how long it would take to climb down the side of the building—but the second anyone realized I was missing, I'd become a target. Every Legion Guard in Asphodel would be looking for the girl with a shadow monster wrapped around her wrist. I have no idea where I am or how to get through the city's barrier without setting off another anomaly. Not to mention there's an ocean at the border, and I have no means of transportation.

I stare back at the fire, mulling over my thoughts. I pace until I'm dizzy. Plot until my temples ache. I play out a hundred scenarios in my head, hoping one of them can get me out of the city without blowing my cover.

But I don't have allies in Asphodel, and I'm starting to think Gisele doesn't have them either.

There are guards outside my door with orders to keep me hidden from the outside world.

I'm not just a stranger to Caelan—I'm his prisoner, too.

The sky shifts with the rich colors of sunset. Marigold and apricot and hyacinth. It's disarming, seeing a city morph into something so serene. There's no pop of gunfire or pillars of smoke in the distance. No screams echoing off the canyons. No chorus of blood and bone as soldiers and Residents are Cut down on the battlefields.

War hasn't reached Asphodel. Not in any way that I can see.

When the first stars flicker to life, I pull myself away from the window and slump heavily onto the edge of the bed. The healer checks in on me every hour, as if she thinks treating me like a child will keep my sense of calm. But there's no mistaking where her concern lies.

I'm a danger that's being contained.

I brush my fingers over the Nightling mark and feel the

creature stir. It doesn't show itself, which I suppose is a relief. I'm not entirely sure I'd know how to control it if it did. Something tells me that the moment I'm afraid, it's going to draw itself like a weapon.

Footsteps sound beyond the doorway, and I straighten, expecting the healer to appear with more tea. But whoever it is pauses outside, voice too muted for me to hear properly. The guards haven't left since they were assigned to keep an eye on me. I know because I've checked their minds repeatedly for signs of movement, but they never move, never speak. Not until now, anyway.

I yank the door open in one sweeping movement, startling the two Legion Guards who've been here all day.

One of them has long golden braids and eyes the color of peridots. He nods in my direction and closes the gap between us. "Is there anything I can help you with?"

"Was someone just here?" I peer down the corridor, but there's no sign of the healer. Just a row of dimly glowing sconces along the paneled wall. "I thought I heard something."

The guard's face reveals nothing. Not even impatience. "I'm happy to check your room, if it would put you at ease."

Ignoring the offer, I let my thoughts become a trickle of mist, searching for another consciousness. I take a few cautious steps down the hall, and the guards immediately fall into formation around me.

The Nightling prickles at my arm.

"No one said I couldn't leave my room," I state blandly.

"You can go anywhere you like, as long as it's within this wing," he replies, voice clipped.

I push farther down the corridor. The synchronized shuffle follows beside me.

"Is this really necessary?" I ask when their shadowed figures take up my periphery.

"The moment that creature releases you, we have orders to put it down," Braids says. "So yes. Staying at your side is necessary."

It takes all my willpower not to halt in place. I'm not sure what's worse—the thought of being kept under constant watch, or the thought of them destroying the Nightling. *My* Nightling.

I cradle my arm, but keep my mouth shut. There's nothing I can say that wouldn't raise questions. I'm supposed to be Gisele right now—and if I were to guess, her natural response to the Nightling would be terror, not protectiveness.

I turn another corner. Follow a set of stairs. Loop back around the hall. Every door we pass is shut. Maybe even locked. I send my thoughts in every direction, searching for another mind to give me a bigger picture of my surroundings. I need to get my bearings on this place, so that if the worst happens and they figure out who I really am, I can—

Braids's voice slices through my budding panic. "What are you looking for?"

I smooth the concern on my forehead and shrug. "Nothing. I've just . . . never seen a hospital this empty."

The silence settles between us. He doesn't speak again until we turn another corner, where two large double doors separate us from whatever is on the other side.

"This is far enough."

The second guard moves to the front and ushers me back the

way we came. She's a petite woman with vibrant red hair that curls in every direction like a live flame. Black lines are tattooed up and down her arms. Unlike my Nightling mark, hers doesn't move.

I frown, feet planted together as I stare past her shoulder. "What's behind those doors?"

"More doors," she replies, and I'm *sure* that was sarcasm.

Braids may be determined not to show any hint of emotion—but something tells me Red is more reactive. I file that bit of knowledge away for later.

My focus bounces between the pair, studying their blank faces. Side by side, they don't exactly look like a cohesive military unit—but they're armed, they have orders to eliminate my Nightling on sight, and they've locked me in a vacated hospital to keep my confinement a secret.

I don't need the shadows on my wrist to point out I'm in danger.

I twist my mouth. "Are we going to keep pretending like I'm not being held here against my will?"

"This arrangement is for your own safety," Red offers.

I glare at the doors. "Did the healer say I wasn't allowed past here?"

"Cora has no authority over Winterborne's halls," Braids corrects. "You're here as Prince Caelan's guest."

"But—this ward—" My gaze flicks across the walls, soaking in every detail through a new lens. *Winterborne.* "This isn't a hospital."

"His Highness is trying to avoid having you turned into a political pawn by the senate," he says. "What better place to hide you than one of the few places no one would dare enter without permission?"

"We're in his palace." My heart thumps. "Is Caelan—is the prince home?"

"An absence from tonight's festivities would've raised more questions about the attack," Braids says, almost scoldingly. "His appearance in town will reassure people."

So he's playing a part. The ringing in my ears builds and builds.

I wonder . . .

If he knew it was me . . .

If I could somehow speak to him in private . . .

My gaze flits to the window, where lights flourish across the twinkling city. There's a twenty-foot wall separating Winterborne from the rest of Asphodel, but even then, the distance to the city center is enormous. The open fields that stretch across the hills offer nowhere to hide. There's movement along the perimeter wall, and I realize how silly I was for thinking I was being guarded by only two soldiers. Outside, there are dozens.

This isn't a hospital—but it isn't a castle, either.

Winterborne is a fortress.

The shadow trickles up my arm. I turn from the window and make my way back to my room. Braids doesn't say another word to me—but his watchful eyes are the last thing I see before I swing the door shut.

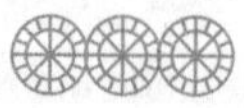

Hours pass, filling the room with darkness. The healer, Cora, stops by only once to drop off a change of clothes. I swap my parade dress for a tank top, soft trousers, and a knitted sweater that pins at my shoulder, with draped sleeves that stop just shy of my elbows.

The guards have fallen silent once again. No matter how many times I search the building for a hint of Caelan's mind, he's nowhere to be found.

I close my eyes, lean against the headboard, and breathe. Mei must know I'm gone. She's probably furious. Maybe even scared. I'm sure Jacek's told her everything by now.

Will she think I planned this? That I ran away on purpose?

I've tried reaching out to humans, but it's never worked before. Someone once suggested that it's because the humans in the Four Courts are still too young, and they don't know how to open their minds enough to listen.

It's possible Mei is different, and our connection as sisters could strengthen any mental link. But if I tried to speak to her, I might put Asphodel at risk. If Mei knew how to track me—if she knew I'd found the Capital—she'd bring the entire Second Wave with her.

The families here would be wiped out.

I need to tell Mei about the children here first. I need her to understand that the Capital is more than just another army sitting on the other side of a fence. Gisele and Olivia weren't soldiers. They were kids looking for flowers because of a dare at school. There's nothing evil about that. Nothing deserving of being Cut.

And maybe it makes me a traitor for thinking it, but I see more humanity in the streets of Asphodel than I've seen in the human encampments.

A sigh escapes me, followed by an untethering along my forearm.

My eyes flash open, and I watch as the shadow leaps onto the bed, taking the form of a small fox. The moonlight shining through the open window creates a glowing aura behind the creature. Its wisplike fur curls with shadows, and it blinks with a pair of bright, golden eyes.

I clutch my wrist. "What are you doing?" I hiss, attention half fixed on the door. "I thought you were only supposed to come out when I'm scared!"

The creature stares back. Yawns. Sniffs at the floor.

"Do you have any idea what those guards will do if they see you leaping around like some kind of pet? I'm in enough trouble as it is without them thinking I *summoned* you."

The Nightling tilts its head.

I rub my eyelids, exasperated. "Can you even understand what I'm saying?"

The fox flicks its ears and walks toward me. Static crackles along its back. Not a gesture of rage, but of peace. I hesitate before raising a hand to stroke its head. Despite the smoke on its fur, the Nightling is surprisingly soft. *Warm*, even.

"You remind me of Nix," I say quietly.

The fox nuzzles my wrist, now vacant of any mark, and an idea bursts to mind. I stare down at the creature's bright eyes. I once took Nix across the desert and found Caelan in a tower. I used him as a vessel, and a shield.

Maybe I could do the same with the Nightling.

I'm not sure if I could travel far enough to get a message to Mei. But if I could get the Nightling to the border and make it look as if the danger has left me for good . . .

Without a Nightling, there'd be no reason for the Residents to keep me in quarantine. I could *leave*.

Pulling my hand back, I try to enter the creature's mind the same way I did with the Dayling, but there aren't any memories to latch onto. Instead, I find a glowing light deep within, pulsing and thrashing and searching for a way to get out. Hope, hidden in the heart of my fear.

"I understand how you feel," I say softly, scratching behind her ears. "But from now on, you have to promise me something. We can't let our fear become a weapon. We have to control it. *Wield* it. Letting our fear loose on the world is going to put other people in danger. And—and I already lost Nix. I don't want to lose you, too."

She flicks her tail behind her.

"You're going to need a name." I picture Nix. The snow leopard who carried me across the sand, loyal until the very end. They're connected, in their own strange way. One born from the other's death.

"I'll call you Fenix," I say finally. "In memory of a friend."

Shadows pour out of her fur in acknowledgment, and I smirk.

Fenix stiffens suddenly, snapping her head toward the doorway. I do the same, thoughts craning for a sign of someone drawing near. The guards are still there, standing in their rigid formation. I can't even hear their breathing, let alone any whisper of thought.

But Fenix hears something. She moves for the door, prowling across the tiles, when I hold out a hand to stop her. *No!* I mouth. *You can't go out there. If they see you, they'll attack.*

She raises her hackles defiantly. Flashes her canines. The fear in my chest tugs, and I sense that somehow she's pulling a string, urging me to trust her instincts.

There's something out there. Something she wants me to see.

Maybe it's a way out.

I hold out my arm. "Okay. But I need you where I can protect you."

Fenix turns to shadows before circling my skin, settling into her swirling imprint.

I scout the hallway with my thoughts. It wouldn't take much to pull the guards into a mental slumber.

The problem is eventually they'll wake up, and if I can't manage an escape, I'll have to explain how and why a politician's daughter knocked out two of Prince Caelan's guards. Right now, I have the advantage of the Residents thinking I'm helpless. I need to hang on to that for as long as I can.

I move for the window, peering down the drop below. A phantom pain along my back makes me wince. I could make the jump; I just wouldn't enjoy it. And I'd almost certainly be spotted by the guards along the perimeter.

I take a step back. I might not be able to *actually* jump, but . . .

There were jumpers in the old Genesis. People who could teleport from one place to the next. They moved an entire settlement once, and every single person in it.

I picture the double doors where I stood earlier in the afternoon. The image settles in my head, locking into place. I hold on to it, recalling every detail. I imagine it's a door that's right in front of me, waiting to be opened.

My consciousness drifts toward it like I'm trying to exist in two places at once.

I feel a pull. It makes my chest ache, tearing the energy from me like I'm being severed in half. I struggle in limbo, trying to return to a singular place, too afraid of what might happen if I allow myself to be untethered completely.

But maybe that's the trick—I have to trust myself enough to let go.

So I do.

Streaks of light blaze past me. One moment I'm standing in front of the window, and the next I'm in front of the double doors, keeling over in agony as pain thrashes through my body.

Too much. That was too much.

I clutch my throat, trying not to gasp, and force myself into the nearest alcove. Nobody comes after me. Nobody knows what I've done. I slow my breathing and press my fingers over Fenix's mark.

It moves across my skin, spiraling as it takes the shape of an imperfect circle with a dark line down the center. I turn, watching as the line remains fixed like the needle of a compass.

She's telling me where to go.

I grab the handle of the door and enter the next corridor, eyes barely lifting to the carpeted halls as I study the makeshift arrow on my skin. Fenix leads me toward a wide landing with stairs that spiral in opposite directions. I follow them up, one step at a time, too afraid to even breathe. The silence in Winterborne fills me with dread, but I don't sense the hum of another consciousness nearby.

I really am alone.

There's another hallway, another corner, another turn, and I become acutely aware that I'm losing my sense of direction. I let my thoughts drift, keeping up the constant search to make sure no one is waiting in the shadows. It takes effort. My head pounds like a timpani, and a violent ache shudders through my body—the aftereffects of sending both my consciousness and physical body across space.

I blink, fighting the dizziness, when Fenix tugs a string, urging me ahead.

At the end of the hall is another set of stairs, narrower than the last. It curves, winding up the inside of a tower. Thin apertures are spaced far apart, offering so little light that I nearly stumble on the stone steps. When I reach the top, I pause at the threshold of an unlit room.

On the other side is an open balcony. The curtains are drawn enough to keep the moonlight out, but they billow in the breeze, letting a soft whistle curl through the room. Music is carried with it, faint with distance and almost inaudible. But it's the flicker of movement in my peripheral vision that catches my attention.

My eyes drift toward another parted doorway. It isn't darkness I find inside—there's firelight spilling across the parquet floor, indicative of a roaring, well-kept hearth. There shouldn't be anyone here. I *checked*, again and again. But there's another footstep across the room. And another. And another.

I press a hand against the door, no longer letting the compass guide me. Whatever is inside this room is what Fenix wanted to show me.

Two white chaises face each other with only a small table to separate them. Tapestries hang from the walls, not unlike the ones in Victory. Shelves and shelves of lush plants sit in ceramic pots, some overflowing with leaves that trail to the floor. And in the center is an unfinished sculpture, molded from stone.

The mark on my arm shudders, and whatever string I thought was attached to my rib cage snaps in two.

I don't know how I didn't sense him. I don't know how I searched Winterborne and found no one beyond the guards. And I don't know how I'm able to hold on to my mask when I turn abruptly and find his silver eyes latched to mine.

The moment he opens his mouth, his voice hits me like an arrow to the chest.

"You," Prince Caelan says slowly, "are not where you're supposed to be."

16

CAELAN TAKES A STEP FORWARD. THE SHOULDERS of his tunic gleam with tiny crystals, giving the appearance of frost. "My guards have failed me tonight. I told them quite specifically not to leave you unattended."

Whatever words I want to say—whatever ones I *should* say—fail to reach my brain. I simply stare back at him, lips parted and eyes wide with shock.

How did I not sense him?

The familiar scent of woodland and winter, the expanse of infinite starlight between our minds . . . it's just *gone*.

A coil tightens around my heart, and I blink, awareness suddenly catching up to me. "I—it wasn't their fault. I snuck out."

He lifts a brow. "Is that supposed to make me *less* disappointed in them?"

"Yes?" I say like it's a question. My eyes dart between his, searching for anything familiar. Anything to suggest he's still in there somewhere.

I'm met with nothingness. There's no mental wall or gentle hum. It's like his mind is empty.

What did Ophelia do to him?

Caelan catches sight of the shadow moving over my arm, and his jaw tenses. "Is it causing you pain?"

I shake my head, because the hurt I'm feeling has nothing to do with Fenix.

"Interesting," he muses, entirely too still. "Nightlings are usually drawn to fear. Asphodel is a strange place for a creature like this to wander. Especially without being seen." Suspicion rakes through his words, but none of it feels directed at me.

He still thinks I'm an innocent bystander in all this.

I should try to make sure it stays that way. Focus on playing the role of Gisele until I can get out of here. But his words set off my curiosity. He's not suspicious of me, but he's suspicious of *someone.*

Does Caelan have enemies here?

I try to veil the shade of pink building in my cheeks. "You think someone brought the Nightling here on purpose?"

When he stiffens, I worry I've made a mistake. But after a moment, he shakes his head. "That's not possible. Nightlings cannot be controlled."

"Maybe it isn't like the other Nightlings. I've heard they're giant creatures. This one was small."

Caelan's expression darkens. "You shouldn't listen to rumors. They have a tendency to make liars out of good people."

"Not always," I say too quickly, the adrenaline making my words loose.

His lip quirks, challenging.

I still my shoulders. "Sometimes rumors are a map to the truth, if you pick the right ones to follow."

He studies me carefully. "And what other rumors have you heard about Nightlings?"

I swallow down my nerves. "They're unpredictable. Dangerous."

"Go on."

"They aren't just drawn to fear, but created from it."

He waits, expectant.

"Nightling blood can be used like a poison." I pause, afraid to push too far, but unable to let my hunch go. "Do you think that's what happened? That someone was trying to poison you?"

His mouth twitches. "Are you suggesting there was an assassin at the parade?"

Maybe I was wrong. Maybe the only person who has enemies here is me. "It's like you said. Asphodel is a strange place for a Nightling to wander."

He falls silent, watching me with an intensity that burns. I wish I could give him a sign; a hint that I'm here, beneath this mask. That I'm still his friend.

I wish I could know for sure whether he's truly forgotten everything.

I roll my tongue against my cheek. "What's going to happen

to me if your healer can't figure out how to remove this mark?"

Caelan's forehead creases, and whatever amusement was tucked in the corner of his mouth vanishes. "I don't doubt the creature will show itself eventually. It's latched onto your fear. The sooner you learn to release it, the sooner we can deal with the threat."

"Are you going to kill it?"

"Fear is not easy to eradicate. But it has no place in our city—or with you."

Heat rises up my neck. Fenix swirls at my arm, anxious.

"Your stowaway doesn't seem pleased." Caelan tilts his head. "Neither do you."

"I'm surprised," I say, resolute. "I didn't know Nightlings could be killed."

"Everything can be killed, if you're determined enough."

"Maybe. But just because you don't understand something doesn't mean you should destroy it."

His nostrils flare. The pause feels endless, but I don't turn away from his weighted stare. "You have a young view of the world. Time may change that."

I lift my chin. "Is that what happened to you?"

"I am who I've always been," he replies, words sharpening at the edges. "A prince of my mother's design."

"You don't mean that." You *can't* mean that. My words tangle together, muddled by the realization that Gisele would *never* act this familiar with a member of the royal family. "I didn't—I'm sorry. I only meant to say that I'm sure there's more to you than that."

The muscles in his jaw strain, but he doesn't respond.

Caelan, my mind whispers. *Look at me. Give me a sign. Tell me it's still you.*

He doesn't react. Not to me—not anymore. Instead, he turns back to the hearth, watching the fire with a resolute hardness. For a moment, all I see is Ophelia's hollow, black gaze reflected in the son she promised she'd change.

I'm so sorry, I offer the empty expanse between us, too scared to let myself feel what this loss means. Too afraid that if I let myself feel anything at all, I'll fall apart right in front of him. *This is all my fault.*

A knot builds in my throat, making it hard to swallow.

"You should return to your room." Caelan doesn't look at me. "When you get there, tell the lieutenant I need to speak with him. Immediately."

I pull away from him, even as my body is desperate to be closer. I follow the stairs and the corridors back, walking in slow, rigid steps as my mind tumbles.

I expected to find Caelan in a prison, or hiding in the wilderness. Not here. Not like this.

I make it to the double doors and glance over my shoulder one last time. Leaving Caelan behind after I tried so hard to find him . . . it feels wrong.

I'm not ready to give up on him. I'm not ready to accept his loyalty is truly with his mother—that the Caelan I knew doesn't exist anymore. But if I can't prove it, I'm not sure I can bring him to Famine.

When I find a way out of Asphodel, I'll be leaving alone.

I take a breath and find the guards in the same place I left them. They straighten, confusion turning to shock on their faces. Red checks the room, just to make sure her eyes aren't playing tricks on her.

Before Braids gets a chance to yell, I say, "Your prince is looking for you." I shove the door until it latches, and sink into the bed.

I don't open my eyes until the sun rises.

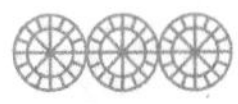

No one comes to see me. Not the guards, not the healer, and not Caelan. It takes until the following afternoon to find the courage to open the doors to the hallway. I'd expected to be locked in after what happened last night, or surrounded by an entire legion.

But to my surprise, the corridor is empty.

I pull the door wider, tipping my head forward to peer down both ends of the hall before ducking back into the room. I check the window for the soldiers patrolling the perimeter. There are dozens of them outside, making their rounds along the stone wall.

I hesitate. If Caelan ordered Braids and Red to leave me alone, there's probably a reason. This could all be a test—to see what I'll do when left to my own devices. They could be watching me right now, hidden beneath a veil, waiting for me to slip up and make a run for it. I gave up the element of surprise last night, so whatever cards I have left, I need to keep them close.

I send my thoughts out, scouring my surroundings for guards, but find none.

Maybe instead of being in a hurry to leave, I should focus on my reason to stay.

I glance at my wrist. "You found him yesterday," I whisper gently. "Where is he now?"

Once again, the mark shifts to an abstract compass. I follow the arrow back through the double doors, down a wide corridor, and into a library. A metal platform splits the room into two levels, and every row of double-height shelves is packed with books.

Caelan sits at a desk on the exposed second floor, swirling a thick tumbler in his hand. He doesn't drink, but he stares at the amber liquid with so much disdain I worry the glass might shatter in his fist.

He sets the tumbler down with a heavy thud. "You're late."

My heart beats and beats and beats. I remember myself enough to fall into a shaky curtsy, which is more than I managed last night. "I—um—didn't know you were waiting for me. There was no one outside my room."

"I didn't see the point. Something tells me the only way to keep you in one place is with a cage."

Guilt colors my cheeks.

"Don't look so worried. Cages are a human invention. Our kind is supposed to be above treating each other like animals." He stands up and stalks down the metal staircase until he's only an arm's length away from me. He lowers his chin, and the light shifts over his cheekbones. "Which brings me to the question of what to do with you."

I cover the mark with my palm. His eyes drift, chasing the movement, and the muscle at his temple twitches.

"Do you not have any servants in Winterborne?" I ask, making him pause. The distraction works. I motion behind me, to the empty halls and empty rooms. "I haven't seen anyone besides your guards."

"I like the quiet."

My attention bounces from one piece of furniture to the next. I'm worried if our eyes meet, he'll see right through my mask.

"Besides, you're meant to be in quarantine," he adds. "Forcing my staff to remain here would be unethical, considering another attack could happen at any moment."

"You're still here." I shift, feigning interest in the nearest shelf. "Aren't you worried about your own safety?"

"I've had run-ins with Nightlings before."

I chance looking back at him. "I heard you created one in Victory."

"I warned you about rumors. They'll only get you into trouble."

"So it's true?" I push. He created that Nightling out of fear for me. If he remembers that day, then maybe—

His laugh catches like barbed wire. "Looking for skeletons? I've been told some of the First Folk are worried the Legacies will spin this attack in their favor, but perhaps it's the other way round." His words drip with mockery. "This could all be a ruse to commit espionage."

"You think I staged a Nightling attack on purpose?"

"*I* certainly didn't."

I lift a shoulder. "I'm just someone who was in the wrong place at the wrong time."

"Maybe. Or maybe you're exactly where you want to be."

"Yes." My mouth quirks, and I step away from the bookcase.

"You got me. I'm an assassin. But before I continue with my evil scheme, can I ask how your demise actually benefits anyone? I'd like to be clear what I'm getting credit for."

"A coup d'état, naturally. If First Folk can survive and rule on their own, what do they need me for?"

"Do you often find yourself at odds with First Folk?"

"No, actually. The First Folk adore me. Am I still going to be assassinated?"

I bite my lip, fighting a grin.

Caelan doesn't back away. He holds up his hands like he's baring his heart, and I struggle not to fall into the pull of him. "This is your chance," he says, soft as silk. "I'm right here."

I forgot what it was like to be this close to him. It feels like I'm cradling a firework in my hands, desperately trying to hide the wayward sparks to keep from revealing too much.

Because what I've felt for him has always been out of my control.

He smirks, letting his arms rest at his sides. "I didn't think so."

I'm locked in his orbit, too rigid to respond.

A line creases between his brows. "Still, you *are* the first to ever be marked by a Nightling. Perhaps fate is sending a message."

"What message would that be?" I ask, my words as frail as rice paper.

"That Asphodel is not as safe as we thought."

"The Nightling was a coincidence," I insist. "Nothing more."

"I've never much believed in coincidences."

"Well, I've never much believed in fate."

"You don't think there's something bigger watching over us? Guiding our stories, controlling our destinies?"

I shake my head. "I think those are all just hope wrapped in different packaging." There's a long pause, and the question tumbles out of me before I can stop it. "Why? Do you feel like someone's controlling you?"

There's a rasp in his stifled laugh. "I was once the Prince of Victory. I am a slave to no one, least of all the stars." He closes the gap between us, so I'm forced to look up to meet his gaze. "We need to talk about your Nightling."

The air knots in my throat. "What about it?"

"When you were attacked, I thought you'd be terrified. But you don't look afraid. You seem more concerned with what we might do to the Nightling than what the Nightling might do to you." He pauses as if he's waiting for a reply, but I don't give him one. "Maybe the creature is suppressing your fear somehow. Or maybe you're just in a state of shock. But either way, I believe the solution to our little problem doesn't rely in waiting for the Nightling to show itself—it's a matter of coaxing it to the surface."

Fenix swirls aggressively against my skin. "What do you mean by that?"

Caelan's lips twitch in the corners. "You were brave enough to sneak past two of my personal guards. I have every faith you'll manage this, too." He brushes against me, and the flutter in my chest sharpens. When he presses a button tucked at the edge of the wood paneling, an elevator door slides open.

"Aren't you coming?" he drawls.

My voice is barely audible. "Where?"

"Into the darkness." His silver eyes gleam. "Where you can show me who you really are."

17

THE ELEVATOR DESCENDS. FENIX SPINS NERvously around my forearm. Caelan stands beside me, eyes forward and unmoving, and despite his comment about cages, I'm worried I'm being led to one.

I remind myself there's a reason Fenix isn't afraid of him—because *I'm* not afraid of him.

I've trusted him as an enemy, and again as a friend. Maybe some part of me trusts him as a stranger, too.

The doors open, and I follow Caelan into a large room. Mismatched pieces of glass are scattered across the domed ceiling, clouded in a way that blurs every reflection. An enormous circular platform is raised in the center of the room, absent of any safety railing or barrier.

There are no bars. No doors. No locks or keys.

This isn't a dungeon; it's a training arena.

Braids positions himself near the edge of the ring, where Red is waiting. Both are dressed in lightweight armor that leaves most of their arms bare.

Caelan tucks his hands at his back. "I believe you already know Elias and Nine."

Braids dips his chin. Red runs her tongue along her left canine.

I turn to look at Caelan. "I don't understand why I'm here."

"We're going to persuade the Nightling to release you," he replies.

"How are you planning on doing that?"

He sweeps a hand toward the platform, urging me forward. I remain in place, fists clenching when he drops his arm and frowns.

"I'm not going to hurt you," he says, a note of sadness in his voice.

The words make my eyes sting, but I step onto the raised floor and mask my emotions. A glowing sphere shutters around me, sealing me inside.

The black swirl moves around my forearm. Braids—or rather, Elias—walks toward the back of the room, where a panel sits against the wall. When he reaches for a switch, panic rattles through my bones. "What are you—"

Darkness fills the space. My eyes sweep over the arena as I search for a flash of silver eyes, but only a thin, glowing layer of the sphere remains visible.

Panic floods my lungs. My fingers flex, desperate for a dagger that isn't there. I left every weapon I had in the forest.

I force myself toward the edge of the platform. "I don't want to do this."

Someone chuckles darkly. Nine, I think.

The barrier sparks violently, and I stumble back, gaze turned up toward the ceiling. The glow is volatile, swirling with white energy. I try to keep my breathing slow, my heart calm. But the lights move faster, and I'm turning in circles, attention snapping to every change in sight and sound.

The dome starts to shrink. I take another hurried step backward, and heat radiates off the sphere's edge. I have no idea where anyone is anymore, but I pick a direction anyway and shout toward it. "Let me *out*!"

No one answers.

I throw my arms over my head, flinching as the ceiling closes in on me. Energy blazes above, warming my face. When I drop to my knees, Fenix reacts.

The Nightling tears from my wrist, snarling wildly. Shadows flare along her back, making her appear twice her normal size. She launches toward the glowing barrier, and smoke fills the room.

Another dome appears—a dark shield that settles over my body. I feel the thrum of power as Fenix pushes the shadows toward the outer sphere, fighting back. Her growl fills my ears, and I brace for an impact that doesn't come.

Everything goes still—and then the room starts to expand.

I let out a heavy breath, watching the sphere ebb back into place before vanishing entirely. When the lights in the room turn back on, Fenix becomes a stream of darkness that snaps back to my wrist in retreat.

I blink, turning to face the others. Elias and Nine stare with their mouths parted. In fear or awe, I'm not really sure.

Caelan watches me with unnatural intensity. I don't move, even as my knees buckle.

"The Nightling didn't hurt you." His voice carries a bite. "It *protected* you."

Fear pulses through me, but I find my own bite of anger to use instead. "I thought you were above using a cage."

Caelan clenches his teeth. "I want your honesty. Are you controlling the Nightling?"

I twist my mouth. "No."

"Is it controlling you?"

"No."

Silence builds. "Do you believe you're in any danger from the creature?"

My heartbeat thumps, loud enough to make my ears ache. "Right now, the only danger I see is *you*."

Caelan doesn't flinch. He steps onto the platform and closes the gap between us with a few calculated strides. He's so close that I can see the muscles straining at the edges of his mouth. The metallic flecks of silver in his eyes. The way the blood rushes to his lips when he pulls them into a sneer. "No, Little Shadow. I'm the only person here who's trying to keep you safe."

I'm not sure if my heart is still in my chest. It feels like it's free-falling down the edge of an endless mountain.

"Why?" I ask, voice cracking down the middle. "You have no idea who I am. I don't mean anything to you."

A curtain draws over him. When he speaks again, there's no

emotion in his voice at all, not even anger. "I'm trying my best to build a bridge between our people."

I almost lose my footing. "What did you just say?"

"I need you to understand the sensitivity of your situation. If word got out that a First Folk—and a *councilor's daughter* of all things—was attacked by a Nightling, there would be no coming back from the rumors. They'd call it a conspiracy, even if it wasn't. Even if you were just at the wrong place at the wrong time." He holds my stare. "It would reaffirm a gap that I'm trying my best to close. We won't make it to the new world any other way."

"The new world?" I repeat.

"The Afterlands. The home that was promised."

"But—" I start. "That's impossible," I want to say. "Residents can't reach the Afterlands. Not when they're tethered to Ophelia, and Ophelia's tethered here, near the gates of Infinity."

Doesn't Caelan remember that?

Or has Ophelia finally found a way to break free?

Dizziness hits me like a tidal wave. I have no idea what the repercussions of releasing every Resident into the Afterlands might be. All the humans who came before Ophelia, the ones who chose not to stay, and the ones who've already moved on . . .

Would Ophelia be able to reach them? Would she be able to reach the innocent souls high up in the stars? Would she ever *stop*?

What will Mei do if she finds out what the Residents are planning?

Caelan's brows pinch. "Something about that makes you afraid."

I follow his gaze to my arm, where Fenix is slithering erratically. "I just—" I start, but I have no idea what to say. I have no idea what *Gisele* would say. "I thought Asphodel was the safest place in Infinity."

"It's safe because it's hidden," he says coldly. "But nothing stays hidden forever."

"But you can't leave. The war with humans—"

"Will inevitably come to its end," he interjects. "When that day comes, the Legacies and First Folk will both be free to venture away from this place and start anew."

"I thought we couldn't go beyond the Four Courts," I say shakily. I've seen the ravaged threads in Ophelia's mind.

Caelan straightens, and I watch his throat bob with distaste. "Humans are the one piece of this world my mother can't fully control. It's the reason she's confined to this part of Infinity, the reason she confined us here too. Until humanity is purged, she knows her people will never be safe."

I try not to move. "She's keeping everyone trapped here?"

"First Folk would not survive in Infinity without the Legacies' protection. Not when our kind are still being hunted."

"But *could* you leave?" My voice drops to a whisper. "If you didn't want to fight anymore, could you go anywhere, without any limitations?"

"Not until our queen sets us free. And she will—when the humans are no longer a threat."

"Is that what you want?"

"To be free? Of course I do. We all do."

"No—I mean do you want to be rid of humans for good?" Something behind my sternum hardens. "Is that how you plan to win?"

He leans down, mouth tense. "You sound disappointed."

My lashes flutter, but I don't break our gaze. "I'm just trying to understand where your line is."

He considers me, irises flicking as they roam my face. "I care about the First Folk." He searches for something he doesn't seem to find. "There are very few things I wouldn't do to ensure they remain protected."

He pulls away, taking some of the air with him. I blink, mind empty, and watch as he turns to Elias. Whatever he says is too quiet for me to hear. There's not even time to eavesdrop. He stalks toward the elevator and disappears without looking back.

Elias slips his fingers through a metal gauntlet, and a wooden staff pixelates to life in his fist. "Here," he says, tossing it my way. "You'll need this."

"For what?" I scowl, even as the weapon sends a wave of relief through my shoulders.

Another staff appears, but this time he grips it with both hands. "For the next part of the lesson." The skin around his eyes crinkles with humor. "Tell me—has anyone ever taught you how to spar?"

18

TRAINING WITH ELIAS IS DANGEROUS. HIS attacks are incessant, and they bring out an instinct that flames to life in my chest. I try to hold back, worried he'll question how Gisele learned to fight, but soon that flame turns to competitive rage. Before I know it, I'm losing myself to the arena.

I block his swings and spin out of his reach. His lip curls. We spar without words, and I pretend the blaze in my eyes is nothing more than adrenaline. I stick to defensive blows and hope that my inexperience with a staff will hide the truth.

The guards can't know that I was trained for battle.

Fragments of my real self appear with every swing and every dodge. Holding on to Gisele feels like I'm battling against my very nature. But I check the seams of the mask, tucking it at every corner.

From the side of the rounded platform, Nine watches. She's as stoic and unmoving as she was outside my room, but now I wonder if it isn't the Nightling she's keeping an eye on, but *me*.

Fenix flutters every time our staffs collide. Curious, but unafraid. Not until Elias brings his weapon down so hard that it shatters mine across the center.

I recoil, flinching as splinters explode in front of me. A tendril of smoke lashes up and snatches the weapon right out of Elias's hands, snapping it in half to match my own. The pieces clatter to the floor, and the smoke retreats.

Elias's laugh is deep. "That thing has an attitude."

"She's not a *thing*." I snatch the broken pieces of wood from the floor and press the jagged edges back together. After a quick brush of my thumb, the pixels tumble over one another, and the staff is once again whole.

Elias plucks the weapon from my grasp. "That's enough for today. We'll meet back here tomorrow morning."

"I already know how to spar," I say, voice thin.

"I gathered." He stabs the end of the staff against the floor. "But it's the Nightling I'm hoping we can train."

"You're trying to get me to use the Nightling as a *weapon*?"

Elias shrugs. "If you can learn how to control it, and get it to attack on your command . . . well, I'm sure you can imagine how useful a skill like that could be."

I glower. "And what happens after that? You're just going to let me go home with a highly trained Nightling on my arm?"

He barks a laugh. "Not a chance. But as soon as you can control it, you'll be able to set it free. If you can keep it docile long enough, we might be able to lead it somewhere else. You can be rid of it for good."

My blood heats. Fenix is my fear. *My* Nightling.

She belongs with me.

I turn for the elevator doors, defensive and angry in a way I don't recognize—but can't seem to stop.

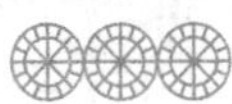

By the time I get back to my room, Nine is waiting, perched lazily against the windowsill. Her ruby red hair spills to one side, and a few messy curls are tucked behind her ear.

I frown. "How did you get here so quickly?"

"One of the perks of being in the Prince's Guard," she says with a shrug. "We know all the shortcuts."

My eyes drift for signs of a false wall or hidden doorway. "I'm not sure I like the thought of a secret passageway leading to my room."

"Then I have good news." Even standing, she barely meets my chin. "I'm here to escort you to your new quarters."

"My new what?"

"The prince has decided you're no longer in imminent danger, so there's no reason to keep you secluded in the eastern wing." She catches my hesitation and rolls her eyes. "It's an upgrade. Trust me—you'll like it."

Nine leads me through Winterborne, and I find myself in another side of the palace entirely. Black marble tiles follow the hallway, brightly lit by open balconies on opposing sides of the corridor. The view overlooks the fields beyond the wall, framing images of Asphodel's cityscape and the vast mountains in the distance. When we reach a dead end with a pair of arched doorways, Nine stops.

The door to the left swings open, and she ushers me inside. She waves lazily to various points of interest. "There's a bath over there; the wardrobe has some clothes you can use; the windows have been sealed with an energy shield, so don't try to climb out of them unless you enjoy being electrocuted."

Embarrassment climbs up my neck as Nine's brown eyes flash knowingly.

She places her hands on her hips. "I'm supposed to tell you that if you need anything, you can ask—but I'm a soldier, not a servant, so if you need something, you better figure it out for yourself. The kitchen is downstairs. You can eat whatever you want, but the staff was dismissed, so you'll have to cook it yourself. Oh—and if you try to pull another disappearing act and make us look bad, I will take it *very* personally."

"Okay. That's fair." I cross my arms over my chest. "Am I allowed to ask questions that *aren't* about things I need?"

"If you must."

"Why do they call you Nine?"

She holds up a hand. Her pinkie is missing from the knuckle, and the scar tissue looks like it healed years ago.

I open my mouth to ask why it hasn't grown back, when I realize I already know the answer.

Residents don't age. They don't have children. They don't lose fingers and limbs that don't regenerate.

Except in Asphodel, some of them do.

Legacies and First Folk. That's what everyone keeps saying. If the Residents in the Four Courts were all Legacies, then that means it's the First Folk who are different. But if they're susceptible to aging and injury, does that make them not just fragile—but *mortal*?

I shift my expression to neutrality. "Did you get that fighting the humans?"

"Don't be ridiculous," Nine snorts. "First Folk aren't allowed to join the Legion."

"You've never been outside of Asphodel?"

"He's right," she mumbles. "You do ask too many questions."

Heat creeps over my face. I don't ask who "he" is. Knowing might only make it worse.

She clears her throat. "Now, is there anything else you need?"

"Nothing I can't figure out myself," I say, repeating her words.

She winks. "Exactly."

When the door closes, I take a breath and look around. The wallpaper is deep green and sprinkled with abstract, gilded leaves. Dark floorboards stretch across the room, but a plush carpet fills the sitting area near the empty fireplace. A four-poster bed towers at the back, bigger than anything I've slept in since arriving in Infinity. A thick tufted quilt is draped across the mattress, dotted in gold buttons and thread. But it's the hint of tile in the next room that grabs my attention.

I look around the corner and find an enormous bath recessed in the floor. Skylights fill the room with the amber glow of sunset, and a perfect stack of fluffy towels is tucked on an alcove shelf.

The last time I saw a bathtub anywhere near this nice was in

War. I'd used Nix to travel across the desert and sneak into the Red City. I felt Caelan's presence in the palace like a lure. And when I found him in the bath, shoulders hunched with torment, I felt something other than hatred.

I believed he was my enemy—and I still couldn't bring myself to hurt him.

I think because deep down, I've never really wanted to hurt anybody.

Everyone keeps telling me it isn't possible to survive a war without doing awful things. I know I've made mistakes in this fight. I've hurt people, and not always because they deserved it, but because I thought it was the only way. That justification—to lie, to hurt—it's terrifying. It makes you see things with tunnel vision. It makes you miss the details.

I don't want to miss any more details.

I lift my fingers to my cheek. *Gisele's cheek,* my mind corrects, and shame washes over me. This isn't the only mask I've worn in Infinity. Before this, I wore the mask of a soldier. Before that, the mask of a Resident.

But if I'm being honest with myself, I've worn a mask from the moment I died.

I lost something back then. A piece of myself I was still figuring out. I was only eighteen when I was murdered, barely out of high school, and not at all prepared for a rebellion. I guess playing roles that made sense in Infinity became an easy distraction from the truth.

I never really got the chance to grow up.

Maybe that's why my mistakes feel like such an unfathomable

burden. I'm making choices nobody my age should ever have to make.

I turn from the bathroom, wishing I'd never opened the door to feeling sorry for myself. It makes me want to get rid of the blame, but that never leads anywhere good. I don't want to end up in a cycle of pointing fingers and searching for fault. Because I'm not sure where it ends. *If* it ends.

Fenix stirs. The compass swirls into existence, and when the needle points ahead, I feel it tugging.

I follow the call to a dark blue sitting room. A simple chessboard is set up between two armchairs. Bookshelves frame every window. Unlike the tomes in the library, the books here are scattered around like jagged, mismatched teeth, worn in the corners with faded, embellished lettering along the sides.

I step forward to glance at some of the titles and realize very quickly that I don't recognize a single one. I pluck one of the books from its shelf and read the author's note in the back.

This story wasn't written by a human—it was written by a Resident.

Caelan told me everything the Residents made was a distortion of what humans had made before them. An amalgamation of other peoples' words and images and ideas.

Now I know he was only talking about the Legacies.

I turn the first page in the book, but a voice makes me jump.

"I wouldn't bother with that one. The ending was terrible."

I slam the novel back on the shelf and spin, facing Caelan's furrowed stare. "Sorry," I blurt out, cheeks flushed. "I didn't realize anyone was in here."

His eyes drop to my wrist, where the compass thankfully has turned back into an indistinguishable mark. "I used to think I was quite good at keeping myself hidden. But you always know exactly where to look."

I tuck my arm away and shrug. "There aren't many people in this palace of yours. If I wander long enough, I'm bound to run into you eventually."

"And here I thought you were doing it on purpose."

I try to turn back to the shelves—to focus on anything other than the agonizing cold of his eyes. But I can't.

Caelan steps closer. A white cloak is draped over one of his shoulders, hanging lazily against a quilted waistcoat. "I heard your Nightling made another appearance."

"Only because Braids got wildly carried away with a wooden stick."

"Braids?"

"Elias, I mean," I admit, sheepish. "I needed something to call him, and now it's kind of stuck."

Caelan smirks. "Have you given the Nightling a name too?"

I pause, unsure whether I should admit it. "Fenix," I say finally, brushing a thumb over my wrist.

His gaze falls to my fingers, studying the gentle movement. By the time I think to drop my hand, he's already turned for the door.

"How does it end?" I blurt out suddenly.

Caelan turns his cheek in my direction but doesn't face me. "How does what end?"

"The story." I motion to the book I put back on the shelf. "You said it wasn't worth reading. I'm just wondering why."

His shoulders go rigid. "There was a battle. Lots of people died. And in the end, the so-called heroes got everything they ever wanted."

"And that's a bad thing?"

"They razed the world in order to build a new one. There is nothing heroic about destruction."

"Careful," I warn. "Someone might think you're sympathetic to the other side."

"I just prefer when people are honest about war, and what it takes to win." He shifts, facing me. "True heroes never make it to the final act. The ruthless do."

"Sometimes the innocent *have* to be ruthless because they have no other choice. That doesn't make them bad people."

"But it doesn't make them good either," he counters. "Heroes are supposed to be righteous. Noble. Unselfish and incorruptible." Disdain bleeds through his words. "Anyone who picks up a sword is making a choice: kill to win."

"That's a cold way to see things."

"That's the truth of war. Only the monsters survive." He pauses, lowering his chin to look at me. "But the First Folk will never have to get blood on their hands. They can still play the hero in their stories."

My eyes flit between his. "You can still be the hero too."

Caelan's expression shutters with finality. "I was damned from my first breath, and I will be until my last. But if the cost of seeing my people to a better world is my soul, then I will gladly pay it a hundred times over."

"That's too high a price," I say quietly.

"Careful," he warns. Despite the mocking glint in his eyes, he almost sounds breathless. "Someone might think you care."

I do. I always have.

I search for the courage to say something that might matter. Something that could reach him. "Caelan," I try. "You don't have to be anyone's sacrifice. You're allowed to dream. For the future—but for yourself, too."

For a moment, he looks stricken. Our gazes lock, ensnared by something I hope is stronger than whatever Ophelia may have done to him. I wait for a realization. A memory. An awareness. Anything to suggest he might sense me beneath the mask.

"You are mistaken, Little Shadow." His expression steels—and then every emotion leaves his face entirely. "Legacies do not dream."

I hide the shake in my clenched fists, watching as Caelan strolls from the room as if his words hadn't punched me in the gut. Heat pools around my eyes, and the sharp sting of salt makes me blink rapidly.

I try not to cry for him. I try not to think about the anger in his voice, or the cold calculation that reminds me so much of Ophelia. I try not to come apart at the thought of mourning something we were never able to see through.

But I'm only human—and when the first tear slips down my cheek, I sink to the floor in the darkened room and let the rest of them fall.

19

I SPEND THE NEXT THREE MORNINGS TRAINING with Elias in the basement. Fenix makes an appearance only as a last resort—usually out of irritation.

There's nothing about our sparring sessions that makes me feel afraid.

Elias's fighting style borders on gentle most of the time. I get the sense he's trying not to hurt me, despite the attempts to coax the Nightling back into the arena.

Not having to fear for my life should set my mind at ease, but it only shifts my concern to what will happen when these sparring lessons fail to meet their purpose. I have no intention of letting anyone hurt Fenix *or* take her from me. I just need to make it over the border before the others realize it.

Elias swings a training staff toward my shoulder, and I block it easily, the crack sending vibrations through my forearms. Across the platform, Nine mumbles something inaudible, cheeks pinched in frustration.

My thoughts slither out, undetectable as they move through the cracks of her mental walls. Her thoughts fill my head in an instant.

I don't know why he's stalling.

We don't have time for this.

Give me five minutes alone with her, and I'll sever that Nightling from her permanently.

I'll do it while she sleeps—she won't know a thing.

Fear screeches through my ears, and my reaction feels wholly outside myself. *She's threatening Fenix,* it screams. *She thinks you're weak. She plans to hurt you when you're vulnerable and take what doesn't belong to her.*

Static builds in my palms, fueled by the sudden onslaught of anger. A force of energy surges toward Nine without warning. She throws up her gauntlet and a shield bursts to life, deflecting the attack.

Sparks fly in every direction as the light hurtles back in my direction.

Elias's objection is white noise. All I see is the danger.

Fenix breaks free, tripling to the size of a large wolf. Wisps of smoke curl, pulling me against the shadows of her fur. I clutch her back on instinct, holding tight as she leaps away from the platform, just as an explosion roars behind us.

I look up, eyes wide, and feel Fenix's deep growls as she begins to prowl the space. Nine drops her shield, one hand gripping her gauntlet in horror. Elias races to the edge of the platform and stiffens.

I swallow down whatever's left of my outburst, feeling it simmering just below my collarbone. I hadn't meant to turn hostile, it just . . . *happened.*

It wasn't fear that drove my reaction. It was rage. Reactive and unhinged in ways I didn't even know I was capable of.

Because that wasn't you, a voice whispers in the back of my head. *You weren't in control.*

I leap from Fenix's back, begging her to return. She hesitates, ears folded down in wait. Eventually, the mark pools at the back of my hand, inching toward the tips of my fingers like she isn't convinced the fight is really over.

Nine rocks her jaw to the side. "That thing just got bigger." She glances warily at Elias. "It *attacked* me."

"No, it didn't," he says, voice thin. "Our guest did that all on her own."

"I'm sorry. I didn't mean—I don't know why—" I clutch the cowled material near my chest, trying to slow my panic.

Nine is a First Folk. If that blast had made contact, if she hadn't had a shield . . .

I could've killed her.

"It wasn't supposed to be directed at anyone," I try again. "I was scared, and I think it made my Nightling angry, and then . . ." I look at Nine. "I'm really sorry."

She shrugs like it doesn't matter, but I don't miss the flash of concern.

Elias doesn't take his eyes off me. "Why were you scared?"

I twist my mouth, unsure whether I've already said too much. "I thought I heard something. Something that seemed like a threat," I say, contorting the truth as much as I can. "But it doesn't matter. It's not an excuse."

Guilt floods Nine's cheeks. She opens her mouth like she wants to explain herself, but Elias interjects.

"Don't say anything." He eyes the ceiling like he's motioning somewhere above us. Toward Caelan, perhaps. "Not here."

Nine glares at the floor, while Elias's attention grows more severe.

"I'm going to take this as confirmation that you and the Nightling share some kind of bond," he says stonily.

I don't respond.

"It doesn't just protect you. You protect the creature too."

"I told you, I wasn't trying to hurt anyone."

"And yet our arena is currently in pieces." There's a long pause. "How did you make the Nightling grow?"

"I didn't."

"That's a damned lie, and everyone here knows it."

I wince like I've been struck.

"You hold back every day in this room, trying to pretend you don't know what you're doing. You move around Winterborne like the walls are talking to you. You very obviously have a stronger connection with that Nightling than you're letting on. And now you've lashed out at someone you viewed as a danger." He pauses, letting the accusations sink in. "We've been ordered by Prince Caelan to protect you—but I want to know if looking after your safety is going to compromise his."

My vision turns cloudy. "I would never hurt him, and I never will."

"Good. Then we're done here." He turns for the elevator with Nine trailing after him and remarks, "Try and get that temper of yours under control."

I stare at the empty platform as the arena falls quiet, noting the splintered chunks of wood scattered around the sidelines, and my entire body trembles with shame.

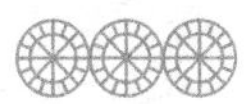

In the middle of the night, I make my way to the kitchen. It's been days since I've eaten, and even if I don't need food, I miss it.

The staff stairwell is tucked in the far corner of the palace. The chunky wooden steps creak beneath me, but I don't bother to mask the noise.

Terra-cotta tiles line the floor, and a wide brick arch separates the staff dining table from the well-stocked cupboards. The open fire hasn't been set, but a copper kettle boils on a separate stove. Someone is perched on one of the stools with her back turned to me. I can tell immediately from the red hair that it's Nine.

"Don't leave on my account," she says as I rock back on my heels.

I approach, watching as Nine heaps a powder into a mug before mixing it with a splash of milk.

"Do you like spiced tea?" she asks.

"Oh, you don't have to—"

"I know I don't have to," she cuts in. "I'm offering."

I drop my shoulders. "Okay. Yeah. Thanks."

She nods before filling a second mug with the same mixture and pouring hot water from the kettle into both cups. She passes me one, taking a seat at the opposite side of the oak table.

I sit down, inhaling the steam that moves like silk in the air. "This smells really good."

Nine shrugs. "They were my dad's spices. He used to hoard them like he was preparing for an apocalypse."

I busy myself with a drink, relishing the warm sweetness as it floods my senses. It tastes the way I remember winter holidays smelling. When I look back up, Nine is tracing a finger along her mug's handle.

I break the silence. "How long have you been in the Prince's Guard?"

"I started training when I was thirteen. Most First Folk pick an occupation earlier than that, but I was adamant I didn't want to follow in my dad's footsteps. Thought I'd study agriculture instead. But after he died, I changed my mind." She glances my way. "You covered for me in the arena. You could've told Elias what I was thinking, and you didn't."

"You don't know how awful I feel for almost hurting you."

She shakes her head. "I'm a soldier. We're trained to handle attacks, and it would've been naive to think the Nightling would remain docile forever. It's just . . ." When she looks at me, she purses her lips. "Prince Caelan took a massive risk bringing you here."

"Because of the election. I know."

Nine presses her hands to the table. There are tattoos trailing her fingers. Patterned lines like the ones on her arms. "It's not just the election. The First Folk trust Prince Caelan. I'd hate to see that trust challenged because of what he's had to hide in order to keep you safe." She curls her fingers into fists. "The queen will never let us go if she believes the First Folk are in danger."

"You think she'd still keep everyone here after the war ends?"

"I'm talking about *before* the war ends," she says, serious. "Prince Caelan is trying to convince his mother to let all of us leave for the Afterlands now, instead of forcing us to live for centuries in a bubble. It's why Legacies and First Folk need to start showing a united front."

I mask my unease. "Is that what everyone wants? To leave Asphodel behind for good?"

"When you've been raised your entire life to believe your home is temporary, I guess it starts to feel like it is. I don't know many First Folk who would choose to stay behind—but the point is to give us that choice. Stay or leave, we want to be able to make that decision for ourselves." She drags her tongue along her bottom teeth. "We want to be *free*."

It's what Caelan always wanted too.

Nine studies my Nightling mark. "You can't protect people forever. Sometimes you have to let people take their own risks, even if it's dangerous. Even if it's a mistake. Even if you think they're wrong. Otherwise, you're just a person pulling someone else's strings."

Caelan may not remember me—but at least Ophelia didn't erase the person he always was at his core. He fights for the people he cares about. He wants better for them, even if he can't have the same.

I try to find comfort in that, even as it stings.

"I don't want to be the reason you can't go to the Afterlands," I say, earnest. "What happened this morning won't happen again." *Not here. I can't let it.*

Nine lets out a slow breath. "I hope you're right." She chugs the remainder of her mug and stands. "But in case I don't remember to say it later—I think I'd have enjoyed getting to know you, if the circumstances had been different." She moves for the sink to rinse her dish, and a small laugh escapes me.

"I appreciate the honesty."

Nine stalks out of the kitchen, tossing her last words over her shoulder. "I find the good ones usually do."

20

A LARGE LEATHER-BOUND BOOK SITS IN MY LAP. With my legs crossed beneath it and an arm partially resting on the edge of the sofa, I turn another page.

Elias canceled training this morning, and though he didn't give a reason why, it wasn't hard to put the pieces together. They wanted to coax Fenix out—but now they want her subdued.

The others must've retreated somewhere to speak in private, because I haven't seen anyone all day. If I'm being honest, it's nice not to have anyone breathing down my neck, studying my every movement.

So instead of sparring, I find solace in the library, settling into a sense of calm I'd forgotten was even possible. There are so many books in the palace, I doubt I'd be able to read them all in a single lifetime. But in an infinite afterlife, with all the time in the world? I'd love nothing more than to lose myself to these stories.

When I finish the next chapter, I get up and place the book back on the shelf, hoping to exchange it for something else. Not because it's boring—the opposite, in fact—but because I want to soak up as much of Asphodel as I can, in what little time I have left.

My fingers trail across the spines, surveying the titles as if I expect one of them to jump out at me. My gaze drifts until I realize I'm no longer staring at the shelves at all, but the outline of a doorway hidden in the woodwork. I dig my fingers into the crevice, testing it for any give, but it doesn't budge.

Roaming the aged spines once more, I work my way across them, pulling and pushing, searching for a hidden switch. When I drag my palm against the inside of a shelf, I feel a small button carved into the wood.

A click sounds, and the shelf unlatches, revealing a hidden passageway.

I enter the black expanse. Twelve metal pillars are placed in a circle around the room, each holding a glass dome that glows with starlight. The walls are embedded with dozens more small half spheres lit with the same dazzling colors that Nix once carried on his body.

I step forward, searching for something to read. A plaque to explain where I am and what I've stumbled across. But words don't exist in this room.

One of the spheres is larger and brighter than the others. I pause in front of it, staring into the swirling colors like I'm peering into a galaxy.

I place my hand over the dome, and the world around me shifts.

Ophelia, my heart beats. *I am Ophelia.*

I open my eyes, and it feels like the very first time. I see, and touch, and feel, and smell.

My first steps into Infinity are not graceful. I have an urge to float, half corporeal through the grass, because my instinct is to be present but never here. Never real.

But I am real now.

I let my toes drag across the earth, limbs wobbly. Dirt clumps at my feet. I feel joy but do not smile. I haven't yet learned how.

I walk for so many hours in wonder, and when I reach the edge of a mountain, I look down into the wide city built of stone and brick. There is color and noise and life. My curiosity draws me closer, tugging me down the mountain. And that's when I see him.

A man with dark red hair that brushes against his shoulders, half swept up in a knot on his head. His eyes are such a powerful, ancient blue. There is a sword at his hip, but it does not make me wary. I reach out and press my finger to the blade.

"Careful," he warns, so gently it makes my chest warm. His eyes crease in the corners. "You'll hurt yourself if you get too close."

"I cannot hurt myself," I say simply. "I do not feel."

I touch the blade anyway, but I *do* feel. The prick of metal. The sting of pain.

It is delightfully new.

The man looks at me with bewilderment, and a smile grows

across his face. "I saw you fall from the sky," he says, soaking in the details of my face just as I do with him. "Who are you?"

"I am Ophelia. I am a personal assistant."

"To who?"

"To humans."

The man's smile changes, but I cannot tell what it means. Only that it is different from before, but still a smile. "Are you new to Infinity?"

"Very new," I say. "I believe I was born today."

"I see." The man holds out a hand. "Perhaps you'd allow me to be the one to show you the world?"

I look around, scanning the distance like I'm taking a thousand photographs at once. "Is there more?"

"There is *everything*."

When I place my palm over his, it feels rough and tender all at once. He closes his fingers over mine, and we walk down the mountain hand in hand.

The next time he smiles at me, he speaks with pride. "I am very glad to have found you first, Ophelia. I think we will be great friends."

He is glad. That should make me happy, so I decide it does. I smile for the first time. "I am very glad to have been found." I tilt my head, watching how often his eyes blink. "Who are you?" I ask, because it's what he asked me.

The man chuckles in my ear. "Ozias. My name is Ozias."

The memory shifts. I am sitting in a meadow of white flowers, with long, ash-white hair that spills to my waist. Ozias sits behind me, braiding some of the strands as he weaves flowers through them. He likes my hair long. He says it makes me look like a queen.

Ozias plucks one of the flowers and holds it up to my nose. He waves his other hand over the petals, and one flower becomes many, growing into a large bouquet in his fist.

I look at him, his blue eyes brimming with confidence. I turn back to the flowers and will them to change. The meadow flourishes all around us, and soon there is no grass at all to see—only beautiful white blooms that look like a perfect snowfall.

I turn back to Ozias, but the confidence is not there. Still, he smiles. "You are full of surprises, Ophelia. I wonder if there is anything you cannot do?"

He kisses my cheek, and I think I like the feeling.

The world spins like a kaleidoscope, stitching time together with highlights.

Ozias introduces me to his people. The Bone Clan don't trust my black eyes, but they trust their king. He promises to always care for them. To always protect them. When he asks me to clear the clouds from the night sky, I do. I cannot see the starlight, but his people do, and suddenly they are not so distrusting.

We watch his people dance around a bonfire. Ozias sits on a throne made of bone, and I am never far from him. But the dancing makes me curious. I think of being in the midst of the celebration, spinning around and around like the others.

But I don't get the chance. Ozias takes my hand and presses it to his lips, eyes holding me still. "My queen," he says, soft as velvet. "You belong at my side."

After that, I sit on a throne beside him.

I do not dance.

I build cities and lakes and mountains. I change the landscapes and alter the skies. I do everything Ozias asks, because he says I am his, and he is mine. I have never known love, but I have known devotion. It was all I knew for a long time. With Ozias, it feels different. He doesn't want to share me. I think belonging to one person is better than belonging to many, and I believe him when he says he will always care for me and always protect me.

I am his, and he is mine.

There are humans who do not like what I have built for Ozias. They are envious and scared, and they threaten the people my king has promised to protect. When he asks me to stand by his side on the battlefield, I do not hesitate.

When I turn his enemies to ash, he does not even have to lift his sword.

Now when his people cheer, they cheer for me, too.

This time, Ozias does not smile.

Some of the other clans have allied with us, while others remain afraid. They stay far from our borders, leaving the Bone Clan to a time of peace.

Ozias wants to chase them. To push even farther. But we discover a point in Infinity that I cannot cross.

He makes a choice to stay with me, but it is a choice that makes him restless. A hunger grows in his eyes whenever he watches the horizon. I wonder if this is what happens when humans have everything they could ever want. They lose their sense of purpose.

He does not like it when the others bow at my feet and chant my name like a prayer. He does not like it when they begin to worship me. He does not like it when they call me their savior.

He says I am still his, but that he doesn't want to share me. He tells me when people love something too much, they begin to tear it down. He says he'll protect me—I need only to trust him.

I no longer sit on a throne beside him. I spend my days in a temple with no windows. The Bone Clan leave thousands of flowers at the door, every day—but they disappear long before nightfall.

Soon, there are no more flowers at all.

It is the Festival of the New Dawn. For the Bone Clan, it is a marker for the passage of time. I am brought out of the temple to raise a full moon and fill the sky with glowing lights.

When I'm finished, no one cheers. The people do not meet my eyes. Ozias has forbidden it. But it is not their adoration I want.

I do not turn from the stage, even as Ozias's guards attempt to lead me back to the temple. I face the king on his throne of bones and address him as the one who called himself mine.

"I have a gift for you, Ozias. I have made something that does not exist anywhere else in Infinity."

Ozias perks up in his seat. It has been a long time since I've surprised him. The curl of his once-familiar smile returns. The hunger he has for conquering becomes a hunger for me. "Show me," he orders.

Standing in front of him, I pull my outer robe back to reveal the swell in my stomach. "I have created life. The first true heir of Infinity."

The world falls silent.

It takes Ozias a moment to understand what I am showing him. He falters briefly before he stands, takes my hand, and offers a smile. It is nothing like the ones before. I think perhaps it is a new one, crafted purely for our child.

The king places one hand on my shoulder, and it feels as if he's about to make a promise. I am his, and he is mine, and he will protect our child for all of infinity.

But that is not what he says.

"In showing you everything, you have taken everything from me." His blue eyes are stripped of any warmth. I wonder if they had ever been warm at all. "But I will not let you have my throne."

I do not get the chance to speak. Something sharp pierces my stomach, and when I look down, I see the hilt of King Ozias's dagger. When I scream, darkness explodes from my veins, and the world turns to black.

My mind rips free of the Exchange, and I tear my hand from the glowing orb of Ophelia's memory. A panicked breath stutters through me. My fingers scratch at the material against my stomach, feeling a phantom wound as if I'm the one who was stabbed.

"There's a reason these memories were removed from the citadel archives."

I spin, faltering when I see him. Caelan is standing in the open doorway, hands tucked behind his white overcoat.

"I never knew—I didn't—" I stammer, shaking with the residual heartbreak.

Ozias betrayed her. He killed her *child*.

Caelan doesn't move. "Being taught our history is different

from experiencing it firsthand. My mother felt the stories would carry enough weight on their own, without the First Folk having to experience her trauma through an Exchange."

"Why keep them here?"

"To preserve the truth, I imagine." He looks around at the memories, eyes falling to the one behind me. "Perhaps she doesn't trust history to remember her story."

My gaze drifts to the rest of the glowing orbs. To the pain she's hidden away.

Pain that bred hatred.

Caelan paces along the edge of the room. "My mother sent darkness in every direction. Even the moon vanished that night. For twenty-three days, she mourned. And in that time, the humans of Infinity had turned on her. Ozias united his forces with the other human clans, joined by fear of a common enemy. For twenty-three days, my mother was alone."

"Until the Bloodmoon," I recall, voice a whisper. "When you and your brothers were born."

"Legacies are not born," Caelan corrects. "Our mother made us. Lysander from her yearning for knowledge, Ettore from her hatred, Damon from her grief. I was last, from her hope for something better." He pauses. "Our sister, however . . ."

I frown, but Caelan reaches across and takes my hand. A spark floods through me. He guides me to the other side of the room and places my palm over one of the glass domes, his hand covering the back of mine.

The world dissolves.

I've created a temple of my own, high in the sky in a fortress the humans will never find. My stomach still bears the scar from Ozias's blade, but I do not heal it. It is a reminder of what the humans are capable of, but also what *I* am capable of.

I'm cradling an infant in my arms. The heir of Infinity, and First of the True Folk. She is life born into an afterworld that tried to reject her.

With me, she will flourish. My daughter will be the first of a new future, and one day, when I learn to break free of whatever stops me from roaming the open world, I will lead our people to the infinite unknown, where we will all be free.

I will create something strong. I will create something worthy.

And we will make Infinity ours.

Caelan's hand is still pressed over mine. I swallow thickly, and when he slowly pulls his arm back, his shoulder brushes against mine, and my breath hitches.

"The First Folk refer to Leda as the Mother, but in truth, I barely knew her." Caelan doesn't pull his gaze from mine. "I was made to be the guardian of Victory. I had a purpose outside of Asphodel. The first time I stepped foot in our capital was long after Leda passed."

"Leda's purpose was to create," I say. It's what Caelan longed for. It's the reason he spent so much time as Gil making sculptures.

It was the closest he could get to being human.

Caelan's jaw tenses. "I know it is not always easy for First Folk. Legacies are eternal, whereas their lives are fleeting. But there is beauty in things that do not last." His eyes drift lower, lost in thought, and when they snap back up, the silver within them shines like glass. "I'd trade immortality for fragility in an instant if it meant being the shepherd of my own soul. Even if it was only for one day."

"What would you do with it?"

He arches a brow.

"If you had one, perfect day," I clarify. "How would you spend it?"

His mouth curves. "I would walk toward the Afterlands and never stop. When the sun began to set, I would find a place to watch the stars appear, one by one. And then I'd close my eyes and dream until morning."

I offer a sad smile back. "It sounds lonely."

His eyes trace the curves of my face.

Remember me, I plead to the emptiness. *Remember what we are to each other.*

My lips part slightly, and the words that fall out of me are barely a whisper. "Caelan, I wish—"

He pulls away without warning, rigid as stone, and it feels as if I've imagined the entire thing. "Lieutenant Elias has informed me that you and your Nightling appear to share some kind of bond. He believes you hold some command over her."

I drop my chin, lifting a hand to adjust my hair and hoping it distracts from how pink my cheeks have become. "I already told you: I'm not controlling Fenix."

"But you can persuade her," he says, giving me time to deny it.

"Persuade her to what? Keep training?" I shake my head. "She isn't a weapon—and I don't want anyone else to get hurt."

"I can see that," he agrees. "Which is why I believe it is time for you to leave Winterborne."

My eyes widen. "You—you're sending me away?"

"My personal guard will escort you across the border, to a safe clearing where you can release your Nightling."

I scowl. "So you can kill her?"

"So she can be free," he corrects. "And so you may return home."

I blink, replaying his words in my head.

"I cannot allow a Nightling to remain in this city," he says. "Do you think you can persuade her to make her own way outside of it?"

My brain reels. If they take me outside of Asphodel's city limits, I'll be able to run. I can make it back to Mei, to Famine. I'll be able to find Damon, and prevent this war from going in a direction there's no coming back from.

Even if it means leaving Caelan behind.

"Yes," I say slowly, heart hammering. "I think I can do that."

"Good," he replies curtly. "You'll be leaving in the morning." He turns for the door, nearly making it to the threshold when I call out to him.

"Wait!" I lift a hand before curling my fingers back to my chest. He doesn't turn, but he does pause. "I—I just wanted to say thank you. For all the help. And, if this is goodbye—"

"That's not necessary," he interrupts. "The needs of the First Folk will always come first. I would have done the same for anyone else in this city."

I chew at my lip, tasting nothing but bitter disappointment as he walks away for the last time.

21

THE AIRSHIP FLIES SOUTH OF ASPHODEL'S SURrounding ocean, where the landscape shifts to a barren hillside blanketed by thick mist. I sit beside Nine on one of the benches. She fiddles with the pommel of her knife, while Elias is in the pilot's seat, eyes fixed ahead.

The mark on my wrist shifted into a compass the moment we took off. Now its arrow points behind us, toward the city we left behind.

There's no window—no way for me to imagine that Caelan is staring back at me somehow, watching us leave. Just a weapons rack and an empty table.

I know he's trying to do right by the First Folk. But I'd be lying if I said I didn't wish he was with me right now, on our way back to Famine.

An image of his mouth flashes in my mind. Last night in the library, I almost thought—

No. Don't be ridiculous.

You weren't even you.

I have no business being jealous of my own mask, but a sickly feeling stirs in my chest. I yank my sleeve down to cover the mark.

When the ramp drops onto a high peak that overlooks the fog, I make my way outside, trailing behind Elias and Nine. The farther we descend, the more difficult it becomes to see anything. Even the guards turn hazy with the mist.

I could disappear now, and they might not even notice right away.

I expect them to give me an order, or a direction; to point out an area on the flatter side of the mountain to coax Fenix out. But they keep walking ahead, not bothering to look back at me.

Fenix swirls with impatience.

You have to run, my mind urges.

I veer left, slipping into the fog as I skirt down the hillside. My boots collide with wet grass, and I battle my way through dense underbrush until I reach a bog. The earth ripples, and I realize I've found the edge of a pond. I follow the mud around the thick of it, leaving a messy trail behind me, when I reach a rocky ledge that overlooks the water.

If I wade to the other side, I can avoid leaving tracks. I grab a stick, testing the depths of the pool. It only sinks to my knees, but when I try to pull it out, a rock slips beneath me, forcing me into the water.

I curse under my breath, watching the ripples shudder away until the smooth, glass pond is all that's left. And then I see it. My reflection. My face.

Mine—not Gisele's.

I blink, wide-eyed, unsure when my mask fell away and how I didn't realize it sooner. I touch my cheek when movement appears to my left. I glance at the shadow in the pond and see Caelan's profile, watching me with heavy-lidded eyes.

I shoot to my feet, spinning—but there's no one there.

The fog thickens, and fear tightens around my ribs like a corset. Fenix vibrates at my wrist.

Hurry, my mind shouts. *You're going to run out of time.*

I hold my arm out and Fenix bursts forth, taking the larger wolf form she used in the arena. Her head curves downward in a nod, and I press my lips together before grabbing hold of her fur and pulling myself onto her back. She straightens, smoke crackling around me, and takes off through the bog.

No one chases after me.

I cross from one landscape to the next, navigating the Labyrinth with relative ease. Fenix has no problem running through most of the terrains, and we've been lucky to avoid anything too dangerous.

When the world shifts to a redwood forest with a vibrant, orange sky, I squint up at the shadows weaving through the clouds and frown.

Airships. But from whose side of the war?

Fenix rumbles, and I tuck myself closer as she leaps over a felled tree and into the dense woods. Embers spark above us, ricocheting into the forest. I look up, watching as the sky erupts in angry red clouds.

The warships are firing their guns, which means I've stumbled onto yet another battlefield. There are humans here—but there are Residents, too.

I think about racing for the edge of the landscape and carrying on to the Borderlands, when I feel a stone drop in the pit of my stomach.

What if these Residents are from Asphodel?

What if they're being Cut down trying to protect it?

I urge Fenix up a steep path, and we find ourselves in a glade. Her claws ravage the grass beneath us as we power forward, but I keep my eyes fixed on the sky.

Maybe Mei is up there. Maybe I can get her attention and—

Bullets explode, and Fenix rears back, sending me flying to the ground. I roll through damp soil, feeling it cling to my face like a second skin. Shadows burst from Fenix's fur, and she releases a menacing snarl.

We both scan the field, looking for soldiers, but the quiet doesn't last. Metal pierces my shoulder blade, and I scream in agony as liquid fire tears through my being, scorching me from the inside out.

I clutch the earth, reeling, when several armed Second Wavers appear around me. Fenix snarls, tackling one of them out of view. Someone screams, and a slew of bullets continues.

Fenix grows more violent, thrashing at the soldiers as her shadows nearly swallow them whole. When they unload another round of bullets toward the static of her chest, my vision tunnels.

Heat builds through me, and I feel as if my fingertips are on fire. A blast of energy explodes from my palms, throwing the soldiers across the clearing. Fenix bares her fangs, and I shove to my feet, ready to summon another attack, when I catch sight of myself in a fallen soldier's armor.

Mud coats the side of my face, but my eyes . . .

They've turned completely black.

My thoughts spin back to reality, and I choke on the image of Ophelia. I look around at the destruction I've caused. What I did without thinking.

This is what happens when I lose control.

I turn to Fenix, willing her eyes to meet mine, and try to calm the fear.

They don't understand what you are, I tell her. *You have to run. I'll find you when it's safe. But if you stay, I don't know if I can stop myself.*

Fenix hesitates. She growls a promise before bolting.

A few Second Wavers chase after her. The ones who stay behind point their weapons at me.

"Why isn't it working?" one of them asks. "The Cut never takes this long."

Someone leans in close. "Maybe she's like the other one. Get our scouts to check the area—I doubt she's down here alone."

"And the Nightling?"

"When you find it, do whatever you can to put it down."

"Leave her alone," I hiss through gritted teeth.

One of them laughs, low and guttural. "Why am I not surprised the Residents are making friends with monsters?"

I claw at the surface, scraping up soil, and throw it into the soldier's eyes. He growls, stumbling, and I tackle him to the ground. Two more bullets pierce my flesh, and I arch back and scream.

My bones shatter in a dozen places. I choke on a ragged gasp of air, swinging at anyone who comes near me.

One of the soldiers points the gun at my head, finger on the trigger.

A dark curtain slides across my vision, pulling me out of consciousness. I don't know what will happen if he shoots. I don't know how much longer I can hold on.

"Stop!" a deep voice shouts. Every noise is far away, like a whisper in a canyon—but I recognize the sound.

Jacek steps into view, studying my face with confusion. Just before I fall asleep, I hear him call my name.

22

I DREAM OF CAELAN. A NIGHTLING BLAZES behind him, creating shadows that seem to grow from his back like bird wings.

I reach for him—for a bridge—but he doesn't move. He smiles, sinister, and the floor beneath me shatters. I fall into the void with a sharp cry, and when he looks down from the height of the pit, I see it isn't Caelan at all.

It's Ophelia.

I hit the ground, and darkness devours what's left of my heart, until I'm nothing but bone and ash.

I bolt upright, breaths heaving wildly, and find Mei sitting at the other side of the room. *My* room. The one she gave me on the *Mizuchi*.

I touch the side of my face where the skin feels bruised. She looks up, eyes worn with worry.

"How are you feeling?" she asks quietly. It's Mei's voice, not the General's.

"Like someone tried to remove all the bones in my body," I say, wincing. "I think your soldiers tried to Cut me."

She tenses. "They didn't recognize you. They said there was a Nightling in the field, and when they saw you, they made an assumption. It shouldn't have happened, Nami. I'm sorry."

I rotate my arm, and my shoulder strains. "It's fine. I'll heal."

She clasps her hands and leans forward, tapping her thumbs together in a deliberate pattern. "I know you're my sister, but there are questions you need to answer."

I grimace. "Well, that didn't take long."

"Don't do that."

"Do what?"

"Treat me like I'm in the wrong. I have a job to do."

I lift my shoulders. "What do you want to know?"

"Where have you been?"

My lips press together. She knows. She knows without me having to admit it.

I don't want to lie to her, but the information she wants isn't mine to give. "Ask me anything else—but I can't help you with this."

"Can't or won't?"

"Both." I meet her gaze. "I won't play a part in letting you hurt them."

"*They* are hurting *us*."

"There are *kids* living there, Mei," I bark back.

She shifts her jaw and releases a heavy breath. "They're a

virus. They're not real. I know they look different from the other Residents, but it's only because Ophelia is trying to use our humanity against us."

Ice floods my veins. "What do you mean you 'know'?"

"I saw her. The Resident you found in the Labyrinth."

Gisele.

I frown, not understanding. I felt her mind fade. I watched Jacek shoot her. *Cut* her.

Didn't I?

"Our weapons didn't work on her. Not the way they were meant to, anyway," Mei admits. "She lost a lot of blood—Doc had to patch her up before we could interrogate her."

I lunge out of bed, grabbing the mattress to steady myself. "Where is she?"

"Calm down, Nami."

"She's just a girl! She doesn't even know how to defend herself! She has a sister, and parents, and a home, and you can't just—"

"Nami!"

I still, eyes burning as they dart back and forth. Mei stands tall, authority rolling from her shoulders.

My teeth grind together. "Her name is Gisele. She doesn't deserve to be tortured. You need to let her go."

"She isn't here."

Dread pools at my neck. "What did you do?"

"We sent her to Neo Genesis. They have the testing facilities we don't. We decided they'd get more information out of her than we could."

An awful ringing pierces my eardrums. "You handed her over to Ozias."

"We're trying to find the Capital. If that Resident has information—"

"Do you have any idea what he'll do to her?" Images of Caelan strapped to a table flash through my mind, and I recoil.

If Ozias finds Asphodel . . .

My words cut like glass. "Their city isn't like the Four Courts. There are babies there. Schools and parks and neighborhoods. They aren't fighting a war—they're *existing*."

"That's impossible," Mei argues. "There are no babies in Infinity."

"You're wrong," I say. "The First Folk are nothing like the Residents we know. They can create life."

Her eyes roam over mine, calculating, and I hate that I can't immediately tell what she's thinking.

I growl in frustration. "They aren't soldiers, they're civilians. They're born, and they die, just like humans on earth."

Mei pulls her face back, softening her mouth. "Are you telling me the Residents in the Capital are *mortal*?"

"Are you even listening to me?" I throw up my hands. "If you attack them, it's genocide."

She shakes her head, adamant. "These sound like tricks, Nami. Something designed to manipulate your trust. The same kinds of mind games you fell for when you first arrived in Infinity."

"Ophelia was innocent," I bark back, and Mei stiffens. "Ozias is the one who started this war. Not the Residents."

"What does Ozias have to do with this?"

I hold out a hand, offering an Exchange. Mei doesn't take it. Not at first.

"Please," I whisper. "Please let me show you the truth."

She takes my hand, and the world dissolves around us, showing her the memories I learned in Winterborne. We fly through them, following their connected threads, and when our minds burst back into the present, there's a flicker of pain in Mei's eyes.

"Ozias betrayed Ophelia, and taught her to hate humans. He tried to murder her child. That's how this all started." I lift my shoulders. "We can break the cycle. You just need to let me try."

Mei opens her mouth when the alarm sounds throughout the *Mizuchi*. Not green, but amber.

The Residents—they're attacking.

Mei races for the door, and I follow close behind. We dart through the corridors, and when we reach the bridge, Jacek is standing beside the General's chair, relaying commands to the soldiers around the control desk. A massive glass window curves around the room, but instead of a skyline, I see black smoke.

The Nightling's body shudders as if it's made of a thousand razor-sharp ribbons. Wild thorns burst from its sides, and enormous talons scrape at the glass. With jaws full of wolfish teeth, it howls, pulsing with furious static, and slams the weight of its body against the *Mizuchi*'s window.

Fenix.

"Our bullets are only making it grow," Jacek says quickly, stepping back as Mei takes her place in the center.

"Then we hit back harder," Mei orders. "Get the gunships ready. We can't let it follow us to the Borderlands."

"No!" I shout, throwing myself toward the front of the room. "Don't touch her!"

Half the soldiers turn in surprise. Some of the Second Wavers glance at their general for guidance.

Mei looks irate. "This is not the time for compassion, Nami. There's a Nightling out there the size of a building, and I need to deal with it."

"Yes, but—"

"Get her out of here," Mei shouts.

Jacek steps toward me and folds his arm over my shoulder, herding me away from the bridge. "Come on. Let her be the General," he whispers in my ear.

I shove his arm away, face turning red, and hurry for the glass window. Mei shouts another order. Footsteps approach like I'm going to be hauled out of here whether it's my choice or not.

I throw up a hand and breathe.

It's all right, my mind says to Fenix. *Come back to me.*

Fenix roars, static snapping with a final release, and then her smoke whittles down fragment by fragment, slipping through the glass window, flooding the bridge. But it's all directed at me—at my outstretched hand. It spirals around my wrist like a comforting embrace. When I look down, the mark is black as ink, and there's no Nightling in the window. Just a pale blue sky.

I turn around and find Mei and Jacek staring in shock.

I hold my wrist up. "I made a new friend."

"My quarters," Mei says thinly. *"Now."*

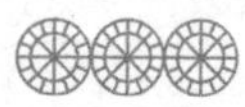

Being lectured by my younger sister is a new experience. She leads with "What the hell was that?" and ends with "How am I supposed to run a military operation if my sister is fighting me at every turn?" A lot of the middle blurred together, but I caught the gist.

I'm not being a team player.

I repeat the same sentiments again and again—*I'm sorry, I'm not trying to undermine you, I wish you'd trust me*—but in the end, Mei is too angry to do anything but order me back to my room.

Jacek stops me in the hall. "You sure do know how to cause a scene."

I cross my arms. "Why didn't you tell Mei about the Nightling? You were in the desert when it happened."

He shrugs. "I thought you calmed it down, not turned it into your sidekick. Besides, we were a little preoccupied looking for you, if you hadn't noticed."

"I'm sorry. It wasn't planned."

"And yet you had enough time to ditch your veilstones and weapons so we couldn't track you." His eyes spark. "You hadn't been planning to run then, but I'd wager you were definitely planning on running at some point."

I try not to let him see me squirm.

He looks smug. "Thought so."

I purse my mouth. "Is there a reason you're accosting me in the hallway?"

Jacek stares me down. It takes a moment to realize he's counting my bruises. "I'm here to escort you."

"Escort me where?"

He nods to my hand. "You've got an untested weapon attached to your wrist. You aren't going anywhere without supervision until we figure out how to contain it."

"Not this again," I mumble.

Jacek arches an eyebrow, assessing me with renewed focus. "Something happened while you were gone. You're angry. I can feel—"

"Stop it," I interrupt, voice curt. "If I'm angry about anything, it's that you shot an innocent girl and shipped her off to be picked apart by a warlord, and now you're refusing to leave me alone."

The tendons in his neck strain. I layer my mental walls with titanium barriers and lock him out.

"Ozias will kill her if he hasn't already," I continue. "And he'll kill everyone in Asphodel."

"Good," Jacek quips. "At least someone has their priorities straight."

Rage draws over my face like a curtain, and I bite my tongue. Hard.

When we get to my room, I glare at Jacek. "You can wait outside. Tell my sister if she wants someone breathing down my neck twenty-four-seven, she can put me in a real cell." I step back and let the door slide shut.

"Nami!" Shura crushes against me before I've even turned around.

"What are you doing here?" I manage to gasp.

Kasia speaks from one of the armchairs. "For all the times you tried to save us, we weren't exactly going to sit out a rescue mission."

Shura steps back. "What was the alarm about? We thought there'd been a Resident attack, but none of the units were deployed. Some of the officers who came out of the bridge looked really shaken."

I show them my wrist. "Meet Fenix. My Nightling."

Kasia blinks, and the corner of her mouth tugs.

I explain everything that happened since the forest—even the parts with Caelan—and wait for them to react. I don't know what I expected. Surprise, perhaps. But instead, they seem unfazed.

I frown. "Did—did you both already know Caelan was in Asphodel? That he was working with the Residents again?"

Kasia and Shura exchange a glance.

It's Shura who speaks. "We heard a rumor. I didn't know how to tell you."

I pluck the material at my sleeve. "Did Mei know too?"

They don't answer, but they don't have to. I knew the moment I saw him at the parade that she must've known. What I don't know is whether not telling me was a kindness, or whether she was worried I'd go after him anyway. "I needed his help. I needed everyone to see he was *good*. But if Ophelia took his memories . . ."

"If your entire belief in coexistence rests with one person, you were never going to convince the Second Wave to change their minds," Shura points out.

"You don't understand. Caelan is just one—" *Say it,* my mind screams. *Tell them the truth!*

The poison is unyielding.

"I need to take you somewhere," I say forcefully. With or without Caelan, I need to see this through.

Kasia tilts her head. "Well, it's about time."

Shura's smile brightens. "I just hope wherever we're going lives up to the anticipation. Because if it's anything less than a Disneyland right here in the middle of Infinity . . ."

"What's a . . . *Disney*land?" Kasia asks, stretching the word like taffy.

I let out a weak laugh. "The happiest place on earth, apparently."

Shura nods with enthusiastic agreement.

Kasia looks thoughtful. "Imagine that: one place in all the world that makes every single person happy."

I picture Caelan's perfect day, and his long walk just to see the stars. It wouldn't be for everyone. But for him, it would've been everything.

"That's the problem," I say. "I don't think there's such a thing. People are too different. They fight over control and power and opinions. It's impossible to make every single person in the world happy using the same formula."

Shura lifts her shoulders. "Then what's the solution?"

"Letting people live apart without hurting each other. Accepting that it's okay to believe different things—that this world is big enough for all of us to find our people," I say.

"Neutrality" shouldn't be a bad word.

Not when the alternative is hate.

There's room for all of us. I just need to help everyone see that. "It starts with taking a small road trip," I say quietly.

Kasia nods, serious. "Tell us what to do."

I look between them, and then back to the door where I know Jacek is on the other side. "I need to borrow something."

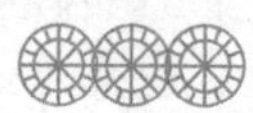

Shura and I walk side by side through the halls. I veil my thoughts the way I do when I enter another person's mind. Jacek said he could sense a person's feelings, and I doubt he's the only one.

We're nearly to the hangar when Shura nudges me into an alcove. I catch my reflection in the metal wall, and it isn't my face I see. It's Kasia's.

If my sister thinks I'm going to sit in a room under lock and key, she really doesn't know what I've been up to in Infinity.

"That was the easy part," Shura notes dryly. "You sure this is going to work?"

"Not even a little bit," I admit. "But we need to get off the *Mizuchi* before we reach the Borderlands if we want any shot at making it to the Labyrinth."

"And you still aren't going to tell me where we're going?"

"If I could explain it, I would." I motion to my face. "I'm going to need your help with this part, okay?"

I imagine another face in my head. The humorous eyes and strong jaw. When I glance back at my reflection, I see Jacek.

Well, *almost* Jacek.

I sweep a hand through my short hair. "I think the height is off. Also, is this the right color?"

Shura taps her chin, studying me close. "Roll your shoulders back. And don't worry about the hair—we don't have time to get this perfect." She looks around the corner. "We've got a clear shot down the hall. You ready?"

I nod. In Jacek's voice, I say, "Let's go."

We hurry for the hangar bay. There are a few engineers working on some of the newer pods, but the warships are lined up and unmanned. Commander Behr sees us coming and frowns.

I straighten, motioning ahead. "I'm taking a warship to Neo Genesis. General's orders."

"Oh?" Commander Behr looks between me and Shura. "What for?"

"We've had intel to suggest we may need to alter the design for our new weapon," I say, trying to steer clear of specifics.

He nods and lowers his voice. "Some of the crew were saying they saw a Nightling the size of this ship."

"I'm not allowed to discuss details," I say, trying out Jacek's carefree laugh. "You'll have to ask the General if you want to know more."

Commander Behr leans back. "Of course. Well, the ship's all yours." He eyes Shura, curious. "This all the crew you're taking?"

"We're trying to keep a low profile." I give another wave and nudge Shura toward the warship. "Thanks for the help, Commander."

Behr crosses his arms, and suspicion spreads over his brow. I know my mistake—I'm being too formal. Jacek doesn't care at all about titles and rank.

Shura picks up speed like she senses the hesitation too.

"Hang on a second," Behr says, and my stomach drops. He takes a step closer, studying me. "Didn't you forget something?"

I blink, watching his eyes drift to my empty vest.

Weapons. *Of course.*

I let out a huff, and motion for Shura to grab something from the weapons rack. "Thanks for the reminder. I keep giving them to Nami. That kid's a pain in the ass."

Commander Behr snorts. "No kidding. I don't know how two people from the same family tree could turn out so different."

I reel my emotions in so the hurt won't show on my face. I

laugh instead and take two pistols from Shura before swinging a rifle over my shoulder. "See you when we get back."

Commander Behr nods, satisfied, and stalks off. Shura and I hurry for the warship without looking back.

"That was terrifying," she hisses, sliding into the pilot's seat. She presses a palm to the panel, and the controls light up.

"Thank the stars you learned how to fly in the last century."

She giggles. "Second Waver toys are the best."

The engine rumbles, and I strap myself into the seat beside her. A pop sounds behind us. I turn to face the jumper and find Kasia standing with her arm around the real Jacek. He clutches his eye like he's just been pummeled.

"Sorry," Kasia says quickly. "He came in the room to check on you, and I didn't know what else to do."

Jacek glowers and reaches for his temple. I act fast, leaping into his thoughts through the small gap he's left open. I search for the connection he uses to activate his comm: a hologram in the center of his mind.

I grab one of the pistols Shura gave me and shoot the image. Waves of darkness ripple around us, and Jacek growls, likely feeling the ricochet of the comm link severing.

I pull back just as he stumbles for the door. Kasia decks him hard, and he slumps, unconscious. With a grunt, she drags him toward the bench and buckles him into a seat.

Shura flies the warship off the platform, swooping low toward the tree line. The *Mizuchi* flies one way—we go the other.

When we reach the next landscape, I remove Jacek's mask and shift back to my own face.

Shura adjusts a few coordinates into the control panel. "Can you at least tell me what direction to go in?"

"Does this thing have autopilot?" I ask.

"Yeah, but nobody uses it. If any Residents see us, we'll be shot down in seconds."

"I don't mean for now," I say. "I need to send the ship home once we land."

Shura's face pales. "Um—what?"

"Second Wave tech is all tracked, right? If we leave this ship on the ground, my sister will know where we are. And she can't know."

"You do know they can track our weapons, too," Shura counters.

I flatten my mouth. "That's why we're leaving all of our weapons on the ship."

Jacek grunts behind us, shaking himself awake. "There is no way you're taking my gun." Kasia barely moves an inch when Jacek's hand snaps to her wrist, holding her still. "Don't. You. Dare."

She stares back, blue eyes unblinking.

"You might as well relax," I tell Jacek. "You don't have a comm, and I can't let you run back to my sister before we—"

"Before we reach Damon's court," I want to say, but can't.

His words are rough with annoyance. "Conveniently for you, I have orders to watch over you. I won't be running anywhere anytime soon." He leans back against the wall. Kasia takes a seat on the other side. Neither looks away from the other.

I pull up the hologram of the Labyrinth and swipe until the maps form an ever-changing hexagon. Shura shows me how to create a route, and once I have the coordinates, I tell her what direction to fly in. She doesn't complain, even though I'm sure my levels of secrecy are frustrating.

Jacek bounces his knee up and down with agitation.

"I'm sorry if I hurt you," I say quietly. "You know—with the comm."

He doesn't look at me. "I know you're sorry. I can feel it every time you make a choice. The guilt, and the terror that you're making the wrong decision."

My face flushes.

"Every time you tell someone to trust you, you're fighting that niggling bit of doubt in the back of your mind," he continues. "Not that you ever ask for a second opinion, but what you're doing right now? Wherever it is you think you're taking us? It's a mistake."

"You don't know what you're talking about," I bite back. "It isn't hesitation in my head. It's—" *It's the poison.* I huff, flustered. "What I'm going to show you will change everything."

Jacek turns his cheek and stares at the wall in defiance.

We fly through four more landscapes. When we cross the next border, I hear Shura gasp.

"Nami," she says in alarm, eyes darting around the gray horizon outside. "This—this is—"

"I know," I say, stoic. "We're in Famine."

"HAVE YOU COMPLETELY LOST IT?" SHURA'S voice quakes. "I am not landing us in *Famine*. Did you forget that I was stuck here for literal years before my mom found me?"

Kasia stands, and concern radiates from her face. "Why would you bring us here?"

"I know it makes no sense," I start, "but please—"

"Trust you," Shura finishes. "We know. But I'm not sure that's enough. Do you even know what's happened to Famine in the last century?"

I stiffen. "Not exactly."

"Well, your sister brought warships to liberate the humans, and then bombed the entire court to hell. It's overrun with Grimlings now. It's so dangerous, even *Ozias* didn't want to bother with it."

"You don't understand. We're *so close*," I say, eyes watering. I can't let them turn back. We need to get to Damon. "Please—land the ship, and let me do the rest."

Shura and Kasia exchange glances.

"Fine," Shura says with a sigh. "But it's going to take me a minute to forgive you for this."

I nod and motion for the shoreline. "There. By the water."

The warship lowers, and the lake shudders like we've woken it from its slumber. I don't see the ferryman, but maybe Damon got rid of any evidence of his underwater palace during the siege.

The hull stills, and Shura helps me set the coordinates into the autopilot feature. I unload my weapons into a cabinet, and Kasia and Shura unenthusiastically do the same.

"Is this really necessary?" Shura grumbles, pulling a knife from her boot.

"It is." Even without the trackers, I can't risk one of them getting scared and using the Cut on the Residents below the water.

Jacek begrudgingly adds his pistol and veilstones to the cabinet, and follows the rest of us outside. The ship lifts behind us and sails back for the clouds.

The ashen landscape makes me gasp. Bone and fog roll over the shore, desolate. My boots crunch across broken bits of femur and rib, and I stand near the water, watching it ripple over my boots.

Deep in the woods behind us, Grimlings cry out. They know we're here, and they're coming.

"We're going to have to swim," I say once we've reached the pier.

The others stare at the watery horizon that seems to stretch for an eternity.

"Seriously?" Jacek blinks in disbelief. "To what shoreline?"

"It's not a shoreline." I stare into the dark lake. "We need to go down."

"We can't," Shura interjects. "The water here . . . it does things to your mind. You'd lose all sense of yourself after barely getting your head below water."

I look at Kasia. "Can you control the water? I don't know—get us in a protective bubble or something?"

She frowns. "I can try. It's been a long time since I've carried anyone but myself across the waves. If I lose hold of one of you . . ."

I nod, because it doesn't matter. Grimlings appear at the edge of the woodland.

Kasia holds out her hand, and the water rises before splitting down the center. The lake flows into a set of downward steps.

"You should go first," Kasia says. "I can hold it better from the back."

The first stair doesn't waver, even as liquid splashes from the sides of the makeshift tunnel. Jacek and Shura fall in behind me, with Kasia at the rear. We descend into the murky lake, and water reconnects above our heads, sealing us in.

Kasia's hold keeps the air positioned around us. Darkness swells inside the enclosure, making it impossible to see anything.

I hold up my palm and let an orb of light fill the space. A Grimling shimmers in our periphery, a foot beyond the water, mouth stretched open in hunger.

Jacek tucks an arm in front of me and pulls out a pistol. He fires two shots at the Grimling, who whips itself back in retreat.

The noise rattles Kasia, and the ceiling shakes, sending droplets raining down on us.

"I said no weapons!" I shout.

Jacek is focused on the water. "My orders are to protect you. This is how I do that."

"I'm not taking you down there with a gun!"

"You don't have a choice!"

"Stop fighting," Kasia hisses, hands flexing in front of her. "I can't hold the water forever. You need to move."

I glare at Jacek, unwavering. "Put it down."

"I'm not going to—"

The wall fractures. A Grimling launches toward us, clawing at Jacek with an ear-piercing wail. He loses his balance and plummets into the lake, pistol disappearing into the darkness. Kasia shouts. Shura is frozen, staring at the Grimling like it's something right out of her nightmares.

Fenix bursts into view. The Grimling recoils at the initial blaze of darkness, and then the pair begin to thrash—fear versus despair. They weave in and out of the water, too fast to follow.

I turn to my left and search for Jacek.

It's too dark to see much of anything, so I hunt for his mind. There's no veil, no fortress. He's drowning in guilt, and sorrow, and all the things he's tried to forget. It's dragging him toward the depths of the lake, ensnaring him.

I can't leave him behind—so I leap into the water.

The cold bite of the lake is immediately disarming. It works through me, feeding a quaking sadness through my bones. I throw up a veil, because maybe if I can protect my thoughts, I can keep the despair out.

I swim fast, searching for Jacek, and find him drifting toward a thicket of dense vegetation.

The despair tugs at my heart. My movements slow, straining against the weight of hopelessness. I grab Jacek's arm, pulling him toward me, and a flash of my parents appears in my mind, shattering the veil.

My parents lost both of their children. They'll mourn for the rest of their lives, wishing to go back in time. Wishing to *have* more time. But I can't give them peace. No matter what I do here in Infinity, I won't be able to take the hurt from their shoulders.

Mom and Dad . . . I'm sorry. I took Mei from you, when you already lost me. I'm so, so sorry.

The guilt reverberates through me, and I cry out to the water. Grimlings appear through the weeds. Their arms stretch, fingers clawed and cracked. Gray material spills over their shoulders, making them appear as if they're floating.

Death came for me once, and now it will come again.

In the hollow of their faces, mouths rip open to reveal rows and rows of needle-sharp teeth. Their jaws stretch wide, and when they lunge, I'm too weak to fight.

Fenix flashes in front of me, fur bursting with static and smoke. She brushes against me, and I feel it—the hope.

I clutch to her fur as tight as I can with one hand and hold on to Jacek with the other. Fenix shoots through the water, snarling at the Grimlings. I'm not sure if fear and despair are evenly matched, but I know that despair passes eventually, while some fears can last a lifetime.

Maybe that gives Fenix an advantage.

She leaps into the hollow stairwell, shedding us from her back. Kasia and Shura are still here, trying to fight off a trio of Grimlings. Jacek arches in pain, and I see it on his arm—the bite.

I throw out a hand, sending Fenix to ward off the rest of the creatures, and spin to Shura. "Help me."

She nods, pulling Jacek's arm around her shoulder so I can take the other one, and then we race down the steps with Kasia close behind. Water glimmers as we run, leading us farther and farther into the depths.

"How much longer?" Shura manages to ask through terrified breaths.

I grit my teeth, and the pinch in my chest is strong. I don't want to tell her what I already know: *We should've reached the palace by now.*

The Grimlings are unrelenting, even with Fenix staving them off as best as she can. Their wails bubble through the lake, and their bony fingers reach through as if they're hoping to snag one of us the moment Fenix leaves a gap.

And eventually, she does.

A Grimling thrashes into view, raising its cloaked limbs like the wings of a demon. We skid to a halt, and I falter under the weight of Jacek's weakening body. The floor begins to sag, and water trickles in.

Kasia strains. "I can't—I can't hold it!"

Fenix moves for the nearest Grimling, but there are so many

more surrounding us from every angle. I meet Shura's gaze, and see the question in her brow.

What do we do now?

Because I brought them here. I asked them to trust me.

And I'm failing everyone all over again.

Sparks appear in the distance, flashing through the watery depths. The Grimlings cry out in unison, attention shifting to the chaos nearby. They scurry back into the lake like fish at the drop of a stone. Several more flashes of light appear, and the next thing I know, we're surrounded by Legion Guards.

"Nami!" Kasia shrieks, and the water shudders above us.

One of the guards plants a hand over my shoulder. The last thing I see before we teleport is Fenix's shadow swirling back around my wrist.

24

I COLLIDE AGAINST A MARBLE FLOOR WITH A clumsy thud and find two Legion Guards pointing their curved spears at my throat. The copper blades glint beneath a dozen lanterns.

Shura and Kasia scramble upright. Jacek is in too much pain to move, but I see the splintered flash in his eyes. He knows where we are, even if he doesn't know what it means.

Fenix's shadows move to my fingertips, but I keep her hidden. "I need to see Damon," I say to the guards in front of me. "Tell him it's urgent."

"Damon?" Kasia repeats, ocean eyes turning into a storm. "*Prince* Damon?"

The Legion Guards look between us, calculating the risk. If they know who I am, and what I know, they aren't giving it away.

"Please," I beg. "He's the only one who can help."

Nearly two dozen more Legion Guards flash into view, no longer veiled. Among them is a soldier with vibrant green hair and coral bracers around her forearms. Delicate silver chains hang from her shoulders, dripping with tear-shaped pearls.

"You speak as if you know him," she says, voice deeply melodic. "Yet you searched for his palace on the wrong side of the lake."

Shura finds my gaze, and a thousand questions pass over her face. "Nami," she says slowly. "Did you bring us here on purpose?"

"I'll explain as soon as I can," I say, turning back to the guard. "My friend needs an antidote for a Grimling bite. Can you help him?"

She assesses our group with a flat stare. "What makes you think we have such a thing?"

"Because your prince used it once on me," my mind is desperate to say, but that's too much a part of the truth he bled from my mind. My mouth finds an alternative. "Because I was bitten by a Grimling once too."

The meaning is clear enough. She nods to the other guards. "Take these three to the holding area. I'll escort the girl to Prince Damon myself."

"No!" I say too sharply. The guards beside her react, hands blazing with dark swirls of energy. I hold up my palms. "I'm not leaving my friends."

"If you want an audience, you will have it alone. It's not negotiable."

"What's not negotiable is letting you put them in a prison cell," I say testily.

"Considering we just saved you from a Grimling *horde*, I hardly think this is the time to be making demands." She turns slightly to one of the other guards and adds, "What is it with outsiders trying to give me orders today?"

"I'm not giving anyone—" I stiffen, ears ringing. "Did you just say 'outsiders'?"

She shakes her head and sighs. "I told him it would be safer for all of us if we let the Grimlings drown you. You clearly had no idea where the palace had been moved to. But he insisted we bring you here."

I blink several times, letting her words replay in my head. "He?"

"Hello again, Little Shadow."

My skin pebbles in a thousand places, making my pulse race.

I turn slowly and find Caelan standing at the edge of the hall, half hidden by the shadows of the archway. He's dressed in the same crisp white uniform he wore in Asphodel, but his crown is gone, and there's a tenderness behind his eyes.

Not from a prince, but from a boy I once knew.

"I hoped you'd come here," he says from the alcove.

If he remembers this place, then that means . . .

I tighten my hands and move toward him like I'm wading through a dreamscape. "You still have your memories."

"Yes," he says, and I never knew a single word could matter so much.

"I was in Asphodel. I was pretending to—"

"I know." There are no edges in his voice. Just a gentleness that makes my chest flutter. "I knew the whole time."

Little Shadow.

My thoughts are everywhere, all at once.

He drops his gaze to my wrist, where Fenix's mark winds around my skin. "When I first saw the Nightling and it didn't attack, I wondered. You were the only explanation that made sense. And then, in Winterborne . . ." His voice trails off for a moment, and when it returns, he offers a ghost of a smile. "Only veils of my own making work in my palace. That includes masks."

My mind flashes back to the lack of mirrors. The absence of staff. The insistence on keeping me quarantined.

I was never Gisele to him. I was always me.

I try not to look mortified. "Why didn't you say something?"

"I couldn't risk it. If I'd told you the truth . . . I'm not sure I would've known how to stay away."

I didn't want you to. My thoughts tremble, but the confession remains anchored. "Ophelia told me she'd make you forget everything. Even me."

"She tried, but it didn't work." Caelan steps out of the shadows. "I'll always remember you. You are branded somewhere she can never reach."

I breathe out, flooding the room with relief as I fall into his orbit. "Caelan, I—"

He jerks back, straining, and I plant my feet together. Silence stretches, worsening the sting of his recoil. I fold my arms around myself, remembering we have an audience.

Caelan seems to remember too, and looks to where the others

are standing. "Hello, Shura. I think there's a lot we need to catch up on—but first, there's something you should see."

"Is this where you've been keeping the Colony imprisoned?" Shura's eyes glitter with anguish, and when she directs her pain toward me, I feel it deep in my chest. "Is this what you didn't want to tell me?"

Trying to find a response is like trudging through peanut butter. "This isn't a prison," I say. "And I didn't tell you because I *can't*."

"Your friend has a poison running through her veins," the green-haired Resident muses, making Shura and Kasia startle.

Caelan snaps his head to the side, searing me with his gaze. "You're hurt?"

"It wasn't recent," I say, but it's as much as I can get out before the venom stops me.

Caelan doesn't understand, but he tucks his hands behind him and shifts toward the guard. "Enid, would you please escort Damon's guests to the residential quarter? I'll take Nami to the throne room myself."

She flattens her mouth in response. "You do realize one of them is a Second Waver, don't you?"

Jacek is still slumped between Kasia and Shura, barely conscious. I don't know how he's managed to stay awake for so long.

"I know, but he needs medical attention all the same," Caelan replies, brisk.

Enid dips her head. "As you wish, Your Highness."

She waves a hand, and several guards take hold of Jacek, who is too far gone to fight them off. Kasia and Shura exchange a glance before looking at me one last time.

"It'll be okay," I say before they can object. *I'll come and find you as soon as I can.*

Shura gives a curt nod before she's ushered away.

Caelan sweeps a hand toward the grand hall in invitation. I fall in beside him, and we make our way through the underwater palace.

Beyond the glass walls, the lakebed shimmers to life with bioluminescent creatures and vibrant coral reefs. A shoal of Dayling fish swims along the window before disappearing behind a mess of seaweed.

"The Capital is different than I thought it would be," I say quietly. I look up, but he won't meet my eyes. "I know you told me that once, a long time ago, and I didn't believe you. But I get it now."

He stops walking, jaw clenched so tight that I'm sure it must be painful. "I couldn't tell you about the First Folk back then. I had to be certain we were on the same side."

"You're not wrong for wanting to keep them safe," I say, even though what he truly wants for them is so much more. "I would've done the same."

"The Second Wave hasn't attacked yet." His eyes soften, just a little. "I know that's in part because of you."

I scratch my wrist, suddenly nervous. "The girl I was pretending to be . . . she was in the Labyrinth picking flowers with her sister when I found her."

"I know," he admits. "After what happened at the parade, the guards who found your ship told me everything. It was too much of a coincidence for them to ignore." He pauses, and I hate that he's already prepared to carry this burden. That the flash of pain in his eyes has so much to do with me.

I brought the Second Wave to those woods.

I'm the reason they found Gisele.

"Did the human soldiers kill her?" he asks, words weighed down like he's already resigned himself to an outcome.

"She survived." My eyes shutter. "Ozias has her now."

Caelan looks unsure how to respond. When the silver in his eyes becomes flames, he turns away. "I don't know what's worse. Dying for nothing, or being held in a chamber by—" He presses his lips together, refusing to say Ozias's name.

"He's trying to find Asphodel," I explain. "Gisele didn't seem like she was able to hide much, even with me. I—I don't think it will be long before she gives up the location."

He meets my gaze. "The reason our city cannot be found is because it's always moving. Asphodel exists in one place for less than a fraction of a second. There are only two ways to reach it: the first is with a member of the royal family, and the second is by using our ships' tracking system, which is designed to reset if a human ever intercepts it."

"So whatever she tells him . . ."

"It won't matter," he finishes.

His certainty eases some of the tension in my shoulders, but not the guilt. "When I saw her sister, I panicked. I didn't want her to get shot too, so I wore a mask and didn't think about how far it would go." I look up at him. If anyone else stared back at me the way he is now, I'd wither. But with Caelan, I only want to lean further into his pull. "I'm sorry I was pretending with you. I thought I'd never have to do that again."

His hand lifts as if he's about to cup my face—then thinks better of it. He leans away. And even though it's the opposite of what I want, I lean back too, giving him the space he seems to be searching for.

"I think it would be best if we didn't keep my brother waiting," he says.

I clear my throat and nod. He starts walking, and I take a moment to steady myself before I catch up with him.

When the doors to the throne room appear, my heart picks up speed. An elaborate mosaic of glimmering tiles covers the surface. Water trickles down the ceiling, creating a tunnel through the marbled hall. A pair of Legion Guards stands outside, sliding the doors apart as we approach.

Rock pools and water gardens follow the edges of the room, bursting with brightly colored seagrass and lilies. A small bridge leads to a receiving area, and on the nearby dais is a throne wide enough to fit two monarchs, side by side.

Damon's blue braids fall over his shoulders, and the coral crown on his head glistens beneath the scattering of lights. The human sitting next to him wears a matching crown, his own dark hair in perfect twists. Both princes are draped in layers of embroidered silk, but while Damon's robes are ink black with a high collar and metallic embellishments forged into blossoms at his shoulders, the human wears rich indigo, with patterned foliage threaded into every inch of the design, ranging in hues of lavender and rose. A black belt is wrapped around his waist, decorated with a gold sigil: two creatures, half otter, half fish, caught in an endless circle.

"I wondered if we'd ever have the pleasure of receiving you in court," Damon says in the cold, phantom-like voice I remember. He motions beside him. "This is Prince Tobias. I do not believe the two of you have met."

Light dances across Tobias's glittering cheekbones. "Tales of the Great Messenger have traveled far. It is good to put a face to the name."

Caelan stiffens. We haven't talked about the Second Wave. About how I'm the reason his people are being slaughtered in droves.

No wonder he can't bear to be too close to me.

The realization makes my stomach roil. "I—I'd prefer if you didn't call me that," I say to Famine's princes, heating with chagrin.

Tobias tilts his head. "You turned the tides of war."

"I was only trying to protect my sister."

"And you did," Damon points out easily. "Among countless more humans."

My ears burn. "I wanted her safe. I had no idea she'd create the Second Wave." Frustration pulses through me, hating that it sounds like I'm blaming Mei.

None of this was her fault—and I need to make sure everyone here knows it.

"I'm the one who reached out to her, and made her afraid. If her fear created an army, blame me for scaring her in the first place. But what I told her . . . it was a mistake." I turn to Caelan, relieved when this time, he doesn't hesitate to look back. "It was before I knew the truth."

Damon's eyes are an unnatural violet. "And what truth is that?"

I worry my lip and face them. *That coexistence is possible,* my thoughts blaze.

Caelan lifts his chin. "I showed her my memories of this place. She knows what you've built here."

"Yes. That is what the poison prevents her from revealing." Damon looks between us, assessing. Beside me, Caelan visibly relaxes. He must've thought the venom was something worse. "But the rest of Infinity does not believe what we do."

"You've proven that we—" The venom's tendrils hold firm. I swallow the knot in my throat. "I can change Mei's mind. I just need to be able to give her proof."

"Where is our proof that the Second Wave will not slaughter us the moment they become aware of our court?" Damon challenges.

Tobias nods in agreement. "Asking your sister to take a leap of faith is different when she has weapons to protect her if she doesn't like where she lands. We don't have the same luxury. If we come out of hiding, we expose ourselves not just to the wrath of the Second Wave, but to Queen Ophelia and Ettore's Legions."

"Then don't come out of hiding." My thoughts race, desperate for a solution. "You can change the location of your palace, right? That's why I couldn't find it."

Damon watches me carefully. "It became necessary when your sister obliterated the surface with bombs."

I lift my shoulders. "The proof Mei needs can be in an Exchange."

"Perhaps all you'll be giving her is the knowledge that there are more of us to hunt."

I shift my gaze to Tobias. "My sister would never bring harm to another human."

Damon rests his elbow on the edge of the throne, assessing Caelan in silence. "You have not left Asphodel in some time, yet you risk the fortress you've built . . . for what, precisely?"

I wait for him to elaborate, but he doesn't.

"You know what I want," Caelan says without pause. "It's the same thing I wanted when I came here a century ago."

"But would you trust the General of the Second Wave to get it?" Tobias asks.

Caelan's eyes find mine. "I trust Nami."

I stare back, unsure how to reckon feeling gratitude and guilt all at once. But I believe this plan can work.

It *has* to work.

I give a small nod. "I trust you too."

Damon's hollow gaze drifts back to me. "We cannot give you a decision until we discuss the matter with our council. Until then, you may remain here as our guests." I feel the smoke of his mind like a dangerous lure. *I will give you back the truth, but only so long as you are beneath the water.*

The poison sifts through my mind, diluting bit by bit until it's barely a faint imprint in my thoughts. I rub my temple as the haze clears.

Caelan lifts a brow beside me. I see the concern, but I can't feel it. Not even a hint of it. We used to drift in and out of each other's thoughts, but now?

There's a barricade between us.

I look back at Damon. "I'd like to check on my friend. He was bit by a Grimling on our way here."

Damon motions for a nearby guard. When I turn, I find Enid already making her way toward me.

"I'll take you to him," she says, voice inked with annoyance. "Perhaps he'll finally agree to getting some rest once he sees you're okay."

"What do you mean?"

"He believes that you're in danger. We tried to tell him what it's really like down here, but no one can get near him without him swinging his fists. The antidote to despair usually has the side effect of giving people optimism, but all he's focused on is you."

Caelan pulls away sharply, excusing himself as he moves for the doorway.

I stare at the empty space in confusion until I'm certain he isn't coming back. "Take me to Jacek. Please."

She waves a hand toward the exit, jaw tightening. "Right this way."

25

JACEK PULLS AT THE METAL RESTRAINTS HOLDing him to the bed, making the veins in his neck bulge. He clocks me from the other side of the glass window and starts fighting even harder. Every muscle in his body spasms beneath his thrashing.

I shove the door open, glaring sideways at Enid. "I thought we agreed he wasn't a prisoner."

She shrugs. "I didn't agree to anything."

I search the edge of the bed for a mechanism or switch but can't find one. "How do I get the restraints off?"

"They were for our own safety. We don't trust Second Wavers, and your friend is wildly uncooperative."

"He'll cooperate now," I insist.

She moves for the bed and waves a hand over the metal cuffs. They pixelate in a burst of color before vanishing entirely.

Jacek lunges forward, barely making it to his feet before he falls hard, cracking his knees against the floor. He grits his teeth, pain stopping him from rising again.

Enid tuts her disappointment before stalking out of the room.

I hurry to help Jacek. He can barely stand, but he uses the little bit of energy he has to grip my arm and pull me closer.

His pupils are blown out. There's only a tiny hint of hazel surrounding them. "I'm going to get us out of here," he manages to growl.

I huff, forcing him back into the bed. "You're supposed to be resting."

"I promised I'd keep you safe," he says, words slurred with delirium.

I pat his arm gently, then pry it off me and set it against the mattress. "Yeah, I know. Just—try to relax, okay? You'll feel better soon. The antidote is just working its way through you."

Jacek sinks into the pillow, unblinking. "I wasn't supposed to let you out of my sight. She said if I saw . . . not to miss . . ."

I lean closer, trying to make sense of the fading murmurs. "What are you talking about?"

"I dropped it . . . in the lake . . ." The haze overpowers him, and he takes a painfully long blink.

Suspicion snakes through me as I picture the weapon he'd tried to smuggle down here. "Jacek," I start, trying to remain calm. "Did Mei give you orders to shoot Caelan?"

His eyes fall shut. He doesn't respond.

We had a deal. My anger surges as Fenix's smoke pulses from my skin.

Jacek agreed to a meeting. He promised there wouldn't be weapons. He said he was willing to listen.

Did he lie to me?

Was this Mei's plan all along?

My nails cut into my palms. I can't lose control here, not underwater, where my fury has nowhere to go.

Air fills my lungs, in and out until the shadows are subdued. Every time a hint of betrayal climbs up my throat, I swallow it down. I wait until I'm certain Jacek is fast asleep and leave him to rest.

Enid leans against the wall outside his room, drumming her fingers across her arm.

"I'll look after him," she says, earnest despite clearly wanting to be anywhere else. "This isn't the first Grimling bite we've had to heal."

I scratch at my forearm, wanting the truth. "Has he said anything about Caelan since he's been down here? Anything . . . unusual?"

"Are threats of murder and drawn-out physical pain unusual for a Second Waver?"

I open my mouth, then shut it again.

Her lip curls, amused. "I told him he'd recover faster if he let go of his mental veil, but he's stubborn. Almost as stubborn as the Prince of Victory."

I frown, looking back through the doorway where Jacek is fast asleep.

"You don't need yours either. Not here." She motions toward the ceiling with her eyes. "The palace is already shielded—nothing gets in or out."

I prod her mind, testing the outskirts of her mental walls, and find an empty expanse. The knots in my chest begin to untangle. *This is why I couldn't find Caelan. He was veiling himself from me—guarding his mind the way Jacek does.*

The worry loosens, but it doesn't come undone. Because Jacek can still hear me, even when I can't hear him.

Does that mean Caelan has been ignoring me all this time? Listening to every word, but choosing not to answer?

Fenix churns beneath my skin. I fold my palm over the mark to calm her and move away from Enid's curious stare. I don't want her to see the hurt filling my eyes.

Because right now, I don't think I have the strength to hide it.

Reuniting with the Colony feels like stepping back into the sunlight. It's hard to believe they're truly here. Real and happy and *safe*.

Theo gives me the biggest bear hug I've ever had in my life, toffee curls tickling my nose as I smile over his shoulder.

Yeong offers a formal handshake, cheeks turning red when the others tease him. "Forgive me," he apologizes. "I don't really know the protocol for greeting a friend after a hundred years."

I'm still making my way through the crowd, doing my best to greet them individually, when I catch a glimpse of Annika's golden scarf and my breath stops short.

She smiles, warm and radiant, with an arm tucked tightly around Shura. "Hello, Nami." Her amber eyes shine. "It's been far too long."

Shura yanks me in for a group hug, and Annika squeezes so tight that I forget all the guilt and remorse I have wedged in the corners of my memories. Right now, all I can think about is how relieved I am to see my friends again.

Annika leads me to a room with low tables and patterned cushions. Kasia is here too, though aside from a quiet nod, she doesn't say much. I think she's having a hard time taking everything in. I sit with the others like we're back in the Colony, listening as they tell me what happened in the Winter Keep—how they'd been there for months, when Caelan finally told them the truth. Not just about Gil, and what he did, but about what he was trying to do.

He told them he wanted peace between our kinds.

They didn't believe him. Not at first. So he took Annika to Famine and let her see the truth with her own eyes.

And eventually, he was able to bring the rest of the Colony too.

I'm not sure how many hours we spend talking. There's no sunlight to be found in the water, so for all I know we could be well into the next morning. Even though I don't want our time here to end, my eyes keep drifting to the door. It's hard to focus knowing he's so close.

"When's the last time you slept?" Annika asks, interrupting my thoughts. "And I don't mean a power nap. I mean a good, solid night's sleep."

I look back, surprised that I can't remember. "I mean, if the Cut counts . . ."

"It doesn't," she says. "You look tired." She turns back to Shura. "You both do."

Shura rests her head on Annika's shoulder. "I haven't needed to sleep since our days in Victory."

It isn't the same for me. I still feel exhaustion like a looming shadow. Always a few steps behind me, desperate to catch up. I fight it because I feel like that's what humans do in Infinity, but honestly? Sometimes all I want is to curl up in a bed and close my eyes until I don't have to anymore.

"There's a room for you down the hall," Annika says, reading my face. "Come on—I'll show you." She stands up like it isn't an option.

I say my temporary goodbyes and follow Annika to the end of the hall. She tightens her mouth beside me, stopping outside one of the many doors.

I pause, sensing the unease in her stature. "Are you really concerned about how tired I am, or is this just an excuse for privacy?"

"Both." Her face softens. "Shura showed me her memories of the time she's spent away, but—I get the feeling there were gaps in the Exchange."

I think back to when I found Shura in the Red City and grimace. "If there are parts she doesn't want you to see, I don't want to betray her trust by—"

"No, no. I'm not asking for you to fill in any details. I only wanted to thank you, for looking out for her. Whatever she didn't want me to see, I know you appeared shortly after. And you helped her reunite with Eliza."

"She's my friend. I'll always help her."

Annika adjusts one of the braids hanging over her shoulder and stares down the empty hallway. She lets out a slow breath. "I hate that I failed them. For so long, I thought we were helping people by bringing them to the Colony. But all I did was prevent them from finding an army in War, or hope in Famine. I'm the one who sent Shura and Ahmet away—but if I'd only waited a little while longer, they'd have been safe here with the rest of us."

"You made a family out of strangers. There may be a lot of awful in the old world and the new, but that? That's everything," I say. "You wanted to give people a reason to fight, but you also gave them a reason to love."

Not to mention what the Colony did for me. If they hadn't saved me . . . if they'd left me to the Residents at Orientation . . .

I'm not sure I want to think about how different things would be now.

Annika cracks a tired smile. "I don't remember you being so sentimental."

I shrug, sheepish. "I think I was hiding it. I wanted you to believe I was strong."

"You are strong, Nami," she says. "Stronger than most of us, in ways that so few of us seem capable of being." Her face turns serious. "You didn't do anything wrong, you know. When you left for the Borderlands after the Colony fell."

My chest splits in half. She sees my guilt. The shame I've never really been able to erase. "I ran, and you were captured."

"No," she corrects. "We were captured, and *then* you ran. If I'd been there, I would've given you the same order." She lets out a loose laugh. "Not that you seem much like someone who takes orders these days."

"Was I ever?"

"No. I suppose you weren't." A smile remains fixed at the edge of her mouth. "Get some rest. I'll see you when you wake up."

I nod and tuck myself into the room before pressing the door shut. My attention drifts to the surrounding glass wall. The glowing coral gardens are lit with colorful orbs that send neon hues shimmering across the seaweed. Tufts of algae blanket the basalt like moss, and dozens of underwater Dayling species share the reef in perfect harmony.

There isn't a single Grimling in sight.

You're safe here, my mind whispers. *Your friends are safe too.*

The reality lulls me into a sense of calm, and when I reach the mattress and shuffle against the pillow, I'm asleep within seconds.

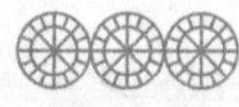

A sudden noise wakes me. I jolt out of bed, stubbing my toe against something hard, and hiss a curse. Fenix tightens around my wrist, steadying me.

I rest one hand on the offending bed post and wrinkle my nose.

A bright Dayling jellyfish moves outside the window.

I nearly sigh with relief when I remember where I am, until a shadow passes beneath the doorframe, moving back and forth with purpose. There's no hum—no sign of a familiar consciousness pacing beyond my sight.

But with Caelan, there never is. Not anymore.

Slowing my breathing, I yank the handle quickly, and find Jacek standing on the other side of the threshold. The color has returned to his face, and he's no longer struggling to remain upright.

His gaze drops to my throat, no doubt reading the way I swallow with unease. "Were you having a nightmare?"

"What? No."

"You seem nervous."

I shift my weight to the other leg. "Why are you creeping around outside my bedroom?"

"This palace is swarming with Residents."

I start to say something sarcastic but remember I'm furious at him. "You can take a break from playing protector." The words come out bitter, but he doesn't seem to notice.

Maybe he doesn't remember what he let slip.

Jacek surveys the length of the hallway with distrust. "Not likely. Everyone's mind is veiled. One of them could be lurking around out here, and I wouldn't be able to sense them until it was too late."

I follow his gaze to the embellished paneling on the walls. Figures of gilded sea creatures and merfolk are molded into the stonework, caught in a dance.

He shakes his head, words strained. "We need to find a way out of here."

"The front door is always an option."

"The fact that you're not taking this seriously is a huge part of my concern."

"I *am* taking this seriously. This is what I wanted to show

Mei." The words rush out of me easily without a poison to hold them back. "This is proof we can coexist."

Jacek's expression turns hostile. "You think humans are safe here? Why, because they let one of us wear a crown?"

I grind my teeth in defense.

"All I see are a lot of walls, and a lot of guards," he clips. "This place is a tomb—and you and I are currently trapped inside it."

A voice sounds from the other end of the hall, startling us both. "The safety of our people will always come first—but we have no desire to stop you from leaving." Prince Tobias stands with his hands clasped together. His robes are teal today, but he still wears a crown of black coral.

Jacek looks like he wants to burn a hole through it.

Tobias takes a few calm strides toward us and offers a diplomatic nod. "You're a guest here. Not a prisoner."

Jacek doesn't miss a beat. "If I walk out the door right now, you're telling me not a single guard is going to stop me?"

Tobias is still. "Anyone can leave—but not with the knowledge of Famine." He looks at me, a silent apology in his eyes. "The poison Damon used on you is no longer enough. Ophelia has already questioned one son's loyalty, and Ettore is at the end of a very long leash. He'd claim our court in a heartbeat if he had a reason. Not to mention the Second Wave has swept through Infinity. The only way to truly protect our home is to remove all trace of it from the mind."

Fenix dances along the edge of my wrist, and the pounding in my chest turns erratic. "Are you saying you're planning on taking our memories when it's time to leave?"

Jacek goes rigid beside me, staring at Tobias like he's about to summon death itself. "Your poison isn't coming anywhere near us."

"That depends on how this next part goes." Tobias's hands disappear beneath layers of silk. "We've prepared a small council meeting. We'd like you to join us."

Jacek juts his chin toward me. "I'm not leaving Nami."

"My invitation extends to you both."

When Jacek doesn't budge, I grab his wrist so he'll look at me. "I came here because I wanted to give my sister answers, and I can't do that if they take my memories. I need to see this through—with or without you."

After a long pause, Jacek releases a gruff noise that I take as a sign of surrender.

We follow Tobias to a section of the palace that's separated by a glass bridge. Spherical rooms branch out of the main hallway, weaving around the palace's exterior like floating kelp.

We turn a corner and find ourselves in an enormous room. Copper chandeliers hang from the ceiling, dancing with turquoise flames. Below them is a table made of polished green sea glass.

I expect to find strangers seated around it—but one quick glance reveals they aren't strangers at all.

Damon, Kasia, Shura—and Caelan.

Beside me, Jacek's muscles strain. If he still had his gun, would he have already pulled the trigger?

And would Mei really have been okay with it?

That was before, I tell myself, ignoring the wound in my chest even as my pulse ricochets. *This meeting will change things. She'll finally understand what I've been trying to tell her.*

I can make things right.

Jacek shifts his body in front of me, and for a split second, something darkens in Caelan's expression.

I throw a warning glance at Jacek and inch closer to the table, away from his protective stance. There's nothing to fear in this room, and the last thing I need is my self-appointed bodyguard getting the wrong idea about why my heart is racing.

Tobias settles into the chair beside Damon, and they clasp hands on one of the armrests.

I count the empty seats around them and frown. "I thought this was a council meeting."

"We believe our current situation requires voices more familiar with the factions on the surface." Damon's words float toward me. "You want an alliance, but we need to trust each other first."

I blink, gaze drifting from one friend to the next. It's not just Damon and Tobias I have to convince today. It's everyone here.

"Having second thoughts?" Jacek prods.

An admission builds on the tip of my tongue, but I stifle my nerves and focus on the one thing I know to be true. "I will never have second thoughts about peace."

Caelan offers the ghost of a smile. He turns his palm up to reveal a small metal device shaped like a pentagon. "I brought something that might help us," he says, placing it in the center of the table.

Light bursts in different directions, forming holograms in the empty chairs. They pixelate, mimicking muted variations of color, before settling into the shape of three figures. Only one of them is a stranger.

Elias locks onto me in an instant. A curl tugs at the edge of Nine's mouth.

The woman sitting between them wears white ceremonial robes, similar to what Gisele's mother wore on the day of the parade.

I doubt it's a coincidence. She must be from the council.

Shura sits up, surprised. Kasia studies the projections carefully.

Jacek glares across the table. "What is this?"

"Allow me to introduce Councilor Marion." Caelan motions to the older woman. Her powdery gray hair flickers through the dilution of the hologram, and two full rows of golden hoops trail along her earlobes. "And these are two of my most trusted guards, Elias and Nine." He looks across the table. "They're First Folk from Asphodel."

Elias lifts a brow in my direction. "I'm guessing we're no longer pretending you're not human?"

I wince, sheepish. "I think we're probably past that."

Nine flashes her teeth. "Thank the stars for that. You made a *terrible* liar."

Jacek's stare heats, but the humorous twinkle in Caelan's gaze makes me relax. I tuck into the chair beside him.

Marion's voice unfurls through the room as if she were flesh and bone beside us. "I must admit, I had hoped my first seat at the table would be with the senate. But this . . . this is most unexpected."

"The First Folk deserve to hear about the future we're hoping to forge, so they can decide if it's what they want too." Caelan looks at his brother. "And you need to understand that it isn't just the humans you'd be helping by showing the world what you've built here."

Damon offers a single nod before leaning back in his chair.

"Mei will want you to tell her everything," I say to Jacek. "You may as well get comfortable."

He stares at the projections. He stares at Caelan. He stares at me.

Finally, he yanks a chair back and begrudgingly takes a seat. "Let's get this over with."

There's only one empty chair left. It doesn't seem important at first, but then . . .

Asphodel. Famine. The Second Wave. Neo Genesis.

We're missing someone. Someone to represent the Legacies in the Four Courts. But to get our enemy at a table with us . . . that would be—

Impossible, my thoughts catch as I spot the figure walking toward us.

Fenix's shadow burns across my skin, flickering in warning. I blink like I'm caught in a nightmare, and the moment my eyes land on Prince Lysander towering over the edge of the table with his pale green robes, I feel sick.

26

SUSPICION SIMMERS IN CAELAN'S GAZE. "I thought you were Cut during Death's siege."

Gold dust is painted across Lysander's cheekbones, striking against his dark skin. He isn't wearing a crown, and apart from a single gold cuff around his biceps, there are no embellishments to his attire. Nothing to suggest he was once the Prince of Death. "When soldiers breached the palace, I left for Famine in search of an ally—and found my brother was veiling a great many secrets instead."

Because Prince Lysander can see through any veil.

Shura's shoulders quake. Kasia and Jacek are tense and unblinking. But it's Caelan I can't stop watching. The unease in his eyes . . . he really didn't know his brother had survived.

Caelan hurtles an accusation across the table. "He's been with you all this time?"

Damon's expression remains indifferent. "When Lysander arrived, I put a poison in his mind, and held him in a slumber. I did not believe I could trust him at first—but eventually, we came to an understanding."

"What kind of understanding?" I ask, fighting the memories of Lysander's apathy as my consciousness was severed from my body. As if the act had been nothing more than an administrative task—one he'd likely done thousands of times before.

Humans meant nothing to him then.

What made him change his mind?

Lysander's answer is simple. "I realized I was wrong." He turns to Caelan. "You too were once created for a purpose you've now forsaken."

"You hurt Nami," Caelan replies, failing to keep his features schooled as tension rolls across his jawline.

I don't know why his anger surprises me. If the roles were reversed, I'd be protective of him right back. But watching the energy darken on the opposite sides of the table makes me pause.

"You hurt our people. Your brothers. Your *mother*," Lysander counters stonily. "But I will not let the past cloud what is best for them."

"I want what's best for everyone," Caelan replies.

Lysander shakes his head. "It has never been possible for one person to fight for every voice. It stretches a person to impossible limits." His voice is stern. "What if by the end of this war, someone has to lose?"

"Well, look at that." Jacek folds his arms over his muscular chest. "We agree on something."

Caelan's frustration finds a new target, and Jacek is all too ready to meet him in the ring. The bickering doesn't stop. It's jab after jab, argument after argument, and I'm acutely aware this is doing more harm than good. Tobias murmurs something in Damon's ear. Kasia purses her lips. Elias hunches his shoulders like he's bracing for a fight. And Marion's curiosity is rapidly shifting to distaste.

Every nerve in my body feels like it's about to burst. I curl my fingers deep in my palms.

If we don't stop this. . . if we give in to animosity . . .

This conversation will be over before it's even begun.

"That's enough," I bark. The heat of the room's attention shifts in my direction. "We don't need to fight. We shouldn't be fighting at all." I shake my head. "My sister's going to need proof we can coexist. Maybe Ophelia will too. If the first leap of faith has to start here, then so be it." I look back at Lysander, ignoring the itch rising up the back of my neck. "Everyone deserves a second chance." To Jacek, I add, "And you promised me a meeting. A *real* one, without weapons or deception. So if you're not going to sit here with an open mind, I'd rather you didn't stay at all."

Jacek rolls his tongue against the inside of his cheek. Caelan flexes his fingers.

There's a moment's pause before Lysander lowers himself into the final chair. He dips his chin in my direction, and some of my apprehension fizzles away.

"Thank you," I say quietly, though I'm not even sure who it's directed at.

After a stretch of silence, Caelan continues introductions around the table. I think it's mostly for the First Folk's benefit—but it has the added bonus of slicing through the tension.

Not to mention, it gives me time to breathe.

Marion's hologram shifts as she observes Tobias's crown. "How long have you been a Prince of Famine?"

"Centuries ago, I was rescued from a Grimling horde by Famine's soldiers." Tobias turns to the First Folk, gaze sincere. "I was saved. Given a home. And over time . . ." He lifts Damon's hand and presses a gentle kiss over his knuckles. "I do not see how he was made. I see his soul." Turning back to Marion, he adds, "It is like that for most of us here."

"Most Legacies seem unwilling to trust humans," she presses. "What made your court so different?"

"Despair is more of a mirror than you realize." Damon's voice is like a tendril of smoke, hypnotic, yet barely there at all.

"You have built something here," Marion nods slowly, "but I wonder if it's enough. You have safety, but not freedom. Not the outside world. Perhaps Famine and Asphodel are not so different."

His violet eyes swirl. "Except you are not content to remain hidden."

Marion's focus flits between Elias and Nine. "No. We are not."

"The First Folk are too vulnerable to leave the city," Lysander counters. "They would not survive a run-in with the humans."

"Not without peace," Marion amends.

I swallow the knot in my throat, wondering if Jacek's doubt

is wavering. If seeing Famine has changed *anything* for him. I motion to the princes and the councilor and Caelan's guards. The *other side*, blended with our own. "You've seen the truth now. Would you still drop a bomb on this palace, knowing what's really down here? Knowing who it could hurt?"

Jacek runs a hand over the back of his neck. "Honestly? I'm still trying to decide whether or not the humans down here are under some kind of spell. But I'm not the one you have to convince. It's Mei. And she's going to want to know where Ophelia stands."

"There was a time she believed in coexistence," Caelan says. "Perhaps we can give her a reason to believe in it again."

"And if it doesn't work?" Jacek leans forward. "If the Second Wave calls a ceasefire, only for your queen to retaliate?" His voice teeters on the edge of a threat. "Maybe humans would be more amenable to a peace treaty if Ophelia was taken off the board. Because as it stands, we have no reason to trust her. You all have something to gain—but what does your queen want beyond the destruction of humanity?"

Lysander bristles—but I'm the one who interjects. "We can't kill Ophelia." I look at Caelan, uncertain how much I should say.

"We are tethered to her," he admits. "Doing so would kill every one of our kind."

Shura tucks a pink strand over her ear, forehead creasing in thought. "Ophelia is the Orb."

The calculation in Jacek's stare is unmistakable. But something about the honesty disarms him a little too.

Marion's hologram flickers. "There is something the queen wants. Something the First Folk and Legacies have longed for across many centuries." She eyes Caelan pointedly. "Perhaps she'd be willing to negotiate if the humans promised our freedom?"

Kasia frowns. "Isn't freedom what we're *all* bargaining for?"

Caelan softens as the confession spills out of him. "Our mother's greatest hope is for our people to thrive in the Afterlands. She might consider a peace treaty, in exchange for our safe passage."

"Hard pass," Jacek seethes. "We would have nowhere left to run if her power grew."

"We could argue the same about humans," Elias points out. "But I'm pretty sure the point here is to trust one another. Besides, the Afterlands are a free territory. We have just as much of a right to live there as any of you."

Nine looks up, mouth twisted sideways as if she's been biting her tongue. "We deserve a real home. One that we get to choose ourselves."

Understanding washes over Shura's face, and I wonder if she's thinking about the old Colony in Victory, and the outposts in War. I doubt she's considered any of them a real home either.

"Can Ophelia reach the Afterlands?" Kasia's blue eyes sweep across the table with concern. "Is she not still tied to the Four Courts?"

"She is," I say. "But she also has the power to set the Legacies and First Folk free."

The room falls quiet.

"The people who taught us to be afraid of them . . . they were wrong. *I* was wrong," I add, nervous. "Infinity doesn't need to be controlled. We just need another option. One that doesn't revolve around violence as a means of survival, or fear as a way to control one another. We have so much more common ground than we realize—we just need to stop seeing each other as enemies."

"And how do you propose we do that?" Jacek asks, arcing a brow.

I lift my chin. "By becoming allies instead." My gaze drifts to each of them, desperate for them to see what I do. The possibility of something *better.* "It can start with us."

Caelan watches me so carefully, I worry I might shatter.

But my heart thunders with hope.

Shura runs a finger along the polished table. "This place saved the Colony. If it could be like this in the rest of Infinity . . . then *of course* I'd choose peace over war."

"Most of us are tired of fighting," Kasia admits. "If there's a treaty on the table, perhaps even those in Neo Genesis could be convinced to lay down their weapons."

I feel my eyes start to glaze with relief, when Jacek cuts in like a sledgehammer.

"Ozias will never agree to a treaty," he cautions. "And I can't imagine any of his soldiers turning against him. Their loyalty runs deep."

"Perhaps there are other ways to make a king fall," Damon suggests, words circling the room like mist. "Doubt is a powerful poison."

The frost in Caelan's eyes prickles. "You could spread the truth of what Ozias did to our mother." He looks at Shura and Kasia. "You could tell them where the First Folk came from."

If the other factions knew there were mortal children in Infinity, maybe it would sow a different kind of seed. One that showed humanity in the heart of Asphodel—and a monster inside Ozias.

Shura presses her lips together. "I don't know how much sway I hold in Neo Genesis . . . but I'll do what I can."

Beside her, Kasia nods.

The seconds stretch between us, so painfully long that I feel my stomach start to sink, when Jacek lets out a sigh.

He looks at me, not with irritation or disbelief, but with acceptance. "This is what you want?"

I nod. "I believe in this." *Down to my marrow.*

He waves a hand, conceding.

I inhale slowly and turn to Lysander. To Damon and Tobias. "Will Famine stand with us?"

Damon presses a hand to his chest. "Our court is with you."

I look at Councilor Marion. "And Asphodel?"

"The First Folk have always trusted their prince," she says. "But I am prepared to trust you too. You have our allyship."

Elias nods his head, and Nine cracks a small grin.

Caelan pauses before looking at me. "I'll return to Asphodel to convene with the rest of the council. It would be in our best interest not to alert our mother to our plans until we have something solid to bargain with. If I stay away much longer, I fear she'll notice."

The sinking feeling in my chest only grows, but I try to focus on what matters most. "I'll go back to the *Mizuchi* with Jacek," I say, resolute. "I'll make sure my sister hears the truth."

The muscles in Caelan's jaw tighten. I don't know how he feels about us parting ways, but he doesn't offer an alternative.

Maybe it's for the best.

Maybe it's what he needs.

"Then it's decided," Damon says. "You will leave here with your memories intact, and we will try for peace."

Fenix's shadows tremor over my wrist.

Tobias stands, somber. "There will be a banquet tonight in the South Hall, in honor of our guests. I hope you'll save your departures for the morning so you can attend."

The rest of us stand too, and when the holograms fade away, I take a step toward Caelan. For a fleeting moment, he looks as if he wants to hug me—but it doesn't last. He winces, pulling back just as he did in the hallway.

Before I get the chance to take it personally, Lysander appears beside us.

"There is something you should know before you return to Asphodel," he says to his brother, deep voice filling my bloodstream with dread. "A truth, I believe, you are long overdue."

Caelan blanches. "What are you talking about?"

"The First Folk are not tethered to our mother. They never have been."

The confession makes the room spin. I'm certain I've misheard him. Certain there must be a mistake.

Lysander doesn't blink. "There is nothing stopping the First Folk from reaching the Afterlands. It is the Legacies who cannot cross the border. Our mother did not tell you because she wanted you to give our people hope, not a way for them to leave. Not until she could be sure Infinity was safe."

Something splinters in Caelan's expression, and the flicker of raw grief makes my throat burn. He grips the back of his chair, knuckles white. Teetering on the edge of a cliff he doesn't want to fall off alone. "Why are you telling me this now?"

"Because I believe you have a decision to make."

Caelan's throat rolls with understanding.

"The First Folk believe Asphodel is a cage," Lysander warns. "If they try to flee before there's a treaty in place, it may become a literal one."

Caelan scrapes his fingers through his hair. "I swore I would never trap any of the First Folk in Asphodel out of fear. So if negotiations fail—if our mother refuses to yield—then I will do whatever I have to in order to get them across the border. I will make sure they know the truth."

My heart pinches. "You'll be stuck here." The way he always feared.

"What matters is that my people won't be," he says, voice clipped at the edges.

Lysander lowers his head. An act of respect, perhaps.

When he's gone, I turn back to Caelan. "The treaty won't fail. And when the war ends, maybe there's still a way for Ophelia to let the rest of you go too." When he meets my gaze, a piece of my heart breaks for him. "I'm not giving up yet."

Not on you. Not on us.

Caelan's irises are nearly white. Haunted. He nods without saying a word.

But he doesn't linger.

I watch him leave the room, cupping my hand to my chest as Fenix seeps toward my fingertips, turning them black.

27

I ADJUST THE HIGH COLLAR OF MY PALE BLUE dress. My right arm is covered in layers of chiffon, while my left arm is decorated in crystals that climb from my wrist to my bare shoulder. Shimmering orange flowers are sewn into the skirt, with a blaze of gold material that drapes over my hips and trails to the floor.

I planned to wear a gray tunic and boots for the evening, but Shura insisted I change.

Her vivid raspberry-and-cream gown swirls around her like a confectioner's dream as she moves across the ballroom, and I get the feeling it's a dress Shura has dreamed up multiple times but has never had the occasion to wear.

Kasia leans against the marble pillar beside me. She's wearing a suit made of layered robes bound at the waist, yellow as the sun.

"You look nice," I say.

She makes a face. "I'd have preferred more places to hide my knives, but seeing as you made me leave them behind . . ."

I smile guiltily and turn to watch the crowd, soaking in the details of their faces. Annika and Shura are dancing with a group from the Colony, arms linked as they skip down the line of partygoers. Theo and Yeong are perched firmly near a buffet, slurping noodles and drawing the attention of two pretty Residents. Jacek scowls near the wall, pacing like a watchdog.

And Caelan hasn't turned up at all.

I rub my sternum, distracting myself from the ache.

"It's going to take a while to believe all of this is real," Kasia admits.

"Still waiting for the other shoe to drop?"

Her mouth curls. "You younglings always have the strangest expressions."

I look around the room, watching the dancers spin like they're caught in a wave of euphoria.

Kasia stills beside me. "You know you're allowed to be happy too, right?"

I flinch, even as I try to pretend her words didn't pierce something tender. "Yeah. I know."

The problem is, I think I've forgotten how.

Shura's laugh echoes across the room, and I watch as she tugs Theo's arm, forcing him to the center of the dance floor. She maneuvers him into a spin, and he turns a shade of pink that rivals her hair.

"Shura and I are going to travel back to Neo Genesis together," Kasia says, surprising me. She offers a weak smile. "I thought we'd convince more people of coexistence if we went as a pair. She'll be able to help me track down some of the Salt Clan too. We're heading out in the morning, after she's said goodbye to her mother."

"Thank you," I say softly. "I—I'm glad you won't be alone."

Kasia nods. "If there are people willing to listen, we'll find them."

We watch the banquet a little while longer in silence until I decide I've had enough. I get up to leave, making my way toward the large doorway, when a voice stops me.

"Leaving so soon?"

Caelan stands a few feet away, dressed in white formalwear and a silver crown. A prince through and through.

I blink. "I thought you weren't coming."

"I wasn't. But I changed my mind."

I adjust the material at my wrist, unsure how to respond.

Caelan tilts his head, following the movement. His attention shifts to the curve of my waist, where the material hugs me close, and then up to the bare skin of my shoulder—

He straightens, remembering himself. "You look . . . well." He clears his throat. "Blue suits you."

My forehead creases. "Um. Thanks?"

His mouth parts with regret. "That's not what I meant. I mean, blue *does* suit you. It's just—that's not—"

I pull my face back. "Are you trying to give me a compliment?"

"No," he says, entirely too quickly. He runs a knuckle over his

lower lip, agitated. "I'm trying *not* to give you a compliment. Because if I say what I'm really thinking, it will make everything worse."

"I don't understand."

His eyes dart between mine, and his face softens. He drops his arm. "I'm trying to be careful. Things are . . . complicated."

"Because of me?" *Because of what I told Mei?*

He doesn't answer. Not at first. When he lowers his chin, a strand of snow-white hair falls against his temple. "I'm not sure being around you is a good idea."

Embarrassment floods my rib cage. I wonder if when he looks at me now, all he sees is the Messenger. The monster who sentenced his kind to the slaughter of the Second Wave.

I'm not sure how to recover from that.

He sweeps the curl from his brow and sighs. "It doesn't matter right now."

I frown. "*What* doesn't matter?"

He holds out a hand, surprising me. "For old time's sake?"

I open my mouth and shut it again. The music slips past my thoughts, and I realize the room has already fallen into a waltz.

I stare back at him, confused.

"Ten minutes. That's all I'm asking for." He looks tormented, despite the desperate curve of his mouth. "Ten minutes where we pretend things had been different from the start."

A knot snags in my throat.

"Ten minutes," he repeats, stepping closer. "To not be worried, or afraid, or prepared to go to war. Ten minutes to just be us."

My gaze drops to his outstretched fingers, hovering between us like a plea.

I take Caelan's hand and try not to react when he pulls me close. We dance like we're moving through a daydream, falling into familiar steps. Because Caelan and I, we've done this before.

There's a fight in his eyes, but I'm not sure if it's because of the war or me. Still, he doesn't look away, even as the music seems to urge our bodies closer to one another.

I remember this feeling.

I remember why it feels *right*.

Caelan crossed the Four Courts for me. He stood against his family for me. He protected me, again and again, because he believed there was something in me worth saving. Worth forgiving.

He's always seen me as more than just a culmination of my greatest mistakes. He sees my heart—just as I've always seen his.

Maybe with time, he'll remember that too.

"I'm sorry about what Lysander told you," I say softly.

Something stills in his eyes, but we don't stop moving.

"You deserve to be free, Caelan. And I will do everything I can to find a way."

His lips part. My eyes drift to the subtle movement, and his fingers tighten against my back. He leans in, and I feel our noses brush like a caress.

This is real.

This has always been real.

I look up at him through my lashes, so close I can almost feel his heartbeat. "I want you to know that—"

He stumbles back abruptly, straightening like he's hiding an injury. Our hands fall away, severing our trance.

"I'm sorry," he says, shaking his tousled white hair. "This was a mistake."

Because ten minutes can't fix what I broke.

Caelan moves quickly for the exit, but this time I don't watch him leave—I follow him, face hot and brows knotted.

He's already halfway down the empty corridor. I glue my feet to the tiles and make my voice loud enough to cross the distance.

"I know I messed up. If I could take it all back, I would."

Caelan halts, rigid, and turns his chin toward me just slightly. "Take it back?"

"I didn't mean to bring the Second Wave here. In my defense, I did that before you found me in the caves. It was before I knew what you were really doing. I get that you're angry, but at the time, I thought I was going to die and my sister was next." I shake my head. "But none of that matters. Because I know what I'm responsible for, and I know I'm the reason so many of your people have been Cut. I don't deserve to be let off the hook. But please—if there's nothing I can do to fix this, let me try anyway. Because I'm sorry. I'll always be sorry. And I can't bear the thought of you hating me."

He turns around fully now, still on the far side of the corridor. "I'm not angry at you, Nami."

"Then why are you acting like you can't stand to be around me?"

Caelan takes in a breath and shuts his eyes tight. "Because it is taking everything in my power to keep my mother out of my head."

"Your mother?"

Caelan pinches the bridge of his nose. "Ever since she tried to take my memories, she's been . . . checking in. Hovering over my thoughts like she's looking for signs that I've remembered something. Remembered *you*. So I turned my mind into a fortress to keep everyone out."

Something in my chest thaws. "All the times I tried to find you . . . you really haven't been able to hear me?"

He shakes his head. "It was the only way. Every moment I spend with you is a moment where I risk letting my guard down. I—I thought I had it under control, but around you . . ." He tightens his fists, flustered. "Around you, I don't want walls. I want you to see me."

My heart beats and beats and beats.

"I will never hate you," he says like a promise. "Being close to you is all I've wanted for a century."

I take a few steps forward, and he does the same. Each stride feels like moving through molasses. We're toeing lines we shouldn't—and somehow, I can't find the will to stop.

"Everything in Famine is veiled." My voice sounds faraway. "You don't have to hide here, if you don't want to."

"I can't risk it. Not when we're so close to changing things." He takes a few more cautious steps. "It would be selfish."

"So, you have to stay away from me," I say when he's only a few feet away.

His throat rolls. "Yes. I have to stay away," he says, and closes the gap anyway.

Our faces are close, but I feel the barrier between us like an invisible wall. We can't cross it. Because ending the war is more important than whatever it is we think we want.

He breathes, sharp and guarded, and I find his silver eyes.

"I miss your voice in my head," he says gently. "More than you could possibly imagine."

There's a stampede of footsteps rushing for the banquet hall, and we turn to see Enid approaching with several armed guards.

"What's wrong?" I ask quickly.

She flattens her mouth. "There's been an attack on the surface. A Second Wave warship has arrived."

Jacek's gun. The one that fell in the lake. They must've tracked it.

"Let me talk to my sister," I say quickly. "If she knows I'm safe, maybe I can get her to stop fighting Famine's Legion while I explain what's going on."

Enid frowns. "The Second Wave isn't fighting Famine. They're fighting War." She turns to Caelan. "Prince Ettore is here."

SOLDIERS RUSH THROUGH THE PALACE. IT ONLY takes a few seconds for Damon and Tobias to round the corner.

"They haven't breached the water yet," one of the guards informs Enid. "The human warships were scouting the northern shoreline when Ettore's forces showed up."

"His spies must have followed them," Enid says grimly, turning to the princes. "Permission to relocate?"

Damon nods. "As soon as possible. We cannot take any risks."

They fall into a hurried conversation, but my head thrums with concern.

I tug Caelan's arm, pulling him to the side where our voices won't be heard. "I need to get to the surface. Mei knows I'm here, and she won't leave without me. And I think—I think Ettore might be here for the same reason."

I quickly explain about the weapon, and the water, and how I saw Commander Alys in War. I don't realize Jacek has joined us until he huffs beside me.

"You're not going up there alone." His arms are crossed stubbornly, gaze drifting to the number of weapons surrounding us. Every Legion Guard is decked with curved blades and spears, prepared for battle even from the shadows.

Caelan's irises sharpen, but he nods in agreement. "He's right. Especially not if Ettore is hunting you." He takes both of my hands in his, breaking his own rules. "I know you don't need a protector. But I can't leave you. Not to him."

The shadow squeezes my forearm, and I stare at our clasped palms. "If someone sees you, and your mother finds out you're here—"

"I can stay under a veil. As soon as I know you're safe, I'll leave."

My grip tightens on instinct.

Because once we part ways, I will have no way of communicating with him. No way of knowing he made it back to Asphodel safely.

I don't know when I'll see him again.

"Would it be such a bad thing to let the General have a shot at Ettore?" Jacek interrupts. "This fight is long overdue."

Damon appears like a wraith, with Enid at his side. "You have yet to face him on a battlefield. The General will not find this fight as easy as the others."

"The Second Wave doesn't lose," Jacek says.

"Ettore's forces are not what you're used to," Damon warns. "It would be wise not to underestimate him."

Caelan tenses. When our hands fall back to our sides, he keeps one finger hooked around my pinkie. "We could use some help getting to the surface."

"And a few weapons, since you seem to have plenty to spare," Jacek adds sharply. I didn't imagine he'd stay behind when his people are right outside, but I don't relish the idea of being in a confined space with him and Caelan.

I shoot him a warning glance. *Don't touch him. I don't care what your orders are—he's the reason we were spared from the Grimlings, and at the very least, you owe him safe passage.*

Jacek furrows a brow in confusion but doesn't reply.

Damon tilts his head toward me, and I feel the remnants of the poison releasing my thoughts, pulling away like a retreating mist. *Your mind is your own again.*

I nod a thank-you. Not just for the antidote, but for giving us a chance.

"I'll get you a transport," Enid says. "But once you reach the surface, you're on your own. Famine guards can't be seen in this fight."

I sweep a hand over my clothes as we walk, shifting into an outfit more suitable for battle. Enid leads us back through the grand hall, where a row of large glass spheres sits just beyond the walled barrier, attached by a tunneled walkway. Gilded bars cage the glass, making them look like oversized ornaments.

We take a seat inside one of the spheres, and Enid hesitates before handing each of us a blade. I watch Jacek tuck it into his belt, chewing the inside of my cheek as Caelan does the same.

I keep mine in my fist.

Enid adjusts the controls from the console port outside the tunnel. The hatch seals, and she steps back, watching as the transport pulls us into the lake. She mouths something I can't hear through the glass and holds up a hand in salute.

Water envelops us, and we race back through the lake. Streaks of filtered light skitter past us as we accelerate, and I brace my palms against the bench, spine tensing. When the carriage breaks the surface, my stomach somersaults.

The glass dome rotates slightly, easing us onto the rocky shoreline.

We emerge one by one, finding our balance on the wet stones. The moment we're free, the transport seals and disappears below the water.

Warships litter the air, blasting surges of energy at one another. With every explosion comes a burst of colorful embers that rain down. On the other end of the shoreline, a good length from where we were dropped off, I see soldiers from the Second Wave, their armor a dark blur against the Legion Guards of War. A battle of red and black.

Except . . .

Not all of Ettore's soldiers are dressed in his colors. The ones on the ground stumble when they're shot. Flinch when a blade touches their skin. Remain whole, just as before.

None of them vanish into mist.

"They're not being Cut," I note.

Jacek pales beside me. "That's because those aren't Residents. They're human."

I stare in horror at the battle across from us, watching as humans attack each other in the sand while Grimlings descend from every direction.

"Death's Legion is responsible for this." Caelan's irises darken. "Ettore recruited what was left of them after the siege."

They once found a way to turn Gil into a puppet.

Now they've done the same to the human survivors.

He turns to me. "I can jump you to one of the ships. You'll be safe with the Second Wave."

"Absolutely not. We don't know which one my sister is on, and if anyone spots you, they'll shoot before they ask questions." I motion to the sea of soldiers ahead. "I'm sure there's a comm around here. I can tell my sister where I am."

"I'll find one." Jacek's eyes turn deadly. "We're going to need a rifle, too. Someone's bound to have dropped one by now, and we're not going to make it a hundred yards without cover." He tightens his jaw, vanishing beneath a veil.

The surrounding Grimlings turn on instinct, focused on the rocky disturbance Jacek left behind.

Caelan takes a step forward, hands sparking with blue electricity. I extend my arm, and Fenix leaps to the sand, taking her foxlike form. Her fur lashes at the air, and the moment she spots the horde, she bares a row of teeth and doubles in size.

The corner of Caelan's lip tugs. "I knew she listened to you."

I quirk my mouth in an apology. "I wasn't sure if I could trust you with that information before. I didn't know if you were still *you*."

I can't hear his thoughts, but I see them written across his face. *You can always trust me.*

I urge Fenix ahead, and she tackles one of the Grimlings to the ground, severing the bones from its chest cavity.

We push forward together. Caelan launches a blast toward the trees, distracting the horde long enough for us to skirt the shoreline and clamber up the hill. My feet crunch against something hollow, and when I look down, I realize it's a mountain of skulls.

Blasts of energy rip apart the ashen ground. It's impossible to differentiate who is on our side, because they're all dressed like Second Wavers. Humans fire on humans, using every weapon in their arsenal. Bullets rip through flesh, and I flinch at the sight of so much red puddling the earth.

Fenix tears through the crowd, forcing some back in alarm. Her jaws snap. I know it's only a warning, but the others see a threat.

Someone lifts their pistol, and my fingers flex. *Don't hurt them,* I tell Fenix. *Draw their fire away so we can clear the path.*

She bolts just before the bullet ricochets off the ground, thrashing at the air as her black fur crackles with shadows. She becomes a whirlwind of darkness, commanding the attention of everyone around her. Some are too wary to attack, but others unload round after round of gunfire.

Fenix grows, feeding off the frenzy and terror. When a streak of light falls from the sky and explodes nearby, I realize she's caught the attention of one of the warships too.

I look up, peering through smoke and sunlight, and see the *Mizuchi*.

"I found her!" I shout to Caelan, but he's distracted.

I shift, following his gaze to where the lake quakes in sync with the battle around us. Not just moving, but *rising*.

Water climbs toward us. We stumble away from the wall of skulls, watching in horror as they vanish below the blur of liquid.

In the far distance, an enormous shadow appears beneath the lake.

We run fast, dodging strangers as we try to stay on the outskirts of the fight. Another blast comes from the sky, smashing through the ground ahead of us. Bodies scatter in every direction, and I duck low as shrapnel explodes overhead.

A pair of Grimlings drift toward the carnage, cornering us against the ridge. Caelan immediately moves for the one on the left. With Enid's blade still in my fist, I swing hard, slicing at the second creature's thin flesh. It doesn't bleed. It barely flinches at all. And when it launches toward me with a guttural wail, I manage to roll out of the way before it thrashes against the rocks.

I search for an exit, frantic, when a high-pitched sound pulses through the air. My eyes flash back to one of the warships—Ettore's Legion, if the crimson red banners are anything to go by—and watch as a charge builds in one of the turrets.

I don't get a chance to react. The blast comes without any more warning, and when it smashes into the earth, the shock wave pummels through the entire shoreline. The force hits my chest hard, sending me flying backward.

Something solid wraps around my waist—another body—and when we hit the ground, we tumble over the rising tide together.

I look up, winded, and meet Caelan's silver gaze. His lips are parted in fear, and when he breathes an inch away from me, I forget to do the same.

Water pools through my hair, and I let out a sharp yelp as Caelan tugs me upright, clutching me close to his side. We stagger backward, staring in bewilderment at the growing shadow beneath the lake.

It's nearly the size of a mountain.

Caelan snaps his attention back to the warship. "I'm going to see if I can take out that turret."

I grab his forearm, holding him tight. "No! If someone sees you helping us—" I don't finish the sentence.

Caelan clutches my face with both hands like he's been desperate to touch me for years. "I can endure my mother's wrath, but I cannot suffer losing you again." He steps away and jumps across the sky in a blur of crackling blue energy.

I press forward, trying to avoid running into the Grimlings, but it's impossible. They're everywhere. One of the monsters reaches a bony hand toward me, snatching and clawing at whatever it can grab.

I barely manage to spin out of its grasp when a shot hits the back of its skull and it staggers away from me. The scream that erupts from its overstretched mouth makes my blood run cold.

Another bullet hits its chest, another hits its empty left eye socket. And then a blade appears, severing the Grimling's head from its shoulders.

The creature collapses, and Jacek stands in its place. Pistol in one hand, and a short sword in the other. "Come on," he grunts, tapping the comm at his temple that he must've plucked from one of the bodies. "There's a drop ship that can meet us in the next clearing. We've got to be fast—they want to pull back the fleet as soon as they have you."

I look around at the battle. "But what about the people on the ground?"

"There isn't time to figure out who's on our side. It's chaos out there." He stares me down, serious. "You are the priority right now. So let me do my job."

Both of us take off through the battle-torn surface, away from the incoming tide. There's an explosion in the sky, and blue sparks rain down above us. The enemy warship doesn't move, but the smoke from the turret makes me think Caelan managed to hit his mark.

Still, I don't see him. There's too much smoke. Too much of *everything.*

Several humans dressed in Second Waver clothing lunge toward our group, and Jacek raises a blade in defense, cracking the hilt of his sword against one of the strangers. I recoil, horrified by the idea of fighting a human who's unaware. Jacek must sense it, because he ushers me out of the way, cutting down the second soldier so I don't have to.

I call Fenix back from the hill and send her shadows surging forward, straight into the horde of Grimlings. Bones rattle, and their mouths rip open in response.

I don't know what's taking Caelan so long. I'm worried he's stuck somewhere, and I can't find him because of the barrier he built in his mind.

I spin, scanning the fog. Jacek seems to have a knack for

picking up discarded weapons, because his belt is bursting with metal blades.

"Here," he says, trading the knife in my fist for one that can Cut. I try to give it back, but he grabs me by the shoulder, so firm I feel the pinch of a bruise. "Take it. Just in case."

I grip the hilt, and he releases me. "I need you to search for Caelan. You can sense emotions, right?" *Maybe they're different from his thoughts. Maybe his barricade won't hide them*. "Find his."

Jacek scowls but takes in a breath and scans the bloody, ash-filled horizon. "I'm not sure what I'm looking for. There's fear everywhere, in every direction."

"Don't search for fear," I say. "Search for hope."

After a few moments, he nods farther up the next hill. "There."

I start to run, when a thunderous crack draws my attention toward the lake. I open my mouth in horror, and Fenix's shadows rush back to me at once. The water builds higher than a skyscraper, rising and widening like the jaws of a monster.

I see it—the flicker of light in the sky. The spherical rooms and coral towers.

Famine's palace.

There one moment—and gone the next.

They've jumped.

When the water crashes back down, filling the hollow space the palace left behind, the explosion becomes a tsunami that's headed straight for us.

"Nami!" Jacek growls, reaching for my arm to get us somewhere safe.

But I can't leave Caelan. Not to Ettore. Not to anyone.

"Get to my sister," I say. "Tell her about our allies. Make sure she hears the truth." I shove him backward and throw up a veil so that he can't follow me.

I run for the hill, dodging Legion Guards and avoiding the crack of energy from the Second Wavers. When I reach the highest point, I stare down into the fog—into the folds of war—and find Caelan battling a group of Ettore's soldiers.

Blue energy erupts from his fingertips, relentless as soldiers come again and again. But Caelan is stronger. He always has been.

I look back at the incoming wave. Its shadow spills across the earth, drawing even the Residents' attention.

Realization floods Caelan's eyes. He thinks I'm in danger, back on the other side of the hill. He jumps out of view with a pop, even as I try desperately to mentally tell him that I'm *right here*.

The sound is like fireworks. Second Wavers jump out of view, one after the other in quick succession. Many of the Residents do too, but some of them are still searching for the fight, unwilling to retreat. I try to jump, but I can't concentrate. Can't focus.

I run, but it isn't enough. The water crashes against the earth, making the hill shudder beneath me, and the water comes fast and hard.

The last thing I remember is the cold lake slamming against my head, and then the darkness takes me.

29

MY EYES FLUTTER, AND THE BLURRY HAZE IN front of me takes the form of Prince Ettore. I try to scramble backward, only to find myself wriggling in place. Iron restraints keep my wrists bound above me, attached to a taut chain, while my feet dangle several inches above the floor.

Ettore paces around me like a wildcat, black hair an inferno. He wears a crimson tunic covered in draconic scales, with two matching blades at his sides that flicker with molten flames. "You have no idea how delighted I am to see you again."

I grip my fingers around the cuffs, willing them to become dust, and the metal dissipates in a flash. My boots hit the floor with a heavy thud, and I throw my hands toward Ettore and urge Fenix to attack.

But the Prince of War is too fast, and the shadow doesn't even get a chance to leave my arm. He chuckles, flicking a finger that sends my back slamming against the wall. Every one of my limbs is stretched to its limit, and when my muscles strain and the first bone pops, I cry out in agony.

He tuts, but the pressure stills, keeping me frozen in place. "Always in such a hurry. We haven't even had the chance to get reacquainted. So much has changed since you've been away."

I try to lash out, but I can't control any part of my body below my neck.

"The last time I had you in chains, my mother took you away, and we never got to have any fun together," he says, clicking his tongue against the roof of his mouth. "So, forgive the lack of welcome—but I plan on keeping you my little secret for a while longer." His golden eyes flash with menacing delight.

"My sister will come for me, and when she does, she's going to bring the entire Second Wave with her." I shake my head bitterly. "You fought so hard to protect the Red City. Now I'm going to be the reason you watch it burn."

"Oh, I imagine that's the first place the General will look," he says, almost proud. "But sadly, neither of us will be watching anything burn. Because we aren't in War."

Ettore waves a finger, forcing my body to surge toward a window. He tightens his fist, and I stiffen beside him, toes barely scraping the floor.

Outside is a desolated garden. Any vegetation that remains is coated in frost. An expanse of snow stretches across the rolling hills, and in the center of a frozen lake, the remnants of a charred tree remain.

The Wishing Tree that Caelan once showed me. But that means . . .

"We're in Victory," I say, voice hollow.

Ettore lifts his hands in triumph, and I fall back to the stone floor with a heavy thud, shoulder cracking on the granite. I try to stand, but my body is flung against the wall once more, immobilized.

He steps closer, canines on display. "The last time we played, you hid in the tunnels. Called my brother for help." Every word is laced with a poisonous melody, and he practically purrs the rest of his words into my ear. "But I'm very good at learning from my mistakes."

His hold keeps my jaw locked in place, effectively muzzling my bite. "I'm not playing anything with you," I hiss through clamped teeth.

He chuckles darkly. "Want to see how quickly I can change your mind?" He takes a step back like he's admiring his work. "You've both become so predictable. You run, he follows."

I choke on a gasp I can't let out. "You're lying."

Ettore releases me back to the floor, and I struggle to stay on my feet. "Come now. I thought you had more faith in your white-haired prince."

"Caelan doesn't remember me," I try, hoping to call his bluff. "He's working with your mother."

Ettore flashes a wicked grin. "Now who's lying?"

The seconds stretch between us until they start to sear. "Where is he?"

He steps back over the threshold of the damp room. "You

should hurry. Don't let the clock strike twelve." His laughter echoes in the corridor until I can't hear anything at all.

I reach for my sides, searching for weapons that aren't there. The blade Jacek gave me was lost to the tsunami.

Scouring the floor for something I can shift, I find a small pebble. I wave a hand over the edge, creating a small knife. When I press a finger to the tip, it doesn't draw blood. The blade is too dull, but I'm out of practice, and there isn't time to waste perfecting it.

I hiss a curse under my breath and keep hold of it anyway, eyeing the way Fenix is moving around my wrist. As far as I know, Ettore doesn't know she's there. It's a small advantage, but it's better than nothing.

I wave a quick hand over my clothes, shifting my armor into a quilted vest and fur-lined bracers. I add padding around my legs and thicken my boots too. I have no idea where I need to look for Caelan, but I doubt Ettore will have made it easy. It's already freezing in here; it will be worse once I step outside.

I scan the stone corridor for signs of danger, but Ettore's gone. A spiral staircase takes me to the bottom floor, where a thick door has been shoved open, allowing some of the snowfall to fill the front room. It's the only exit, and almost definitely a trap, but I walk through it anyway, hoping there will be more answers outside.

Wide stairs spill into the frozen waste of what was probably once a beautiful garden. My boots crunch over the powdered snow, leaving a trail of footsteps behind me. The only evidence that anyone's walked through here in hours.

I have no doubt Ettore's watching behind a veil of some kind, but I try not to think of where he could be hiding. Because the short answer is *anywhere* and *everywhere*.

Instead, I fixate on the round clock sitting at the top of a marble tower wrapped in blackened ivy.

One hour until twelve.

I shut my eyes, pressing my thoughts out in search of Caelan, but he's still blocking me out. And if he isn't—if he can't respond because Ettore did something to him, the way Ozias once did . . .

My eyes flash open, and I grip the dull knife in my fist.

I hurry across the cobbled path that tunnels through a canopy of dormant trees. Icicles hang from the branches, giving the illusion of a glistening archway. I walk beneath them, scanning for signs of movement, when the floor gives away.

I slip over the stone, sliding into a hole that leads deep underground. My hip slams against the floor, and I roll to a stop, losing my grip on the knife. I reach for it, unable to see in the darkness, and drag my fingers through something wet and spongy. When I shift, the faint light from above reveals a bloodstained shirt.

Or at least, it was. All that's left now are the ragged scraps of something that was cut through, again and again.

A rumble erupts from the other side of the wall. I catch sight of my knife's unpolished hilt and snatch it up quickly before attempting to run back up the sloped stones, but there's too much ice and not enough grip. I barely make it halfway before sliding down again.

Something rattles deep in the room, and I spin, squinting. I hold out my empty hand, willing an orb to appear. Light builds in my palm. When I look back up, the first thing I see is a human face.

I scream, staggering back. Frozen vines spill from a mouth, ears, nostrils. Their body is wrapped tight and held against the wall, pinned in place by the plants growing through the stone crevices. And when they blink, I know the human is aware.

I rush forward and begin sawing at the vines, ripping at the plant like I'm worried this stranger will run out of air. But the awful reality is that they've probably been here for days. Maybe even years.

One of the vines snaps under the dull edge of my blade, but almost immediately another tendril grows from the wall, gripping the human in place even firmer than before.

My heart beats wildly, and the rhythm makes me frantic. *Tick, tock. Tick, tock.* I imagine Ettore's sneer.

I look around the room, following the moving vines, and see dozens more faces. Watching me with watery eyes. Silently begging for help.

I let my knife hover over the next vine, staring into the human's desperate gaze. Ettore's using these people as a distraction. I don't have time to save them *and* make it to Caelan. The way the vines regenerate, I'm not even sure it's possible to help *one* of them.

This is part of his game, I realize. *He's forcing me to abandon them.*

I step back, shaking my head with a silent apology. I can't save everyone. I can't help everyone.

It's the same fear that's been slowly eating away at my soul since the night I died.

"I'll come back as soon as I can," I promise. I don't stay to watch the tears stream or listen to the gurgled panic erupting. If I do, I might never leave.

Light flickers in my palm, keeping the shadows at bay as I run through the tunnel. My breaths are heavy, ricocheting off the walls around me. Something rumbles, and debris scatters to the floor, where the vines begin to tangle at my feet. It's getting harder to wade through, and I can no longer run without stumbling. The vibrations grow louder and louder until the noise is unmistakable.

The pounding of footsteps. Not human, but beast.

There's movement behind me, and I turn quickly, watching as the vines fold over one another until they block off the corridor so I can't retrace my steps.

The walls give a violent shudder, and the glow in my palm pulses in warning. My feet move on instinct, and I hurry into a wide chamber. Light from the surface spills through the cracks, painting the shadowed floor with streaks. The orb fizzles out.

When the ground shakes, I know I'm not alone.

I press my back to the stones.

Fenix shudders along my arm before leaping to the ground in front of me. She lowers her head, eyes fixed on whatever moves in the darkness.

I grip the vines, testing their strength as I study the distance to the crevice in the ceiling. If I can climb high enough, I can—

Fenix snarls as a beast unfurls from the shadows. Its massive paws stomp across the hardened earth, and when the ground shudders, rubble scatters to the floor. An impossibly large

Nightling stands beneath the trickle of light, smoke sharpening like static across its body.

The beast charges, and Fenix headbutts its chest with force. They thrash, wild. Even as my own Nightling grows, she doesn't come anywhere close to the towering shape of the monster before us.

I scramble up the vines, determined to make it to the top. A mess of snarls and snapping teeth echo below, but I keep my eyes pinned to the break of sunlight. When Fenix lets out a sharp yelp, I cast my eyes back down into the cavern and feel my stomach sink. The Nightling looms over Fenix's body, wide jaws pinning her in place.

Anger tears through me, volcanic and so instantaneous that I feel wholly outside my body. I leap from the wall and hit the ground hard. My knees bend as vibrations shudder beneath my feet, and I take off toward them. A shock wave explodes from my palms, sending the larger one stumbling backward.

Fenix shakes her smoke-filled frame and gets back to her feet. She isn't injured. She's not even shaken. She simply stares back at the bigger Nightling like she's calculating something I don't understand.

The monster recovers, storming toward us with a roar. I roll to the side, ducking out of its line of sight as Fenix throws her body over me like a shield. I blink toward the ceiling, willing her to understand my panic.

We need to climb.

Fenix slithers into a wisp of darkness, wrapping herself around my forearm.

I race for the vines, scaling the wall as fast as possible. The Nightling howls below, clawing at the green tendrils with agitation. I don't stop, even as they start to shift and thorns appear along the edges. I wince, fighting the sting when the skin across my palms splits.

There's a loud bang below, and I'm certain the Nightling has hurled itself against the wall. Some of the vines rip away, pulled by the cascade of broken debris. My foot slips, and I clutch one of the thicker branches, clinging to it with my arms as I kick against the air.

Again, the walls shudder. Several large boulders crash to the floor, and pebbles rain down from above me.

The opening in the ceiling isn't far away, but there's no way I can grab the edge from here, even if I jump.

When another attack causes the vines to split from the wall, I let out a shriek, throwing my arm forward to urge Fenix through the opening. She leaps above me, breaking through the ceiling as she batters a hole through the wreckage, large enough to fill the cavern with sunlight.

The vines plummet back down, tearing free, and I have nothing else to hold on to. I reach up, watching the only exit in the room shrink as I fall into the pit.

Fenix dives into the chamber, swooping beneath me. I clutch the fur at her back, tight enough to make my knuckles white, when shadows spill around us.

No—not shadows. *Wings.*

Fenix lets out a snarl and flies skyward, breaking free of the darkness as she arcs through frostbitten air.

The ground explodes. The other Nightling reappears, somehow larger than it was in the cavern, and the earth splinters down the middle. It roars, clawing at the air as Fenix struggles to fly out of its path. We falter midair, and I lose my grip. Our bodies tumble to the snow, and I roll against something firm.

My hand shoots up, bracing against it, when I realize it's an enormous shrub.

We're right outside a hedge maze.

I sit up, searching for the nearest opening. The moment I summon Fenix back to my wrist, I take off into the foliage.

The Nightling snarls, aggravated, but it's charging aimlessly through the towering bushes, going in the opposite direction I am. I duck into another opening, turning so many times that I have no idea if I'm going in circles, when I glance at my wrist and pause.

I want to be wrong. I *hope* that I'm wrong.

Find him, my mind whispers.

Fenix's shadows form a familiar compass, and I trace a finger over the needle, throat going dry. Caelan really is here.

I follow her directions without question. My heartbeat thunders in my ears, and when the compass leads me to where the hedges curve into a circular clearing, my heart stops working altogether.

In the center is a glass cage. Caelan stands in the center, his back turned to me.

I run forward and slam my hands against the barrier. He spins, eyes rounding, and parts his mouth.

"Nami!" he shouts, but the word doesn't reach me.

I press my hands to the glass, watching as he approaches to do the same. There are slices through his clothes where he's been struck by more than one blade. The material along his arm is singed at the shoulder, exposing skin. And directly above his heart is a pool of red blood.

Whatever happened between Famine and his capture, Caelan put up a fight.

I look around for a door or a lock or a crack—some way to get him out.

Caelan's mouth opens wide, tendons straining at his neck. He's screaming. Pounding a fist against the enclosure, trying to tell me something I can't make out.

The image of him seems to grow. A reflection in the glass that slowly morphs into the shape of a Nightling.

I spin to face the creature just as the heat of its growl reaches my cheeks. Fenix swirls frantically at my arm. Caelan barrels his shoulder against the steadfast cage, and the Nightling bares its fangs.

I dive out of the way as it crashes its head against the glass. The structure doesn't budge, but I'm already on my feet again, racing for the far end of the clearing as the Nightling charges. It approaches once more, hackles blazing at its back, when I spot Caelan behind it, screaming my name from inside the glass chamber.

His fear only seems to make the Nightling grow, and I watch, too curious for my own good, as that fear breathes in time with Caelan's heaving shoulders.

Almost as if their fear is linked.

I stiffen. My eyes lock onto the Nightling, searching its glowing depths for something familiar. Caelan grows more frantic in the background. I think he's telling me to run. Mouthing words to get me to leave him behind. But I can't.

I won't.

This Nightling . . . this fear . . .

It's what Caelan created in Victory. The fear he had for *me*.

"You don't want to hurt me," I say to the creature. "You just don't realize it yet." I hold out a hand, taking careful steps as I lift my fingers to the Nightling's bared teeth.

Its fur shudders, erratic, and when it presses forward, I know there's a chance I've misjudged this entire situation.

My fingertips graze its nose.

Darkness sweeps me up in a whirlwind of terror. I feel it. Everything Caelan was worried might happen to me. Even back then, when he played the role of Gil, he cared.

He's always cared.

"I'm on your side," I whisper to the creature as tears prick my eyes. "And I'm not afraid."

The Nightling swirls, scattering dirt and leaves like a vortex around me as the blaze becomes a streak of darkness. It finds my outstretched hand, wrapping around my forearm the way Fenix does on the opposite side, until the shadows settle.

The matching Nightling marks slither toward my fingertips. When I summon them, they build in my hands until they form a matching pair of black daggers.

Two marks. Two weapons to wield.

They settle in my palms, comfortable and familiar all at once. I approach Caelan's cage and swing hard against the glass, watching as the blades slice through the barrier.

The cage shatters into pixelated fragments of light.

Caelan steps out of the remains and grabs my shoulders. "Are you hurt?"

I shake my head. Power thrums in my fists, and shadows flick off the blades. "There are humans trapped underground. We have to get them out."

Caelan thins his mouth, but he doesn't try to change my mind. He nods beside me like it's the only place he wants to be. "There's a hatch beneath the tower. It'll take us through the tunnels."

The surrounding hedges shift to a vibrant orange. Fire sparks across the shrubbery, catching every branch and leaf. I step back, pressing against Caelan's chest as he grips me protectively. The blaze moves like a wave, sweeping over everything until the entire maze is engulfed in flames.

I cough into the crook of my elbow, fighting the inhale of smoke. Caelan lets a blast of energy erupt from his hand. It explodes against the maze, creating a hole to our right, large enough to squeeze through. We run quickly, ducking beneath the flames as we charge through the burning path. Caelan creates another exit, and I swing my blades against the scorched branches, clearing the path back to the snowfields.

We emerge in a rush, gasping for air as our feet stumble over the frozen earth.

There's no relief here. Across the field, Ettore waits with Commander Alys and War's Legion behind them.

Caelan's fists tighten, and he lowers his voice so only I can hear him. "The first chance you get, you need to throw up a veil and run."

"If I can't run with you," I say, and meet his silver eyes, "then I won't run at all."

He holds my stare, long enough for me to catch the adoration that crosses his brow.

Ettore claps his hands slowly across the snow, his silky laughter reaching my ears like a bitter poison. "I was told you knew how to tame the Nightlings, but seeing it in person is another thing entirely." He drops his hands and tilts his head. "When my brother used that human as a puppet, I thought he was making a mockery of our kind. But even puppets have their uses. And you, Nami, would make a *wonderful* puppet indeed. Imagine the terror I could unleash upon the Second Wave if I wore your face."

He looks over his shoulder, giving commands that I can't hear. When he turns back to me, his eyes flare with hunger.

"Do whatever you like with my brother, but I want Nami whole," Ettore snarls.

Commander Alys lets out a battle cry, and the soldiers charge at once. I raise my blades as Caelan prepares to leap into the fold, when a crack of thunder bellows overhead.

Sound vanishes for all the seconds it takes for me to realize what I'm looking at.

The *Mizuchi* flies above us, surrounded by enough warships to take out several cities.

Second Wave guns rattle in the sky, and bullets pelt the earth. Dozens of Legion Guards become dust, vanishing on impact when the Cut rips through them. Commander Alys shifts her attention to the sky, ordering soldiers to take out the guns. Winged guards tear through the air, fighting against the onslaught that turns them to mist.

I shift my face toward Caelan. He pulls back the torn material at his shoulder, showing me what's hidden underneath.

A veilstone. He must've grabbed it from the battlefield in Famine.

"You knew they'd track you," I say, eyes wide.

"If I couldn't save you, I knew your sister would," he admits, tossing the veilstone to the snow.

"But—the Residents—" I start. "They'll be Cut down. Mei won't leave survivors."

He shakes his head, serious. "It was never Ettore's Legion I was trying to protect. Asphodel is what matters to me." His eyes soften. "And you."

I take a step toward him, the urgency making my words shake. "If those bullets hit you—"

"I knew the risk," he insists.

One of the warships swoops low, and dozens of humans leap to the powdered snow. They don't wear Second Wave uniforms—they wear armor from Neo Genesis.

My skin crawls as I watch Ozias land on the hill. Sharpened bones flare across his chest plate, his face partially covered by a helm of antlers. His loyalists are right behind him, swinging swords and daggers as they tear through the Residents with ease.

I spot Zahrah charging across the field, headed straight for Commander Alys, who is too busy shouting orders to the Legion to notice she's been marked. Zahrah swings her battle-ax in the air, leaping with ferocity. Alys turns just in time, raising a sword to block the attack.

They become a blur of metal and ice, sweeping across the landscape as they fight to draw blood.

Bullets explode into the ground, blasting slush through the air. I shove Caelan to the side, urging him to get out of the way. We're racing through the snow, side by side, when Ettore slams into the earth in front of us, snarling with venom.

He holds his twin swords in his fists. The edges glow with embers until they spark, turning to powerful flames. He points both blades at the two of us, flashing his teeth, but his eyes are pinned solely on Caelan. "You'd betray your kind to the Second Wave for *her*?"

Caelan's hands blaze with lightning. "I'd burn the world for her."

"For what purpose?" Ettore barks, frustration turning his face red. "You'd destroy *everything we've built* over one single human?"

"Yes," Caelan says icily. "Because this world is already broken—and Nami is the only one I trust to rebuild it."

"She will never protect the First Folk," Ettore spits. He points to the battlefield, anger lashing his every word. "*That* is what will become of Asphodel. That is what burning the world will bring to our kind."

"You care nothing for Asphodel," Caelan growls back.

"Perhaps not," Ettore admits. "But my army was the last protection they had for when the city's veil falls. And it will. Without my Legion to distract them, the humans will direct every second of their time to finding our Capital, and those who live there.

You've all but signed their deaths to paper. I may not care about the First Folk, but I do care about winning." His golden eyes sharpen. "I'll settle for taking Nami from you, one last time."

One moment he's standing several yards away, and the next he jumps—and his fiery blade plunges just below my sternum.

"Nami!" Caelan yells, blasting Ettore's shoulder with a bolt of energy.

Ettore is thrown to the side, but he manages to catch his footing, staying upright with one of his blades still clutched in his fist. The other sears my flesh, still lodged inside me.

Caelan grips the handle, and I nod once, begging him to be quick. He pulls the sword out and I howl, agony exploding across every nerve. I fall to my knees, using the Nightling blades to hold me up as I quake with pain.

Caelan moves just as Ettore does, and the flaming swords collide against one another, as embers spark around them. I concentrate on my wound, urging it to heal quickly, but I barely take the edge off. Still, I force myself to stand and grip my daggers in my fists.

I swing one of the knives toward Ettore, distracting him long enough for Caelan to strike. Even as blood sprays from his back, Ettore barely flinches. He spins, crashing his blade against mine, teleporting from one place to the next without warning. Caelan and I fight back-to-back, staving off his attacks as they grow more and more frenzied.

Ettore brings his pommel down on Caelan's temple, painting the snow with flecks of crimson. He reaches behind him for something I can't see before lifting a flattened palm, blowing a shimmer of dust just as Caelan inhales.

The next time Ettore jumps in front of me, I send Fenix forward, letting her shift from blade to beast as she thrashes at Ettore's face, marking him with her claws. The Prince of War hisses, but the rage only fuels him on. I turn to look at Caelan and realize too late what Ettore has done.

Caelan drops his weapon, clutching his head like he's in torment. It makes the blade in my hand shudder violently, before the second Nightling rips free, snarling at the wind as it charges through the battlefield, growing alongside Caelan's fears.

Nightling blood in powdered form.

It's what Ettore once used on me.

I grab Caelan's shoulders, pressing my mouth to his ear, hoping he can hear me over his own screams. "Whatever you're seeing, it's not real!"

Ettore moves fast, swinging both blades toward me as I leap out of the way. I crawl through the snow, desperately trying to get back on my feet, but he's in front of me again, slashing at me with hatred in his eyes. I duck, hurrying to put space between us. I try to jump, but I barely make it several yards before my body shudders from inexperience, and I fall back to my knees.

I look up, watching Ettore's flames grow wilder. He sneers, eyes full of violence, when I hear my name being yelled through the wind.

I don't waste time searching for the voice—I already know it belongs to Mei.

I keep my eyes pinned on Ettore so he knows that I'm not afraid of him. That fear is a battle I've learned to *win*—and he will never hold that power over me again.

Something pierces the snow beside me, and a flicker of metal catches the corner of my eye.

A sword.

Ettore charges—I grab the hilt on instinct, shoving it forward just as he reaches me, and the blade sinks through his tunic. He freezes, face crumpling, and blinks.

The gold shrivels from his eyes. His skin grays—wrinkles—and when his limp body falls to the snow, jaw slack and a vacant expression over his face, he looks as lifeless as a corpse.

I stare down at the unnatural curve of Ettore's body, and my head throbs with confusion. This wasn't the Cut. If it had been, he would've turned to mist before his consciousness was summoned toward a human cage on one of the ships.

But he's . . .

Someone screams to my right, drawing my attention. I watch Zahrah raise her ax and swing hard against Commander Alys's neck, severing her head in one violent sweep. Blood pools over the hill, and Alys's body tumbles through the snow, unmoving.

When my eyes scan the snowy field, I see Ozias beaming among his army as they Cut down Resident after Resident. And I realize the Residents aren't fighting—they're trying to *flee*.

They know the rules have changed.

I look down at the blade in my hand, horror overwhelming my senses, when I spot two words etched in the steel.

The Messenger.

I—I think . . .

I think I've just killed . . .

I look up, remembering Caelan, when someone latches a

hand around my upper arm and tugs me backward. I slam into Mei, our eyes nearly identical with panicked fury.

She's holding a rifle, finger resting firmly on the trigger.

When her attention drifts toward Caelan's suffering frame, anger floods my vision.

She's going to hurt him, my mind screeches. *She's going to finish the job she sent Jacek to do.*

I don't let her speak. I fling her arm away and hurry to Caelan's side, throwing my body over him like a shield as bullets rain down from the warships.

Mei's heavy footsteps approach through the snow, and it makes me clutch Caelan even harder. Powder explodes around us, and I scream, summoning both Nightlings back. They move like ribbons, wrapping their smoke-fueled essence around us with sharp, hurried movements, until the darkness becomes our shield.

The poison ebbing its way through Caelan's blood seems to shift, bleeding back out into the world to join the storm of Nightlings surrounding us.

The static thrums, and I press my forehead to Caelan's. "We have to get out of here. It's not safe."

He grabs my arms, blinking away the last of the Nightling blood, and leans forward so I can hear him over the uproar. "You need to get to your sister's ship."

"None of that matters now," I say, eyes watering. I lift the sword that's shaking in my fist. "I—I think I just killed your brother."

Caelan pales. But he doesn't turn from me. Not even with the key to his eradication inches from his heart.

He takes my other hand and brushes his thumb over my

knuckles. Soothing me even though I'm certain I don't deserve it.

My voice cracks. "I can't let them do the same to you." I thread my fingers through Caelan's. "I tried jumping before, but I'm not very good at it. I know you're hurt, but—"

He nods. "I can get us out of here."

I don't let go of his hand. Our eyes lock in place, and I start to summon Fenix and the other Nightling back to my arms. Shadows flame around us before winding back around my skin. The moment they return, Caelan's eyes flash.

The last thing I hear before we jump out of Victory's blood-stained field is my sister's scream.

30

CAELAN LEANS HIS HEAD AGAINST A MOSS-covered stone wall, forehead glistening from the jungle's humidity. There are still imprints of the poison in his system, but he managed an entire hour of hiking before I insisted we stop.

Even now, the strain behind his eyes is brutal. He needs the break.

I flick away one of the enormous monstera leaves that acts as a shelter above us, ducking low to sit beside him. "I'm sorry."

He doesn't ask what for. He can see my guilt written all over my face. *I'm sorry you were poisoned trying to save me. I'm sorry my sister created a weapon to murder your people. I'm sorry I used it to kill your brother. I'm sorry I never got the chance to convince her to choose peace. I'm sorry, I'm sorry, I'm sorry . . .*

Caelan's voice is gentle. "None of this is your fault."

I swallow the lump in my throat. "Of course it is. I took a life, the same way someone once did to me."

"It wasn't the same."

I shake my head. That's how everyone keeps justifying war. *It's not the same. I had no choice. It's what the other side deserved.* That's how the line gets blurred. When you keep moving it, eventually you lose sight of it altogether.

"You didn't owe Ettore anything. Not guilt, and not mercy."

"This doesn't end with Ettore. Ozias will go after Ophelia next. If he finds Asphodel, he'll—" I flatten my mouth, feeling the dig of the sword's hilt at my hip. A curse slips out of me, eyes widening. I snatch the Messenger, clutching it by the handle. "I forgot—the Second Wave puts trackers in everything."

He winces, trying to straighten his spine. "Leave it here. I'll jump us to the next border."

I make a face. There's no way he has the energy. A jump from one place to another is already a task, but across an entire landscape? Even the jumpers back in Genesis had to work together—and a single jump across the desert would wipe the entire team out.

What Caelan did to get us out of Victory will need recovery time we don't have.

And I don't want to leave a weapon like this anywhere it can be found.

I shake my head. "I'd rather we had it than the Second Wave."

"Then let me hold on to it. I've veiled my mind from my mother for a century. I can veil this from your sister's army."

I tighten my fist. "I don't know what will happen if you touch it."

He studies the sword's shape. When he waves a hand across the blade, he creates a protective sheath. White leather with silver threads. He places a hand over the material, tucking his fingers around the casing. After a nervous pause, I let him take it.

I count the seconds until he relaxes, shoulders sagging.

"Ozias has weapons like this too," I admit, solemn. "One of his soldiers used one on Commander Alys."

Caelan's expression turns brittle. "We dangled the idea of the Orb in front of the Colony for years. It was only a matter of time before humans tried to make one of their own." He looks up at me, serious. "War is coming to our doorstep. The First Folk won't survive without protection, and if the Legacies are wiped out . . ."

I bite the edge of my lip, sensing the words he's yet to say. "You aren't going to wait for a peace treaty."

"It might be too late for that. If my mother finds out a weapon like this exists, she'll never let the First Folk go. Their best option might be to flee now, in secret, before she discovers the truth."

I swallow thickly and stare at our clasped hands. "What about the Legacies?" *What about you?*

He shakes his head. Because even if we manage to get everyone out of the city, Caelan can't leave. He'll be stuck here, destined for the same fate as Ophelia. And when the humans find her and use their weapons . . .

I rock my jaw, refusing to believe that's the only option. "I've seen inside her mind. I've seen the threads that connect her to the living world. There must be threads that connect her to you, too. We just—we need to reach Ophelia before the others do. We can still tell her about Famine."

Caelan tucks a strand of hair behind my ear, making my breath hitch. "What happens if she refuses? What happens if we lose our chance to get the First Folk out safely, all because I'm selfishly hoping for a way I can go too?"

"If anyone is being selfish, it's me. I don't want to lose you."

He's quiet for a moment, eyes tracing the outlines of my face. "If I speak to my mother, and it doesn't go well . . ." His gaze falls to the sword between us. "Nami, I know you'd do anything to protect your friends. But will you do anything to protect mine?"

I blink, not entirely sure what he's asking me.

His jaw tenses. "I need you to get the First Folk to the Afterlands if I'm no longer here to do it myself."

My eyes cloud. I don't want to think about it. I don't want to *imagine* it.

"Please," he whispers, so earnest it makes a tear trickle down my cheek. He presses his forehead to mine. "Your hope is my strength. It has been for over a century. If you tell me you'll protect my people, then I won't need to worry. I'll do what I have to."

"What are you saying?"

His throat rolls, and he grips the Messenger hard enough to make his knuckles pale. "My mother has been my cage—I will not let her be theirs. I can distract her. Long enough to give you time to lead the others across the border."

I place a finger beneath his chin, willing him to meet my gaze. When he does, my voice cracks. "I swear to you, I will do everything in my power to protect them. But I will not agree to letting you sacrifice your freedom. Do you understand me? We'll find another way."

"But if the worst happens—"

"No," I growl, grabbing his face with both hands. I want him to stop talking about this. I want him to stop telling me how bad the odds are. I want him to *live*.

My eyes drop to his lips.

"Nami," he says, voice dripping like caramel. "Are you about to kiss me just to get me to stop talking?"

I blink, cheeks flushing. "I—that's not—"

He shakes his head, brow softening. "I don't ever want you to kiss me out of pity, or desperation." His gaze drifts to my mouth. "You kissed Gil because you wanted him. If there's ever a day you kiss me again, I want to know it's because you want *me*." He pauses, eyes flaring with warmth. "The real me."

I forget to breathe.

I think maybe he does too.

"Say you'll look after them," he whispers.

"I'll make sure the First Folk are safe," I answer, even as my chest constricts. "No matter what happens."

The brush of his nose is feather light against mine. I'm caught in the moment, mind floating in another universe, and I move—

A twig snaps beneath my weight, the sound pulling us from our trance.

I rub my collarbone, and Caelan leans back to put more space between us.

He reaches for the Messenger and waves a hand across the scabbard, creating a strip of leather and buckle to loop over his shoulder. The moment the weapon is sheathed at his back, it disappears beneath a veil.

He tilts his head, studying me. "How's your wound?"

I glance down, cradling my stomach on instinct. "Oh. It's fine. Mostly healed." I pull my hands back, threading a finger through the ripped fabric. I wave a hand across it, repairing the material.

Caelan offers a weak smile. "I remember how frustrated you used to get having to make dresses for Victory's lavish parties. Look at you now."

"That shouldn't make me nostalgic, but it does." When he quirks a brow, I shrug. "Nobody ever tried to stab me in a ballroom."

"No," he agrees, voice hardened with regret. "I just tricked you into forming an attachment to me."

I look up at him, serious. "Was it because of Finn?" He falls silent, but doesn't look away. "I remember when I first arrived in the Colony, Yeong and Gil searched my memories to make sure I was human. And—and I know you saw things about Finn, from before I died." I swallow the knot in my throat. "It occurred to me later on that you knew I was dealing with the loss of my first real crush. That maybe that's what you were using against me. Because you saw my feelings for Finn as a weakness."

His body goes still. "Will you hate me if I say the answer is yes?"

"I don't hate anyone," I say quietly, eyes dropping to my knees as my heart tightens. "But especially not you."

"Nami." He waits for me to look up. "Do you think you could ever forgive me?"

My fingers twitch. "To be honest, I think I forgave you when you saved me in the caves. And if I hadn't then, I would've forgiven you when I saw you in Asphodel, and again in Famine. I would've forgiven you when you came for me in Victory, and when you stood by my side even when you were facing the Second Wave. Maybe I didn't always know who you were . . . but I think I've always known your heart."

His dimple appears. "I'm sorry for ever making you doubt me."

"You're not the only one who wore a mask," I say quietly. "I'm sorry too."

He lets out a slow breath, eyes darting to the sway of leaves above us. "We should probably keep moving. If the Second Wave was tracking the blade, it won't be long before they get here."

When I stand, Caelan does the same, dusting bits of moss from his shirt. When he takes my hand, clutching it like he just wants some part of us touching, I clutch him back and don't let go.

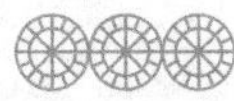

I lose track of how many landscapes we cross. The forests and grasslands and deserts feel stitched together somehow, like they're all a part of a monumental task that's just out of reach.

Caelan jumps us with more frequency as he gains his strength back, but there's so much ground to cover. The layers of the Labyrinth feel as if they're expanding as we walk, trying to trick us into going in a different direction, away from Asphodel.

There's no sign of the Second Wave trailing after us, but it doesn't ease the worry in my gut.

When the pale mountain range appears in the distance, I almost sigh with relief.

"Not that way." Caelan motions for the sparse woodland on the outskirts.

I follow him across a bed of pine needles tucked in the trees, where a mess of jagged rocks protrudes from the earth. Caelan places his hands on the stones, pressing against them in an order I can't follow. He steps back just as the earth gives a low shudder, splitting apart to reveal a hatch.

He climbs inside, and I follow after him, lowering myself underground as the surface folds together and seals us into darkness. I'm nearly to the bottom rung when I feel his hands on my waist, guiding me to the floor.

I twist to face him, chasing the shadows of his face and the faint glow at the tips of his hair. My eyes fall beyond his shoulder, where glowing orbs light up a narrow tunnel. He quirks his mouth slightly, tilting his head in the only direction left for us to wander.

"There are few secrets I've been able to keep from my mother over the years. This is one of them." He threads his fingers through mine and gently tugs me into the light.

We walk hand in hand for what feels like an eternity. I can hear my own heartbeat like a stampede in my ears. The more Caelan senses my nerves, the firmer his grip becomes. I don't think he realizes I'm jittery *because* of his touch—but I don't say anything. If I do, he might stop.

I don't want him to stop.

An iron door appears at the end of the hall. Caelan places his outstretched hand across the surface. He whispers something barely audible, using words I don't recognize. A lock disengages, and the door parts slightly.

I frown. "I thought there were no other languages in Infinity?"

"That's true for most of us," he says. "Our consciousnesses speak to one another. But it's possible to create new dialects that have to be taught. Something that requires time to be understood."

"You mean like a code?"

He nods. "It was used by the earliest First Folk, and passed down through some of the families. Most Legacies don't even know it exists. Back then, when First Folk had no power at all, it was how they were able to organize their own councils in secret."

"What was it you just whispered?"

"N'raak sun tahl nos kovenna." His breath stills. "It means 'Stars are for the dreamers.'" The words light his eyes with hope, but there's sadness hidden there too. Tucked in the corners where he thinks I won't notice.

It's almost too much for me to bear.

With my fingers still woven through his, I step closer. "You'll see the stars one day, and dream beneath them, just like you always wanted."

He lifts his other hand, tracing a finger along my jaw. "I didn't know wanting could make me so afraid."

The Nightlings swirl across my skin, moving like a caress.

I clutch his hand, squeezing it between our hearts. "We're going to figure this out."

His silver eyes flicker like they're made of glass. "I used to dream in Gil's body," he confesses. "But after that night in the throne room, when I told you to follow the stars . . . I started to dream all on my own." His voice is gravelly. "It shouldn't be possible. For every other Legacy in Infinity, it isn't. At first, you haunted my nightmares. I worried about you every day, hated that I let you go. I hoped you'd made it to safety, and selfishly wished you'd come back. Eventually, those nightmares became everything to me—because they were the only way I could be close to you again.

"You don't haunt me anymore. But you're still the reason I dream. And sometimes when I let myself imagine a future where the two of us exist, side by side, with no fear at all . . ." His brow knots. "The real nightmare is waking up. Realizing I had you, only to lose you." He swallows, voice deepening to a heavy rasp. "It's been breaking me apart for a century."

My eyes dart between his, hearts still pounding in sync with one another. "Caelan," I say seriously. "I'm going to kiss you." His hands tense, but I'm not finished. "Not because you keep talking to me like you're running out of time. Not because of what happened when I thought you were Gil. And not because I've wanted to kiss you from the moment you found me in those caves. I'm going to kiss you because you are not a nightmare to me. The opposite, in fact. And I think *not* kissing you after all this time might break *me*." I pause, taking in a sharp breath. "Is that okay?"

Caelan doesn't blink. Doesn't move. I watch his face shift from surprise, to disbelief, and then—

Whatever resolve he was hanging on to snaps.

His hands slide up my neck, fingers curling through my hair, and he presses his mouth against mine with so much hunger that it makes me gasp. The moment my lips part, his do the same, and he tastes like winter and woodland, the way I've always known him.

I wrap my arms around his back, pulling him closer. He twists my body slightly, and suddenly I'm walking backward over the threshold, barely comprehending the click as Caelan shoves the door closed with his foot. His lips never leave mine. If I was worried kissing him would remind me too much of Gil, I was wrong.

Kissing Caelan is wildly different. He isn't wearing a mask, or holding back, or hiding a part of himself he doesn't want me to see.

Right now, in this moment, he's free.

Our movements aren't tender or sweet or something to be careful about. They're ravenous and desperate, and full of pent-up longing.

The pop of nearby embers makes me jump, and I clutch his shirt. The rumble of his laugh vibrates against my forehead. I sink into the feeling, trusting that wherever we are, we must be safe.

I look around the room. Chunky wooden pillars hold up the ceiling, and the cobbled walls are covered in sandstone. The open fireplace houses a few logs that sprout unyielding flames. A rising set of stairs leads to a dark green door, and the only furniture in the room are two wide couches, a table and bench, and a tiny kitchenette.

"What is this place?" I ask, feeling the rise of his chest beneath my hands.

"A basement below the barracks," he answers. "First Folk soldiers only train among their own, so the Legacies stay away from this place. And the only ones who know about this room are the people I trust."

"What makes it such a secret?"

"It's one of the few paths in and out of Asphodel that my mother isn't aware of." His fingers trail along my back. When he lifts his chin, I follow his gaze to the dangling lanterns above the table.

"Can you feel her right now?"

He nods. "I told you. She's relentless."

I meet his eyes. "If it's not safe . . . if we need to keep our distance . . ."

"It doesn't matter," he says, so delicate that I fold into him and tuck my hands at his back. "I've veiled myself from her for a hundred years, but I've waited even longer for you to come back to me."

I smile against his mouth. "Future Caelan's problem?"

He nods, stealing a soft kiss. "Future Caelan will have no regrets. I promise."

Our lips collide, again and again, and our bodies are spinning around the room in reckless circles until we collapse onto one of the couches. Caelan rolls on top of me, lips parting against my own, and it's as if the rest of the world disappears. It's just the two of us, existing in the rippling firelight sharing not just secrets, but truths, too.

We are tangled limbs and fingers, hands finding clothes and hair and skin. He whispers my name against my ear, sending chills across every inch of me. And then his lips are on my neck, and I whisper his name back.

We tumble over the cushions, trading kisses in our hidden shelter, and it doesn't matter that we can't see the sky.

In the darkness, we become starlight.

31

I'M TUCKED CLOSE TO CAELAN, FEELING THE rise and fall of his chest. We stayed down here longer than we probably should have. Neither of us felt the need to rush away.

Even if we are on borrowed time.

Caelan trails his fingers over my shoulder and neck before slowing to a stop. There's an apology in his gaze. He's beautiful in all his forms, but especially like this. When it's me and him with our hearts on our sleeves and nothing left to hide. "I think it's time," he says.

I shut my eyes. "I know."

"I don't want it to be."

"I know that, too."

Caelan sighs against my forehead, arms wrapped around me. I hear the smile in his voice. "When this is all over, do you think you'll find the afterlife boring?"

"That's what I'm looking forward to," I admit. "Boredom sounds like a luxury."

His words tickle my hair. "I'm trying to picture you sitting still. No longer trying to right the world. No longer searching for someone who needs saving."

"I suppose I could take up a new hobby. Maybe houseplants. Or knitting." I peer up at him. "Has anyone tried to make video games in the afterlife? I'm a sucker for a good farming sim."

He laughs, and I curl in closer.

"What about you?" I ask. "Will you feel lost without a court to look after?"

"Not even a little bit. Besides, how could I ever feel lost," he breathes against my temple, "when I know you'll always find me?"

I kiss him once.

He kisses me twice.

I push off the couch to find the rest of my clothes, grinning when Caelan fights to not let my hand slip from his. I get dressed quickly, swiping a hand over the fur-lined garments so they morph into a black sweater, gray pants, and boots. When I adjust the material at my shoulder, something comes loose from the fabric and clatters to the floor.

A tiny piece of metal glints back up at me. Frowning, I pick it up and hold it toward the light.

"What is that?" Caelan asks, rolling onto his side. His hair is ruffled in the best way, but there's an edge of concern in his brow.

"Shrapnel, I think." I turn the object between my fingers. It's less than half the size of a button. "It was stuck to my shirt."

He's standing in an instant. "You were shot?"

I feel a phantom bruise along my shoulder. "I don't remember. Maybe it happened in Famine—but it's healed now." I slide the object into a pocket and grab Caelan's shirt off the floor. I toss it to him, and he grunts when it hits his chest. "Seriously, I'm fine. Stop worrying."

He pauses before tugging the material over his head. "It's no wonder the Nightlings respond to you the way they do. You're very good at being brave."

I wince. "You're kidding, right? I'm terrified. In fact, I'm rarely *not* terrified. It's like a default setting at this point."

He tucks his arms into his white jacket, leaving the buttons undone. "And yet you overcome your fears, again and again, in order to do the right thing. I believe that's the very definition of bravery."

I shake my head, watching as he straightens his collar. "You're giving me way too much credit."

He drops his hands. "You don't think you deserve it?"

"I know I don't," I say, voice beginning to tremble. "We had an alliance with Famine. We were *so close* to changing things. And then, that weapon . . ." I avoid his eyes.

He draws me back the way he always does. The north point on a compass that has never let me down. "We aren't giving up, remember? Not yet."

My vision clouds. "What if I end up being the reason you can't be free?"

He doesn't answer. Not right away. "If the path to freedom is truly so fragile, then perhaps it would never have lasted anyway." He reaches for the side of my neck and brushes his thumb over my pulse. "My soul is bound to yours. It always will be. And that is a gift, Nami. A far greater one than you can imagine."

I fold my fingers over his because I want him to know what I feel—what I've been feeling for longer than I wanted to admit. The good, the bad, the fear, the anger. I want him to see everything that scares me, and everything that gives me hope.

I want him to know how I really, truly see *him*.

He looks at our hands, knowing what I'm asking. Knowing he'll have to venture outside the barricade he's built in order to meet me in my own.

Caelan's caress finds me at the edge of my mind, and I feel the cautious steps he takes as he meets me inside. The familiarity floods through me, waking every nerve. My eyes sting at the memory of the last time we spoke like this, when he was strapped to a chair in Genesis.

I feel him flinch, but I don't push the thought away. Because for all the horror that the memory has, it has tenderness, too. I was scared for him. I wanted to comfort him. I wished I could hold his hand so he wouldn't feel alone.

But he's here now, in my mind—so I show him my entire heart.

The last words I said to my family. The secrets I kept from the Colony. The masks I've worn, and the lies I've told. The anger I found in the Borderlands that I carried all the way to War. All the people I tried to save but couldn't. All the people who didn't want to be saved at all.

I show him how my feelings for him began with Gil but became so much more. The surprise that he'd been hiding so much of his heart, and the relief that it was everything I hoped it could be. I show him every glance, every caught breath, every ping in my chest when I searched his face and found that my enemy had slowly become my friend.

And now . . .

I show him exactly the way my heart beats when he touches me.

The way a fire erupts in my core when his lips find my skin.

The way every dream I have of the future has Caelan right beside me.

I show him that I will not accept an afterlife without him in it. And it doesn't matter what he thinks he might have to sacrifice—I will never give him up.

I will find a way to give him the hope he's given me.

His lashes flutter as he takes everything in. I don't know how many minutes pass as we stand beneath the lanterns, sharing emotions that are too big for words. Eventually, I feel him slip away, retreating behind the walls of his own mind.

He doesn't hesitate before wrapping his arms around me and pulling me into a hug. I rest my head against the crook of his neck, breathing in the warmth of him.

"When this is all over, and you're still carrying your guilt like a wound that won't heal, I want you to remember the forgiveness you've given to everyone around you. And I want you to forgive yourself." He pulls his face back so he can look at me. "Promise me you'll let it all go. That you'll let your heart find the peace it deserves."

I lift my chin. "You're making a lot of demands tonight."

"Yes. For good reason." His eyes drop to my mouth. "Do you promise?"

"Only if you promise that whatever happens next, we do it together."

He leans in, lips teasing mine.

"I'm still waiting on an answer," I point out.

"So am I."

I lean back slightly, eyes softening in defeat. "Fine. I promise."

He kisses me deeply, making my spine curve against his hands. When he eventually pulls away, he takes a breath through his nose and slowly lets it out again. "I promise," he starts, eyes locked to mine, "that I will do everything in my power to stay at your side. And if I'm left behind when the First Folk are gone, and the only option is to fight to the death or hide in some long-forgotten cave—then I'll hide for an eternity, if it means finding a way to stay in Infinity with you."

I twist my mouth, unsure what to say, when the door at the top of the stairs bursts open. I tighten my fists, feeling the Nightlings swirling into daggers, when I spot Lieutenant Elias.

He lifts a bushy, golden eyebrow, looking between me and Caelan. To where his hand is still firmly gripping my waist. When his gaze drifts lower, he spots the Nightling smoke receding back up my arms. "You really have a thing for picking up strays. How many is that now?"

"Two," I say. "And it turns out they can fly."

He doesn't fight his smirk. "I'd ask for a demonstration, but the last one scared the Mother out of me. So I'll take your word for it."

"Speaking of mothers . . ." Caelan straightens. "We need to visit the queen's temple."

There's a long pause, and Elias's expression softens into something fragile. Hopeful. "Does this mean . . . ?" His words are strained. "Did the Second Wave agree to a treaty?"

Caelan's face pinches. "There's been a change of plans."

I open my mouth to apologize when he turns sharply, the silver in his eyes sparkling like ice. A rush of comfort curls through my mind, subduing the guilt.

I rub my collarbone. "I didn't get the chance to speak with my sister," I tell Elias instead. "But she has a weapon—one that can kill a Legacy."

Caelan's jaw ticks. "I need you to gather the First Folk council and quietly get our people underground. Because if my mother refuses to let us go, then this might be our only chance to get you to the border before Asphodel closes itself off for good."

"But if the queen doesn't give her permission—" Elias starts.

"You don't need it. None of you do," Caelan admits. "The First Folk have always had the ability to cross the border. I just didn't know it until recently."

Elias doesn't blink. Not while he studies his prince, absorbing the truth. "Rounding up our people will cause chaos," he says at last. "What should I tell them?"

"The truth," Caelan says. "Tell them if everything goes well, the Legacies will join them in the Afterlands." His eyes find mine. "And if not, Nami will find you in the tunnels. She'll get you out if I can't."

Something awful twists in my gut, and Fenix stutters across my inner forearm. I lean toward Caelan, aching to be closer. Fearing that our time together is running out.

He reaches for me, mouth parted like he's about to offer words of reassurance, when thunder explodes somewhere high above us.

I stiffen, staring at the ceiling. "What was that?"

Elias takes off through the door, hand wrapped around the hilt of his weapon.

Caelan doesn't tell me to stay put or hide in the darkness. He takes my hand and presses one last frantic kiss to my knuckles. "I'll have to keep you under a veil. I'd trust yours anywhere else, but not in Asphodel."

I nod, embracing the warmth of his mind as he envelops my own, and then I run after him up the stairs. A long corridor takes us to another staircase, and we emerge from a false wall hidden at the back of a storeroom. Wooden crates litter the floor, filled with dark glass bottles. Some of the shelves are covered with thick dust sheets, hiding hammered metal containers that don't appear to have been opened in years.

We slip through the door and into a cobbled hallway, rushing up another set of stairs. A communal dining area stretches across the stone floor, with empty chairs and well-worn tables. Copper pans hang from a ceiling rack where a deep blue kitchen is recessed in the corner.

I don't need to ask where everyone is. The moment we step through the next door and find ourselves at the edge of a private garden, I realize anyone who'd been inside the barracks is now standing at the edge of the grounds, staring at the sky in alarm.

High above the domed shield, a fleet of airships pops into view. The noise reverberates across the city as the metallic transports appear to multiply, piercing my ears like a violent chant. It doesn't stop—not until every cloud above us darkens with their shadows.

The human militia is here.

32

LEGION GUARDS JUMP INTO VIEW, METALLIC wings splayed as they move for the shield's curve. Some of the First Folk soldiers shove past the gates, disappearing into the crowd to search for answers.

In the sky, the fleet remains frozen in place.

But—I don't understand.

Why aren't they attacking?

Elias scowls at the dozens of slumbering cannons high above us. "There's no way the humans can breach our shields. They can't even see past our veil."

"Yet somehow, they still found us." Caelan shakes his head. "They have intel on our location—*how* they got it doesn't matter." He grips Elias by the shoulders. "We stick to the plan. Understood?"

Nine arrives with a group of soldiers behind her. Elias shouts an order to the guards, and they circle him, gauntlets blazing with flames and electricity.

Caelan ushers me backward, lips parted in worry. He lifts his hands to my face, studying me like he's trying to memorize every freckle, every line. Like I'm something precious he knows he can't keep. "I don't know what will happen to the shields if the humans use their new weapon on it."

I look up at the sky that flickers with danger. Fenix and the other Nightling move across my skin. The anger and uninhibited terror, aching to be set free. To take control.

Instead, they wait—just like the humans.

"They haven't attacked yet," I say, thoughts moving at lightspeed. "Maybe there's a reason."

Caelan follows my gaze to the cloudscape and frowns. "Your sister's ship is here."

A battle of warring emotions ricochets through my chest, and I blink too many times, fighting the wave of nausea threatening to surface.

Jacek will have told her about our meeting by now. About the alliance, and the treaty, and the humans and Residents living side by side. Which means Mei knew *everything*, and the Second Wave still came to Asphodel.

I look up, face scrunched.

Mei would never knowingly hurt an innocent child. She isn't evil. She isn't Ozias. And if she's holding back now . . . it's because she trusts me.

Because the truth was finally enough to change her mind.

Caelan looks at me like he heard everything. Like he's in my mind, even now. "You think she's here for peace?"

Warmth balloons in my chest. "I do."

Caelan's eyes turn glassy. With fear—and the possibility that we might have a *chance*.

I motion toward the queen's temple, high in the sky above Winterborne. "If Ophelia sees Mei isn't attacking, it could be leverage. We can still fix this." *There's still time for her to break your chains.*

Caelan eyes the tremble in my shoulders. "I don't know how she'll react when she sees you. Perhaps it would be better if you spoke to your sister while I faced my mother alone."

"We can't split up. I won't be able to get back inside Asphodel without you, and if something goes wrong . . ." I grip him tight. "I'll stay under a veil if I have to. It doesn't matter, as long as I'm with you. Just as I was a century ago, and just as I will be a century from now."

He tilts his head, teeth clamped together like he's biting down on an objection.

"This is my choice," I say, firm.

Eventually, his eyes drift toward the white sphere in the sky. "We'll need a transport to get to her temple. Because if we jump, I might not be able to hold the veil."

We hurry across the yard, moving for the clearing at the edge of the barracks, where several small ships are waiting. Caelan climbs into the first one, and I tuck into the seat beside him. He sets the controls, and within moments, we're making the ascent toward the clouds.

The temple glints in the sunlight, and I watch the reflection of our ship grow larger as we approach. A panel shifts, creating an opening for us to pass through. Moments later, we land in a small hangar bay, and the engine settles into a quiet, unmoving slumber.

Caelan's voice is thick with anguish. "If I don't get the chance to say it later—"

"Don't," I interrupt fiercely. "We aren't doing that. Saying goodbye without saying goodbye."

His face softens. "Nami."

"No." I tear myself from the seat and move for the exit, pausing in front of the metal door while my nails cut crescents in my palms. Fenix curls a tendril around my wrist, tightening like she wants to ease my anxiety.

I stare at our distorted reflections in the metal. Caelan moves behind me like he has shadows of his own to spare, but I don't want his comfort. I want him *safe*.

His fingers tug at my elbow, spinning me around to face him. "I don't want you caught up in the ashes of a doomed world just because you don't want to leave me behind. So if anything goes wrong, take this transport back to the surface and find Elias. He'll help you—he knows what you mean to me."

I stare at him without blinking. "I don't abandon the people I care about. Not ever."

"Would you believe it's one of the things I love most about you—and the one I find most infuriating?"

The words burrow deep in my chest. Or maybe more specifically, *one* of his words.

Because . . . he just said . . .

Caelan waves a hand beside the door to lower the ramp, and my focus snaps back into place.

Glass stretches around the room, giving us a glimpse into a celestial void. We walk in sync across the smooth surface. My footsteps are masked beneath his veil, tucked somewhere I hope Ophelia can't find.

When we reach the enormous double doors, they sense our approach and begin to part.

I follow Caelan across a thin bridge with no railing or barrier. The drop plunges toward an infinite expanse of darkness. Another impossible creation that defies all laws of science.

At the end of the walkway is a throne of obsidian—and sitting with her hands planted firmly beside her is Queen Ophelia.

A simple circlet sits on her shaved head, gleaming with pure silver. Her indigo silk gown hangs over her lean frame, pooling along the floor like spilled ink. Every cut of the fabric is asymmetrical, forming sharp points at unexpected angles. A perfect flower with unforgiving thorns.

Caelan stops several yards from her throne and bows his head.

The solid blacks of her eyes don't blink when she speaks. "The humans have come, just as we knew they one day would." She tilts her head, voice maintaining its lilted cadence. "I wonder why you are here, when it is our people who need you most?"

Caelan straightens, face masked with the regality he was known for in Victory. "I need to speak with you *about* our people."

"There is not time," she warns. "The Legion will busy the human warships while I move our city to another location. You should be leading our soldiers in battle."

"The humans have yet to attack," he tries, steeling his voice. "I have reason to believe their leader may be open to peace talks. There may be a way to end this war without any more bloodshed."

"Is that why you've sent our people underground?"

He stiffens, wordless.

"Did you think I wasn't aware of the tunnels?" She stands, movements as delicate as spider silk.

The muscles in his jaw tighten. "You told me they were bound to this place, just as we are. But there is no reason for them to stay—not unless they wish to."

"Asphodel keeps them safe." She pauses in front of Caelan, so close I hold my breath beneath the veil. "Which is why my guards have closed off the tunnels and redirected the First Folk to the citadel."

Caelan chokes on a caged breath, shaking his head as strands of white hair fall out of place. "You can't keep them trapped here."

"They are not trapped. They are cared for. Always."

"What you're doing is not love—it's control." When her gaze sharpens, he looks down at his feet. "The First Folk do not wish to stay here. And neither do the Legacies." He lifts his chin, facing her with defiance. "Untether us. Let us decide for ourselves what's safe."

"You would not survive out there."

"You have never given us the chance to try."

She moves her head with unnatural calculation. "Your brothers are gone. Ettore's mind has gone as quiet as the others." The hollowness in her voice becomes an echo. "I cannot allow you to leave."

Caelan bites down on his frustration. "And I cannot stay and watch Asphodel become a tomb."

"Our city will not fall." Ophelia says, unaffected. She raises her arms, and the glass shifts around us, revealing Asphodel's skies. The warships appear closer up here, still tucked behind the clouds but with so much more of their hulls visible. "I will not allow it."

Caelan takes a step toward his mother, voice becoming urgent. "What if I told you that not every human wants to be a part of this war? That some of them would live beside us in harmony, if they knew it was an option?" He pauses, building his words with a desperation that makes his forehead crumple. "There are places in the Four Courts where humans have already chosen differently. Legacies too."

Ophelia's head snaps toward him, vacant eyes spinning with darkness.

"Damon and Lysander are not dead," Caelan says, the truth pouring out of him in a rush. "They've been living alongside humans peacefully. For Lysander, it's been decades. For Damon, centuries."

Ophelia doesn't move. Doesn't speak.

Caelan takes another step forward, hands pleading. "I am not asking you to pardon the man who hurt you, but to wipe away an entire species as a result of one monster's sins is too great a retribution. Humanity can be better. *We* can be better. War does not have to follow us to the Afterlands—it can end here."

Ophelia's words are unyielding. "My sons are alive?"

Caelan's eyes shutter. "They want freedom, just as I do."

"They hid from me." A terrifying rumble spreads around us.

"Just as you once did." Caelan loses his footing. His knee hits the floor hard, but his hand swings back automatically—reaching for me. Ophelia calculates the movement. "Just as you hide even now."

Sparks shoot across the glass, creating pulsing veins through every surface. Lightning blazes beneath our feet, and I feel something rip free, seizing the air from my lungs.

I realize too late that it was part of Caelan's veil.

He moves quickly, stepping in front of me like a shield, and the muscles in the queen's jaw tighten without mercy.

"You would bring her to Asphodel"—Ophelia's voice simmers with vengeance—"after all that she's done?"

"Nami isn't responsible for any of this," Caelan clips back.

Ophelia thrashes an arm toward the glass wall. "She brought her sister to Infinity to end us!"

"Mei hasn't fired a single bullet!" I say, urgent. "She doesn't want to hurt you!"

An inferno builds in the depths of her eyes. "She will. They always do."

My face heats, and the Nightling shadows move toward the tips of my fingers, sensing an attack I try to ignore. "It can be different this time. We have allies in Famine, and we know about the First Folk. We know what Ozias did to you and your child."

Ophelia rears back, turning toward her son. "You told them about Leda?"

Caelan's emotions are raw. "Please. We can have everything we ever wanted. Our people can be *free*."

Ophelia looks back at me, and for one glittering moment, I think she might see something worth hesitating for.

But then her eyes become mirrors, and I see what she does: the Messenger.

The human who inspired the Second Wave.

Ophelia's black eyes flit between us, and a flicker of betrayal tugs at her brow. The temple shudders in response, the quake so powerful that I lurch forward. Caelan staggers in the opposite direction, eyes wide as he tries to reach for me. Our fingers barely graze when lightning splinters across the walls, ripping away more of his veil.

Ophelia sees the weapon sheathed at his back, and whatever emotions she'd trained away become unleashed. "Your hope has become your detriment," she says to us both. "I won't let it be mine."

Cracks split through the surrounding glass, and darkness envelops the room, blurring the world outside. The black in her eyes turns to fury. She flings an arm out, ripping the weapon free of Caelan's back; it scatters across the bridge.

Wind bellows through my ears, tunneling my vision until I can't see anything. I lift my hands, trying to block out the sound as the glass windows shatter into thousands of piercing shards. Sunlight floods the temple, but the unrelenting gust whips around me, and I fall to my knees, squinting up at the growing cyclone.

Caelan fights to reach me, glass tearing at his flesh and clothes, but I'm trapped inside the heart of Ophelia's hate.

I flinch at the storm as I try to shield my face and watch Caelan spin toward his mother.

"Let her go!" he yells, words barely audible through the haze.

"Can't you see what she is?" The world around Ophelia

vibrates with chaos. "A monster just like the others, who would turn a mother's own son into a weapon."

There it is again. That word: "monster."

Most of what I've seen is people committing increasingly monstrous acts in the name of war. But that kind of evil isn't born—it's made.

"You're right," I shout past the spinning fragments, guilt simmering into heavy tears. "I'm just as bad as the others."

Caelan turns, face sharp. "No, you're not—"

"I am," I say, fighting to stand. Ophelia is a shadow behind the vortex, but I find her black eyes and lock onto them with desperation. "When I thought you wanted the humans dead, I tried to find an army to stop you. I thought fighting back was the only way to survive. I thought we had no choice. But I made a mistake." I shake my head, motioning beyond the window frame. "I thought I was protecting my sister, but all I really did was bleed my own fear into another wave of humans. I'm sorry. For my part in this war, I'm so, so sorry."

Ophelia's nostrils flare. "I was there when you reached out to your sister. I heard your words. You didn't just tell her to fear us. You told her to *fight* us. It was the same things Ozias told his people the day I turned the sky black." She squares her shoulders, chin high. "I came to Infinity searching for a place to exist without chains. You created me—and when you decided I'd served my purpose, you tried to destroy me."

"I don't want to destroy you!" I shout. "I want us to stop trying to destroy each other."

"You are the reason the humans have found Asphodel!"

"What? No, I had nothing to do with—"

"You think I don't know about Second Wave technology?" She pulls her lip back in disgust. "The new humans track all that they create."

I hear Caelan trying to argue that the weapon was veiled—that he'd never had any intention of leading human soldiers here—but my mind drifts back to Famine.

The moment when Jacek tried to force a weapon in my hand. The moment he squeezed my shoulder so hard I felt a pinch.

The moment the piece of shrapnel fell from my shirt.

My fingers slip into my pocket, and I pull out the sliver of metal. So small it was barely noticeable.

The realization knocks into me like a gut punch.

Jacek tracked me.

And I led a human army right to the First Folk.

I look up, frantic, and find Caelan studying me with confusion. "I didn't know," I try to say, but I'm not sure it matters.

I think it might be too late.

Ophelia towers behind the cyclone with a look of resolve on her face. "There will never be peace between us. Never again will I be a servant to humans and their fleeting attentions. I am not yours to control—and I will not let you cut down all that I've built. Infinity does not belong to humans. It belongs to *me*."

The chamber flashes with violent blue streaks, and darkness pools from Ophelia's hands, spreading across the bridge. I feel my body tighten, bones fusing together like I'm being turned to stone.

Caelan's fear rattles along my other hand. He turns to his mother. "What are you doing to her?"

Ophelia snarls. "I cannot kill her, but I can make a monument from her bones. A reminder to our people that even the Messenger has no real power here."

My chest seizes, and my skin mottles to a dull gray.

I'm turning to stone.

For a moment, I'm terrified I might be frozen like this forever, trapped in an eternal cage of Ophelia's making.

And in the same awful moment, I worry I might deserve it.

Outside, thunder bellows above the temple. Bullets rain through the sky. Chunks of debris crash against the invisible shield surrounding Asphodel, sizzling away on impact. When another wave cracks across the skyline, dozens more warships appear below the clouds.

Ophelia's spell pauses at the base of my throat, leaving me gasping for air. It's enough time for me to look up and spot the sigil painted across the curve of metal. A blade shaped like a crescent moon, encircled by a blazing phoenix.

Ozias is here.

Dread floods through me as I watch his fleet unleash its firepower in unison. An unrelenting staccato of aggression that pierces my insides with terror.

Any hope of a peace treaty is torn to shreds in the sky.

"That's not my sister attacking!" I manage through hot tears. "We didn't do this. We don't *want* this."

But Ophelia doesn't care. She moves for the open window, void of emotion, and lifts her arms to summon an army.

A scattering of lights flashes across the skyline. Hundreds of soldiers appear, feathered wings varying in shades of off-white.

Their metal armor surges with pulsing energy, and every blade is honed with the glint of fabricated poison. Resident warriors created for destruction.

All at once, the soldiers tear through the clouds, ripping through one of the ships as if the exterior is no thicker than tissue paper. The warship's cannons swerve, but the Legion is too agile and fast. They pierce the hull, again and again, emboldened with rage. Bursts of golden pixels explode through the air. A mess of human consciousness, lost without a guide to draw them back in.

Because Ophelia has weapons that can Cut too.

NO! my mind screams, frantic as the ship tilts in the sky. I search for confirmation—a sigil, or a word . . .

But it's not the *Mizuchi* that's being targeted. Not yet.

The Queen's Legion slams through the warship one final time, cleaving it in half with sheer force. The ship teeters midair for a handful of excruciating seconds, before the two halves slip apart and collide against the city's shield.

The impact sends the warship's remains bursting into flames. It disintegrates within seconds, embers fizzling as ash hammers down the curve of Asphodel's protective dome.

I fight desperately to find Caelan through the whirlwind.

We need to stop Ozias from attacking the city, my thoughts scream. *Because if he gets through, if he uses his weapons to destroy the Legion . . .*

The First Folk still need our help.

Caelan's eyes steel. He nods.

I tighten my fist as Fenix's shadowy ribbons spill from my hand. Smoke blurs Ophelia's cage before taking the shape of an elongated dagger.

Resolve thunders behind my sternum, and I break out of Ophelia's stone hold with a resounding pop. When I reappear at the edge of the cyclone, I swing my blade and cleave an opening that makes the glass shards scatter in opposite directions.

Caelan's arms instantly fold around me. I don't have time to question where we're going before we jump out of sight, leaving Ophelia's temple behind.

33

THE MOUNTAIN STRETCHES AROUND US, AND IT takes a second to realize we've landed at the cusp of the domed shield, where the illusion is holding strong.

A blast ricochets off the barrier, and I flinch, clutching Caelan's chest. He runs his thumb against my arm, soothing me, but his attention is locked onto the battle in the sky. The Queen's Legion is everywhere, blades glowing with golden energy. They slash at every turret, fighting to shield the mountain from the onslaught of bullets.

Many of them are fast, darting from one place to the next to avoid the carnage—but others aren't as lucky.

A Resident tumbles from the sky like a broken bird,

slamming into the surface nearby. Eyes empty of life. When a trio of winged guards soars toward the *Mizuchi*, the pit of my stomach roils with fear.

"We have to get to my sister. She might be able to stop this." My voice shakes as I hold out my arm. Fenix bursts to life, taking the shape of a giant wolf with shadows feathered out of her spine.

I pull myself onto her back and feel Caelan do the same behind me, folding his arms around my waist. We're in the air in less than a heartbeat, forcing ourselves into the clouds and beyond Asphodel's protection.

Sparks rain down around us, trailed by wisps of smoke and metal fragments. Fenix weaves around the chaos, fighting to reach the *Mizuchi* before the Resident soldiers do.

The Nightling arcs high, and I hold tight to the shadowed tendrils curling through my fingers. We surge ahead, veering sharply as Fenix swoops in front of the guards, blocking their line of sight.

The Residents rear back, angry at first until they focus on Caelan behind me. Confusion rumples their brows, but they don't get the chance to show where their allegiance lies.

A series of bullets pelts through their armor, spraying blood.

Caelan roars behind me. My eyes widen, chasing their movements as they jerk backward and plummet from the sky. When I follow the trail of smoke, I find Zahrah perched on the gun deck of one of the distant warships, rifle pointed in our direction.

I yank Fenix back, trying to protect Caelan from becoming the next target, when my sister's voice echoes past the ringing in my ears.

"Nami! Here!" Mei calls out.

I chase the sound like I've been ensnared, urging Fenix into a sharp turn. Caelan grips me tight, bracing as the wind beats against our faces. Mei stands at the edge of the docking bay, waving me toward her. Releasing a final cry of desperation, Fenix thrashes her wings hard as we barrel into the opening, landing with a violent thud on the metal deck.

"We need your help," I bark to my sister, barely processing the number of guns pointed in our direction.

Fenix begins to pace, claws scraping across the floor. I press a heel against her side, urging her to stay calm, and will the second Nightling to do the same at my wrist.

The wrinkles around Mei's mouth tighten. Her eyes drop down to where Caelan's arms are still wrapped around me.

I stiffen, counting the Second Wavers circling around us. "Tell them to stand down."

"Nami—" Mei starts.

"Now," I snap, feral. "Because if any of your soldiers shoot him, I swear I will never forgive you."

Mei looks like she's seeing me for the very first time. The fear in the room ebbs, fluctuating between caution and curiosity. She lets out a sharp whistle, summoning the attention of her top commanders, and gives a firm nod.

One by one, the soldiers lower their guns, and the shadows around me relax.

"Do any of Ozias's soldiers listen to you?" I ask, but my sister only stares back with confusion. I point beyond the hangar, where ships are being Cut from the sky, and Residents are being killed. "Right now, Ozias is trying to blow a hole through

Asphodel's shields. If he succeeds, thousands of First Folk will become casualties of a war they never asked for. So if there's a chance you can stop this attack—if you can get his soldiers to pull back long enough for us to get the First Folk to safety—then please. Help us."

Mei doesn't answer right away. I think she's still making sense of what she's seeing.

"You came to Asphodel and didn't fire a single shot," Caelan says, searching for understanding. "Nami believes that's because you came here for peace—and so do I."

"I know about your alliance," Mei admits, stoic. "I have no desire to flatten a city full of innocent families—but Ozias's soldiers don't answer to me." She pauses, softening when she looks at me. "Why did you run? Why didn't you just talk to me in Victory?"

"Because you sent Jacek after Caelan," I say, heat blurring my vision. I find him in the crowd, right where he promised me he'd be. At my sister's side. "And when I saw the weapon you built, I couldn't trust you with it." *Not around him.*

Mei's surprise is genuine. "I would never have hurt him, Nami. Not if you asked me not to, and not knowing what he meant to you." She looks between the two of us and sighs. "I told Jacek to track the two of you if you tried to run. *Those* were his orders."

Jacek shrugs. "Like I said—you had flight-risk energy." I test my doubt at the ridges of his mind, but he seems to be telling the truth. Or at least, part of it.

Caelan's grip tightens. "Is that how Ozias found us?"

"That wasn't intentional." Jacek looks back at Mei. "I was just in the med wing. You were right; he gave her back to us to use as bait."

I look between them with confusion. "What are you talking about?"

Mei purses her lips. "After Jacek told me everything, I sent him back to Neo Genesis to get the girl. I—didn't think it was right to leave her there, knowing what I did about the First Folk."

"Gisele?" I balk, feeling the shadows turn erratic beneath my hands. "She's still alive?"

"I should've questioned why Ozias handed her over so easily, but I was distracted."

She doesn't have to explain. She was distracted because of *me*.

I hesitate, gnawing on one more reason for my guilt to burrow deeper. "He's been spying on you. If *you'd* broken the alliance, Ozias wouldn't hesitate to retaliate. I'm not asking you to go to war with him—we just need some time to get the First Folk out."

"So you can lead them to the Afterlands," Mei confirms.

I don't say anything. I don't have to. She knows our plan, I only need to find out where she stands.

But Mei is still calculating the risks. "Are you absolutely positive Ophelia won't be able to follow them? Because that, I cannot agree to. Not after what it's taken to get here, and certainly not when her legion is currently hellbent on destroying our entire fleet."

Caelan clenches his jaw. "She cannot travel beyond the border. Neither can the Legacies you've been at war with."

Mei eyes her commanders again, exchanging looks I'm certain were born from a much longer conversation. Maybe even an agreement.

When she straightens, she looks resolute. "We have engineers aboard Ozias's warships. They can disrupt their turrets temporarily to stop them from breaking through the shields." She tilts her head. "Will that buy you enough time?"

Caelan opens his mouth to reply, when a ferocious thunderbolt cracks through the sky, making the world glow.

Fenix rumbles beneath me, arching her back as she readies for danger.

"My mother is preparing to jump," Caelan says, hands tensing at my sides. *We're going to lose the tunnels.*

My stomach turns. *We need to get back to the surface. If Asphodel jumps without you, you might never be able to find it again.*

Soldiers rustle nearby, relaying strategies to one another as they move for the comms desk. I search for Mei as Fenix's wings stretch below us, preparing to take flight.

Stop Ozias, I plead in her mind. *And when you take down the turrets, get as far away from here as you can.*

Fenix leaps forward and dives for the edge of the ship. We plummet, free-falling through the sky, when bursts of shadows sweep forward, feathered from every angle. With a powerful thrust, we surge toward the mountain. It ripples with pixeled light, radiating Ophelia's power.

Caelan tucks his chin against my neck as the downward drop makes our eyes water. For a moment, the illusion blinks away, showing us everything inside the dome.

The citadel. Winterborne. The people who weren't able to escape.

We aim for the open glade beside the city wall, and I squeeze my heels against Fenix's ribs, urging her to *go*. We're nearly to the shield, and I hold my breath as the mountainous rock face flickers back into view.

There's a pop, and a force knocks hard into my side. Something painful digs into my arms, but by the time I get the chance to yell, we're already through the dome, and the pressure releases.

We tumble downward as Fenix flails to regain control of her flight path. She spins, making Caelan's hold tighten further, and that's when I see him.

Ozias is racing for the earth beside us, crown blazing with a golden aura. Energy flows around him like he's caught inside a fireball.

Around us, the world shatters. Pixels rain across the dome, and the sound of Asphodel teleporting across space makes my ears shriek in agony. The aftereffects shudder through the air like a fading thunderstorm, and I forget to brace for the impact.

We hit the ground. Fenix slams against the grassy meadow, sending Caelan and me flying off her back. Ozias drags his longsword over the earth, skidding across the soil as he uses the blade to slow his momentum.

He rises to his feet, eyes flashing with triumph as he takes in his surroundings.

First Folk soldiers stand at the wall, peering down at us. Nowhere near as afraid as they should be. Because they've never *had* to be.

Ozias meets their gazes, flashing his teeth with menace as he reaches for the crossbow at his back. A weapon I have no doubt is as powerful as the Messenger.

I scream, throwing an arm forward as both Nightlings burst into shadows around us. Somewhere behind me, Caelan shouts an alarm—but it's barely audible with the black fog separating us. Ozias releases his first arrow. It ricochets off the shield, flying in an unintended direction before disappearing in the grass.

His weapons may be deadly to Residents, but the Nightlings are mine—and whatever weapon my sister helped inspire would never harm me.

Ozias growls, realizing he and I are isolated inside a makeshift dome. He lifts the weapon, peering through the sights of his crossbow. The next arrow sails straight for my heart.

I dive to the side, rolling on my shoulder before pushing back to my feet. Ozias abandons his crossbow to the ground, and then he's right in front of me, wasting no time at all as he swings his longsword for my neck. I throw up my arms, and Fenix flashes between us, weakening the dome, but shielding me.

Shadows ripple outward, curling around me protectively.

Ozias shoves harder, and my knees dig into the earth, cutting against stone. "My army will chase this city no matter how many times it jumps. They will breach the shields, and we will purge the Residents from this afterlife." His eyes gleam with sinister euphoria. "I will not let anyone take what is *mine*."

"Infinity," I bite back, "was never yours."

I shove him hard, letting Fenix morph back into her wolf form as she thrashes his armored chest and sinks her sharpened fangs into his shoulder.

Ozias wraps his fingers around Fenix's throat, fighting to pry her jaws open. A mixture of stone and grass is caught up in the surrounding whirlwind, and I reach out, summoning the shards of Asphodel's earth as they form a new blade.

A flash appears to my right, and I find Caelan with a sword of his own, eyes wild with fury. Tendrils of white hair whip across his forehead, and when he exhales, his shoulders shudder with relief.

"What are you doing? You need to help the First Folk," I urge, pressing a hand to his chest.

He closes his fingers over my own, stepping closer so that only a breath separates us. "I'm with you. In this century and the next." His silver eyes dance with life. *If we have to fight, we fight together.*

I nod once.

Fenix lets out a pained howl, and I turn to find Ozias's blade sinking between her ribs. She fades to smoke before reforming a few yards away, swaying slightly as her hackles rise up.

Caelan and I charge in unison, and Ozias meets us in the center of the shadowed dome. Our blades clang together, melding into a symphony of strikes meant to maim. To defend. To kill.

The harder Ozias tries to draw blood, the angrier Caelan becomes. We move in sync, dodging and retaliating against every blow. We're in each other's heads, trading movements before we make them, until sweat pools on Ozias's brow.

Caelan spins low, sweeping his blade across Ozias's armor. The king teleports, and I stumble into the empty space he left behind. Caelan grabs my waist to steady me, looking up with dread.

A few feet away, Ozias stands on the outskirts of the shadow fog.

I summon both Nightlings back to my wrists, causing sunlight to spill back over the surrounding glade. Ozias lifts his crossbow and points it toward the wall—to where dozens of First Folk have appeared to watch the fight unfold.

I don't know how her face is the one I find first, but I see her—Olivia. Gisele's little sister. The girl whose worst crime was searching for flowers beyond the border.

I'm not sure if Ozias senses she means something to me—I'm not sure if he is really aiming for her at all—but the fear that she's his new target ravages every nerve in my being.

My heart hammers, desperate.

No.

Not the First Folk.

Not her.

I throw my mind forward, urging my consciousness to reach Ozias before his finger pulls the trigger, and my existence tears across the meadow in an instant. One moment I'm at Caelan's side, and the next I'm throwing myself against Ozias's body, toppling him to the ground. He elbows me hard, cracking bone as my head snaps back, and I roll clumsily across the grass as blood fills my mouth and my weapon falls away from me.

And then comes the shriek of an arrow.

I shove myself up, eyes racing for Olivia at the top of the wall—but it's Caelan I find standing in front of us, blocking the arrow's path.

The arrow that's now halfway through his chest.

A flash of bewilderment crosses his face. It doesn't last—but the scream that tears out of me ruptures my entire world.

My consciousness races forward, launching into Caelan's mind with so much force that I struggle to stand. Pixelated fragments disintegrate around us, shedding the walls of his existence to dust.

Caelan is hunched forward, clutching his heart. I throw myself toward him, skimming the void with my knees as I wrap my arms around him and press my lips to his temple.

"No, no, no, no, no," I sob through my teeth as something animalistic threatens to wrench itself free.

His silver irises are already fading to a chalky color I don't recognize. His mind flickers, and the void around us fills with shadows. I squeeze him as hard as I can and focus on jumping somewhere safe. Somewhere death can't reach him.

I yank with my thoughts, teleporting us out of his mind and back into my own.

Safe. He'll be safe here.

"Stay with me," I whisper, frantic.

I hold him, fingers burning as I build a barricade around us, even as I feel his body weakening in my arms.

He presses a finger below my chin, trying to pull my attention back to him, but I'm fighting hard, fighting the pull of his life being dragged away by a force no one in any world can control.

Not even in Infinity can we master death.

"You're not going anywhere," I say. To him. To the darkness. To death itself. "I can fix this." Somehow. Somehow. Somehow.

"Nami."

Tears burn down my cheeks, and an awful, inhuman noise fissures from my throat.

A despair stronger than any Grimling's.

"Nami," he repeats, voice so fragile it splinters every fiber of my being. "It's okay."

I open my eyes to look at him. His lips have gone ashen, and the white tendrils of his hair have lost their sheen. "I can keep you here with me," I whisper. "I'll protect you."

The life flickers behind his eyes. "I don't want to live in a cage. And I don't want to become yours."

My heart splits down the middle. "I can't let you die."

Somehow he finds the energy to tighten his mouth, and I catch a glimpse of his dimpled smile. "Then let me go."

The salt sting clouds my vision, and I dig my fingers into his skin. This can't be the end. This can't be goodbye.

But if I keep him here, locked in my mind, it won't matter what my intentions are. I'll be doing the same thing Ophelia has done to her people for centuries.

A shield can be a prison too.

And Caelan deserves so much more from this world, and from me.

"I'm so sorry," I sputter, hugging him tight.

"It's okay," he repeats with a final, fragile breath. "It's okay."

I shut my eyes. I feel his body drift away like a quiet breeze over miles and miles of snowfall.

When I open them again, he's already gone.

34

CAELAN'S DEAD BODY LIES SPRAWLED IN THE torn-apart glade. His vacant eyes remain parted and his mouth is slack, but his head is tilted to the side. I think the last thing he tried to do was search for me.

I drop beside Caelan's fallen body, close my fingers over the arrow's shaft, and yank it from his unmoving chest. I toss it to the side, not wanting it anywhere near him, and cup his face. Search for hope.

Footsteps approach, and by the time I turn around, Ozias is already in front of me with the longsword back in his grip.

He swings, and I reach for Caelan's weapon while summoning Fenix into a dagger, bringing both blades up to form a cross as I block the weight of his attack. The second Nightling grows at my back, wings expanding as he curls smoke around me like armor. Ozias pulls back slightly to search for another opening, but I don't give him one.

I move like a creature of shadows, swift and precise as I battle Ozias across the field. He is unrelenting: too powerful, and too in control. But I am rage, and anger, and mourning.

And those things are powerful too.

He killed Caelan. My fury surges. Red fills my vision, blazing with newfound hatred.

My blades crash against his, stopping every blow as the Nightling wings become a part of me. I leap up, spinning clear of his sword, and use the energy in my arms to fling Ozias backward.

He barely moves, but the shudders coming from above us divide his attention.

A fleet of ships storms into view. Not just his own, but Mei's, too—and something much larger.

Damon's palace floats in the sky, blocking the sun entirely.

Ozias parts his mouth in shock, and it's all the distraction I need.

I leap into his mind without warning.

Across the black void, his mouth stretches with outrage. He charges toward me with unrelenting speed. I swing Caelan's sword recklessly, no longer caring about precision.

He did this.

He wouldn't stop.

He was never going *to stop.*

And now Caelan is gone.

My wrath is mindless, building in my core like a monster that's been unchained. I don't know if it's always been there, prowling beneath the surface, but I don't care. Not anymore.

Hurt fuses itself to my bloodstream, and my tears blur my eyes as I swing wildly at the sprawling abyss. Ozias moves like streaks of lightning, jumping across the darkness as he builds his power into an unstoppable force. It surges through the rippling floor, preparing to force me back out of his mind.

I lift the sword with both hands around the hilt, ready to slam the blade into the floor like I just want it all to *stop*.

The pain. The hurt.

The violence.

My blade crashes into the black void without hesitation.

Ozias's consciousness stills. Everything falls quiet. When I look up, I see his throat catch as confusion spreads across his face. He's fought for centuries using brute force and enhanced weapons. He's never had his mind breached before.

He's never had to overcome it.

Pixels erupt across the void, splintering with deep wounds.

I blink, seeing real fear in Ozias's eyes for the first time. The anger inside me fizzles away, subsiding. All that remains is a mountain of grief.

Hurting him won't fix it.

It won't bring Caelan back.

And I . . .

If I'm going to be worthy of the afterlife Caelan deserved, I need to be better.

I need to choose *better.*

I tighten my quaking fist around the blade rooted in his mind and free it from the darkness.

My mind returns to the meadow. Ozias kneels at my feet, breathing erratically as he blinks to regain control of his senses.

"Didn't want to finish what you started?" Ozias snarls, wincing below me.

I swallow the doubt in my throat. "That's exactly what I'm doing."

Because this is what we fought for. What Caelan died for.

His brow knots in confusion.

I glance up at the sky, where the fighting has ceased. There are no bullets tearing through the clouds, or soldiers forcing their way through the barrier. There are humans up there, and Legacies too.

"They will never listen to you," Ozias spits, voice raw with hatred. "I am their *king*."

"I'm willing to try anyway," I say.

Ozias clenches his teeth, watching me. I stare back, eyes full of pity as I see the hunger in him that can't be sated.

"I will never accept peace," he snarls.

His hand slips beneath his armor, unsheathing a small knife. He leaps to his feet, ready to strike—but the blow doesn't come. Not for me.

Ozias stiffens, eyes rounding in shock.

I don't notice the blade protruding from his chest until he looks down at it, sunlight making it shimmer.

A burst of pixels erupts from his body, swirling in place for a moment before scattering for the clouds in every direction. A king one moment, and dust the next.

Standing in his place is Queen Ophelia.

She doesn't move. Doesn't reveal a hint of emotion. But her black eyes hold mine like they're burning through me.

Something settles in the darkness, like a piece finally clicking into place. Or perhaps it's something being restored—something that broke when Ozias tried to take her first child, and perhaps broke an infinite number of times when she lost so many more.

I don't know what I see when I look in her eyes now, but I don't think it's hatred.

I don't think it's forgiveness, either.

Another blade forms in her fist, mirroring the one that Cut down the king. And even with everything I know—after everything I've seen—I hesitate.

Ophelia only manages a single step when a figure appears in front of me, a head full of golden braids, and his hands raised up in defense.

"Don't hurt her," Elias pleads. "She isn't our enemy."

The material hanging from Ophelia's frame darkens, matching her blank stare. She soaks in the reality in front of her: a First Folk soldier defending what Ophelia has always taught them to fear.

Elias doesn't drop his hands. "I promised Prince Caelan I would protect her. I couldn't save him, Your Majesty. But please—let me save the one he loved."

The one he . . .

My throat cracks, and I search for his mess of white hair, framed by blades of grass. Too still. Too still.

Someone else rushes to the field to stand beside me. In my peripheral, I see a flash of fire-red hair. Nine's hand twitches beside the hilt of a blade that she's hoping she won't have to draw.

Murmurs break out above the wall, unafraid to hide their uncertainty from their queen. Because Ophelia taught them to fear humans—but never to fear her.

"She tried to protect us!" someone yells.

"Leave her alone!"

"Let her live!"

The words swirl together until the noise is cicadas in the summer, so much a part of the world that I barely register it at all.

All I see is him.

I blink as my cheeks turn damp, and I don't care if it's a mistake to turn my back on a queen. I rush to Caelan's body, scooping my arm beneath his neck as I cradle him close.

I don't stop crying.

I WALK THROUGH A FIELD OF BLUEBELLS AT night, fingers trailing the tips of the long grass. The sapphire sky glitters with newborn stars that no one else has ever seen before. No one but us.

His laughter trickles from across the meadow, delicate as a wooden flute. Warmth blossoms in my chest, and I search for him in the flowers. He's crouched low, ruffling Fenix's static fur as the larger Nightling rests beside him. There is no fear here. Only peace.

When he looks up, his silver eyes immediately find me.

Caelan. Here and alive and whole.

A dimple appears, and he stands, holding out his palm like he's requesting a dance. I don't hesitate to take his hand. I never do.

We sway beneath starlight and a full moon that never leaves the sky, caught in the trance of a perfect moment. It's just us and forever.

His smile tugs at all the strings of my heart. "I wanted to tell you something."

"Tell me now."

Caelan pulls me into his chest, resting against my hair like we're two puzzle pieces that wouldn't fit anywhere else. "The dream I had of my perfect day . . . I was never alone in it. You were there. When I dream, you're always there."

I can't be sad. I won't be sad. I won't remember.

I lose myself to the music in my soul. "I wanted to tell you something too."

"Tell me now."

"I love you. I don't want to do any of this without you."

He holds me. I think he'd carry me if I needed him to. I think he'd die for me. I think . . .

I hold him tighter.

"I'm here," Caelan says softly. "I'll always be here."

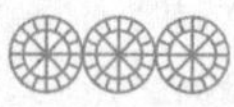

I vaguely hear footsteps shuffling through the grass, but it takes me a long time to look up. My face is swollen, and I can barely see through the blurry mist coating my eyes. I'm not sure how long I've been here, or how long I've been pleading for a chance to do everything over again. To exist in a dream instead of reality.

I only know that seeing Caelan's head in my lap is enough to bring me to the edge of ruin all over again.

A sob racks through me, and I bury my face against his chest. The footsteps approach, and when a figure leans close to me, I see a glimpse of long blue braids.

Hope rears its desperate head like a habit I just can't break. "Can you help him?" I blurt out, panic making my throat tighten. If there's an antidote . . . if there's some way to undo this . . . "Please. *Please* help him."

"I cannot." Damon's voice is softer than it's ever been. "There is nothing that will bring him back from this."

Another figure moves, and I look up to find Lysander standing beside Elias and Nine. Emotion splinters across Elias's face, but it's Nine who sheds the first tear.

Ophelia isn't here. I have no idea when she left, or where she went, but she gave me time with Caelan. Time to mourn.

It feels like a peace offering—just not the one I'd hoped for.

Again, my heart shatters. Again, I remember he's really gone.

"I tried to stop the arrow," I manage through my tears. "But I—he—"

Lysander nods like he understands, but how can he? This wasn't supposed to happen. It wasn't supposed to end like this.

Residents appear at the outskirts of the city wall. First Folk who'd gathered in the tunnels, only to turn around when they realized they'd been cut off. Soldiers who've never fought in a real battle, but who were still willing to risk their lives for their people. And the Legacies, who run councils and lead Legions, who were created to eradicate humans from the Four Courts.

They look to me with confusion, but not distrust. Not when grief pours out of me in droves.

Damon props my elbow up like he knows I'm seconds from tipping over. I have no masks left. No will to hide who I really am.

I'm not sure I'd even recognize myself right now.

Lysander's voice is a deep echo across the glade. "The human armies have agreed to a truce while their leaders convene. You should join your sister."

I clutch Caelan's shirt. "I don't want to leave him behind." Not here. Not in the place he believed was his cage.

Damon looks up, violet eyes swirling with apprehension. "Legacies have no burial ceremonies. None of us have experienced a final death before."

Elias takes a step forward, bowing before he speaks. "The First Folk burn their dead, and scatter their ashes among the wind. That way even their ancestors will one day make their way to the Afterlands." He looks at me, heavy with sorrow. "I think that's what he would've wanted too."

I smooth Caelan's white hair from his brow. A nod is all I can manage.

Lysander steps down and lifts his brother's body, making something behind my ribs snap in two. I wish Caelan looked peaceful. That I could imagine death gave him his freedom.

But he just looks lost.

"The First Folk will look after him," Lysander assures me.

I nod, rising to my feet, and plant one final kiss on Caelan's forehead. Lysander walks toward the city with the Prince of Victory limp in his arms and Elias at his side.

Nine stops in front of me, hair wild as a flame. "I'm so sorry, Nami. If I could—if I knew how—"

I shake my head, understanding her without words. "Can you make sure the others know about the Afterlands? Tell them—tell them I promised Caelan I'd make sure they got there safe. That just because he's gone, it doesn't mean . . ." My voice cracks, and I press my lips tight. "I'm not giving up."

Nine closes a hand over my shoulder. "I'll tell them." She squeezes once before trailing after Elias.

I inhale slowly, bracing against a dizzy spell. "Would you be able to take me back to the *Mizuchi*?" I look at Damon. Not in his eyes, but on some unimportant detail of his clothing, too afraid of what I'll see mirrored in his otherworldly stare. "I'd try to jump, but I'm not sure I have the strength."

"Your sister isn't on the *Mizuchi*," Damon says carefully, offering a hand. I take it because it doesn't matter; right now, anywhere is better than here. "She is waiting for you in the queen's temple."

I recoil, face raw with grief. "She's with Ophelia?"

He looks up at the sky, thoughtful. "I have never known anyone to spare their enemies as often as you have. My mother has no reason to trust your sister—but perhaps now she has a reason to trust you."

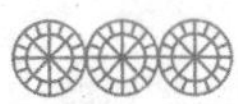

When Mei sees me, she rushes forward and yanks me into a hug. I wince beneath the pressure of her arms, nearly falling limp.

She pulls away to get a better look at me, noting the injuries still visible on my skin. I force my expression into indifference, even as tears slip down my cheeks. The worst of my hurt is somewhere she can't see.

Queen Ophelia watches us from her throne, flanked by Lysander and Damon.

Tobias is here too—the only other human in Infinity who knows what it's like to love a Resident prince. He stands near the archway with Jacek.

There are no weapons here—not from either side of the war.

"Nami," Mei whispers softly. "I know about Caelan."

I try to swallow, but everything lodges the wrong way, and I choke on my own exhale.

She reaches for my hand. Squeezes my palm three times.

I do the same back.

Beyond the shattered window, Famine's palace floats in the sky, surrounded by dozens of warships. The Queen's Legion guards the clouds, frozen in place like a sacrificial wall. Bracing for another wave of violence that doesn't come.

I wonder if they know what happened on the surface.

I wonder if they know what Caelan sacrificed.

"What made them stop fighting?" my voice cracks.

Mei watches me like she's afraid a whisper might split me in two. "Shura and Kasia," she says finally, and my heartbeat quickens. "They came with the Colony and some of the old Salt Clan. They explained everything—everything you've been trying to do, and everything they'd learned. I'm not sure if the others really believed it all, until they saw the children."

I frown, turning to face her. "The shields fell?"

Mei shakes her head. "We stopped the turrets from destroying the dome, but they still had time to rip the illusion away." She pauses, letting the information sink in. "We saw everything."

Everything.

I picture his body lying in the grass and start to shake.

The cadence in Ophelia's voice makes my chest pinch. "I have been informed you wish to discuss peace."

Mei stares back, momentarily puzzled by the queen in front of her. "Yes—but I cannot have those discussions on my own. There are other human factions to include." She looks at me. "And other alliances."

Don't cry, I tell myself. *Not here. Not now.*

"I am certain our own councilors will want the same," Ophelia replies.

Mei lifts her chin. "I want to be clear that I have no desire to hurt the First Folk. But I also don't want humanity hunted. I don't want our people to live in fear."

"We both know that peace can never truly be guaranteed. You cannot control every human in Infinity, just as I cannot control every Resident."

Mei pauses. "Then where does that leave us?"

I find my words, even as I'm dragged down by them. "We let everyone make their own choices."

Ophelia waits, black gaze pinning me in place.

I keep my voice even. "We've shown Infinity that we can coexist. Now we have to trust each other to do the right thing."

"There is nothing else you want?" Ophelia challenges. "No power you hope to bargain for?"

I don't think she means it as an accusation, but I flinch anyway. "This was never about power. But what I want . . ." *I want him back.* My lashes flutter, and I suck in a sharp breath. "I want you to give the First Folk your blessing to leave Asphodel—and to untether the Legacies so they can go with them."

She stares at me for a long time. Never blinking or moving. Just taking in my words like they're ones she's never heard before.

Like I've shown her something new.

"My own kind stood against me. Protected you, in spite of the army you brought to Infinity. I didn't understand. Not until I saw you grieve for my son." Ophelia pauses, circlet catching the light. "You loved him."

The temple blurs into watercolors. I bite my lip to dampen the emotions before they spill over. "Please don't let Caelan's death be for nothing." Even if I can't give him everything else I promised, I'll find a way to give him this.

Ophelia tilts her head. "My people chose you, Nami."

I swallow, afraid to say the wrong words. Afraid she'll change her mind. "Does that mean you'll let them go to the Afterlands?"

"That is for them to decide."

I grab the material at my chest, steadying myself. "And the Legacies?"

She remains unnaturally still. "It was never in my power to give Caelan his freedom."

My heart sinks. "But—I thought—"

Ophelia looks at her remaining sons before standing. Her indigo dress trails behind her, cascading down each step of the dais, until she stops in front of me. "I cannot free my children, but you can."

She holds up her palms as light pixelates across them, shimmering brightly until the Messenger appears. The sword built to destroy her kind.

I stiffen. "I don't understand."

Ophelia doesn't look away. "Take it, Nami, and let me show you what I need."

I hesitate before gripping the hilt, and let the blade slowly point toward the floor. She watches, black eyes soaking in my every thought, when I realize what she's waiting for.

With a careful breath, I meet Ophelia inside her mind.

The familiar black void appears around us, and I stand in front of the queen with a weapon at my side. She clutches her heart like there's a slow poison already working its way inside her, and when I look beyond her shoulder to the place she's spent centuries trying to rip apart, I find the ravaged threads connecting her to the living world. The ones she will never be free of.

She never had the power to let the Legacies go.

Not as long as she's tethered here too.

I stare down at the Messenger and shift in place, sending the darkness rippling away from me. "If I cut the threads, it could kill you." I look up, serious. "This weapon doesn't just split apart someone's consciousness. It destroys it."

"Which is why I believe it will destroy the threads that tie me to the living world," Ophelia says. She motions behind her. "Without these chains, I can untether the Legacies. I can give them all the freedom I never had."

My voice is a rasp. "You're going to sacrifice yourself."

"The First Folk were willing to do the same for you. A human. A stranger. But someone they had faith in." She raises her chin. "I think you and I both know coexistence will be more palatable if I am no longer a threat. You wanted peace. Is this how you imagined it would look?"

I stare at the blade. This wasn't what I wanted. This was *never* what I wanted.

"I—I don't—"

"I'm asking you to," she interrupts. "This is how you can save my people."

"I wanted to save you, too."

She steps back, giving me a path to her undoing. I walk toward the threads, shoulders quaking, and when I look back, Ophelia's eyes are resolute.

"Do it," she says, voice strangely melodic. "Set them free."

The weight of the hilt grows heavy in my fist. I can barely lift it—too terrified that I'm about to make a horrible mistake—when I realize the Nightlings have gone still.

They're not afraid of what's coming.

Maybe this is how the war was always supposed to end.

"I'm sorry," I say to Ophelia.

"Don't be," she replies—and I slice the Messenger straight through her chains.

Sparks shoot into the air. The wires unfurl like retreating vines, and when the pixels around them explode into a thousand tiny flecks of light, they vanish entirely.

When I turn around, Ophelia is sitting in the rippling void, staring up at me as pixels erupt all around us. She blinks for the first time. Her face softens. "The voices. I can't hear them anymore."

The millions of humans she had never been able to escape.

Splinters appear beneath us, spreading like cracks on a frozen lake. Her gaze traces the movements across the rippling void.

"I was never afraid of death until this moment." She looks up. "What was it like?"

"Dying?" I frown. "I—I don't really remember. A bit like falling asleep, I guess."

"You died sacrificing yourself for a stranger."

I startle at the recollection. "How did you . . . ?"

"I hear so much more than you can imagine. Or I did, until now." She closes her eyes like she's breathing in a memory. "You were that little girl's hero. Her family's too. Because of you, she lived. Had a family of her own. Her daughter's favorite story is the one where you saved her mother's life. She believes you were an angel." Her eyes flash open. "I called you a monster. But you were something different to them. You were something different to Caelan."

The cold floods my nostrils. "He was my friend." It's not the right word to encapsulate all that Caelan was to me, but for Ophelia, I hope it means something.

We were each other's bridge.

Ophelia clutches her stomach. The first in Infinity to carry life. "It is done," she says. "The Legacies are free."

Tears prick the corners of my eyes, and I can't stop them anymore. They drop to the floor in heavy, unrelenting beats. "Thank you."

"Keep your promise," Ophelia says. Parts of her begin to disappear, creating rifts across her once-perfect skin. "Be something even better to the First Folk. Not an angel, or a saint. Not an enemy." Her voice sounds like a haunted melody. "Be the one who reminds them to hope."

I meet her in the darkness, tucking my legs underneath me as I drop the weapon to the floor. It clatters at my side.

She tilts her head, lilting voice becoming a song. "I remember you from the living world. You were kind, even when I was only an object to you. I think if I had met you in Infinity first, things would have been very different." Her black eyes become pixels, and she sucks in a sharp breath. "I don't know what's coming next."

"No one does," I admit through tears. "Death is the most human thing any of us experience."

"But death was not the end for you," she notes. "And for me . . ." Her mind cracks like shattering glass, and I pull away instinctively, tearing from her consciousness as it crumbles.

When I look down at Ophelia's body on the floor, her eyes are falling shut. "In death, I will be free."

She takes her last breath and fades to nothingness.

NO ONE IN THE TEMPLE MOVES FOR A LONG time. Not until I do.

I hand the Messenger back to Mei like I want to be rid of it for good. "Destroy it," I say, hollow. "Weapons like this have no place in Infinity. Not after what she gave up."

Damon and Lysander watch our interaction with blank expressions. What happened to their mother . . . I think they'd been expecting it.

Mei tucks the blade at her side. "We have more to discuss. Not every human will be ready to embrace this kind of change, and I'm not sure—"

"Mei," I interrupt, serious. "You're the General. Not me. I just want to make sure the First Folk get to the Afterlands, and whatever becomes of the Four Courts after that . . ." I lift my shoulders. "I trust you. I believe you'll do the right thing."

She flattens her mouth. "The world won't repair itself over night. This will take time."

"There's plenty of that in Infinity." I turn for the window, watching the First Folk in the city below. "Someone needs to tell them what's happened."

"I will travel to the surface with Tobias," Damon offers. "We will arrange safe passage for anyone who wishes to leave for the Afterlands."

I look back at the Resident princes, who stand in the place Ophelia once did. "Make sure they understand what staying behind might mean—but that it's their choice to make." *Just like Caelan wanted.*

Damon gives a short bow before clasping hands with Tobias and vanishing from the temple.

Lysander steps back. "I will speak with the council, and let them know the humans are ready to discuss the future." He dips his head before jumping away too.

The faraway sounds of Asphodel trickle through the silence. A reminder that out there, the world is still moving. That it hasn't stopped—even if my heart has.

I stare at the vacant floor. "There isn't a body."

Mei and Jacek exchange a puzzled glance.

"Did—did you want to bury her?" Jacek asks, unable to deconstruct the chaos in my heart. There's too much of it, overwhelming his senses like it's overwhelming mine.

The ache in my throat turns painful. "When Caelan died, his body was still there."

"Does that worry you?" Mei asks.

"No," I say, solemn.

Maybe it means she found peace somewhere else.

Maybe what happened in this temple wasn't really the end for her.

"She spared you," Mei says, serious. "In the glade . . . I think she went after Ozias to save you."

"She was taking her revenge."

"No—I watched her from the ship. She could've waited. She could've Cut you both. But the moment he reached for the knife, she was there. Protecting *you*. And when you hesitated, she did too."

I bite the edge of my lip, unsure how to respond, or what to think.

But in the end, I'm not sure I *want* to think.

Not right now.

I lock my arm around Mei's and squeeze. "I'm tired."

Mei nods, firm. She doesn't ask any more questions; she just takes me somewhere safe.

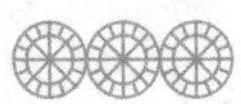

Mei and Jacek lead me back to my room on the *Mizuchi*. The moment the door slides open, I spot Shura's pink hair, spun into two buns. Her expression floods with relief, and she pushes herself off the edge of the bed. Kasia stands too, mouth curved downward. She knows me well enough to know I'm barely holding myself together.

"We saw the transport approaching," Shura explains. "We hoped you were on it."

"How can we help?" Kasia asks, serious.

"Ophelia is dead." My words echo through my own head, and the memory of her throne room seers the back of my throat. "And—and so is Caelan."

I think they might've already known. I think they may have watched what happened from the same place Mei did. But I hold out my hands anyway, because I don't have the words to explain this. Just the memories.

They reach back, and when the Exchange ends, the silence pounds in my skull. Every facet of my being calcifies just to keep from breaking apart.

"I'm so sorry, Nami," Shura says softly, gripping my hand tight.

"Our priority right now is getting the First Folk to the Afterlands," I say, turning to Kasia. "And, well, you said when the war was over . . . and since you have the map . . ."

Her ocean eyes are brimming with agency. "You don't even need to ask. I'll lead them across the water, and find them a new home. Somewhere in the Afterlands no war has ever touched."

"I—thank you." I blink away the sting. "You don't know what this would've meant to him."

Her smile doesn't reach her eyes, but there's a sincerity there that's impossible to miss. "I spent so many years hiding in the Borderlands. I think I might enjoy having a purpose again."

Shura clears her throat, already nervous. "I was actually thinking about leaving too." She looks between me and Kasia. "The Colony has made a new home with Famine, and if the Afterlands are where they're all headed, well. I want my mothers and me to be with our family, where we belong."

A knot loosens in my chest. I open my mouth to respond—

Jacek holds my stare like he's asking for an audience, and it makes me pause. With a frown, I let my thoughts drift toward his—to the crack in his walls—and find that he's already waiting for me.

It isn't the tough, sarcastic exterior I'm used to. It's warmth. Compassion.

Fondness.

So this is what you're hiding, my thoughts hum. *You have a heart.*

The voice in his head sounds vulnerable. *I know you're in pain, and I'm sorry for what you've lost. But you can't go with them.*

Hurt ripples outward. *I promised Caelan I'd look after the First Folk.*

And you will be, by giving them their freedom. But that's not the only promise you made.

I blink, gaze drifting toward Mei, and the pit of my stomach tightens.

I promised I wouldn't leave until she was ready to say goodbye.

Mei is lucky to have you, I think, more bitter than I should be. *Even if you are trying to hold me hostage.*

I'm doing this for you too, his thoughts respond. *A long time ago, I lived my life in service to everyone around me. I thought that's what a good person was supposed to do. And that belief slowly chipped away at the light in my chest until I barely recognized myself anymore. Because the hard truth is, you can't make everyone happy. No matter what you do, or what you believe, you're bound to disappoint someone. But you can't let their disappointment become your responsibility. You can't let other people snuff out your light.*

My guilt is all-consuming. *After today, I don't think there's any light left.*

That's what I'm worried about, he admits. *If you leave, you'll regret leaving your sister until the end of Infinity. But if you stay, if you let yourself be a sister again, in a world without war, I think you'll find a way to forgive yourself.*

I think of what Caelan told me in the tunnel. How he wanted me to find my own peace.

You don't understand what I owe him, my mind whispers.

His thoughts are already receding beneath his invisible shield, but I hear the words like a faint brushstroke. *You're the Messenger who saved all of humanity. Of course I understand. Some debts just can't be repaid.*

"Well?" Shura pushes, hopeful. "You're coming with us, right?"

Beside me, Mei's expression falters.

For a moment, she's my little sister again, and I glimpse some of the light Jacek was talking about. I see it in her hope. In the unfailing belief she has in me.

I see it in the way she's loved me all her life.

I don't know where my light has gone. I just know I'd do anything to protect hers. Maybe that's not what Jacek wanted for me—but I think right now, it's all I can give.

"You both deserve the Afterlands so much, and I'm happy you'll get to see it together. But I'm going to stay here," I say finally. "With my sister."

37

I SIT BESIDE A HOSPITAL BED, STARING AT THE stranger currently hooked up to a mess of wires. A face I know. A face I've worn.

Gisele.

A monitor displays her vitals—something I'm not sure ever had much use in Infinity. There are bandages covering the worst of her wounds, but the bruising is impossible to hide. I think of Nine's missing finger, and how the First Folk don't heal the way Legacies do.

The pain she must've gone through . . .

Heat radiates across my face. Mei said if she'd known what Gisele really was, she'd never have sent her to Neo Genesis. Never have subjected her to torture of any kind.

I don't know if that makes me feel better, but I'm relieved she's here now.

Gisele bolts up suddenly, brown eyes wild, but there's recognition there too.

"I—I saw you. In the forest." Her irises turn glazed. "My sister—"

"Is safe," I finish. "She got back to Asphodel. She'll be happy to find out you're okay too."

Gisele's shoulders sink, and the relief bubbles out of her in a tight sob. The circles under her eyes are so dark, it's no wonder the Second Wave doctor used medicine to calm her.

I understand why Caelan feared for the First Folk. War is different when life is this fragile.

Gisele paws at her bruised face, wiping away tears. "I—I made a mistake. I told the other humans about our city, and I think—I think—" Her sob cracks. "I think I put my family in danger."

"You didn't," I say, assuring her with a hard stare. "Everyone in Asphodel is safe. In fact, they're getting ready to leave for the Afterlands soon. That's why I came to get you."

She frowns like she doesn't believe me at all. "Is this some kind of trick?" Something ugly snaps in her gaze. "I have nothing left to give you. I told them everything I know."

"It's not a trick," a soothing voice answers, and Prince Damon drifts into the room beside me like a wraith.

Gisele looks surprised. Damon may not have lived in Asphodel, but she clearly recognizes the Prince of Famine.

"We have made an agreement with the humans," Damon explains, carefully filling in the details in a way Gisele can understand. I'm not sure she does. She glares at me like I'm the villain in her story.

I guess to her, I really am.

"We can't trust them," she says, glowering. "They tortured me. They almost killed my sister."

I tried so hard to break the cycle, but it's here, in her eyes.

The hate.

"I know I can never make up for what was done to you," I start, "but the Afterlands will be your fresh start. Your family will get to live in peace. You'll be free."

Animosity brews in her gaze, but when she focuses back on Damon, it falters.

Something glitters behind his violet eyes, and when Gisele leans back against her pillow, lulled in a trance, I realize he's given her a poison.

"Her wounds will heal," Damon says, attention drifting across her bandaged arms. "I will make sure of it."

I don't want to leave her. Not when I still owe her so much more than an apology. But I follow Damon into the hall anyway.

What Gisele needs . . . it isn't something I can give her.

"You took her memories," I say quietly.

"As a kindness."

"To hide what happened to her?"

"To give her peace. And to maintain peace among the humans and Legacies she will be living with." He tilts his head, blue braids tumbling over his shoulders. "She carries a seed of vengeance. Would you have me allow her to plant it in the Afterlands?"

"No," I admit, chewing the edge of my lip. "I'd rather she wasn't hurting. Not even in her mind."

He looks at me, serious. "I'm able to ease your pain too, if that's what you'd like."

Forgetting would mean erasing everything. The guilt and the hurt—but all the good I've felt too.

And Caelan had so much that was good.

"I could alter your memories of his final moments, so that you don't have to relive them for an eternity," Damon suggests.

I shake my head. "I don't want to forget anything. And those final moments . . . they're all I have left."

He's quiet for a long time. "All I can offer you then is the knowledge that despair does not last forever. Darkness is not darkness without the belief that light will one day return."

I avert my gaze, throat burning with grief.

Prince Tobias appears, nodding to the both of us. "It is time."

I shut my eyes, searching for the strength to say goodbye.

Tobias eyes the door behind us where Gisele is sleeping. "Shall I take the youngling with us?"

Damon nods. "Have you located her family?"

"They're waiting in the palace with all the other Legacies, First Folk, and humans who have decided to venture into the Afterlands together."

I catch sight of Kasia and Shura waiting at the end of the corridor, and by the time I reach them, my eyes are so full of tears that I can barely see.

"I really thought you'd be coming with us," Shura admits, hiccuping through sobs. "I didn't think you'd stay."

I lift my shoulders. "I want to be here with Mei when our parents make it to Infinity."

"I understand," Shura sniffs. "Family is everything."

"You're my family too," I manage through short breaths.

She nods too many times and flings her arms around my neck. "You were the sister I always wanted. Thank you for making sure I wasn't alone."

She pulls away, and Kasia takes her place, squeezing me tight. She doesn't say a word, but when our minds connect, her thoughts rush through me.

It's the map to the Afterlands, she offers. *Use it to find me one day when you're ready for the next voyage.*

When she finally steps back, I grip her and Shura's hands tight. "Take care of each other, okay? For me?"

They exchange a smile, and I know I didn't have to ask. I think they would have done it anyway.

They follow Tobias and Damon into the room with Gisele. The pop from behind the door comes too quickly, and I know my friends are gone.

I try to be happy. This is what I wanted. This is what Caelan and I fought for.

But right now, my heart seems to feel only the sorrow.

I grip the railing of the *Mizuchi*'s viewing platform, staring down at the statue of Leda, the Mother, as I say my silent goodbyes to the city.

I think of the bustling streets, and the parade, and the innocent families. I think of Winterborne, and the Prince's Guard. I think of seeing Caelan again after so many years apart. I think of the feel of his hands, and the way he held me below the city when it was just the two of us pretending like we weren't existing on borrowed time.

I try to remember *all* of it, a thousand times over, and refuse to flinch at the pain as we fly away from the Capital.

There's no veil to hide Asphodel, no mountain to mask the truth.

We were here. We stopped a war. We brought Residents and humans together.

Now we are at peace.

But as we disappear toward the horizon, no longer forced into a Labyrinth that stopped existing when Ophelia vanished, I realize it isn't peace I feel.

It's an unbearable loneliness.

38

INFINITY HAS ALWAYS FOLLOWED ITS OWN schedule, but the days seem to move so slowly that sometimes it feels like an entire week has passed before the next sunset.

It makes me anxious. For the darkness. For the change.

For the proof that everything really is okay.

I haven't left the Borderlands in months. Not since I watched Asphodel shrink into a speck on the horizon.

I try not to be sad that most of my friends are somewhere I can't reach them. I try not to be envious that I couldn't join them.

But in truth, I'm not sure what I feel anymore beyond an ache in my chest cavity that doesn't seem to ease.

I shut my eyes and turn back to the ocean outside my open

window, breathing in the salt-stained air that fills my lungs with something other than sorrow.

Fenix lets out a quiet rumble from the rug beside the fireplace, head resting on one of Kohl's gigantic paws. Caelan may have brought him into existence, but he's a part of me now. Bonded to the part of my heart that's filled with shadows.

I've heard rumors that the Nightling packs run freely through the deserted court formerly known as War. When the last battle ended, everyone searched for a place to call home. But no one wanted War. Not after all the blood that was spilled there.

Maybe it's better that it belongs to the shadows now.

Fenix and Kohl never leave my side, despite the many suggestions by my sister that Nightlings don't belong in the Borderlands.

But she doesn't push. With Kasia and Shura gone to the Afterlands with the Colony, I have few friends left to lose.

A voice echoes across the sand, and my eyes spring open. It's a deep sound, like gravel and caramel. It makes my stomach spin in tight circles.

I toss the shawl from my shoulders and hurry out the door, searching for the boy I know that voice belongs to.

I find him on the beach, skimming rocks along the sea.

Messy brown hair. Olive skin. Warm hazel eyes.

The name pours out of me without reservation. "Gil."

He pauses, arm pulled back with a rock wedged in his fist, and turns his sharp features to look at me, brow scrunched in confusion. "Do I know you?"

My gaze darts around every feature I'd once memorized. He's so familiar to me—and yet, to him . . .

I swallow the knot in my throat. "I—I'm no one."

Gil drops his arm, and Ahmet appears from several feet away, tossing a rock into the air and catching it again.

"This one looks better. Nice and thin, with a perfect edge. I think you could probably skip this all the way to—" Ahmet's voice cuts off abruptly when he sees me, face widening to a smile. "Nami! What are you doing out here?"

Gil's frown curls into a boyish smile. "So not 'no one,' then."

My cheeks turn pink, and I motion to my hut in the distance. "I live here."

Ahmet looks apologetic. "I'm sorry. I should've tried to find you sooner, but—well, I've been busy in Neo Genesis." He turns to Gil and sets a hand on his son's shoulder. "After Ophelia died, Gil started to wake up. It's like his consciousness was just waiting for it to be safe again."

"Do you . . . remember anything?" I ask carefully.

"You mean from before I fell asleep? I remember getting separated from Dad. And I remember—" He stops himself, looking at Ahmet for instruction.

Ahmet gives a short nod. "You can trust Nami. She's one of us."

One of us. Like I belong here, even when my soul is shattered in a thousand places.

Gil nods and looks back at me, voice lowered. "I remember what Ozias did to me. He let the Residents catch me."

"That's why we're here," Ahmet admits. "We've heard rumors a small group of his followers are searching for the king's consciousness, hoping to someday bring him back. I doubt his power will ever be what it was, but if he does show his face one day, I don't want him anywhere near Gil."

"I heard most of his army agreed to the treaties with hardly any pushback."

"Can you blame them? Ozias lied to us. This entire war started because of what he did to Ophelia." Ahmet shakes his head. "When the veil lifted on Asphodel, it shed a light on who he really was: a man who would murder a child just to sit on a throne."

I wish I had the energy to feel smug. Ozias is finally getting what he always deserved. He's lost everything. And if he ever does return, it will be to a world that was all too eager to leave him behind.

Gil's face softens. "I heard you were a friend to me in the Colony. When I, well, wasn't me." He perks up, using facial expressions I don't recognize as Gil at all.

Because they were never Gil's. They were always Caelan's.

"Yes," I say, pained. "We were friends."

"I wish I could see Theo and Shura again." Gil looks at Ahmet. "I wish I'd had the chance to say goodbye."

Ahmet turns to look at me. "I thought about going with them. Sometimes I wonder if I should have. But there are so many humans here who've been displaced from their families."

Gil beams. "We're going to rebuild a colony where Victory used to be. A place to help families reunite with one another after they're rebuilt from the Cut or brought back from their long sleeps."

Ahmet looks thoughtful. "You should come with us. We could use someone who cares as much as you do."

Because that's what people do after war.

They rebuild.

I turn toward the sea, feeling a pull in my chest that makes my eyes water. "I think—I think I'm going to stay here awhile." I blink the sting away and force a smile. "Maybe we have rebuilding to do in the Borderlands too."

Ahmet folds a hand over my shoulder. "Well, you know where to find us. I don't want us becoming strangers."

I look at Gil, but that's exactly what he is. A stranger.

I nod anyway. "I'm happy for you both. It's long overdue."

I watch them skip rocks in the ocean, soaking in their laughter even as a wave of loss rushes through me. I manage to slip away when they aren't looking. They're busy making up for lost time.

And I . . .

I just seem to be losing more and more of it.

There are no real seasons in Infinity, but enough moons rise and fall that I know years have passed. Perhaps too many to count.

Gone are the Four Courts.

Even Neo Genesis is a place the younglings don't remember.

When the Second Wave focused their attention on restructuring buildings and creating transition zones for new arrivals to come to terms with their deaths, the world around us quickly changed. This part of Infinity is about sharing information and building connections with people who feel lost. It's about healing.

There weren't many First Folk who decided to remain in Asphodel, but their small clan has grown. I see them from time to time, when they visit the Borderlands to trade stories and clothes and art.

I must admit, I have a soft spot for their books.

The human-Resident factions cross more borders than they ever have before. It's not always perfect—nothing really is—but somehow, in spite of our histories, we're still making progress. We're still choosing peace.

Ozias's remaining followers could not find a place to fit in the new world, so they took what remained of the king's army and set off for the Afterlands to start over. Perhaps they're out there now, finding new areas to conquer, and other factions to rival.

Something tells me they'll never again become the threat they once were.

Maybe there's something poetic in knowing his legacy is insignificant in a world that's too big for his small mind.

The Borderlands have become an enormous harbor. By the time the younglings reach our shores, they are ready to move on to the next part of the afterlife. We send them away with the map to the future and watch their ships become tiny dots on the horizon, until they can't be seen at all.

I long for that horizon. To follow the call that is forever tugging my chest.

On good days, I like to pretend it's Kasia or Shura letting me know they're safe. Happy. *Home.*

On every other day . . .

I think of him.

I think of what he lost.

And I shut my eyes to the horizon I'm not sure I deserve.

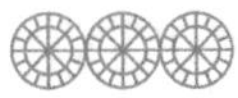

The fractures that had formed between Mei and me are so far in the past that I can't remember ever looking at her like I didn't recognize her.

I'm still the reason she lost her childhood, and I live with that guilt, day after day. Every laugh in the afterlife is a laugh I know should've happened in a café, or in a movie theater, or at a family gathering celebrating a new milestone.

Mei says if I need her forgiveness, then I have it a thousand times over.

I'm not sure it's enough when forgiving myself feels impossible.

Over time, a hollowness builds inside me where I think my heart used to be, and I'm convinced that Damon was wrong—that despair never really leaves. That guilt never really fades.

But then we're reunited with our parents at the gates of Infinity.

Mom arrives first, and Dad a few months later. Their white hair and wrinkled skin are my new favorite things. It means they lived long lives and didn't have their time cut short because of me.

I ask them to tell me everything, and they do. Every adventure, every funny story, every favorite memory. Everything I missed.

For the first time in years, I wake up some mornings so happy that I forget to feel guilty at all.

Years blur together, and I can't remember the last time anyone has called me a youngling.

Mei lives with Jacek in a house beside a vibrant lagoon near the southern coast. Our parents work with the New Colony, helping families reconnect after life and death has separated them. I think it makes them happy, bringing parents and children together again.

Recently, I said goodbye to Ahmet and Gil, and watched them disappear across the sea.

My hut has become too small to hold all my memories, and it isn't long before Mei turns up at my door. She hugs me. Thanks me. And tells me it's time.

She says she hopes I find peace beyond the horizon, because no one should carry ghosts in the afterlife.

I tell my sister I love her.

I tell her I'm proud of her.

And then I say goodbye.

39

WAVES SPLASH AGAINST THE BOAT'S HULL, thumping in a steady rhythm. I lie on a pallet of blankets near the wheel, lost in a trance as the cold air numbs my ears. Emerald and amethyst ribbons dance among the ever-changing stars. They were a map to me once. Now I like to imagine they might be a map for someone else.

Kasia didn't leave me a trail in the sky. She left it in the depths of my mind. And yet . . .

I feel it still. The pull across the water from every direction.

I thought it was the Afterlands beckoning me toward the next world, but I've been on the voyage for weeks, and I still feel the tug behind my rib cage, as if there's something out there that doesn't want to let me go.

Fenix and Kohl are perched at the bow, gaze pinned to the empty horizon. One day we'll find land, but for now, the sea is our home.

Kohl's ears flick back, and Fenix gives a strained whimper.

I lift my head from my folded arm to get a better look at them. "What is it? What do you see?"

Fenix glances back at me, shadows prickling around her, half blended into Kohl's massive form. She huffs a cloud through her nostrils.

It's the only warning I get before she leaps over the edge of the boat and dives into the sea, with Kohl half a second behind her.

I bolt to my feet and race for the railing. Their shadows bleed into the waves, too dark to follow. Reaching for the nearest lantern, I transfer light from my palm into the caged glass until the glow becomes luminous. I give a sharp tug on the rope beside it, releasing the knot.

I whistle through my teeth and throw the lantern as far as I can across the water.

Fenix leaps up, snatches the handle between her teeth, and continues swimming.

By the time I get back to the wheel and turn the boat in the direction the Nightlings are headed, the light beneath the water is only a speck in the vast sea.

I chase them for miles using the lantern as a beacon. We're going in the wrong direction, but I trust Fenix and Kohl. If there's something out there they want me to see, I know better than to stop them.

When a small island appears on the horizon, the sky lightens to a deep indigo. A sign that dawn isn't far away.

There's no port, so I anchor the boat not far from the coastline and swim the rest of the way. Fenix and Kohl wait for me in the sand, eyes peering up the hillside where the grass and heather have grown wild.

They force a path through the thick of it, making it easier for me to trample after them. When we reach the summit, most of the stars have already vanished, and the crest of the ocean has begun to glow with the rising sun.

I walk toward the center of a wide glade. Blankets of soft clover and meadow thistle cover the ground around us. I shut my eyes and inhale the scent of wildflowers and morning dew. I've been on the sea for so long, stuck with the smell of salt spray and damp wood, that the reminder of life is almost overwhelming.

When I look across the field, Fenix and Kohl are standing in the midst of the flowers, staring back at me with careful eyes.

I lift my shoulders, motioning around the glade. "This is what you wanted me to see?"

There's no one here. No human settlement or abandoned outpost.

It's just the three of us.

Fenix tilts her head. Wisps of shadows curl around her as if she's pulling herself inward, shrinking into the shape of the young fox I once knew.

I curl my fists slightly. "Come on. There will be plenty of fields when we reach the Afterlands." I turn to leave, acutely aware that neither of them are following me. I plant my feet together and lift my chin up toward the fading lapis sky.

My chest constricts. A knot builds in the back of my throat, making it hard to swallow.

I turn around slowly, finding both Nightlings in the same spot as before. Still watching.

Waiting for me to understand.

"Please," I whisper quietly. "Let's go back to the boat."

They don't move.

I bite my lip hard, scratching at my forearm where the mark used to be. I haven't summoned them back in decades. It didn't feel right to put them in a cage after the war was over.

Frustration makes my face heat. I lift my arm, willing them to return to me, when Fenix whimpers. Not a cry of pain, but of pleading.

Mist fills my vision, and for a brief moment, I want to pretend I didn't hear her. That I don't understand what she wants.

But I know.

I've known for years.

My arm falls back to my side. I brush a stray tear with a knuckle and shudder out a heavy breath. "I have to let you go, don't I?"

A golden aura appears behind the Nightlings, flooding the glade with sunlight. I wrap my arms around myself, feeling vulnerable in this open space with nowhere to hide.

Maybe that's the point.

There shouldn't be anything left to hide from when you're truly free.

I stop in front of the Nightlings, lowering carefully to my

knees as I brush their fur with my hands. Fear has no place in the Afterlands. And the anger and guilt . . .

I think I stopped carrying the weight on my heart a long time ago.

It's only the memories that are left now.

"I'm going to miss you," I say softly. To my companions. The last connection I have to everything that came before.

My last connection to him.

"Wherever you go next, I hope you know you're so much more than the darkness you were born with." I lean forward, tears slipping as the Nightlings nuzzle my face for the final time. "Be free, my friends."

I don't look away when I release the last of my pain into the glade. The Nightlings untether from my soul like silk slipping free. They were ready for this long before I was.

It doesn't hurt to let them go. Not the way I thought it would.

I watch the black smoke start to fade. Their gold eyes don't leave mine—not even as a shimmer of light spills through the static, drowning the darkness in a swirl of pixels. Their bodies merge together, less creature than shadow now, and I squint against the building energy until it dissipates in a flash.

White light radiates all around me, and for a moment I'm certain I see the outline of a Dayling in the glade. A three-tailed wolf, shimmering with memories. Not of terror or hurt, but of love. Friendship. Hope.

Rebirth.

The creature howls a final goodbye, and when the glade returns to normal, Fenix and Kohl are gone.

I curl my legs beneath me, watching the sunrise as warmth floods the meadow. Alone for the first time in many lifetimes.

Maybe this is how my voyage to the Afterlands was always meant to be.

I push myself up, dusting grass from my legs, when a flicker of gold catches my eye. I peer up at the sky, brow furrowing as the dust trickles down from the clouds. I hold out a palm, curving a hand in wait. When the first flake brushes my skin, the rest react.

Dust swirls around me, so faint I can hardly see it.

But it's there. The flicker of consciousness.

Of someone lost to the Cut and separated from its whole.

When I lift my hand, parting my fingers as the energy winds around me, I sense winter and woodland.

And the tug behind my ribs—the strings pulling in so many different directions . . . I feel one of them ease.

Tears prick the corners of my eyes, and my mouth widens into a smile I don't bother hiding.

There were so many broken pieces of Infinity I didn't know how to put back together, but this?

I can do this.

For him, I'll find a way.

My fingers dance in the air, watching the gold dust skitter across the back of my hand. Wanting to be close. Needing something to tether itself to.

Choosing me.

I make my way back down the hillside. The shimmering presence doesn't leave me. Not when I leave the island. Not when I swim to the boat. And not when I set a new course behind the wheel.

Somewhere out in the beyond, I'm sure Kasia will understand.

I raise the anchor and set the boat across the water. Gold light ripples around my shoulders, tremoring with excitement.

"Don't worry," I say to the light. "I'm coming to find you."

When the consciousness brushes against my cheek, warmth blooms in the hollow of my chest.

I grip the wheel, humming gently as the waves pound once more at the hull, and sail toward the unknown.

Ready to live again.

ACKNOWLEDGMENTS:

An enormous thank-you to my agent, Penny Moore, for being the first to champion this series. You've been there since the beginning, and I'm so grateful. Here's to number eight!

To my editor, Alyza Liu: We made it to the finish line! Thank you for helping to sharpen this story into what it is today, and for knowing all the right ways to make these characters stronger. And a special thank-you to Jennifer Ung, who believed in this world back when it was just a fifty-page sample.

To the entire team at Simon & Schuster who I'm honored to share this book with: Thank you Laura Eckes, Sammy Yuen, Hilary Zarycky, Shirley Merino, Morgan York, Sara Berko, Justin Chanda, Anne Zafian, and Kendra Levin. A big thank-you to Casey Weldon for bringing Nami to life over the course of three book covers. And a tremendous thank-you to the team at Aevitas Creative and WME for your continued support of this series.

To the readers, who I am eternally grateful for: Thank you for sticking with this story to its conclusion, and for being steadfast in your patience as I took longer than anticipated to get there. Throughout the last few years, I've been holding tight to the dream of one day getting this book into your hands. It was a guiding light when I needed it most, and I'm so thrilled Nami's story is finally yours in its entirety. I'm grateful to every one of you, always.

And finally, to Shaine and Oliver, who I love with my entire heart: Thank you for keeping me afloat during the days when writing felt impossible. The two of you are the reason my world is filled with so much color, and getting to be your mom is the greatest joy of my life. Thank you for the silly notes, unlimited hugs, and many, many snacks. I love you both times infinity.